Breaking Rules

RULES DUET

BOOK ONE

ANASTASIJA WHITE

This book is a work of fiction. Names, characters, locales, businesses, events and incidents are products of the author's imagination or are used fictitiously. Any resemblance to actual person, living or dead; events; or locations is entirely coincidental.

The author acknowledges the trademark status and trademark owners of various products, and/or brands referenced in the work of fiction. The publication/use of these trademarks is not authorized, associated with, or sponsored by the trademark owners.

Developmental Editing: Melanie Yu, MadeMeBlushBooks, https://mademeblushbooks.com/

Line Editing: Beth, VB Edits, https://vbeditsromance.com/

Edited by The Fiction Fix, https://thefictionfix.com/

Edited by Caroline Knecht, https://reedsy.com/caroline-knecht

Cover Design by © Leila @ Opulent Swag and Designs, https://www.opulentswagand designs.com/

This book is intended for an 18+ audience.

For trigger warnings, strongly advised to visit https://shor.by/BRB1

ISBN 978-609-08-0790-3 (ebook)

ISBN 978-609-08-0789-7 (paperback)

ISBN 978-609-08-0793-4 (special edition, paperback)

To the ones who have found the strength to walk away and to the ones still searching for it.
To every heart that has been battered and bruised but still held onto kindness and never stopped dreaming.
To every soul that has been made to feel small, please never forget that you deserve love without fear or cruelty.
You are not alone.
You are not broken.
You are not what they did to you.
You are worthy of healing, happiness, and love that feels like the warmest hug. A love that reminds you that you as you are have always been enough.

This is for you.

Playlist

"my tears ricochet" - Taylor Swift
"Take What You Want" - Post Malone feat. Ozzy Osbourne & Travis Scott
"Broken Smile (My All)" - Lil Peep
"Elastic Heart" - Sia
"Rain" - Sleep Token
"Shameless" - Camila Cabello
"LABOUR - the cacophony" - Paris Paloma
"Seven" - Natalie Jane
"we can't be friends (wait for your love)" - Ariana Grande
"My Boy Only Breaks His Favorite Toys" - Taylor Swift
"Will you cry?" - Gracie Abrams
"DIRTY LITTLE SECRET" - Nessa Barrett
"Look After You" - The Fray
"Dusk Till Dawn" - ZAYN feat. Sia

Find the rest of **BREAKING RULES** playlist here:

Author's Note

Hi, hello, hey, my beautiful readers!

First of all, **THANK YOU** so much for giving a chance to Bella and Xander's story. This book is different from my already published works, as it's way angstier and emotionally darker. Also, it's my most favorite couple I've ever written and it speaks volumes considering this book was first written in 2021. It's a very rewritten and reworked version and I'm beyond proud of it.

Writing **BREAKING RULES** wasn't easy. The themes of parental neglect and mentally&physically abusive relationships are heavy, and they should be treated with care and respect. I did my best to tell Bella's story with all the love and sensitivity it deserves. She's my Phoenix—the one who rises from the ashes stronger, braver, and more confident than ever. I really hope you will love her just as much as I do, and as Xander loves her.

This book contains some very sensitive topics, so please check the trigger / content warnings before you continue. It includes: mental abuse, physical abuse, sexual abuse, mention of suicide. For a full list of triggers and content warnings, please visit: https://shor.by/BRB1

There's nothing more important than your mental health.

Ana.

CHAPTER 1

I'm Stuck

BELLA

July

A SLIGHT CHILL RUNS DOWN MY SPINE, MY SCALP prickling as I take in the extravagance of the grand ballroom. Even though it's only open to the Boston City Warriors football team, this party is the last place I want to be.

"Isabella." I whip my head around at the sound of my boyfriend's voice. Jake stands a few feet away, his brows furrowed. "Hurry up," he tells me.

I scurry over to him, and he quickly takes my hand and pulls us farther into the room.

Taking deep breaths, I try to calm myself. No matter how many times we do this, it never gets easier. I'm just *me*. He's a superstar. We don't quite fit.

The sounds of champagne flutes clinking together and laughter surround me as soft music plays in the background, setting the mood without getting in the way of conversation. We're here tonight in honor of the team's new quarterback, and the excitement is palpable. According to the snippets I catch as we pass, tonight signifies a new chapter for the Warriors. Considering how often I've heard the words

"Super Bowl" since we arrived, the team definitely expects the new guy to make a difference.

When those words are muttered for what feels like the hundredth time, I let out a sigh.

Jake scowls over his shoulder. "Stop sulking. You look hot."

The black bodycon dress he chose for me hugs my every curve. It's a bit too revealing for my liking, but it was a gift, and I didn't want to hurt his feelings, so I donned it without complaint—same with the stilettos already pinching my feet.

I wish I'd stayed home.

As I take a step forward, skirting one of Jake's coaches, my mother's words float through my mind: *Keep your back straight, Isabella. You look like a gremlin. Stop embarrassing me.* On instinct, I pull my shoulders back and put a smile on my face, silently repeating the words I've heard since I was little: *Look good and keep quiet. No one cares what you think or how you feel.*

"Thank you," I say quietly.

Jake presses me hard into his side and kisses the top of my head, inhaling deeply. "Your perfume smells delicious."

"It's my magic," I joke awkwardly, making him snort. "Now will you tell me why you wanted me here so badly?"

He scans the room, as if searching for someone. "It's a welcome party."

I ignore the annoyance flaring to life inside me. "Yeah, I know. You've got a new quarterback. Alex Walker? Is that his name?"

"*Alexander* Walker." He drapes an arm around my waist. "He's the reason I wanted you here."

Confused, I frown up at him. "Why?"

"Because he's a beast on the field. I really think we're gonna rock the league this season."

What does any of that have to do with me?

With a smirk, I tease, "Are you fangirling over some dude?"

"*Fangirling*?" He stops in his tracks and narrows his eyes. "You'll understand everything real soon."

"If you say so."

The moment we sit at our designated table, he starts talking with his teammate Omar Williams. Jake doesn't bother to introduce me to him or the woman beside him, who keeps a protective hand on her baby bump.

"Hi." I plaster on a smile, but the second our eyes connect, she looks away.

With an exaggerated sigh, she presses her lips into a thin line and surveys the other guests.

Wow. It's not that I expected people to be friendly to me, but I didn't imagine they'd be outright rude either.

I'm just a girlfriend...not a fiancée, and definitely not a wife. They probably figure I'm in Jake's life temporarily, so why would they waste their time bonding with me? I understand the logic, despite how shitty it is. It costs nothing to be kind.

I peruse the venue, not really taking in the details. It's exactly what I expected. Everything is coated in the team's colors, red and white, with the Warriors logo—a silver shield—displayed here and there. I'm not interested in this new guy either. If Jake says he's good, then I'll take his word for it.

Honestly, I don't know a whole lot about football. I've mostly avoided anything having to do with the sport since Jake and I broke up when he graduated from high school. We got back together six months ago, and I've made little effort to learn since. I have zero interest, so why bother?

The music comes to a stop, and we all turn to the small stage, where the general manager holds a mic, a million-dollar smile on his face. "Thank you so much for coming tonight," he says.

I try my best to listen to him, but none of the jargon makes sense, so I tune it out. The only time I pay attention to football is when Jake is on the field, because that's what's expected of me.

"Let me introduce our new quarterback, Alexander Walker!"

With a sip of my water, I watch a guy in a tailored suit join the general manager on stage. He's tall, muscular, and very lean. His hair is dark, but I can't make out his features from here. He thanks the crowd for the warm welcome and says how excited he is to join the team.

Once he stops talking, I put my glass down and turn to Jake. His grayish blue eyes are glued to the scene, and only when I touch his elbow does he turn to look at me.

"I need to use the bathroom."

"Now?" He frowns. "Can't you wait a few minutes? Everyone will look at us."

"I'm sorry." I give him a frown of my own. "I can't wait." Without giving him time to respond, I stand and head toward the bathroom. What I really need is a few minutes to myself.

And that's exactly what I get. Everyone is out there, eager to talk to the new QB, which means there's not a soul in the bathroom when I walk in.

In front of the mirror, I rest my hands on either side of the sink and blow out a breath. How the hell did I get myself into this situation? At a party where I don't fit in, wearing a dress I don't feel comfortable in, with a person I don't recognize anymore. The last part leaves a bitter taste in my mouth, because I couldn't have imagined that would be the case when I agreed to get back together with Jake.

He was supposed to be a bridge to an easier time in my life, when I was happier, but nothing is the way I thought it would be.

I was fourteen when Jake and I struck up a friendship. He was two years older. For a long time, that was all we were: friends. Eventually, though, he confessed his feelings for me. He was my first love, just like I was his, so bumping into him seven months ago almost felt like destiny.

Especially since that encounter happened in a coffee shop I frequented but he'd never been to before. He only popped in because he was meeting a teammate who lived nearby.

We reconnected right away, and within weeks we were officially dating. Three months later, he asked me to move in with him.

When Jake and I started dating again, it felt like the emptiness I'd been carrying around for six years had finally disappeared. Like when he kissed me, I was no longer lost.

Two months after I moved in, though, it hit me how much he'd changed.

The door to the bathroom bursts open, and an elegantly dressed woman steps inside, ripping me out of my thoughts. I hastily wash my hands, flashing her a smile when our eyes meet in the mirror. She smiles back before she walks into one of the stalls. I dry my hands, then take a few deep breaths, mentally preparing myself to return to Jake's side.

I just need to get through tonight. It will be fine.

When I return to our table, my boyfriend is nowhere to be seen. Brow furrowed, I weave through the crowd, searching for him.

"Isabella, over here."

I crane my neck and spot him with the new quarterback—*Alexander* Walker—and with another steadying breath, I head his way.

"There you are." Jake grabs my hand and yanks me in so my back collides with his chest as he splays his palm over my stomach. "This is why I wanted you to come tonight," he says, his hot breath fanning over my cheek. "So you could meet Xander."

Xander? Surprise washes over me. Alexander is Xander? Jake's friend and teammate from college? Eyes narrowed, I take him in.

Like Jake, he has dark brown hair, broad shoulders, and a muscular chest. Even the blue of his irises is similar.

"Babe, come on, it's Xander! I talk about our wild college days all the time!" my boyfriend says, grasping my arms.

I barely register his words. I'm too caught up in studying his new teammate.

"Isabella?"

"I-I—" I stammer, wetting my lips. *Goodness, Isabella. Get a grip!*

Xander's lips lift in a cocky grin, and he dips his head so our eyes are level. "Done eye-fucking me yet?"

Heat creeps into my cheeks and neck. He didn't say that, did he? Right in front of Jake?

"I wasn't," I grit through my teeth, staring daggers at the guy.

He huffs out a laugh. "You obviously were."

"Sorry to break it to you, but you're not as observant as you think," I hiss, not bothering to look at Jake for his reaction. "You're being inappropriate."

"It was a joke," Jake says in a low voice, his fingers sinking into my belly. "He's messing with you."

His sharp hold makes me wince, and embarrassment settles in my chest, making me shift my weight from one foot to the other.

"Sorry," Jake says to his friend. "Give her time to get used to you before you joke like that with her."

Xander studies me for another beat, then shrugs. "I'm sorry about the joke, *Isabella*."

When he says my name, a tingling sensation that has nothing to do with Jake's hand on my stomach spreads across my skin. *Oh my God. What's happening?* I've never reacted to a person's words in such a visceral manner.

Shaking off the thought, I extend my hand, and his fingers gently curl around mine, lightly skimming along my palm and down my wrist. Instantly, my core throbs. *What the hell?* I cross my legs at the ankles and do my best to ignore it. It's neither the time nor the place. And, a thousand times more importantly, he's not the person my body should be reacting to.

Slowly, I free my hand from his and give him a smile. "It's nice to meet you, Xander."

"You too, Isabella," he murmurs, glancing between Jake and me. "Are you going to join us at the club later?"

"The club?" I ask, tilting my head to look at my boyfriend. "I thought we were going home after this."

"No. The guys are going clubbing, baby."

Jake's reply is nonchalant, and my heart squeezes painfully. This isn't how I imagined my night ending.

"Now that this jackass has joined the team, we need to celebrate. It'll be a blast."

"As long as I have a woman in my bed by the end of the night," Xander says, sneaking a glance at me.

I roll my eyes, annoyance poisoning my mood.

Jake snorts. "Like the good old days?"

"Like the good old days," Xander confirms, but his smile slips almost instantly. His jaw ticks, and he balls his hand into a fist at his side, his knuckles turning white before he shoves it into his pocket.

Clubbing? That is so not my scene. But... "Do you want me to go?"

"Nah. It's just the guys tonight." Jake whirls me around. "And I figured you wouldn't want to go anyway. You never come with me."

He's right. I'd much rather stay out of his limelight. But why bring me here only to ditch me for his friends?

I shouldn't be surprised. He'll choose clubs, parties, and posh events over me every time.

"Sure," I mumble, faking a smile.

Softly, he presses a kiss to my lips. Then he spins me back around, holds me against him, and dives back into a conversation with Xander as if I'm not here. With a sigh, I lean against him, preferring my own thoughts over their conversation anyway.

I don't fit in, and Jake does nothing to help me feel welcome. Rather than a partner, I've become an accessory to show off, so he can brag about how he won back his high school sweetheart. So he can praise my beauty anytime someone comments on how good we look together.

Beautiful to everyone except myself.

The conversations, laughter, and music turn into white noise. All I want is to be far from here, to be home, curled up with a romance novel or watching my favorite anime or even out for a run.

Anything would be better than this.

CHAPTER 2
A Beautiful Menace
XANDER

July

ISABELLA TURNS HER HEAD TO LOOK UP AT MILLER. "JAKE, maybe we can—"

"Baby, not now." He dismisses her and brings his gaze back to me.

In college, he always bragged about how beautiful his ex-girlfriend was. I figured he'd pay her more attention now that he has her back.

"Remember sophomore year, when Coach made the whole team run after he caught us drinking?"

I nod, my neck stiff. "It's hard to forget. I thought I was going to puke my guts out on the field."

"Some of the guys did. It was fucking gross." Miller scrunches his nose and looks away, seemingly lost in his memories.

I clench my hand in my pocket and consider making a run for it. I'd rather talk to anyone else at this party.

Isabella is still standing between Miller and me, her back pressed to his chest. Her expression is blank as she stares off into the distance. She'd been silent for a solid ten minutes when she finally spoke, but when Miller didn't even let her finish, her features turned vacant again. It makes me wonder if she's even paying attention to what's happening around her.

She's even more stunning than I expected. In college, Miller always went on about how gorgeous she was, but words don't really do her justice. Her body is flawless. Her little black dress fits her like a glove and emphasizes her round tits and toned legs. Her long brown hair cascades over her shoulders in soft waves. And her eyes? Dark blue, like sapphires, and framed by long black lashes. They're gemstones that hide all kinds of secrets, like the deepest waters of the ocean.

He doesn't deserve a girl like her.

I tighten my hold on my glass and shift my focus to the people around me as the smile I've been working to maintain slips off. I'm thrilled to be playing for my hometown team, to be close to my parents again. On top of that, it's great for my career. The Warriors are one of the strongest teams in the league. Signing with them has opened doors for so many possibilities, for so many milestones and achievements I've yet to hit.

It's all good, with the exception of the person standing in front of me.

Despite all the reasons I should've immediately jumped at the chance to sign with the Warriors, I hesitated, and Jake Miller is the reason why.

I've spent twenty minutes with him tonight, and I'm already on edge. If the asshole could shut up about our past, being around him might be bearable. But he's been on it since the moment his girl joined us.

I need to collect myself before I do something stupid.

"Hey, man. Coach wanted me to find him," I say, cutting Miller off midsentence.

"Sure. I'll be over there"—he jabs his thumb over his shoulder—"if you want to come join us later. I'll introduce you to the guys."

With a nod, I wander off, mulling over his choice of words. *I'll be over there*, not *we*. It only reaffirms my impression: His girlfriend is nothing more than a prop to him.

I sneak a glance over my shoulder, to where Miller and Isabella settle in at a table. She has a faraway look on her face as she trails her finger around the rim of her glass. The other women at the table don't pay her any attention, totally immersed in their own conversation. They even have their backs turned to her, keeping their distance in every sense. Jake is talking to a couple of our teammates, his hand draped over the back of Isabella's chair, a reminder to everyone that she's his.

Clenching my jaw, I move farther into the room, searching for Coach. Not because he wanted to talk to me, but because I needed a break from Miller.

"Hey, Coach," I say as I step in front of Ezra Wilson. He played for the Warriors, a Hall-of-Famer tight end, and he's the best coach the team has had in years. His leadership and the bonds he creates with his players are unmatched. "How have you been?"

A lopsided grin splits his lips. "Pretty good." We shake hands, his grip strong and firm. "I just talked to our general manager. We have big plans for this season. You think you're up for the challenge?"

"Always, sir."

"Good to know." Coach nods, his deep brown eyes crinkling at the corners. "I saw you talking to Miller. Feel good to be playing with a college buddy again?"

College buddy? I fucking hate him.

But I keep that to myself. Instead, I say, "Yeah, it's like the good old days." I've gotta keep the lie going, because playing for the Warriors is important to me. I swallowed my feelings and played nice with Miller in college. I can do it again.

"I think you'll be a good fit."

"I'll do my best."

A ruckus behind me makes me look over my shoulder. Jake is laughing about something, his head thrown back. The room's decor tints his face red and white, and I'm instantly thrown back to a different room, one full of the same colors.

I blink, my hand involuntarily tightening around my glass.

There's blood—so much blood. The glossy white tiles enhance the vibrant scarlet hue. A metallic smell hits my nose, and a wave of nausea crashes into me. It can't be... Please, fuck, no... Please—

"Xander?"

With a harsh inhale, I force myself out of the memory. This is not the fucking time or place for that.

"Sorry, Coach, what did you say?"

Coach studies my face before he nods and gives me a knowing smirk. "Go have fun. Once training camp starts, I expect everyone to be on their best behavior, so take advantage of the opportunity to let loose. Get to know your new teammates, make friends."

"Thanks." I take a step back, realizing my fingers are still trembling. "Have a great night."

"You too."

I turn, desperate for fresh air but knowing I have to play the game. *This is your job, Xander. Focus on it.* So I force a smile, banish the disturbing images that haunt me, and center my attention on the people who matter.

I can do that.

"WHERE DID YOU DISAPPEAR TO?"

I jump at the voice and spin around. When I see who it belongs to, I grit my teeth.

Miller tips his head, signaling over his shoulder. "Ready to go?"

"Sorry, man. I had some catching up to do." I look from him to Isabella, who stands beside him, her fingers locked in his. "Did you change your mind?"

Her beautiful blue eyes widen, and her puffy lips part. "What? Oh, no, no. I'm tired anyway. I better go home."

"Nothing is better for a restful night's sleep than our bed, right?" Jake suggestively arches an eyebrow as he drapes his arm over her shoulders and pulls her to his side.

"Right." Isabella's cheeks redden, and she clutches her purse to her stomach.

Her gaze flickers to mine, and a thrill rushes down my spine.

What the fuck? Something about her draws me in, and it's not just her beauty.

"I'll walk Isabella out, and then we can go," Jake tells me.

I lick my lips. "Do you mind if I come with you? A few minutes outside will do me good."

"Sure." With a shrug, he starts for the exit.

As I follow, I keep my eyes trained on her. His head is bent, his lips at her ear. My body temperature ratchets up at the sight of him touching her, and not in a good way. I slip a finger beneath my collar and pull on it slightly. My neck is stiff, just like my muscles.

When I taunted her about the way she looked at me, it was to see how Jake would react. His dismissal was exactly what I expected. Her reaction, on the other hand? Priceless. She *can* stand up for herself, be hostile. *A beautiful menace.* Yet here she is, allowing him to control her.

Once outside, I lean against the wall, hands in my pockets, and watch him help her into a waiting car. This is not the Jake Miller I know. I'm not buying into this caring boyfriend act. No. He has just mastered the skill of playing the role.

Did I make the right choice, coming here? Do I have it in me to forget what happened? To finally let go of our past?

I don't know.

THE AIR inside the club is stifling. Already, my shirt clings to my chest. I undo another button and then down my whiskey in one go. At the prickle of awareness over my skin, I look up and lock eyes with a blonde. She has her hair pulled up in a high ponytail, her shimmering gold dress exposing her deep cleavage. She smiles at me, and I smile back.

I'm not leaving this place alone. I need a distraction.

A booming laugh to my right makes me wince. Jake and some of our teammates are lost in conversation, a few girls squeezed between them—though the petite redhead isn't so much *between* as she is plastered to his front, her ass on his lap. My annoyance flares hot. It's not my business, and this is as far as it has gone, at least that I'm aware of. Still...is this why he sent Isabella home?

Fuck, that woman is messing with my head.

I rise to my feet and make my way to the VIP bathroom. Inside, I lock the door and stare at my reflection. My hair is tousled on top, damp with sweat. Angling over the sink, I splash icy water on my face and let it slide down my cheeks. The relief is minimal, but it's immediate, so I do it again.

I live with guilt, carry it with me wherever I go. Not even therapy helped me deal with it. The past still tortures me, while Miller looks like he's been living his best life. Nothing bothers him, and now he has his girl back, the one he never forgot, even when he was fucking his way through college.

Asshole.

My body tenses, my jaw rigid and my muscles quivering. The anger inside me bubbles up. Fuck, what I'd give to make the world see the real Jake Miller.

I'd do anything.

I'd do...

An idea flashes in my mind, and the details fall together quickly. Lips curving up, I grip either side of the sink and reassess my reflection.

This is it. What I need to move on, to escape my past. Why didn't I think of it sooner?

I don't need to tolerate Miller. What I need is to make him pay, to expose him for who he really is.

My chest expands, and I feel lighter than I have in years.

Oh, I know what I'm going to do.

And Isabella is going to help.

CHAPTER 3

Xander

BELLA

July

I sit up in bed, eyes bleary, and scan the room. My heart beats insanely fast, making me clutch my hand to my chest.

On my nightstand, my phone buzzes, my best friend's face displayed on the screen. As I answer the call, I drop back onto the mattress. "Hey, Meg."

"Hey. Did I wake you up?"

"It's fine. Don't worry about it." I pull the phone away from my ear with a yawn and check the time. Nine a.m. "How are you?"

"I'm good. Thought I'd call to see how you are. I see your precious boyfriend had a real night out." She clears her throat. "If you went to the team party together, how come he ended up at the club?"

"It was just the guys, and I didn't want to go anyway." I glance at Jake's side of the bed and find it empty. My stomach twists.

Where did he spend the night?

Meg grunts, bringing me back to the conversation. "Why are you with him?"

That's a question I find myself asking more and more often. With every passing day, it becomes clearer that Jake and I are too different.

"I don't know," I breathe out. "I really don't."

Her sigh makes the phone line crackle. "If you're looking for a reason to break up with him, you should start reading the blogs."

That twisting in my stomach turns into a ball of dread. "Did he make headlines again?"

"Not really, just seen with the Warriors' new quarterback and a few other guys." She lowers her voice, her tone sympathetic. "You've been together for six months, living together for three, and as soon as he has a spare minute, he goes out. And he's always photographed with girls. He's clubbing like he's still single."

Bile rises in my throat at the mental image. "You think he's cheating on me?"

"I don't know," she says, sounding defeated. "I haven't seen actual proof, but I don't have a good feeling about it."

I toss the blanket aside and get out of bed. "Maybe it's not like that."

"It definitely *looks* like that." Her tone softens further. "Is everything okay? You can tell me."

If only that were true. For years, I kept so many secrets, and after a while it became a habit. It's easier this way—at least people don't pity me. They can't resent me for my past or blame me for my mistakes if they don't know about them.

"Everything's fine. He and I were happy before. I want to see if we can be like that again."

Meg is quiet for a long time. Finally, she says, "Just remember, you don't have to be with him if you're not sure he's the one. I know finding an apartment you can afford on your own will be tricky, but I can help you look. Your happiness is important."

She hit the nail on the head. Since I started having doubts about my future with Jake, I've looked for apartments when I can, but I can't afford a single one on my own.

Ugh, if only I hadn't been blinded by his affection and given up my apartment so quickly.

"Thank you," I murmur as I step into the closet. "Can I call you later? I want to change my clothes and wash my face."

After we hang up, I put my phone on the shelf and pull on a pair of shorts and a loose tee. Then I head to the bathroom to start my morning routine, hoping it will help me clear all the thoughts about Jake racing inside my skull.

As I pad down the stairs, I check my email on my phone. Since I finished college, I've been working for my cousin as an event organizer while also helping him with paperwork and bookkeeping. We have three birthday parties scheduled this week, and from the look of the request lists, I'll be busy. Honestly, it's exactly what I need to distract myself from—

A shrill sound pierces the air, and the thought dies abruptly. Frozen at the bottom of the stairs, I strain to listen. So far, the house has been quiet. Deserted, even. I assumed I was the only one here. Now, a moan floats through the air, then comes the clatter of something heavy hitting the wall.

What the actual fuck?

My face and neck flush impossibly hot, and fleeing to the bedroom crosses my mind. I cringe at the thought, push myself from the railing, and slowly head toward the guest room. A foot from the door, I stop, realizing it's not pulled all the way closed. If I want to, I can peek inside. Do I want to, though?

Screw it. If my boyfriend is cheating on me, I should know.

With a palm pressed to the door, I silently push it open. As soon as the people on the bed register, relief hits me like a tidal wave. It isn't Jake. It's Xander and a blonde I don't recognize.

Mesmerized, I watch as Xander moves his hips faster and faster. His neck, back, and arms are covered in the most incredible tattoos, so many drawings and whimsical lines blended together. A drop of sweat runs down his back, straight to his butt...and damn, his ass is perfect.

My heartbeat quickens; my nipples harden. Heat crawls up my neck to my cheeks, and my knees wobble.

Why the hell am I so turned on? I shouldn't be here. I shouldn't watch them...and yet I can't make myself take a step back.

Xander wraps his arms around the girl's waist and flips them around so she's on top.

I nibble on my bottom lip, shifting a little, my panties dampening. Dang, I would've—

A breath gets stuck in my throat. Xander is staring at me with a sly grin on his face. *Fuck.*

Pursing my lips, I take a step back and quietly close the door. *Shit.* How am I going to explain what I was doing? I can always say I came to check on the noise but didn't see anything. Yup, that's what I'll say.

I definitely didn't see his dick.

My cheeks flare hot again.

Really, Bella?

As I force myself down the hall, a thought strikes me. Where is Jake? He wouldn't have just given Xander his key so he could fuck in his guest room. My boyfriend must be somewhere in the house. I take a deep breath and head to the living room. Immediately, I'm met with loud snoring, and a mix of relief and annoyance swirls in my stomach.

Jake is lying on the couch, still dressed in his shirt and black pants from yesterday.

I cross my arms over my chest and take him in, wondering yet again what I'm doing. We dated in high school, and after he went to college, I rarely saw him. I was perfectly fine without him in my life. In this moment, I can't remember why I took him back. It certainly wasn't so he could dismiss me when I spoke or ignore me when it suits him and then expect me to play along and pretend to be a happy couple.

The past should stay in the past. Isn't that the rule I've always lived by?

Foot tapping, I bite the inside of my cheek. Should I help him get to our room? Should I wait for him to wake up? Maybe I should leave him like this and go to lunch with Meg, just to unwind. He'll be mad if he wakes up and I'm not here, though, so in the end, it's better if I stay.

With irritation running hot in my veins, I slowly shift closer to the couch and remove his sneakers. He mumbles, turns onto his back, and continues sleeping as if nothing happened.

"What a great way to spend my morning." I pull a blanket from the back of the couch and cover him with it.

Straightening again, I scan the room. I love this place. I love the decor. Jake had no interest in decorating, so I chose the dark blue throw pillows, the gray curtains, and the black coffee table.

I clasp my hands and rock back and forth on my heels. If I'm being honest, I agreed to move in with him in the hopes I wouldn't feel so lonely. It was too quiet in my apartment, my mind too loud. Since I was a little girl, all I've really wanted was for someone to care about me. It's a craving deep in my soul.

A sudden snore tears me out of my thoughts. With a sigh, I saunter to the kitchen, resigned to waiting for Jake to wake up. I might as well make breakfast. But first, I need coffee.

THE RICH AROMA of freshly made coffee fills the kitchen. Closing my eyes, I take a sip and savor the bitterness with a dash of almond milk. Perfect.

"So, you like coffee, and you like watching people fuck."

Eyes flying open, I gasp when I come face-to-face with Xander.

He stands in front of me with a cocky smile on his full lips. "Which do you prefer? Porn or—"

"I prefer not to find random people having sex in Jake's guest room, especially when I had no idea someone was here at all." I glare at him.

Brow arched, he says, "Did you think it was Jake?" The asshole is shirtless, his tattoos fully on display, black pants hanging low on his hips.

"That's none of your business." With a slow exhale, I bring my mug to my lips again. *Patience, Bella. Patience.*

"If you thought it was your boyfriend, your reaction was pretty indifferent. I would've expected you to storm in and—"

"He wouldn't do that to me." My conversation with Meg comes to mind, and I swallow hard.

"Wouldn't he?" Chuckling, he stalks closer. He props a hip on the kitchen counter beside me, standing so close, his body heat soaks into me as my cheeks redden. "Is there any chance you can make me a coffee too?"

"A coffee?" I repeat dumbly, suddenly transfixed by his features.

The lights last night were gaudy and harsh. Here, in broad daylight, I finally get a good look at him. His tousled, deep brown hair is a bit longer on top and shaved at the sides. His dark blue eyes are flecked with green and dancing with mirth. Rather than a full beard, like Jake, his chiseled jaw is covered in a light stubble.

"Yes." He breaks into a smile, his pouty bottom lip a bit fuller than the upper one.

Staring at him for this long is a problem. The more I look, the harder it is to take my eyes off him. He's astoundingly handsome.

"You're eye-fucking me again."

My stomach twists. What the hell is wrong with me?

He's not wrong. I can't help but gawk. He's standing incredibly close to me, and he's half-naked. He smells like sex, and he looks like it too.

"So, about that coffee?" Xander breaks the silence again, mischief dancing in his eyes.

"Make it yourself," I grumble, moving away from him. His charm is playing on my nerves, crawling under my skin with an ease that scares me.

"You're feisty, just like I thought you would be." He takes a step closer.

His hot breath ghosts across my skin, spreading tingles through my body. Chin lifted, I glare at him, trying my hardest not to get lost in his eyes. They look like the sky just before a storm breaks, deep and captivating.

"Like you thought I would be?" I put up a front to keep him from seeing just how much he affects me.

This encounter is so bizarre. Jake is asleep in the next room, and

I'm ogling a half-naked guy I don't even know, one whose very existence sends arousal flooding through me. I want to know more about him. Pressing my palm to my chest, I absentmindedly trail my fingers over my collarbone, the fluttery sensation in my stomach growing more intense. It's absolutely uncontrollable, like an itch I can't ignore.

I need to get rid of it.

CHAPTER 4

The One That Got Away

BELLA

July

"WHAT DOES THAT MEAN?" I FORCE THE WORDS OUT AS I blink. Pulling myself out of the daze he put me in, I take my hand off my chest.

Xander is staring at me, lips tipped up like he's amused. "Miller used to talk about you, and you're exactly how I expected you to be."

He talked about me? I want to ask him to explain. Instead, I say, "How close were you two in college?"

"We were *best* friends." He props his hip against the kitchen counter again. The move draws my focus to his tattooed chest.

With a thick swallow, I drag my attention to my feet. I don't want him to think I give a damn about the ink rolling across his skin.

"You're doing it again, Isabella."

He says my name like he's tasting me. He has to stop, or my panties will be soaked. Again.

"Doing what?" Only now do I realize that, although my gaze is zeroed in on my feet, to him, it probably looks like I'm staring at his groin.

"Looking at me like you wish you were the one in that guest room with me."

Arrogant asshole.

I bring my gaze back to his face, giving him my best withering look. "You wish."

Dammit. Why did I look at him again? Instantly, his eyes captivate me. I slug down the last of my coffee then turn to the coffee maker. I need a distraction, even if it means doing something totally contradictory.

"Do you still want that coffee?"

"Oh, *now* you're offering?" He shifts beside me, the noise subtle. "Yeah, I'd love that."

"Cool. Go sit at the table." Anything to put some distance between us so I can stop embarrassing myself.

Brushing past me, he rounds the kitchen counter, all swagger. Then he plops himself down on the high stool. His gaze bores into me, but I refuse to let it bother me. It doesn't. It shouldn't... *damn him*.

"Why are you here?" I ask, remaining focused on the coffee maker.

"In Boston? Did you forget I'm the new quarterback for the Warriors?"

I roll my eyes. "Ass. No, why are you *here*, at Jake's place?"

"Miller was pretty drunk by the time we called it quits, so I made sure he got home. It was late, so rather than having the driver take me home, he told me I could crash here." Xander props his head on his knuckles, the cords of his arm muscles flexing.

"*Crash* here?" I peer over my shoulder, one eyebrow cocked.

He grins at me, his blue-green eyes sparkling with a devilish glint. "And smash some pussy in the process."

Jealousy I have no business feeling wiggles in the back of my mind. With a huff, I turn to look at him. "Do you know the girl's name?"

There isn't a hint of embarrassment on his face as he shakes his head.

I scowl in disgust and disappointment. "You're impossible."

"I'm exceptional."

"At what? Being obnoxious?" I fill a clean mug with coffee from the carafe.

Smirking, he leans back on the stool. "You don't know me. I wouldn't be so quick to make assumptions."

"I'm not *assuming* anything; I'm speaking from experience." Straightening, I lift my chin. "I've known Jake since I was fourteen. Now, almost a decade later, I've had plenty of time to get to know guys like you."

"That's funny," he says, forearms on the counter, "you may *think* you know a little about me, but *I* know a lot about you, remember?"

I add a splash of almond milk to the coffee and set the mug in front of Xander. Since he keeps bringing it up, I might as well ask. "And what exactly do you think you know about me? This is the second time you've said it, but you've yet to elaborate."

He shrugs. "You're the one that got away."

Confusion worms its way through me. *The one that got away? What is he talking about?*

"That's what Jake said back then. He said you broke up with him, and he was obsessed with you. I've always been curious about the girl who had Miller at her mercy."

Though his tone is serious, I can't help but burst into laughter.

"He was never *obsessed* with me. He was fine after our breakup. He was a total manwhore in college."

One side of his mouth tips up into a smirk. "Sounds like you were spying on him."

"Nah, some of my friends went to school with him. When they came home from winter break, they told me all about what he'd been up to."

I never needed to ask. My friends always made it a point to tell me all about my ex and his endless conquests.

I put my own mug in the kitchen sink and peer at Xander. "How's the coffee? Up to your standards?"

He takes a sip, and as he pulls the mug away, he swipes his tongue over his bottom lip. A radiant smile blooms on his face. "It's perfect."

"Glad to hear it." My tone is far too shaky for a casual interaction. I clear my throat. "Um, how long are you planning to stay?"

"Miller said I could stay as long as I'd like." He takes another sip, hiding his grin behind the mug.

"Are you going to take him up on that offer?" I already know the answer. The guy is here to torture me, plain and simple.

Head dropped back, he barks out a laugh. "Of course! Why would I leave?"

"Wait...where is your girl?" Only now does it hit me that the blonde hasn't joined him.

God, I'm ridiculous. How is it possible that I'm so caught up in him already?

"She's not my girl, as you already know, and she left." He takes a gulp of his coffee and stands up. "I thought she might make you uncomfortable, since you saw her naked and all."

"Asshole," I grit out under my breath as he saunters closer.

"You better get used to me." He sets his mug in the sink, hovering close, his proximity sending tingles all over my skin. "I'm going to be around...a lot."

I swallow my nerves. "Games are the only team events I participate in. Last night was an exception. I don't know most of his teammates, and that will now include you."

"You're forgetting something. I'm not just his teammate—I'm his friend."

"And? That means nothing."

"Maybe, maybe not." With that, he spins on his heel and heads to the doorway. "I'm really looking forward to getting to know you better, Isabella," he says, his tone low and husky. "In every way possible."

Unbidden, heat swirls in my lower abdomen. I'm a fucking mess. This guy seriously has the audacity to hit on his friend's girlfriend? Jake let him stay the night, and this jerk repays him by flirting with me?

With friends like Alexander Walker, who needs enemies?

"Stop it, Alexander. Stop being so inappropriate."

"It's just the way I am." He pauses at the threshold to the kitchen, turning back to wink at me. "And my friends call me Xander."

"I'm not your friend."

"You will be."

Then he's gone, leaving me in peace. As I wash both mugs, my mind drifts back to the guest room, visions of the way he slammed into the blonde plaguing me. How he wrapped his thick arms around her waist and turned them both around. How his deep blue eyes peered at me, devouring me...

My whole body is flushed by the time I tamp down the thoughts.

After turning off the faucet, I dry my hands and take a few deep breaths. Then, cursing myself inwardly, I head upstairs. I need a shower. This wet puddle in my panties is aggravating me, and considering how much Xander riled me up, I'm more than frustrated.

As the bathroom fills with steam, I gradually relax. Without a tight rein on myself, though, my mind once again returns to my run-in with Xander. Why the hell is my body reacting to him like this? What's with the weakness in my knees? The heat spreading over my skin? The rapid beating of my heart? My body is betraying my mind again, and I don't like it.

Plus, I have a boyfriend. I have an active sex life, and all my needs are satisfied.

Pressing my back to the glass shower wall, I breathe in and out. I have to banish these thoughts. *Permanently*. I'm not entirely sure about my future with Jake, but I'm not the type of girl who cheats.

"Get yourself together," I whisper, my emotions in total disarray.

I thought the water would release the tension in my muscles, but I was wrong. After I dry off and dress for the day, I feel more on edge than I did before.

Since I haven't seen any sign that Jake is up, I take my Kindle from the nightstand, settle on the bed, and dive into the book I started yesterday, about a girl and a famous Formula 1 driver. It's wild, really, the parallels between the story and my own life. It's easy to relate to the way the heroine struggles with being in the spotlight.

Maybe it wouldn't be such a challenge if Jake's groupies hadn't dragged my name through the mud. They hate that I'm his high school sweetheart, and they want me to die a slow and painful death

—their words, not mine. All I see on social media is how I'm not good enough for him, how I'm just a basic bitch. I can't win, and I'm beginning to think I don't have the strength to handle the criticism much longer.

Despite how hard I fight to stay immersed in the story, my thoughts keep wandering back to Jake, to Xander, though thankfully not in the way they were before. No matter how good-looking Xander is, he's off-limits.

CHAPTER 5

Say No

BELLA

July

"WAKE UP, BABY."

When I crack my eyes open, I find Jake peering down at me warmly. Apparently, I fell asleep reading.

"How long have you been sleeping?"

With a yawn, I shrug. "I don't know. When did you wake up?"

"Twenty minutes ago. I fell asleep on the couch last night." With his meaty hands gripping my sides, he hauls me to his chest. Instantly, I'm engulfed in the scent of stale alcohol and sweat.

"Yeah, I found you when I went downstairs for coffee." I put my hands to his chest and push back, my nose wrinkled. "You stink."

"I do?" He laughs, adding a bit of pressure, pulling me into him with ease. A second later, he's flipped over onto his back, and I'm straddling his legs. "It's the best thing in the world to wake up and find my girl waiting for me at home."

I wouldn't call my experience *the best*. Finding my boyfriend passed out drunk after a night of partying isn't exactly a dream come true.

"How was the club?"

"It was fine." He runs his hands up and down my sides absentmindedly. "I'm glad you came to the party with me. It would've been awkward if you weren't there, since the rest of the guys brought their wives and girlfriends."

"Don't get used to it. You know how I feel about...all the fancy events, being in the spotlight. I don't like it."

"But you're stunning. Literally every time our photos show up online, the captions call you 'Miller's gorgeous girlfriend.'"

Annoyance singes my veins, and a dash of sadness finds its way under my skin. What's the point of being beautiful if my soul is ugly? If it's so damaged that anyone who gets too close will see right through me?

"I wish you'd join me for team events and parties more often. They're important to me."

Defeat washes over me, but I force a smile. "I know. I'll try harder, I promise."

With a hand on the back of my neck, he pulls my face down for a kiss. He runs his tongue over the seam of my lips, urging me to open for him. Persistent and pushy, just like he always is.

Instead of giving in, I straighten my back and frown down at him. "I told you, you stink. I have no desire to kiss a bottle of...rum?"

"Whiskey." His face splits into a smile. In a swish, I'm on my back, and he's hovering over me. "Let's take a shower."

"I already did." I hold his gaze and watch the way his pupils dilate as he zeroes in on my lips. "Go. I'll wait for you here."

"Isabella," he whines, grinding his erection against my leg. "I kinda have a problem here."

"Yeah? It's probably not as bad as the problem *I* had downstairs, when a half-naked guy strolled into the kitchen."

Jake's face contorts in confusion.

"Xander," I clarify.

He blinks twice, then bursts out laughing. Rearing back, he hops off the bed. "Xander is something else. Where is he?"

"In the guest room, I think."

"I told him he could stay," he says, shedding his clothes. "With that motherfucker, the Super Bowl will be ours. I'm a hundred percent sure of it. His stats are fantastic, and his dedication on the field is spectacular."

"Never seen you so enthusiastic about another player."

"Walker is one of the best quarterbacks in the NFL. I just appreciate talent when I see it. Besides, he's my buddy."

"Uh-huh...he told me you were best friends in college." I scratch my cheek.

"We were." A strange glint flashes behind his eyes, but it instantly disappears. There's more to the story than he's letting on, but I'm not about to ask him. For now, I just want him to take a shower so we can go downstairs and eat. I don't want to go alone.

"Hurry up. I'm starving."

"My shower offer still stands." He takes off his briefs and straightens proudly.

I chuckle. *Indeed, it still stands.*

"Go. I'll order lunch."

With a wink, he strides to the bathroom buck naked. I take him in, my focus landing on his butt. Another vision of Xander and the blonde pops into my mind like I'm reviewing a play.

Before I can stop myself, I've compared Jake's ass to Xander's, and my boyfriend isn't the winner.

What the hell is wrong with me?

"Order pizza," he says as he closes the door. "Get two. I'll see if Walker wants to stay."

Just my luck. With a palm to the face, I fall on my back. Staring at the ceiling, I allow myself a few seconds for a pity party. Then I sit up, unlock my phone, and order the pizzas.

Thoughts swarm in my head like bees in a hive. I have two options: I can complain and act like a baby, or I can be a grown woman and stop worrying about Jake's friend.

I like the second one better, so I'll stick to that.

JAKE AND XANDER are sprawled out on the sectional, the coffee table in front of them littered with pizza boxes and empty beer bottles.

"Babe, can you go upstairs and get my phone?" Jake says as I return with the plate of snacks he requested. It's not the first time tonight he has ordered me around.

"Why don't you get it yourself?" I respond, setting the plate of cheese cubes and ham on the table.

"Isabella, please. Do it for me." He gives me ridiculous puppy dog eyes. "Please?"

Irritation hot in my veins, I open my mouth to tell him to fuck off. But with a deep breath, I rein in my anger and snap it shut again.

"*Fine.*" I head to the hallway.

"Thanks, babe," he calls out as I hit the stairs. "See? She never says no to me," he murmurs.

I pause halfway up the stairs. He's not lying. Fuck, I hate that I'm doing this, but I can't stop myself. The need to be convenient was instilled in me at a young age, and now I'm struggling to break free. Plus, it's easier to go along with things than to make the kinds of changes that would make me happy. For now, I'd rather hide inside my head, in the worlds of the books I read, in the anime I love.

I deliberately take my time using the bathroom, fixing my ponytail, and steadying my breath. Once I'm a little calmer, I go back to the living room, and both men home in on me when I enter.

"What did I miss? What were you talking about while I was gone?" I ask, putting Jake's phone on the table.

He doesn't touch it. Maybe his request was just an excuse to boss me around so he could show his friend what a pushover I am.

I skirt the coffee table, intending to sit on the couch, but as I pass him, Jake bands an arm around my waist and pulls me to him. Caught off guard, I flail, nearly falling on top of him. He bursts out laughing while I plop down on the cushion beside him and glare.

When his laughter subsides, he gives me a smug smile. "We were talking about college. Our buddies, girls, that kind of shit. Xander and I have *a lot* to catch up on."

"Definitely." His asshole friend smirks. "I've got all kinds of stories about your boyfriend. I could tell you everything, even the dirty secrets."

"No, thank you." I hold his gaze, making him chuckle.

I'm not particularly interested, and after Jake spent the night partying with his friend, who ended up fucking a girl in this house, this whole situation makes me uncomfortable.

Even so, I can't help but dig for information. "So, how was the club?"

"If I'd known the clubs in Boston were so much fun, I would've signed a contract way earlier." Xander barks out a laugh, picking up his beer bottle. "Good booze, hot chicks."

"He knows what he's talking about, babe." Jake hauls me to his chest, his palm instantly on my breast.

Cheeks flaming, I glance at Xander to make sure he didn't see. I slant my body away from Jake and fidget in my seat, my heart sinking. It's like he doesn't respect me at all.

"I can't remember the last time I had that much fun," my boyfriend says, oblivious to my discomfort. "It definitely reminded me of the good old days."

"I'm happy to hear that," I mutter, my tone belying the sentiment. "Meg saw you on the blogs."

"Meghan is nosy," he grouses.

Eyes narrowed, Xander looks from Jake to me. "Who is Meghan?"

"My best friend."

"Ah. Will you invite her to the dinner Jake mentioned?"

I click my tongue. Shit. I forgot Jake invited friends over for dinner next week. Usually I wouldn't mind, but he told them I'd cook without asking me first.

"Yes," I say, picking at an invisible speck on my pant leg. "I'll invite Meg."

My boyfriend guffaws. "Don't get ahead of yourself, Walker. She's not exactly your type."

"Is she pretty?" Xander shifts his gaze to me.

I lift my chin. "She is."

His lips stretch into a smile. "Then she's my type."

"Oh, please," Jake argues. "The chick from last night? *She's* your type. Meghan? Hell no."

I push his palm off my thigh and untangle myself from him.

"What?" he groans. "I didn't say anything bad. She's just not Xander's type." Beer bottle dangling from his fingers, he waves dismissively. "But you can invite her. I might invite a few more people too."

"*Thanks,*" I snap. "Though I beg to differ about Meg. Based on the girl I saw this morning, blondes *are* his type."

Jake stiffens, his expression stony. "Come again?" he says.

Shit. I had no intention of telling him I saw his friend hooking up.

I open my mouth to respond, but no words come out. While nerves skitter through me, Xander is smiling from ear to ear.

"It's my fault," he says lazily. "Remember the girl from the club?"

"Of course," Jake snickers. "You were all over each other."

"Well, you said I could use the guest room...and I did. We weren't exactly quiet, and Isabella walked in on us." His eyes dart my way for a split second. "She probably thought it was you."

My stomach bottoms out. "I didn't," I say, voice shaky. The back of my neck goes hot. "I told you I didn't think it was Jake."

"Guys, you're giving me a headache." With a groan, Jake leans back against the couch and faces me. "What happened?"

I sigh, shoulders deflating. "When I woke up, I went downstairs for coffee. I heard noises in the guest room, so I figured I'd make sure everything was okay. As soon as I realized there were people in the bed, I closed the door." *If his asshole friend tries to sabotage my story, I'll kill him.*

"I noticed her and figured I should check on her. Found her in the kitchen, and we had a *lovely* talk. Right?" His lips stretch into a sly smile.

My expression isn't nearly as bright. "Right."

"Okay." Jake shrugs. "Though I would prefer you didn't creep on my friends."

A scoff escapes me. Seriously? *I'm* the one he's going to criticize? "What?"

"Be honest. Did you think it was me? Is that why you went in there?" he asks, pinning me in place with his stare.

I shake my head, a cold sweat breaking over my skin.

"Then you shouldn't have gone in there at all."

"Dude, it's not a big deal. She heard noises, so she checked. It's only natural."

Xander's firm tone shocks the hell out of me, and a lump lodges itself in my throat.

"If you say so," Jake grinds out. He surveys me as silence fills the room.

God, I wish I could disappear into the couch.

"Am I allowed to ask for Isabella's help?" Xander says, pulling me out of my thoughts. "Or have you changed your mind now that you know she's seen me naked?"

"Of course you can ask her. I suggested it myself." Eyes closed, Jake takes a deep breath. When he opens them again, his expression is gentle. "Baby, I'm sorry I overreacted."

"Uh-huh." It's my go-to response when it comes to his tantrums. I just want to move on. "What kind of help are you talking about?"

"I bought a house. The remodel is finished, and I bought furniture, but something is missing." Xander gives me a cute smile. "Miller said you're into interior design, and I love what you did in here. He suggested I ask you for help."

"He was praising your style like crazy." Jake gives me a wink.

God, his mood swings annoy me.

"Please, baby, help him. Preseason starts in a week, and he'll be too busy to deal with it himself. I know you're helping Ben on a few projects, but you've got plenty of free time, right?"

Say no. It's the only thought in my mind, pulsating through my head. Nothing good will come out of this. Licking my lips, I survey my boyfriend, thinking of an adequate way to turn down the project.

Jake watches me with a determined gleam in his eye that tells me he's not willing to negotiate. I can't say no.

My shoulders sag. “Yeah, I’ll help you.”

“Awesome.” Xander grins at me. “I’ll pay you, obviously.”

On second thought, maybe this project is exactly what I need. I can start saving money, and I can build my portfolio.

“Nah.” Jake waves him off. “She’s doing it for fun. She’s not anywhere near professional level.”

I drop my chin and focus on my lap. The words don’t hurt. I’ve dealt with so much worse throughout my life. Still, the shame engulfing me is strong enough to make my breath hitch.

“That doesn’t matter,” Xander says, pulling my attention to him. Eyes locked on mine, he nods once. “I’ll pay for your time, Isabella. I really appreciate you saying yes.”

I flash him a small smile and lean back, doing my best to disappear into the couch. For a long time, I stay there, listening to them talk about the upcoming season, worrying about what it means that I’ll be working with Xander.

CHAPTER 6

Not His Type

BELLA

July

"WHAT WAS UP WITH YOU TODAY?"

Jake slips beneath the covers, his sleepy eyes landing on me. "What do you mean?"

"I thought you liked Meg. Why were you so insistent on her not being Xander's type?" I take off my tee.

"You really want to have a conversation about another girl when you're half-naked in front of me?" He smirks, locking his arms behind his head, his gaze never leaving my body.

"Actually, yeah, I do." I take off my sweatpants and slip into a dark blue satin nightie. Hands on my hips, I stare back at him, though my expression is one of annoyance, not excitement. "Since when is Meg not good enough for a guy like Xander? What's so special about him?"

Frowning, he drops his hands. "God, you're no fun."

"You spent all night clubbing, then spent today bossing me around like I'm your maid—"

"Why are you so moody? And since when do you have a problem with me hanging out with my friends?" he rasps, conveniently ignoring the second part of my sentence. "You never want to go out, so I didn't think it was a big deal."

His brow is furrowed with confusion. My reaction surprised him. Normally, I put up with his bullshit. This time? It's different, and I don't know why.

"I have no problem with where you go. Nightclubs, private events, restaurants—whatever. You're not my property, so I'll never tell you what to do." Chest constricting, I work up the nerve to tell him what's really bothering me. "But I don't like how you treated me today. It's like you don't respect me, like I'm only here to satisfy your needs."

Unwilling to let him see me cry, I turn and storm to the bathroom. Once the door is closed behind me, I survey my reflection, taking in the tears forming in my eyes. I turn the faucet on and splash icy water across my face. Tears are a weakness, and I refuse to let anyone see me like this. After a few deep, calming breaths, I finger-comb my hair and assess myself in the mirror again. The girl looking back at me is filled with sadness and defeat. *Typical.*

Growing up, I learned the easiest way to survive was to please those around me. It was the only way to stop my mother's constant berating. Plus, it felt good when I made people happy, when they were kinder to me.

Respect, though, is a whole other thing, as Jake has proven time and time again.

When I finally collect myself and return to the bedroom, he's playing on his phone, unbothered.

Without a word, I slip under the covers and turn my back to him. I don't want to talk to him, and I certainly don't want him to touch me.

"Isabella." He turns off the bedside lamp. "What do you want me to say?" Rolling onto his side, he wraps his arm around my waist and pulls me to his chest.

"Nothing. If you don't think you did anything wrong, I don't want you to say anything," I mumble, closing my eyes. I don't need forced or fake apologies.

"I'm sorry. I didn't think about how my actions and words would affect you." He nuzzles my neck, going for affectionate.

All I feel is numb. This reaction isn't new. He acted like this in high school, too, so I shouldn't be surprised. Men never change. My stepfather is a prime example of that.

"Thank you for saying that," I whisper, though I don't believe him for a second.

"Listen, babe, about Meghan. She's great—beautiful and smart. It's just...Walker has no interest in anything but casual sex."

I huff. "Still, what you said about her wasn't nice."

"Let me put it this way. Walker will fuck anything that moves, and if she's hot, it's a bonus. Do you want your best friend hooking up with a guy like him? I was just trying to protect her."

"A guy like him?" I wriggle around to face him. "What's the story there? You said he's your friend, but you don't exactly speak highly of him."

With a long sigh, he runs a hand down my hip. "Xander and I were roommates in college. We both had dreams of going pro, similar beliefs and values, that kind of thing. Honestly, he was like a brother to me."

"But...? What happened?"

Jake rolls onto his back, not saying a word, his eyes trained on the ceiling. "A girl happened. We wanted the same girl...and she chose me." He sighs. "We argued, even fought at practice once. Coach said if we wanted to stay on the team, we needed to figure our shit out."

"What did you do?"

"We talked. I dumped the girl, and Walker and I patched things up. Bros before hoes, as they say," he chuckles.

A wave of nausea rolls through me at the disgusting phrase.

"For me, at least. Apparently, not for him. A few weeks later, I found out he banged her the day I broke up with her."

"Then why are you still friends with him?"

"We won the championship that year. It brought us together again. He's not a bad guy, honestly. We were kids, and he apologized. We're good." Finally, he looks at me. There's a smile on his face.

Something is off, but I can't pinpoint exactly what. Maybe it's the way Xander behaved today in the kitchen. Is he going for a repeat performance?

My heart thumps loudly, echoing in my ears. Should I mention Xander was hitting on me? Now that Jake has roped me into decorating his house, it'll be impossible to avoid him.

I decide to come clean.

"Xander was flirting with me," I breathe.

Jake's expression remains passive, and he doesn't speak.

"Um, he knew I saw him with that girl, and when he came to the kitchen afterward, he was all flirty. Smiling, making suggestive comments—"

He huffs out a laugh. "It's in Walker's nature—he's a flirt. I'm not even sure he knows he's doing it most of the time. Plus, you're not his type." He drags me on top of him until I'm straddling his hips. "You are a gorgeous brunette. He always goes for blondes. Also, you're smart, kind, and compassionate—and he likes snobby bitches with no brains."

"Was that a compliment?" Just a moment ago, he swore his friend would fuck anything that moved.

"Of course." He slinks his hand up under my nightie, groaning. "Are we done talking about this?" He cups my breast. "I want you."

Sex. It's why I'm still here. For years, I've used it as a distraction from my worries, to create the illusion that I'm loved, even when I know I'm not. When Jake fucks me, I feel something other than emptiness. But is that really enough to make me stay?

"One second." I hop off the bed, round the end of it, and put my phone on the charger. When I take a step back, I bump into Jake, who silently snuck up behind me.

He snakes his hands around me, pressing my back against his chest, and an intense shiver runs down my spine.

"It wasn't nice of you to leave me alone," he whispers.

"It was just for a couple seconds." I lean back, resting my head against his shoulder.

"No, it wasn't." He glides his hands down my nightie. "You

refused to shower with me earlier, so this time was too much." His shaky breath tells me everything I need to know about how much he wants me.

Turning around, I wrap my arms around his shoulders and give in. If nothing else, at least he's the best sex I've ever had.

COFFEE IN ONE HAND, my phone in the other, I scroll through social media. I don't have any plans for today. When I started working for my cousin, he was reluctant to give me much responsibility, so my days were dull. Frustrated by it, I convinced him to give me a heavier load. Eventually, he started trusting me with more and more tasks, and the more I worked, the clearer it became just how much I love interior design.

One day, I was lying on the couch in my old apartment, staring at the wall, when I realized a big painting would breathe some life into the living room and make the place stand out. I searched for ideas online and browsed stores in hopes of finding the right piece. When I discovered a beautiful painting of La Sagrada Família to hang in the spot, it dawned on me that I'd found something I was good at, like a missing puzzle piece clicked into place. My love for sketching and admiring interiors finally made sense.

My phone buzzes, shaking me out of my thoughts. When I see the DM request and the Instagram handle, my heart stutters in surprise.

XANDER:

Hey Bella. What are you up to?

I'm almost certain he's called me "Isabella" each time we've spoken. Now he's suddenly switched to a nickname very few people use? Why the change?

With my bottom lip caught between my teeth, I stare at my phone and consider ignoring him completely.

Fuck it.

ME:

Hey. Just had a call with my boss. What about you?

XANDER:

Miller said you have the day off.

ME:

Has your coach never called you on your day off?

XANDER:

Yeah, I guess he has...

ME:

XANDER:

Rolling your eyes at me? After I covered for you in front of Miller? Rude.

ME:

Is there a particular reason you're messaging me?

XANDER:

What if I miss you?

My lungs seize, and I jolt so violently I almost spill my coffee.

ME:

Have a good day.

I put my phone facedown on the table and sip from my mug. This guy is getting on my nerves already, and dammit, I'm stuck working with him.

My ringing phone brings me back to reality, and the unknown number flashing on the screen taunts me. What are the chances it *isn't* Xander?

Slim to none, that's for sure.

I slide my thumb over the screen. "What?" I bark. "I wished you a good day."

"What if it wasn't me calling?" Xander's laughter rumbles in my ear.

"It *is* you, so I don't see any point in speculating about what-ifs. What do you want?"

"You agreed to help decorate my place, but you have no idea what my house looks like," he murmurs, unbothered by my rudeness. "How about you come over?"

"Today?"

"Yeah, preseason starts in a week. After that, my free time will be limited," he says. "But I'm available today."

"You're lucky I have nothing important going on." I blow out a breath and stand up. "Send me your address."

"No need for that."

A knock at the front door startles me, making me jump.

With a growl of frustration, I stomp to the door and throw it open. On the other side, Xander stands dressed in a white T-shirt, light blue jeans, and white sneakers, a Cheshire grin on his face and his phone still pressed to his ear.

"I thought it'd be better to pick you up myself."

CHAPTER 7
In Your Dreams
BELLA

July

"Do you always do whatever you want?" I ask as I stab the button to end the call.

"Most of the time." With a smile, he slips his own device into his pocket and leans casually against the doorframe. "I'm happy you agreed to help me, Isabella."

"Good for you. I, on the other hand, already regret it," I mutter, stepping aside. "Come on in. I need fifteen minutes to get ready."

As he passes me, I'm enveloped in the scent of cinnamon and sandalwood with a hint of tobacco.

"Wait for me in the living room." I close the door, then dart for the stairs. I'm halfway up when I realize he's following me. I whirl around and glare, a finger pointed at him. "You. Wait. In. The. Living. Room."

"I can help." His blue eyes sparkle, making my heart go pitter-patter all of a sudden.

"Thanks." I tamp down on the reaction and erect a wall of annoyance. "But I'm fully capable of getting ready on my own." I turn and stomp to the second floor without looking back.

Inside my walk-in closet, I slip my hands in the pockets of my shorts and survey my options. I don't want to give Xander the impression that I'm dressing up for him, so I settle on a light blue floral dress. It's lovely but casual and relatively modest. Once I've stepped into a pair of black flats, I give myself a once-over in the mirror, add black mascara to my eyelashes, and collect my hair into a messy bun.

As I step into the living room, Xander stands. "You look incredible."

"Thanks." I smile. Rather than crass, his compliment is sweet. If he kept all his flirty comments to himself, it'd be so much easier to work with him.

Xander opens the front door and gestures for me to walk outside first. "When I called Miller for your number, he was at the gym. You don't go with him?"

Brows knitted, I wait for an innuendo, but his expression is placid. "No. He's got a routine, but I like trying new things. I never really stick to just one activity."

Xander chuckles. "Why? Do you get bored easily?"

"You could say that. I like variety. I'm open to everything. Free weights, yoga, Pilates, or just running."

"Yoga? You must be really flexible," he teases.

There's the flirtation. *Ass.* I roll my eyes and lift my chin, heading for the gate. "Ask Jake."

"Maybe I will."

I bite the inside of my cheek to keep from saying something rude. He's a flirt, a player on and off the field. Yet my cheeks burn every time he makes these kinds of comments.

On the other side of the gate, he places a hand on my lower back and guides me to a Porsche Cayenne. "Your carriage awaits, Your Grace," he announces. "Like it?"

"It's just a Porsche," I say. I have no interest in boosting his ego.

"*Just* a Porsche?" He arches an amused brow. "It's a Cayenne Turbo S E-Hybrid Coupe."

A huffed laugh escapes me. "*Okay.*"

With a shake of his head, he opens the passenger door for me. As he rounds the hood, I sneak a glance at him, only to find he's watching me. He doesn't look away as he slips into the driver's seat.

Shit. What did I get myself into?

"Did it take you long to find a house or...?" I ask as he starts the engine.

"My dad is the one who found it. He helped me get the process moving pretty quickly."

Hands in my lap, I tuck my chin. "Oh, okay."

"I'm pretty close with my parents, and they live nearby. It's nice to have their help, you know?"

"Yeah, I guess." In all honesty, I struggle to imagine it. I'm not close with my mom, though I am lucky to have a good relationship with my Aunt Millie and her son.

"You aren't close with your family, are you?" He side-eyes me, his smile falling.

"Not really." I look out the window, hoping he gets the hint to drop it. There's no way I'm going to be friends with this guy.

"I'm sorry. I love my folks, so I guess I assume everyone else feels the same way about theirs."

"Definitely not me." The second the words are out of my mouth, I silently chastise myself. I don't talk about my family issues with anyone. Not even Jake.

"Okay. I'm sorry for asking." Xander gives me a small, genuine smile.

I return the gesture. "It's fine, honestly. Most people do love their parents. I'm just not one of them." I avert my gaze, focusing on the road this time.

Thankfully, he does the same. A comfortable silence fills the car, and the rigidness in my muscles ebbs.

For the rest of the ride, he lets me be, and I appreciate that more than anything.

The home we pull up in front of is a one-story mahogany brick house with huge windows and a light gray roof.

Lips stretched into a smile, I turn to look at the owner.

"What? Do you like my house?" he chuckles.

"A little. There's a lot riding on what's inside." I unfasten my seat belt and clamber out of the Porsche, eager to get a better look. The house isn't as big as Jake's, but it's cozier, at least on the outside, with a neat lawn and a beautiful magnolia tree in the corner. It's warm and inviting like my aunt's place—just looking at it sends a rush of comfort through my veins.

As we approach the house, I realize that I'm nearly a head shorter than Xander.

He stops to unlock the front door, and as he pushes it open he holds out an arm. "Welcome to my humble home."

The moment I step inside, I'm assaulted by the incessant barking of a dog and the click-clack sound of nails on hardwood floors.

I freeze, hands clasped, unsure what to expect.

"Don't be scared," Xander says, his mouth a little too close to my ear. The rasp of his soft, velvety voice goes right through me. "Milo is a big sweetheart."

An orange and white corgi appears then, barreling toward me. When he reaches me, he bounces, his tail wagging. His face lights up, as if he's smiling at me.

Oh my God. I sigh in relief, and then I burst out laughing. Kneeling, I hold out a hand so he can sniff it. "Hey, buddy."

He licks my fingers, the sensation making me squirm and squeal with laughter.

"Milo, that's enough. I can't even close the door."

I stand and take a few steps forward. The dog, having discovered his owner is home, has lost all interest in me. He darts for Xander and whines, demanding attention.

"One minute, boy." Once the door is firmly shut, he crouches and loves on his dog.

I can't help but smile. It's so sweet and genuine, it warms my heart. I had a cat when I was little. Back then, knowing something was waiting for me at home, that something noticed me, was more meaningful than just about anything else.

"How did you end up with Milo?" I ask, trying to distract myself from my memories.

"My sister gave him to me on my twenty-fourth birthday. He's only a year old. Still a puppy, really." Xander gets to his feet. "How about we go to the living room?"

"Sure."

As soon as I step inside the living room, I stop in my tracks. White walls and a light wood floor are a great contrast to the room's forest green, black, and light gray accents. The room looks...nice. Why does he need me?

"Xander?"

"What?" He turns to me, a mischievous smile on his lips.

"Your living room looks like it was already decorated. The paintings are gorgeous, the throw pillows, the curtains. Why am I here?" I fold my arms over my chest, pursing my lips in an annoyed pout.

With a nonchalant shrug, he says, "Did I say which room needed to be decorated?"

"*No.*" I draw out the word as I scrutinize him. He's plotting something, but I don't know what. Or am I reading it wrong? Is it possible that Jake's story about their past is clouding my judgment? Is he being honest about needing my help? Or is this just a way to get close to me?

No. It's ridiculous. I'm being ridiculous.

"Follow me." With a wink, he strolls past me, Milo on his heels.

Goodness, this man will be the death of me.

Taking a deep breath, I follow, not allowing myself to look at his perfect ass in those jeans.

"What do you think of this?" He stops at a closed door and turns the knob.

I peek inside, and my heart instantly leaps into my throat. There's a spacious shower. The toilet looks new, but the tile isn't finished, and the walls haven't been painted.

"Erm." I clear my throat. "What happened to your designer? You definitely had one, based on your living room."

Smirking, he rocks back on his heels. "My father hired her. Things were great at first. We discussed my style, she chose items I really liked, and she worked with the contractors. But then I found out she'd been fudging the numbers and skimming money off the top."

"Oh," I say lamely. I nibble on my bottom lip, and Xander's gaze instantly darts to my mouth, his eyes flashing. The sudden change in the air has goosebumps scattering across my skin. Swallowing my nerves, I clear my throat. "I'm sorry that happened. Did you sue her?"

"No. I threatened to, but she returned every penny she took." He chuckles dryly. "She decorated everything except for this room. Think you can help me finish it?"

Head tilted, he watches me, like he's truly worried I'll say no.

I sigh, my shoulders sagging. "Okay."

Grinning, he holds out a hand. I slip my palm against his, but when an electric current runs up my arm, I pull back.

But Xander seems unbothered, closing the door to the bathroom and peering at me. "So, what's next?"

"Do you mind if I look around? So far, what I've seen is mostly Scandinavian, but I want to really get a feel for it, so I can ensure the bathroom flows well with the rest of the house."

"Go ahead. I'll be in the kitchen. I need to feed Milo." With far more cheer than the moment calls for, he saunters off. Halfway down the hall, though, he spins on his heel to face me. "You should start in my bedroom. I'm sure you'll love it."

I raise my eyes to the ceiling and groan. "Go to hell, Xander."

"Only if you keep me company." With one more wink, he disappears.

I shake my head and breathe through the annoyance streaming through my veins. I need to set boundaries, show him I'm not okay with his jokes. When I finish the tour, I'll talk to him and make myself clear. For now, though, I need to look at his bedroom, and I'd be lying if I said I wasn't curious about what I'll find.

CHAPTER 8
Boundaries

BELLA

July

When I step inside Xander's bedroom, I can't hide my smile. My expectations weren't wrong. His bedroom is an authentic example of Scandinavian style, and it's gorgeous.

The wall behind his bed is exposed white brick, the rest are painted a light gray. The ceiling is white as well, enhancing the natural light streaming in from the windows. The floors are made of light wood, but a large area rug adds some warmth and softness.

The king-size bed is made up with a solid gray comforter, two big pillows, and three decorative throw ones. The beautiful simplicity warms my insides. Jake desperately wanted a four-poster bed and sulked like a child when I didn't agree. Xander's bed, on the other hand, is something I'd choose for myself.

His room smells like him, sandalwood and cinnamon and just a hint of tobacco. Maybe there's even a little vanilla, complementing the velvety, woody blend perfectly.

The bed is flanked by nightstands, and on the opposite wall stands a built-in bookcase. My smile grows bigger as I scan the book titles and peruse the photos scattered across the shelves. There's a picture of

Xander as a child. Even then he was handsome, though when he was a little boy, his hair was blond.

Is that why he prefers blondes now?

Shaking my head at my own stupidity, I step away. I assess the walk-in closet next, then the office, the guest room, the living room, and the second bathroom. Finally, I head to the kitchen, where I find Xander sitting on a stool with his phone in his hand, Milo lying on the tile.

"I was right," I say. "The whole place is Scandinavian. All clean lines, simple forms, and neutral colors. I like the dark green and black accents that make certain elements stand out."

"Yeah, my designer was good at her job...just not very good at keeping her hands off my money," he says, setting his phone on the countertop. "What's next?"

"I'll need some time to find pieces that will work for the space. I'm no professional, so I'll need to do some research before I create a design plan. Once I have that done, I'll show it to you, and if it looks good, I can get the bathroom finished."

Head tilted to one side, he says, "When do you think you'll have something for me?"

"On Friday. Oh, that reminds me. You're coming for dinner on Saturday, right?"

"Planning on it." A sly grin lifts his lips.

"Great." I fidget with the hem of my dress. Why does he always have to look at me like that? "I think Jake invited Marco Garcia and a couple other people."

"The more the merrier." His gaze darkens. "I'm a lucky guy."

"Why?" I pinch my brows together.

"I'll have a date with you on Saturday, and maybe even Sunday." He chuckles, his eyes sparkling with mischief. He's goading me, thinking he'll get a reaction, but I've had enough of his flirting. It's too much.

"Okay, this has to stop." I round the counter and tower over him, my hands on my hips.

"What has to stop?" His eyes bore into mine, and there isn't a single sign of regret in them. He's enjoying this, and that only pisses me off more.

"Stop flirting with me. Stop making all those suggestive comments." My heart hammers against my rib cage, and a sudden wave of dizziness overwhelms me. Nine times out of ten, I'll do anything to avoid conflict. It's what I'm best at: keeping quiet and letting things roll off my back. Now, though, I'm done tolerating his behavior. "If you can't, you'll need to find someone else to design your bathroom."

He gives me a once-over, his eyes ablaze.

My cheeks flame, and my chest tightens as anger gets the best of me. He brings out a tough side of me, one I didn't know still existed. My mother did all she could to kill that particular trait in me, but apparently it just went into hiding.

"I like this fierce side of you," he finally says, his tone soothing. "It's sexy."

"God, Xander." I shake my head and take a step back. "I'm your friend's girlfriend. Your *teammate's* girlfriend. Don't you see your flirting makes *me* uncomfortable? It's disrespectful to *me*. You're confusing and annoying."

A beat of silence passes between us before his deep blue eyes narrow on me, their hint of green nowhere in sight. "Okay," he says with a lift of his shoulder. "If it bothers you, I'll stop."

"Yes, it bothers me." I tuck my hair behind my ears and sigh. "So please, keep your words to yourself."

He stands, forcing me to take another step back, and extends his hand. "I'm sorry for my behavior. I was wrong. Let's start over, okay? I'm Xander. It's very nice to meet you."

I shake my head. This is ridiculous, but I find myself slipping my hand into his anyway. "You too."

A violent zing of energy rushes from the tips of my fingers to my veins, my heart, almost making me jolt.

I swallow and slowly retract my hand.

"Just to be clear. We set boundaries?"

"We did," I confirm.

"Okay." He shrugs again. "Just so you know, if someone's gonna cross them, it won't be me. From now on, I'm your friend, Isabella." His voice drops an octave lower, sending shivers down my spine. "*A friend.*"

"And here I was hoping you could be serious for more than one minute."

A smile blooms on his lips. "For you, I will." He searches my face and arches an eyebrow. "Do you want a ride home?"

"No, thanks. I'll call an Uber."

He dips his chin. "If that's what you want."

"I'll have ideas ready to show you on Friday."

"I can't wait." The smile he gives me is far too adorable for such a big man, particularly one who's as big of an asshole as he has been.

I wet my lips. "Um, I better go. You don't need to walk me out."

"Okay." He slides back onto his stool and picks up his phone. "See you, Isabella."

"Bye," I tell him, finally forcing my feet to move. Though I was frozen in his proximity, once I'm halfway across the room, I'm hit with an intense desire to run. But if I do, he'll know his closeness affects me, and I won't give him the satisfaction.

The moment someone knows they can snare another with their words or actions, they have all the power. There's no way I'll show him my weaknesses, my vulnerabilities. I made that mistake when I was young, and I paid the price. Never again.

Once I'm outside, I breathe in and out to calm myself down. My reactions to Xander have drained me of my energy, and I don't have the first clue why. He isn't the first guy to irritate and annoy me. He isn't the first person who has made me feel uncomfortable, not the first man I've found myself attracted to. But with him, it's different. I'm resisting not only his flirting, but also his attempts to get to know me, and I'm not sure what scares me more.

I pull my phone out, but before I can navigate to the Uber app, I decide a walk will help me clear my head. It's a thirty-minute walk to Jake's, and by then I'll have surely calmed down.

As I head down the street, I call Meg.

"Hi," she says by way of greeting, her tone subdued.

My hackles raise instantly. "Hey, what's wrong?"

"Liz has been an ass all day. It's been exhausting dealing with her."

"Did you talk to her about it? All this stress can't be good for you or your business."

"I tried, and nothing changed. She got dumped again, and somehow it's my fault. Again. God, I hate it." Meg groans. "Please tell me something good."

"Are you free on Saturday?"

"I think so. Pretty sure Netflix will understand if I reschedule our date so I can hang out with you."

With a shake of my head, I laugh. "Will you come to dinner at Jake's place? A few of his teammates will be there, nothing big."

"Sure. Sounds fun."

"Thank God. I don't know if I could survive it without you."

"Why is that?" she asks.

"Xander will be there too." I sigh. "Alexander Walker."

"And? That new quarterback is the hottest guy I've ever seen. What's so bad about him?"

"I've known the guy for two days, and he's already the most annoying person I've ever met."

She laughs. "Really? I didn't have him pegged as an asshole. Guess I won't flirt with him then."

My heart sinks. He's not an asshole. That's half the problem, but I don't say anything about it to Meg.

"I'll text you the details."

Once I've tucked my phone back into my purse, a strange feeling wiggles its way to the pit of my stomach. I'm weirdly possessive over a man who has the innate ability to make my skin crawl and dampen my panties simultaneously. The idea of something happening between Meg and Xander brings me a bucketful of unease. It's probably because I want to keep her safe. The last thing I want is for her to get her heart broken.

Yeah, it's definitely just that. At least, that's what I tell myself.

CHAPTER 9
Fuck, She's Beautiful

XANDER

August

A ZING OF EXCITEMENT WORKS ITS WAY THROUGH ME AS I approach Miller's front door. He played right into my hand with this dinner invitation. I may not have an end goal fleshed out, and I may not know how far I'm willing to go to make my plans a reality, but this dinner will only help me move in the right direction. For days, I've been trying to decide what I want more—to put everything behind me, or to put my college friend through the wringer.

The only thing I know for sure is that I can't afford to damage the Warriors dynamic or my own reputation.

I joined the team to advance my career, and if I end up exposing Miller for who he really is in the process, I'll be ecstatic.

For the most part, I've put the memories of college out of my mind. But since I arrived in Boston, they keep sneaking back in, especially flashbacks of the day I found her. The nightmares still haunt me from time to time, but I'm twenty fucking five now, and I was determined to let it go. Then I met Jake's girlfriend, and all that changed. This woman is the key to his downfall.

The question is: Can she be an accomplice, or will she be collateral damage?

I knock on the door and take a step back. I'm twenty minutes early, and hopefully I'm the first to arrive.

"Xander?" Miller says when he appears, a broad smile on his face. "You're early. Come on in."

"I was bored. Figured I'd come hang with you." I step inside wearing a lopsided grin.

His expression is genuine, while mine is anything but. Gotta love Jake Miller though. His ignorance is laughable, and the apology he gave me did nothing by way of mending things.

Or am I the issue? Maybe I'm just a hopeless idiot who refuses to bury the hatchet.

"Am I the first one here?" I ask as I step past him.

"Yeah." With a shrug, he wanders to the living room.

I follow him, taking in a table set for six people with drinks and appetizers. "You caught me on my way to the kitchen. I'm headed to check on Isabella."

Check on her? This dinner was his idea. He has done nothing but talk about it, yet he left his girlfriend to do all the work?

"Where you been?"

"At the gym. Got home about twenty minutes ago. Just got out of the shower." He runs a hand through his damp hair. "Isabella is a big girl. She doesn't need my help."

"If you say so," I mutter, making sure he hears me.

The tips of his ears go pink, but he doesn't say anything.

When we step into the kitchen, Bella stands with her back to us, rummaging through a cupboard. Her long brown hair cascades down her back, ending right around her shoulder blades.

"Babe, Walker's here." Miller stalks over to her, his face split into a grin.

She's in a white dress with an open back and thin straps, so when her shoulders tense, I see it. She's visibly uncomfortable, but based on the way Miller places his hand on the naked skin of her back and slides it down to her ass, he's oblivious.

With his hand splayed over her hip, he pulls her into his side and nuzzles her neck. "I'm here, so I can help." He looks at me over his shoulder, a smile still playing on his lips. "Walker can help too."

I keep quiet, propping myself up against the wall and folding my arms over my chest.

Bella closes the cupboard with a thud and takes a step away from him. She peers over at me quickly, then zeroes in on Jake. "If you really wanted to help, you would've come home sooner. Like four hours ago. Now? Everything is ready."

A frisson of satisfaction zips through me as I watch her stand up for herself. The sight is not only entertaining, but delightful.

"Isabella." Ignoring her cold stare, Miller steps into her, his arms winding around her waist. "You're the best woman in the world. Everything you do is perfect. If I were here, I'd have gotten in the way."

"Flattery won't get you anywhere." With her hands on his chest, she tries to push him away.

He doesn't budge. He's at least twice her size.

"You asked me to organize dinner then disappeared for the entire day. I don't know why you think I'd want you loving up on me like this."

His grip on her waist tightens, his fingers digging into her sides. I clench my jaw, and discomfort floods my system. My whole body goes rigid as he angles in so they're nose-to-nose.

"I'll make it up to you, babe. I promise." He evens out his tone, trying to mask his irritation. "Anything you want."

"Right now, I don't want anything. In fact, I'm thinking about going to my aunt's." With a huff, she wriggles out of his embrace.

A groan of disapproval slips from Miller, but this time, he lets her go.

"Your guests will be here any minute." She spins to her right and picks up a bowl of salad before heading out of the room. As she passes me, our eyes meet, and she nods, acknowledging my presence for the first time today.

Good girl. I keep the thought to myself. I can't say it aloud, no matter how tempting it is.

"What's gotten into her?" Miller mutters under his breath.

Eyes narrowed, I stare at him. Is this motherfucker really that stupid?

When he catches me watching him, he blanches. "Um, do you want something to drink?"

"No, I'll wait for dinner. The food smells delicious." I push off the wall. "Should we go to the living room?"

"Yeah, sure." He threads his fingers through his hair, his gaze wandering over the kitchen. "Let's—"

The knock on the front door pulls him out of his thoughts, and he storms out of the room, muttering something about Isabella being difficult.

For a minute, all I can do is watch him go. This dinner promises to be way more interesting than I anticipated, and I'm here for it.

When I eventually make my way to the living room, I find Miller and Isabella talking to a petite blonde with a short bob. Her short green dress hugs her body, emphasizing her thin waist and round breasts. She's gorgeous. Still, my thoughts stray to Miller's girl.

As if she knows I'm thinking about her, Bella turns her head, and our gazes instantly lock. Her lips part slightly, and she sucks in a breath.

Hands stuffed into my pockets, I turn on the charm and head over.

"Izzy, your food smells absolutely mouthwatering." The blonde's gaze darts to me. "Oh, hey."

"Hey." I stop beside Bella, making sure to brush her arm with mine as I hold out a hand to her friend. "I'm Xander."

"Meghan." She takes my offered hand, her green eyes roaming over my face. "It's nice to meet you."

"You too." Pulling back, I peer at Miller on Bella's other side, who's urgently whispering something in her ear. "Are we waiting for someone else?"

Miller gives me a smug smile that makes me want to punch him in the teeth. "Garcia. He should be here in a few minutes. He's bringing one of his recent conquests. Not sure what her name is."

Meghan looks from Miller to Bella, her brow creased. "Izzy, do you need help in the kitchen?"

"I need to use the bathroom." Bella stalks out of the living room, and her best friend follows.

When we're alone, I squint at Miller, and his smile only gets bigger. "Women," he says. "Gotta love 'em."

If this is love...please, God, save me from it.

THE MORE TIME I spend in Miller's company, the less I understand what Bella is doing with him. I swear, there are no two people on Earth more different than they are, and *fuck*—she's so much more than he deserves.

"Damn, this cheesecake is perfection." Meghan slumps back in her chair, putting her palm on her stomach. "I'm full."

"My girlfriend is an incredible cook." Miller covers Bella's hand with his, an arrogant smirk on his face. It's not the first time tonight he's acted as if the compliments on her delicious food belong to him too. It's almost like she doesn't exist separately from him, like any of her achievements instantly become his.

"Let's make a toast." Garcia holds up his rocks glass. "To Isabella. This dinner is a ten out of ten."

"To Isabella." We all raise our glasses, and as we sip our drinks, a pleasant silence lingers.

"That's my girl." Miller sets his glass down and plants a kiss on Bella's cheek. Her face is an emotionless mask, her body rigid as he pulls away with his chest puffed out. "I knew this dinner would be a total success."

I scoff. "You realize you've taken credit for everything your girlfriend did tonight, right? All you did was invite us."

Miller's jaw ticks, and he rolls his lips together, holding my gaze.

"Still, it *was* a great idea," I add. The last thing I need is for him to think I have a problem with him.

"Thanks, Walker." He forces a smile before he changes the subject.

"Kennedy," he says to the woman Garcia brought with him, "what do you do for a living?"

Wine glass in hand, she glances at Garcia. "I work in marketing." Her red curls cascade down her shoulders as she tips her head back and downs the rest of her drink. When she straightens again, she scans the table, her eyebrows knitted together. "Is there more wine?"

"There should be a bottle in the kitchen." Miller turns to Bella. "Can you refill Kennedy's glass, baby?"

"Oh, it's fine." Kennedy pats at her lips with her napkin. "I can drink whiskey like everyone else."

"Isabella doesn't mind." Miller drapes his hand over his girlfriend's shoulder and pulls her to him. "Please, baby."

Meghan and Garcia, who sit on either side of me, shift in their seats, and the tension in the room thickens.

Bella's chest rises and falls rapidly, her cheeks flushed with annoyance. The question flashes in my head again: Why the hell does she stay with him?

"Sure." Face blank, she pushes herself away from the table, dislodging Miller's arm in the process.

When she returns with the bottle, we're all silent.

"Thank you so much," Kennedy mutters, looking down at the table as Bella refills her glass.

When she turns in her chair with an apologetic smile on her face, her elbow connects with Bella's hand, causing the wine bottle to tilt, and its contents spill down the front of Bella's white dress.

"Oh my God!" Kennedy jumps to her feet, her mouth open and her hand pressed to her breastbone. "Isabella, I'm so sorry. I didn't—"

"It's fine," Bella says in a shaky voice. She forces a wobbly smile onto her face as she sets the bottle on the table and bolts from the room.

Meghan stands and looks at Miller. I swear, if looks could kill, he would be bleeding out on the hardwood floor right now. "Where do you keep your mop?"

"Isabella made this mess; she—"

"Jake. Let your girlfriend change her clothes. Please," she hisses, her glare never leaving him.

"Should be in the laundry room." With a grunt, he stands and follows Meghan to the kitchen.

Beside me, Garcia is talking to Kennedy in a soothing tone while she cries, distraught over the incident. They don't even glance my way as I stride out of the room. I head toward the guest bathroom, since she didn't dart up the stairs when she left. When I find the door slightly ajar and the light on, relief settles over me. Inside, Bella stands in front of the mirror, her hands on either side of the sink and the water running.

I meant what I said at my place—I want to be her friend. When she confronted me, it hit me that making her uncomfortable just for the sake of proving myself right isn't worth it. Yes, she can stand up for herself. I don't need to creep her out with my flirting to make a point. If I want her help, I need her to trust me.

I close the door behind me, and she meets my eye in the mirror. No tears, no trembling lips. She just stands there, breathing heavily.

"Miller was an asshole," I say.

"Not the first time," she grits out. "Won't be the last."

"His reputation is everything to him. When something goes wrong or doesn't fit his idea of perfection—"

"I've known him for a decade, Xander. This isn't new."

"Your boyfriend doesn't respect you."

Her jaw goes tense, and her eyes narrow in what looks like anger, but only for a heartbeat before all emotion seeps out of her again. "It's not like that."

One brow cocked, I take a step closer. "Where is he, Bella?"

"In the living room."

"And why is he there? Why didn't he come find you? Didn't he notice how upset you were?"

"He knows I need a moment to myself." Every word is sharp, cutting.

"You and I both know that's not why. He's not here because he doesn't care." My shoe squeaks on the tile as I take a step closer. "He said it was your fault. He was going to leave the mess for you to clean up once you came back."

She presses her lips so tight they lose all color; a deep wrinkle forms on her forehead. "Whatever," she says on an exhale.

Whatever? My blood rages, and my skin itches. Why is she so fucking calm about this?

"You don't deserve to be treated like that." I put my hands on the countertop on either side of her, caging her in. Warmth spreads over my body, and I swallow, suddenly nervous. "You're gorgeous, kind, smart. He's an idiot."

Bella bites her bottom lip, trying to suppress a smile. "Thank you."

"You're most definitely welcome." With every second I stand here, my heart beats more wildly. What's going on with me? "Will you meet me tomorrow for coffee?"

"Coffee?" she asks, head tilting.

"Yeah, at my place." With a step back, I push my hands into my pockets. "I looked at your suggestions. They're fucking incredible. I want to discuss next steps."

"Really?" She turns off the water and whirls around to face me, her lips turned up and her eyes suddenly bright. "Since the only response I got was a thumbs-up emoji, I was sure you hated it."

"Sorry." I shrug and give her a sheepish grin. "How does eleven sound?"

"Perfect."

For a moment, she just smiles at me, and all I can do is smile back. Her puffy, cherry-red lips and impeccable makeup make it hard to look away. Fuck, she's beautiful.

I step back first. "I better go. We don't want your boyfriend to burst in and wonder what the hell we're doing."

"That would be awkward." She smirks, but as she lowers her gaze and takes in her stained dress, her expression falls. "I need to go upstairs and change."

"Sorry about that." I ease open the door and step into the guest room. "You looked stunning in that dress. You still do."

We walk down the hallway together, and when we get to the stairway, Bella pads up slowly.

"See you tomorrow, Bella," I call out from the landing.

She looks at me over her shoulder. She knows I'm not leaving yet, but the understanding in her expression tells me she gets what I'm saying.

"See you tomorrow."

Feeling lightheaded, I turn on my heel and return to the living room. Everyone at the table looks at me.

"Sorry, I needed to use the bathroom. Is there any chance I could get a cup of coffee?"

"Sure," Miller says, brow wrinkled as he studies me. "It's already brewing."

"Great." I slide back into my seat and smile, a new plan taking shape in my head.

The night of the welcome party, I had a rough idea of how I wanted things to go. Now, I'm certain I'm on the right track. Exposing him to Bella and making her leave him might be the perfect way to play this. Taking away the person he deems his would absolutely be the sweetest revenge.

CHAPTER 10
Perfect Match

BELLA

August

It was barely eight a.m. when I headed out for a run. With so much disappointment built up inside me, it was the best way to let off some steam.

I should've stood up to Jake. I'm still frustrated with myself for letting him treat me that way. That dinner was his idea, and yet he did nothing to help me. I should've left the moment he came home from the gym.

When I returned to the living room, dressed in sweatpants and a loose tee, he turned on his supportive-partner persona, promising to buy me a new dress to replace the ruined one. He fell all over himself gushing about the cheesecake I'd made, but the act fell flat. He only behaved that way because his teammates were there. His reputation matters more to him than anything—that hasn't changed since high school.

The moment they left, though? He warned me I should've been more careful and chastised me for not cleaning up before I left to change my clothes. None of it hurt me. I let it roll off my back, head low, nodding as if I agreed.

I've survived way worse.

It's impossible to hurt me anymore, after all the pain I endured as a child, but he succeeded in making me angry. The idea of not causing trouble was drilled into my skull until it was all I knew. It taught me to bottle up my emotions, to retreat inside myself and only show the world what they wanted to see. Last night, the urge to stand up for myself tore me apart, but my brain kept insisting I should be silent.

It came as no surprise that my brain won the battle. Again.

I slept in the guest room on the first floor, though I lay in bed for hours, mentally slapping myself for staying at his place at all. I should've gone home with Meg. When I remembered Xander and his blonde fucking in the bed I was tossing and turning in all night, my emotions only battled more violently.

All my muscles are sore and achy when I come back from my run, but my mood has improved a ton. After a quick shower, I dry off, collect my hair into a high ponytail, and put on a floral dress.

I sneak out of the bathroom quietly, hoping to leave without having to speak to Jake.

"Babe?"

Fuck. Heart plummeting, I turn.

Jake sits up in bed, rubbing his eyes. "Where are you going?"

"To meet with Xander. He picked out a design, so now we need to discuss next steps." I step in front of the mirror and quickly apply some mascara before I turn back around. "What are your plans today?"

"Dunno," he groans, falling back onto the mattress. "I figured I'd hang out with you."

"I won't be gone long," I tell him. "Two hours, max."

"Okay." He yawns. "I'll be waiting for you. Do we have anything to eat?"

"There are leftovers." I shuffle close and give him a quick peck. Before I can back away, he catches my wrist and pulls me on top of him. Brows pinched, I press my hands to the mattress and push myself up. "What are you doing?"

"How about a quickie?" His hands slide down to my hips, keeping me firmly in place.

A quickie? This motherfucker. First, I'm still angry with him. Second, I don't have time for that.

"Sorry. I need to get going." I try to wiggle out of his grip, but he only holds me tighter. "Jake, this isn't funny."

With a roll of his eyes, he releases me. "You don't have five minutes for me?"

"Five minutes?" I snort and sit up. "We're never that quick."

He breaks into a smug smile. "You're not wrong there."

I stand and head for the door. I've just stepped over the threshold when he calls my name. Turning, I lift a brow in question.

"Are you sure Walker is planning to meet up with you? He left with Meghan last night."

Though my stomach rolls painfully, I keep my expression neutral. "He picked the time. If something changed, I'm sure he would've texted." Besides, Meg spent all night throwing glances at Marco—not that Jake noticed.

"Unless he's too busy fucking your best friend."

With a shake of my head, I go down the stairs and proceed to the front door. I've wasted too much time with him.

JUST AS I park in Xander's driveway, my phone rings, my best friend's name flashing on the display on the dash. "Hey, Meg."

"Hey, babe. Doing okay?"

"I'm good. Heading into Xander's place to discuss the design ideas I sent him."

"I didn't expect him to be such a nice guy after what you told me." She giggles. "He gave me a ride home after dinner, wished me good night, and made sure I was inside before he drove off."

"Weren't you drooling over him a week ago?" I tease, climbing out of my car.

"The guy is hot, yeah, but I figured he'd be a dick. Either way, I'm not interested in him."

"Is that so?" I arch an eyebrow. "What about Marco?"

"Fuck off, Izzy. I don't get involved with taken men."

"Kennedy isn't really his girlfriend. At least, not exclusively."

"Do you wanna talk about it?" she says, her tone going soft. "About last night? Please say yes. Then I can ask about what happened between you and Xander in the guest bathroom." Now she's teasing me.

I freeze, the air around me evaporating. "Meg, I'm—"

"Relax. I'm not judging you."

"He's Jake's friend, and I'm helping him with his second bathroom. That's all."

"Okay," she says flippantly, clearly not believing me. Before I can double down, though, she changes the subject. "Do you have plans on Tuesday evening?"

"I don't think so," I say, somewhat absently. I'm too caught up in studying the peaceful, quiet home in front of me.

"How about we go shopping then? And dinner."

We make plans, and once I've ended the call, I head to the front door. I knock, then take a step back and smooth out the invisible wrinkles on my skirt.

I'm met with persistent barking, and I smile—Milo. When the door slowly opens, Xander appears, wearing nothing but briefs, his hair a mess and his face creased with sleep lines.

Warmth pools in my belly.

"Good morning," I mumble, keeping my attention fixed on his face.

"Morning. Come on in." He steps aside to let me in. "I'm sorry...I overslept."

"It's okay." I bend down to pet Milo's soft fur, and I swear the dog smiles as he leans into my palm. With my focus fixed on Milo, it's easier to avoid gawking at all the bare skin Xander has on display.

"You can wait for me in the living room or in the kitchen. I need a minute to wash my face," he says softly.

"Sure." I straighten and quickly snap my gaze up until I'm looking him in the eye. "Don't forget to put on clothes."

"Wh—Oh, *boundaries*. I forgot about those." He nods, sporting a faux serious expression.

"Stop being sarcastic."

"Whatever you say, Bella." Chuckling, he turns around and heads to his bedroom.

And dammit, I can't resist. Breath held, I take in his broad shoulders, his fine ass, his muscular thighs—which are covered in tattoos. He's too gorgeous for his own good, too good for my own misery.

With a sigh, I head to the living room and settle on the couch, taking my phone out of my pocket and skimming through my emails. From the looks of it, my Monday will be incredibly busy.

"Have you had breakfast?" Xander joins me, and though he's wearing pants, his chest is still bare, his ink and muscles on display. Probably to taunt me.

"Nope, but I'm not hungry." I hop off the couch and put away my phone. "You promised me coffee."

As I follow him to the kitchen, I give in to temptation again and assess his form. He's a total mystery to me. One moment, I think he's a jerk. The next, he's a kind and loyal guy who has strong connections to his family.

Who's the real Alexander Walker?

"What have you been up to this morning?" Xander heads straight for the coffeepot.

I climb onto a stool at the bar-height table. "I got up early, went for a run."

With his back to me, he fiddles with the coffee maker. "What did Jake do?"

"He woke up as I was heading out."

He laughs, but it doesn't reach his eyes when he looks at me over his shoulder. "Did he talk you into a quickie?"

Stomach sinking, I take an exasperated breath. "I thought we agreed on boundaries. And regardless, whether or not Jake and I had sex is none of your business."

"You're boring." With a smirk, he shakes his head.

"I prefer to be boring."

"Really? Because if I had to guess, I'd peg you as a wild little thing."

Fighting the urge to slap some sense into him, I pull my shoulders back. "One more word about my sex life, and I'll leave. For good."

With a lift of his shoulder, he turns his back to me and mumbles, "Sorry."

The kitchen falls into comfortable silence, the only sound coming from Milo, who's snoring in his dog bed. Xander moves around the kitchen with ease, setting two mugs on the table, as well as a plate of cookies.

"You sure you don't want something to eat?" He returns with a bowl of oatmeal and a single slice of whole-grain toast for himself.

I suppress a smile. Instead of a cocky asshole, he's acting like a guy who cares about his guests.

The coffee in front of me is rich, its scent a bit earthy. Eager for the hit of caffeine, I pick it up and take a sip.

"So," he says. "How do you like my coffee?"

Silently, I hold his gaze, giving myself a moment to enjoy the delicious bitterness on my tongue. "It's amazing," I say eventually. "And you weren't wrong. Our tastes are similar."

"Soon, you'll realize I'm always right." The deep timbre of his voice sends shivers down my spine.

To keep things on track, I ask, "Can you show me what you liked?"

"A little patience." He tosses me a wink and takes his phone out of his pocket.

I hide my smile behind my mug. The eagerness clawing at me is enough to make me want to jump out of my seat and yank the device from him so we can get to the fun part.

"This." He puts his phone on the table and pushes it toward me. "I want this."

"Oh." I blink at the photo, a bit disoriented. I sent him five design ideas, and he chose the one I like the most.

"*Oh?* Do you not like it? I figured you would, since you included it in the options." Xander leans away, his brows pulled together.

There's no stopping the smile that splits my face. "No, I do—it's my favorite, actually."

Just like with coffee, our tastes are aligned. It's strange. When I decorated Jake's house, every choice was a battle, and it took a ton of compromise to finally get it done.

"We like the same coffee; we like the same bathroom design," Xander muses. "You're my perfect match, Bella."

My traitorous heart stumbles over itself, but I ignore the sensation. "Those are just coincidences."

His lips tip up in a confident smirk. "No. The more you get to know me, the more you'll see I'm right."

I take a deep breath and let it out slowly, banishing the strange tingling in my extremities. "Matches burn, Xander. Keep that in mind."

For a long moment, all he does is watch me. My heartbeat quickens under his penetrative gaze, and my cheeks start to burn.

Finally, he puts me out of my misery. Leaning forward, he props his cheek on his knuckles. "Don't worry about money. There are no limits. The most important thing is quality."

"Great." I swallow around the lump in my throat. "I'll find items that fit this design and let you choose from the options before I order. If everything goes well, I expect your bathroom to be ready by the end of next month."

"Two months for one bathroom?" He cocks an eyebrow at me, though the expression is all tease.

"You'll be busy with football, and I have a job. I'll be working on this during my personal time. Plus, it takes time to find the right pieces."

"Got it. You're the boss." He takes a sip of his coffee, holding my gaze.

"Glad you've finally accepted that."

"I think I might surprise you once you get to know me better."

"You already have." The words are out before I can stop them. Throat tightening, I avert my attention, choosing to watch Milo instead. "Well," I say eventually, knowing there's no reason for me to linger, "Jake is waiting for me."

He nods, standing. "I'll walk you out."

As I follow him to the door, I can't help but wonder what his plans are for today, though I keep my questions to myself.

He's not my friend. He's my client.

On the front porch, I turn and give him a small wave. "Have a nice day."

"You too." He smiles at me, but I've only taken a few steps when he calls my name. "Bella?"

Pausing, I peer over my shoulder. "Yeah?"

"I'm hosting a party to celebrate the start of preseason."

"Okay." I shrug. Jake doesn't need my permission to go anywhere. "Jake will be—"

"I want you to be there too," he says before I can finish the sentence.

Nerves skitter through me. He's specifically requesting I attend? "I don't—"

"Please," he insists quietly. "You can bring Meghan. Whatever you need. I just want you to come."

It's so unlike me...but I want to go. I don't want to dig into why, at least not now, so I dip my chin. "Fine."

His face lights up with a smile.

"But..." I hold up a finger. "Jake won't like it that you invited me."

"He'll live," he says, his tone easy as he gives me a wink.

"You're unbelievable." With a snort, I turn and stride to my car.

In the driver's seat, I take a minute to assess his house again. Naturally, he's still where I left him, his shoulder propped against the doorframe, staring at me with an intensity that makes my stomach flip. Since the moment I met Xander, my life has been turned upside down. It's changing in ways I never thought possible, and yet I've done nothing to stop it.

It's almost as if I'm enjoying it.

CHAPTER 11

Lonely

BELLA

August

"ARE YOU SURE YOU WANT TO GO TO THE PARTY?" JAKE stands behind me, hands on his hips, while I apply my makeup.

I meet his gaze in the mirror, rolling my eyes in annoyance. "You've already asked me that." I put my eyeliner into my makeup case and turn around to face him. "If you don't want me to go, then say that. Just say the word, and I'll figure out something else to do with my weekend."

"That's not what I meant." He runs a hand through his dark brown hair. His white T-shirt is so tight, it strains against his pecs, his long legs clad in slim black jeans.

"What did you mean, then? You've been asking me if I want to go for days. Honestly, it feels like you're the one who wants me to stay home."

He shifts, his attention darting away for an instant. My questions make him uncomfortable. It's the only confirmation I need—he doesn't want me to go.

He heaves a sigh. "I don't like the idea of Meghan being there either."

I barely keep myself from laughing. It's an excuse. His problem has nothing to do with Meg.

"Xander invited her, not me."

That's a lie. Xander suggested inviting Meg to keep me company, and I agreed.

"I know." He shakes his head, his mouth twisted into a scowl.

"Don't worry. I won't keep you on a leash," I snap. "You can do what you always do when you go out: pretend I'm not there."

His expression turns from confused to mischievous in a blink. "In that dress, there's no way I can pretend you're not with me." He closes the distance between us and spins me around, sliding his hands to my ass. "You'll be the most beautiful girl in the club tonight, babe. I should be on the lookout. What if someone tries to steal you away from me?"

An image of Xander flashes before my eyes. *Fuck*. I shouldn't even be entertaining the idea.

"Don't be ridiculous." I take a step back. "Give me ten minutes, and I'll be ready to go."

"You look ready to me." He licks his lips, eyes burning holes into my body as he sweeps them over me.

My anticipation for tonight's party has made me impatient, and the desire in Jake's gaze only heightens my annoyance.

Luckily, I'm saved from turning him down when a knock sounds at the front door.

I take another step back, and he raises his eyes to the ceiling. With a harsh exhale, he stalks away, mumbling under his breath about Meghan always being on time.

Shaking my head, I return to the mirror. I check my reflection one more time, and a thrill shoots through me. This short black dress is effortlessly simple, with a darted bodice, cutout waistline, and a mini skirt. I'm wearing more makeup than I usually do, the dark liner around my eyes making my blue irises sparkle.

I stick my phone and my red lipstick into my clutch and secure the clasp. It's too small to fit anything else. I blow a kiss to my reflection, then twirl around and head downstairs.

"Wow." Meg whistles as I step into the living room. "You look amazing."

"I could say the same about you."

She's wearing a red dress that barely covers her butt, showing off her long, tan legs. She's dressed to impress, and I know exactly who she has in mind—Marco. Coincidentally, he is coming to the party alone. He and Kennedy "didn't work out."

"I'm gonna show up at the club with the two hottest girls in town." Jake loops his arm around my waist as he sneaks up behind me. "No, not the town—the country." He kisses my cheek. "Let's go."

As we walk across the street to the club entrance, I'm on the lookout for paparazzi or reporters, but it's quiet. Strange.

"Walker rented VIP sections in two clubs," Jake says, as if reading my thoughts. "One under his own name, the other under an alias. We're at the second one. No one knows about it, trust me."

"He's a smart boy," Meg comments. "You always make headlines when you go out."

He grunts a response and tugs me toward the entrance.

The bouncer lifts his chin and gives Jake a "Hey, man," as if they're buddies.

"Do you know him?"

"Connor?" Jake purses his lips. "Yeah. He's here all the time."

"Oh, that's right," Meg says. "This is one of your favorite clubs, isn't it?"

My stomach twists painfully. I didn't know any of this, which shows how *close* I am with Jake.

"You could say that." Smirking, he pulls the second set of doors open, revealing the dance floor. It's huge and packed with people. "Damn! This ought to be good."

Instantly, my anxiety kicks in, and my heart rate skyrockets. My hand goes sweaty in Jake's, and I have to fight the urge not to shake him off.

Xander said this would be a small gathering, but the VIP section is almost full.

Jake drags me along behind him, chin lifted as he scans the crowd.

"Man, this party is fucking amazing!" His voice booms over the music as we climb the stairs to the roped-off area.

Xander is at the top of the stairs, shaking Jake's hand. When he focuses on me, the back of my neck goes hot. His hair is mussed, his forehead covered in a thin sheen of sweat, like he's been dancing.

"I'm glad you like it." Xander tips his chin to the dance floor. "Does the King of Parties approve?"

"You bet I do," Jake laughs, finally letting go of my hand.

I force myself to take a deep breath. The air is thick and warm, and already I'm itching to get out of here. This club, the loud music, the alcohol—it's so not me, even if I loved it in the past.

"It's good to see you again." Meg smiles at Xander as she steps up beside me. She gently brushes my hand, as if to give me reassurance. "Thank you so much for the invite."

"You're welcome." He smiles warmly at her, then shifts his gaze to me. "Hey, Bella."

His deep voice sends shivers down my spine, as if he's whispering in my ear. All it takes is my name on his lips to get me all excited.

Dammit.

"Hey." I take in the VIP crowd. "Nice party."

"I hope you enjoy yourselves. The bar up here is open, and the crowd is full of very cool people."

"Isabella doesn't like crowds." With a chuckle, Jake wraps his arm around my shoulders.

"Why?" Xander eyes me, the corners of his mouth drooping.

"I just feel more comfortable with fewer people around." It's the truth. After what happened in New York when I was thirteen, I'm not the biggest fan of crowds, but I've learned how to live with my dislike. Honestly, crowds allow anonymity. Being a faceless person among many others means I can be myself, especially here, where I don't have to worry about paparazzi popping out at any moment.

"Then it's a good thing we're up here and not down in that

madness." Xander studies the dance floor then zeroes in on me, his ever-intense scrutiny a physical caress.

A fluttering sensation in my stomach makes me dizzy. I look away from him and catch Meg's gaze.

She puts a hand on my arm. "Wanna get a drink?"

"Sure." I glance at Jake. "Are you coming?"

"There are a few guys I want to catch up with." He pats my shoulder, but his attention is fixed on a group of guys across the room. "Go ahead. I'll join you in a bit."

"Okay."

I entwine my fingers with my best friend's and let her lead me away, her warm skin comforting me. As the bartender brings our drinks—a few shots of tequila for me and a cosmopolitan for Meg—Marco appears, his focus trained on Meg.

My best friend is totally oblivious to his attention. This is half the reason I took Xander up on his offer to invite her. It's her chance to get to know Marco better.

"Hey." He gives me a polite smile, but when he turns to Meg, the expression shifts into a lopsided grin. "Hi, Meghan. It's nice to see you again."

"You too," she chirps, turning to get a better look at him. "How are you?"

They launch into easy conversation, and after a few minutes, I tune them out, focusing instead on the music. I nod my head to the beat as I survey the VIP section. Only then do I realize Jake is no longer here, and neither is Xander. *Where did they go?* I swear they settled on one of the couches with a few other guys just a few minutes ago.

I pick up one of the two shots of tequila on the bar and toss it back. I don't have a particular plan for tonight, other than to have a few drinks and dance and sing. I haven't done anything like this in months, not since my relationship with Jake went public.

Don't get me wrong, I'm beyond happy for him, and I'm happy to be his cheerleader once he steps onto the field. He deserves all the praise he's getting from sports journalists, agents, and coaches.

But I loathe all the photoshoots that make women crazy about him. Even worse are the paparazzi who follow us. Staying in the shadows suits me better, and I'm fine with it, at least most of the time.

Tonight, I want to let loose a little. I want to feel like my old self. Not that I've ever had much of a chance to be carefree, thanks to my dearest mother and stepfather. Though I told Jake he could pretend I wasn't here, I secretly hoped we could spend the night dancing and having a good time together. Yet he slipped away the first chance he got.

And now I'm here. I'm surrounded by people, my best friend by my side, but I'm even lonelier than usual. How pathetic is that?

CHAPTER 12
Without You
BELLA

August

After downing my fourth tequila shot, I slide off the barstool and follow Meg downstairs to the dance floor. The EDM makes my body buzz with excitement. It's catchy, with just the right beat for dancing. The bass reverberates through me, making my heart thump fast and hard as a gazillion goosebumps scatter across my skin. I make my way through the crowd, swaying my hips to the rhythm. So senseless, yet so good at the same time.

I have no idea what time it is; it's so easy to lose track in a place like this. From the moment Meg and I hit the dance floor, Marco has kept us company. I excuse myself and order another shot, and as I make my way back to my friend, I search for Jake. I still haven't seen him or Xander.

Whatever. I'm annoyed, but I don't want it to ruin my mood, so I choose to focus on having a good time with my best friend instead.

When a palm lands on my butt, I spin, expecting to find my boyfriend. Instead, a sloppy drunk stranger is here.

I step back and shoot him a glare. "Excuse me?"

"Sorry, but the way you move your hips is just soooooooo sexy. I couldn't help myself." His lips ease into a goofy smile.

I tell him to get lost, annoyed that my boyfriend isn't at my side to do it for me. How sad is it that Jake is here, yet I need to deal with drunk guys on my own? He'd rather hang out with his buddies than me.

I need to find him. He should've at least checked on me—no, he should *be* with me.

Muscles tense with frustration, I stride over to Marco and tap his shoulder.

He squints at me, a smile playing on his lips. "What's up?"

"Have you seen Jake?"

"I have," Meg cuts in. She jabs her thumb over her shoulder. "He was over there a few minutes ago. I noticed him while you were upstairs."

"You're the best." I press my sweaty cheek to hers and kiss the air.

"Do you want me to come with you?"

"No, I'm fine." I march in the direction Meg pointed, trying to politely squeeze past others on my way. I'm so focused on pushing through the crowd that at first the sight in front of me doesn't register. When it does, I zero in on Jake, who is talking to a girl with red curls. He has his arm casually wrapped around her waist, and her palm is pressed to his chest.

Hands balled into fists, I storm straight for them, only stopping when I'm a step away.

The girl is the first to notice me. She knits her brows together in confusion, clearly unaware of who I am. "Can we help you?"

Rage turns my vision red. "How sweet. *We*," I grit out.

That's when Jake finally notices me. As if in slow motion, his eyes widen, and in one move he releases the woman and takes an abrupt step away. If only I had showed up a few minutes later—he would've probably had his tongue down her throat.

"Fuck you, Jake." Turning on my heel, I storm to the exit, ignoring him as he calls my name. I have no interest in hearing his excuses.

"Bella?"

At the sound of the familiar voice, I come to a stop. Xander stands with Meg and Marco, exactly where I left them. Where did *he* come from?

"Isabella!" Jake yells catching up to me. "That wasn't what you think." He grabs my hand and spins me to face him, his grip tight enough to make me wince. "Regina is just a friend."

A bitter laugh escapes my lips. "Do you really expect me to believe that?"

"Why would I lie?" With every word, his voice gets higher, and he digs his fingers into my flesh. "If I ever cheated on you, do you think I could keep it a secret? The truth always comes out. Always. I wouldn't risk our relationship, I swear."

"What's going on?" Xander steps up to us, standing tall beside me.

"Isabella saw me with Regina and thought I was cheating on her," Jake snaps, his face red with anger.

"If she were just a friend, you wouldn't have had your arm around her. You wouldn't have looked like you'd been caught with your pants down," I grind out, my voice trembling. Unbearable hurt finds its way into my heart, crawling under my skin. Nothing I do will ever be enough. All my life, I've known this. I'll never have love. I'll never be cared about. I'm disposable, easy to toss when people get bored. "That was why you didn't want me to come."

"Don't be ridiculous," he barks, practically vibrating.

Potent fury sinks into me, locking my muscles, making my body tense.

Hopeless, I glance at Xander. His eyes are trained on Jake, his irises a stormy blue.

"Regina hangs out with the team all the time. She is just a friend. Nothing more."

Xander looks down at me and gives his head a slight shake.

A wave of confusion washes over me. Is he trying to tell me Jake is lying? My emotions are all over the place, and the fact that I've been drinking only makes the situation more complicated.

"I want to go home." Shoulders pulled back, I clear my throat and look at Jake. "Without you."

I need space. I need time to consider what I want from this relationship. *If I even want to stay in this relationship.*

"What is that supposed to mean?" Jake demands, a frown etched onto his face.

Xander steps in front of me like a human shield and puts his hand on Jake's shoulder. "I'll take Bella wherever she wants to go. The two of you can talk tomorrow."

"Walker, what the fuck?" Jake swats at his friend's hand, shifting a little so he can see me.

"Trust me, this is the best solution. Give her time to think. Get your shit together." He squares his shoulders, straightening his back. His body, so close to mine, emits power, making my heart beat faster.

Xander is standing up for me. Holy shit. This is the first time in my life someone who isn't Meg or my aunt or Ben has done that.

"She clearly doesn't want to listen to you right now."

Jake curses under his breath and focuses his attention on me. "I expect you home tomorrow morning."

I snort. "You *expect* me?"

"Why are you looking at me like that? How can we fix things if you're—"

"Bella will be home tomorrow," Xander says, "if she's ready to see you. But you can't force her."

Jake's nostrils flare, his lips twisted into a deep scowl. "Fine." Wheeling around, he makes his way upstairs to the VIP section.

Xander turns to look at me and angles in close. "Ready to go?"

"Y-yeah, thank you," I stammer, hand pressed to my chest. I'm still stunned. Nothing makes sense.

Quickly, I snap myself out of it and head for the exit, eager to get away from this place.

Why am I still with him? I should find an apartment and move out.

Meg rushes over to me, clutching my hands in hers, searching my face. "I'm so sorry."

"It's fine." I sneak a glance at Marco, who stands a few feet away from us. "At least one of us can still have a great time."

"Izzy..."

My chest tightens at the concern on her face. "Don't worry about me. I'll rest and think things through. I promise." I wrap my arms around her shoulders and hug her tight. "Call you tomorrow."

"I'll be waiting," she whispers. "I love you."

"I love you too." I kiss her cheek and step back.

With a hand on my back, Xander leads me through the throng of people. The music is loud, echoing in my ears, spreading through my body.

When I agreed to come tonight, I didn't expect things to play out this way.

As soon as I step outside, I take a deep breath, letting my shoulders slump.

"I'm sorry, Bella." Xander's deep, penetrating whisper in my ear sets my whole body on fire, enveloping me in warmth.

I assess him. "Don't be. It's not your fault."

He shrugs. "Where am I taking you? Or do you want to go home and stay in the guest bedroom?"

Only then does it hit me. *Shit*. I drop my head into my hands and resist the urge to cry.

"Hey." He grabs my wrist. "What's wrong?"

"I don't have keys." I hold up my tiny purse, nibbling on my bottom lip.

Xander looks me up and down, and a gentle smile blooms on his lips. "Milo will be thrilled to see me back this early, especially with you in tow."

My heart surges at the idea. The anger coursing through me is dampened by the confusing emotions that only stir when Xander is involved. I honestly don't know how to deal with them. I'm a mess, and I feel exposed. It's not how I want to feel, especially alone... with him.

"I'm not sure," I drawl, head down, inspecting my shoes.

"I am." Again, he puts his hand on the small of my back and ushers me down the sidewalk. Once we climb into his Porsche, I stare blankly out the window. Being distant with him should help. Otherwise, I'm liable to do something stupid.

"Did you have a good time?" Xander asks as he pulls out onto the road.

With a scoff, I turn to him. "Oh yeah. I *especially* enjoyed finding my boyfriend with another girl. It was the highlight of my night."

"I'm glad to see the real Bella is back." He smirks, though he remains focused on the road. "So sarcastic. Why do I get the feeling you're only like this with me?"

The nerves that always plague me in his presence are back. He's got me there. Something about him makes me irrational.

I ignore him and answer his first question. "I enjoyed my time on the dance floor. Meg and Marco kept me company, so that was good."

"Even though you don't like crowds?"

I groan and look out the window. After everything that went down, why did he have to bring that up? And more importantly, why does he sound like he cares?

"Like I said, I'm more comfortable in smaller groups, but it's not like I can't be in a crowd. I've had years to get used to it." I fold my arms across my chest.

"Years?" he asks. "What happened?"

Hints of that old panic bubble up inside me, but I force them down again. "I don't want to talk about it. I hardly know you."

"Okay." That's all he says; he doesn't push me to open up.

The farther we get from the club, the more curious I get. Xander left his own party to help me. He stood up for me despite his friendship with Jake. They've been friends for close to a decade, and they're teammates. Still, he picked me.

"Why did you do that?" I swallow my nerves, locking my hands in my lap. "It was your party, but you left it for me. Why?"

"Because I have my own plans." He winks at me, a smug smirk playing on his lips.

I frown, annoyed by the secrecy. "Are you going to enlighten me?"

"I don't want to talk about it. I hardly know you," he quips, using my own words against me. *Smart-ass.*

"Whatever." I straighten in my seat and watch the city pass by out the window.

"I did what was right," he says eventually. "Miller is an arrogant asshole who can't look past his own selfishness. He gave you zero reason to believe him, and the fucker didn't even apologize. He said he didn't cheat on you, but his actions make it look as if he's lying. Then he expected you to instantly believe him."

I am stunned. That's what I've been thinking. It shouldn't be like this. Jake is the one who should be cognizant of my feelings, yet Xander is the one who gets me.

Suddenly, his comment about how I would have to be the one to cross my own boundaries comes back to me, along with a sense of dread.

I'm afraid I just might do that.

CHAPTER 13

Good Night, Isabella

XANDER

August

As my house comes into view, I discreetly study Bella. She's fiddling with her fingers, her teeth sunk into her bottom lip. Is she nervous? Does she regret coming home with me? I never know with this girl; I can't anticipate her moves, and it's throwing me off.

As if she can feel my scrutiny, she peers my way. "Thank you. For everything."

I clear my throat. "You don't need to thank me."

She nods. Her eyes are empty, like she's here physically, but mentally she's somewhere else, lost in her thoughts. "Xander?"

I park in the driveway and lean toward her. "Yeah?"

She parts her lips, a deep sigh escaping them. *Fuck me.* Teasing her is fun, but when she reacts like this, I start doubting my brilliant idea. I go out of my goddamn mind when she's around.

"I don't think I should be here," she says, her voice hoarse.

"Are you afraid of me, Bella?"

Her cheeks go pink at the sound of her name on my lips.

I tighten my hold on the steering wheel before I do something I'll regret. This is not the time to put my cards on the table. I have to play them right. Otherwise, I'll risk my place on the team, and all the hard work I've done to get where I am will have been for nothing. My attraction to her can't overshadow my mission.

"Of course not," she says, leaning back to put space between us.

I don't move. The distance will be beneficial for me too. "Then why?" I ask, admiring the deep blue of her irises. "What do you want to do?"

"I..." She trails off, wringing her hands.

"You're welcome to stay, or I can take you wherever you want to go." I push my door open but stay seated, waiting for her answer. "So, what will it be?"

With a shake of her head, she unbuckles her seat belt. "I'm staying."

I follow her to the front door, my attention wandering over her body. It's hard to focus on anything else when this girl is near me. The blood in my veins turns into lava; I'm a volcano ready to explode. My skin is buzzing, and my hands itch to reach out to her. I've always been levelheaded—I pride myself on that trait—but Bella makes me stupid.

As I pass her to unlock the door, my arm brushes hers, and tingles spread over my skin. *Okay, noted.* I can't control my thoughts or my body's reaction to her.

Fuck.

I step aside and follow her in. The foyer is lit only by the moonlight that streams in from the windows, allowing me to watch Bella, who's standing like she's worried she'll bump into something in the darkness.

I slip closer to her, my mouth an inch from her ear. "Do you want something to drink?"

"No, I'm good," she whispers, her hair grazing my cheek as she backs up a fraction.

"Okay. But I do, so will you keep me company?" I take a step back and turn on the lights.

Her eyes instantly shut, her bottom lip protruding in an adorable little grimace. "You should've warned me," she huffs, cracking one eye open.

"You're too cute. I just couldn't help myself." I wink at her.

"You're the second guy who's told me that tonight," she mutters.

Told her what? Was some asshole bothering her at the club?

"Let's go to the kitchen." She shuffles away from me. "I guess I could use a cup of coffee."

I blink, frowning. "Coffee? It's practically the middle of the night. Won't it keep you up?"

"It helps me sleep better than any sleeping pill," she replies. "Where's Milo?"

As soon as the words leave her mouth, a shuffling sound comes from the living room. Milo appears then, yawning and looking disinterested.

"Hey, cutie." Bella crouches and gives my dog a scratch between his ears, making his little tail wag.

"Milo is a guy. Don't call him *cutie*."

Giggling, she stands. "But he *is* cute."

In the kitchen, I check Milo's food and water while Bella sits at the bar-height table.

As I start the coffee maker and pull a lowball glass from the cupboard, I can feel her watching me.

I make her coffee the way she likes it, then set it in front of her. "Here you are." Then, glass in one hand and a bottle of whiskey in the other, I sit next to her.

Bella sips her coffee, and I down the whiskey in one go, relishing the way it burns.

"Wow. If you're not careful, you'll end up on the floor. How many drinks did you have at the party?" she asks, turning to get a better look at me.

"None." I shake my head, pouring myself another drink. "If I had, I wouldn't have gotten behind the wheel."

"Why are you drinking now?" Bella mutters, a pensive expression on her face.

"I wasn't in the mood then. I am now."

"What changed?"

"You're here," I confess.

A flush works its way up her face, making my smile widen.

It only lasts a second, though, because her words from earlier pop into my mind, and anger floods my veins. "Did someone bother you at the club?"

"Just a guy who tried to get my attention by touching me." She shrugs, taking another sip of her coffee. "He was just drunk. I can take care of myself."

Fuck. This woman baffles me. No matter how hard I try, I can't read her.

"I can't figure you out. What drives you to make decisions? What motivates you? One minute, I think I understand, but then *bam*—you surprise me again."

"It's because you don't know me. At all."

"*Yet*. I don't know you yet," I correct her, pouring myself another drink. I toss it back, then drag the back of my wrist across my mouth. "What about Meghan and Garcia? Is it just me, or were they flirting?"

Bella sets her mug on the bar and yanks off one stiletto, then the other. "God, my feet are killing me," she groans. "Oh yeah. And who knows? Maybe it'll turn into something more."

"Relationships are overrated," I say into my glass after I fill it up once again.

She chuckles, the throaty sound sending electricity down my spine. "That's why you're single?"

No, I'm single because I can't imagine being involved with someone for real. Not after what happened in college. Not after I discovered how easy it is to fundamentally hurt someone. Destroy them, even.

Not after I learned how one stupid decision could so thoroughly change a person's life.

I twirl the glass in my hand, banishing the dark energy billowing inside me. This is not the place for it.

"I don't do relationships. Everyone knows that."

"And I'm sure every girl you meet thinks she'll be the one to change your mind."

"There isn't a woman in existence who could make me change my mind. Dating sucks." I sip from my glass. "Besides, why would I commit myself to one girl when I have a horde of them following my every move?"

"You're disgusting." She twists her lips, and a crease forms between her eyebrows.

"I'm a realist." I lift my glass. "A lot of men think the same way. They just don't have the guts to admit it aloud."

Bella traces the rim of her mug with one finger. "Is Jake cheating on me?" she whispers without looking at me.

The pang in my chest takes me by surprise.

I turn to face her fully, and, sensing my scrutiny, she looks my way. Looking into her eyes is like staring into the deepest ocean...one full of sadness and melancholy.

I swallow my nerves and push the bottle away. Getting drunk is definitely not on my list of things to do tonight. "He and Regina are friends, I know that. They flirt—I saw it myself when we went out after the team party—but she knows he has a girlfriend."

She nods, lips pressed together and eyes downcast. "It's just... Ugh, don't mind me." She stands abruptly and schools her expression. "Where can I sleep?"

And now she's running away from me.

"With me." I grin at her as I stand and collect our glasses.

"Xander." With an exasperated breath, she bends down to grab her heels. "I'm serious."

It takes everything in me not to stare at her ass in that tight dress. "What makes you think I'm joking?"

"Because you are." She straightens, her arms folded over her chest, her stilettos dangling from her fingers. I'm enjoying her annoyance a bit too much, but there are still limits to it. I don't want to scare her away completely.

"Okay, you got me. It was a joke." I saunter closer. "You know where the guest room is, right?"

With a nod, she turns and shuffles out of the kitchen.

I stick her mug and my glass in the dishwasher before stopping in my bedroom to grab a T-shirt for her. In the guest bedroom, I find her sitting on the bed, cast in the dim light of the moon.

Unbidden, a memory overtakes me.

The hallway is dark, but I continue blindly, following the sound of water running. The door to the bathroom is slightly ajar. I'm sweating —a sudden pain in the back of my throat makes it difficult to swallow. The sense of dread that hit me when I got her message lingers.

I place my hand on the door and push it open. My knees almost give out when I see the blood on the floor.

Oh my fucking God. No!

I blink, forcing myself to return to reality and loosen the choke-hold I have on the shirt in my hand. "I brought you a tee, so you have something to sleep in."

A small smile tugs at Bella's lips. "Thanks."

"Do you often sit in the dark like this?"

"Sometimes," she says with a shrug.

"You're weird."

"I don't think so. I've done it for as long as I can remember. I don't need to feel or think. I can just be. I can enjoy the quiet and the calm..."

Something in her voice bothers me. Without thinking, I stroll into the room and sit beside her.

"I'm not usually the prying type," I say, setting the shirt on the bed. "But...did something happen to you when you were a kid?"

"It's a long story." Shoulders drooping, she picks at the comforter, avoiding my gaze.

"Perfect. We have the entire night ahead of us." I scoot over until my shoulder touches hers. "Talk to me."

Bella waits a few seconds before saying anything. I can see the moment she decides to open up to me, because she straightens her back and looks me in the eye. "My father died when I was five. My mother raised me alone until she met Kevin. I was ten. After that, my whole life changed."

The meaning behind her words makes me see red. "Did he do something to you?" I ask in a low voice.

She takes a deep, shaky breath. "It's nothing. It's in the past."

"Hey..." I gently wrap my hand around her wrist, turning her to look at me. "That doesn't mean it won't help to talk about it."

"Xander." My name is a warning. She doesn't want to discuss it.

Her defiance only fuels my determination. "If this man did something to you—"

"Stop!" she bites out. "It's in the past. End of story. I have no desire to revisit any of it."

Though fury roils violently in my gut, I force my muscles to relax. I put my hands on top of my head, locking my fingers. All I can do is breathe through the urge to punch a hole in the wall.

Fuck.

"But—"

"I asked you to stop," she says. "Please, let me leave the past in the past."

Taking a deep breath, I unlock my fingers and stand. "Fine."

Face tilted up, she gives me a blank look, as if she's completely unbothered. It shouldn't be like this. She shouldn't be so chill about being treated so poorly by her parents. Or Miller.

But she made herself clear, so I keep my tone even as I say, "Good night, Isabella."

It takes all my strength not to slam the door behind me. I don't know how to help her, and fuck if that doesn't make my head hurt and my chest squeeze tight.

CHAPTER 14
Family Matters
BELLA

August

The moment I open my eyes, I regret it. With my gloomy mood, even the sunlit room is annoying. I pull a pillow over my face and fight the urge to scream into it. If I do, Xander will definitely think I'm nuts.

Though, if the way he left so abruptly last night is any indication, he already thinks so anyway.

His response is exactly why I don't talk about my past. The smallest memory can rip through my entire body, every vein and muscle. Sorrow. Fear. Misery. I do my best to keep the emotions locked away in the back of my head. I don't want to give them power over my mind or my life. I survived it. It's easier not to talk about it.

Even though it's gut-wrenching to deal with alone.

I sit up in bed and take in the room. I gave it a cursory glance the first time I was here, but now I take my time cataloging the details. The room has a full-length mirror, a gray dresser, and two nightstands. Xander's bedroom is cozy and eye-catching, but this one has its own aura. I feel good here. Lighthearted, even. It's like just stepping into the space eases my worries.

I dress quickly, eager to get out of here before Xander can ask more questions, but when I pass his room and discover his door is open, I tense. *Shit. Is he already awake?* I creep to the door and peek inside. Apparently it's my new habit, watching him when I shouldn't.

Xander is lying on his stomach, hugging a pillow, and Milo is fast asleep in his own dog bed. For a moment, I watch the gorgeous man breathing steadily. I study the tattoos on his back. So many drawings, entwined together with colors and lines—a dream catcher, a wolf, hands clasped together in prayer, a lion. I can't make out some of the smaller tattoos from here.

I sigh. He was right when he said I'm weird. I'm watching the guy sleep—admiring him, even—while he isn't mine. He's Jake's friend, his new teammate. I can't allow myself to think of him as anything more.

Cursing myself for getting caught up in him, I turn and head back down the hall. I only make it a couple of steps, though, before a deep, gravelly voice startles me, making my heart lurch.

"Bella? Are you leaving already?"

Inhaling deeply, I steady myself and return to the doorway. "Yeah."

Xander sits up, his brown hair messy, his jaw covered in scruff. "What time is it?"

"I have no clue."

With a groan, he leans over and snags his phone from the nightstand. "It's eight. That means you got, what? Five hours of sleep? And you're already running away?" He raises a brow. "Stay. Miller's probably still asleep. You'll wake him up, and he'll be moody."

"I barely slept." And I'm not going home yet. That's out of the question.

"The bed wasn't comfortable enough?" He throws his phone onto the mattress beside him.

"It's not that. My mind wouldn't shut off, and I never sleep well in new places anyway."

"That's why I suggested you sleep with me."

I roll my eyes. His teasing bothers me less by the day, and I'm not sure that's a good thing.

"Come here. My bed is warm, and I have excellent cuddling skills."

"Cuddling skills?" A laugh bubbles out of me. "You're unbelievable."

"Nah. I just know what I want, and I'm doing everything I can to make it happen." He grins at me.

"In that case, it's a good thing that I also know what *I* want, and it definitely doesn't include you." I push off the doorframe and slip into my shoes. "Thank you for your help. It means more than you know. Truly."

"It's nothing," he says with a hint of a smile. "I hope you feel better."

"I do." I leave it at that. Truthfully, my life is too complicated to explain. A man who's so close to his family could never understand what I've been through.

"I'll call you tomorrow. I found a rug I think you'll like."

He nods, and a second later he's back on his stomach, a pillow pressed to his chest.

"Bye, Xander," I murmur.

"Bye." His voice sounds muffled.

A weird twinge pierces my heart. The reason Meg is my only friend is simple: I built a wall around myself a long time ago. If I don't let people get close, they can't see through the façade I've created. They can't see how damaged I am. I've known Xander for a matter of weeks, and already he's picked up on far too much. That scares the shit out of me.

On my way to the front door, I pull my phone out of my purse and order an Uber. I'm in desperate need of time with the people who truly love me, the people I'll do absolutely anything for. I hope they're awake.

It's eight forty a.m. when I knock on my aunt's door. When she doesn't answer right away, I let out a quiet curse. Aunt Millie is an early riser, but with my luck, today is the day she decided to sleep in.

Before I can come up with a plan B, the door swings open, and I come face-to-face with a sleepy Ben. He blinks, then blinks again. Then he breaks into a smile.

"Bella? What are you doing here so early?" He steps aside to let me in.

I plant a quick kiss on his cheek as I pass. "Can't I miss my aunt and my favorite cousin?"

"I'm your *only* cousin," he huffs. "And I'm not buying that shit. You look like you came here straight from the club. What happened?"

My stomach sinks. I should've thought about what it would look like to show up first thing in the morning dressed like this. "Does something really need to have happened for me to come visit you?"

Ben just folds his arms over his chest, lifting his chin.

Fine. I hate how easily he can read me. "Jake and I fought last night. We were at a party, and I left."

"What did he do?" Ben steps around me, his expression full of disdain. He has never liked Jake.

While he starts the coffee maker, I sit at the table, fold my hands into my lap, and tell him the story.

"God, Bella, I told you it was a mistake to get back together with him." He frowns at me, his expression full of pity. "And I should've talked you out of moving in with him."

"He was so persuasive, going on about how much he loved me and missed me..."

And secretly, I guess I hoped reconnecting with Jake would take me back to a time in my life when I was happier. I wanted to fill the void in my chest. But of course, I don't tell Ben that.

"And does he love you?" He sets a mug of coffee in front of me. "I can't imagine a man so deeply in love would do something like that. Where did you sleep? Meg's?"

"No. I slept at Xander's house."

Ben drops the spoon he got out to stir sugar. It falls on the floor with a ding. He's staring at me, wide-eyed and slack-jawed.

"What?" I ask.

"Wasn't it Xander's party?" Ben picks up the spoon and drops it into the sink.

"It was," I confirm.

With a sleepy groan, he slips into the chair across from me. "Did he give you his keys?"

"No. He stood up for me. He told Jake to cool off, to give me some time. Then he left the club with me."

"Wow, maybe people really do change. In college, he was a first-class asshole. The Xander I knew would've never taken his friend's girl's side. Never." Ben's face lights up with a smile, but it dies as quickly as it appeared. "Though maybe there's another reason he was being such a gentleman."

"What's that?"

"Keep in mind, I transferred in when they were seniors. Plus, I never hung out with the football team, but I heard rumors. Jake and Xander were more like frenemies than friends. They were always competing for the same girls—like, so competitive I'm surprised they didn't lose their spots on the team." He leans back, holding his mug.

"Jake told me they had problems because of girls."

"Problems?" He laughs heartily, barely avoiding spilling his coffee. "Ask your boyfriend who broke his nose senior year."

My stomach sinks. "Xander broke it?"

"According to rumors. Though maybe you should ask him." He takes a deep breath, leveling me with a heavy stare. "Be very careful with Xander. Maybe he's changed. Maybe he's a better man now, but I wouldn't put it past him to use you to get to Jake."

"Oh." I set my mug on the table, worried the coffee will only worsen the way my stomach churns.

"*Oh?* What does that mean?"

"Xander flirts with me all the time. At first, he'd make comments that made me uneasy," I say quietly. "I told him to stop, and he did. For the most part."

"Did you tell Jake about it?"

"Yeah. He dismissed me. Said I'm not Xander's type. Said he's a natural flirt."

"Xander definitely got around in college. Yeah, that was a long time ago, but I still don't like this situation." He leans across the table and covers my hand. "Don't let this dude get into your head."

Before I can respond, my aunt appears. "Bella! What a pleasant surprise."

"Aunt Millie, I'm sorry if I woke you up." I stand and wrap her in a tight hug.

"Oh, I've been up. I'm glad you're here. I barely see you lately." She returns the hug and kisses my cheek before she steps back and looks me over. "This dress looks wonderful on you. What have you been up to?"

"I was at a party." I shoot a glance in Ben's direction, silently communicating that I don't want to talk about my argument with Jake. I don't want Aunt Millie to worry about me. "I stayed with a friend and thought I'd stop by and see you on my way home."

"Do you have time for breakfast?" She ambles into the kitchen and opens the fridge.

"Yeah, I'd love that." With a smile, I drop back into my seat. "I have the entire day."

"Must be my lucky day." She shoots me a wink.

My insides light up in the way only she can make them. Dear God, I love this woman.

I stay with them until seven p.m., avoiding the inevitable as long as possible. Jake texts several times, asking when I'll be home, and Xander checks in as well, telling me that Jake called him. I ignore them all.

Jake's house is the last place on Earth I want to be, but after dinner I call an Uber and head there anyway, working up the nerve to face the issue now that I've spent the entire day running from it.

CHAPTER 15

Lies

BELLA

August

WITH A DEEP INHALE, I KNOCK ON THE FRONT DOOR. SINCE I don't have my keys, I can't slip in. That means I'll have to come face-to-face with Jake immediately. I have no idea what to say or what I want from him. Apologies, maybe? Explanations? Reassurance? I still haven't processed what I saw last night.

When he appears, he breaks into a relieved smile and hauls me into his chest. I let myself relax into him, winding my hands around his torso. He's my Jake. My friend. My first love. I want to give him a chance to explain himself, and I'm willing to listen.

"Hey," I mumble into his T-shirt.

"Hey, babe." He kisses my forehead before tilting my chin up to look at him. "You have no idea how worried I was when you didn't respond to my texts. I'm so glad you're finally here."

He guides me inside, where the TV is turned up loud and a pizza box lies open on the coffee table. Seriously? I don't expect him to grovel, but he's acting as if nothing happened between us.

My chest pinches as I take in the room.

Am I overreacting?

We sit side by side on the couch, and I turn to look at him. "How was the rest of your night?"

"I went home right after you left."

"Really?" A bolt of surprise hits me. He's the guy who closes down the club, and as pissed as he was when I left, I figured he'd really let loose.

"Babe, I don't fucking care about the party. After you left, I realized what I'd done," he mutters, hanging his head low. "I left you all alone for the whole evening. I didn't think about what it must have been like for you. I was a selfish, arrogant asshole."

Stunned, all I can do is blink. I didn't think I'd get any sort of apology. It's so not like him. But here he is, acknowledging his wrongdoings. Wow.

He turns to face me and grasps my hands. "Regina is just my friend. She works at the club. If you went out with me sometimes, you'd know her too. I...I flirt with her, but it doesn't mean shit." He leans in closer, peering at me through his dark lashes. "Do you trust me?"

Unbidden, a memory swirls in my head.

My mother sits at the kitchen table, a glass of prosecco in her hand. She's staring at me with displeasure written all over her face.

"You want something from me, but you never want to do anything in return. You're an ungrateful little bitch, Isabella. You only care about yourself. So, no, you can't go to Disneyland with Meghan and her family." She waves her hand dismissively. "Go to your room. I can't even look at you right now. You're ruining my mood."

I leave the kitchen; my eyes are trained on the floor. There are no tears—they dried up long ago—but I feel emptier than I usually do. Meghan's mom called mine and asked if I could go with them. She even offered to pay for me since it's Meg's birthday. My mom called me into the kitchen and glared at me as she told Meg's mom that no, I couldn't go. Once she hung up, she told me it was my fault. I wasn't doing enough. I never do enough, no matter how hard I try.

She's never happy with me.

I should do more. Help more. Be useful. Stop causing trouble.

Can I really be angry with Jake for flirting with this woman when I'm never there for him? When I refuse to go to parties and always skip the club?

No, I can't.

I should be putting more effort into our relationship.

"Y-yeah," I stammer. "I trust you."

With a grin, he scoops me up and pulls me into his lap, pressing his lips to mine. Relationships take work, and they can be complicated. Both partners need to make the effort, to be more understanding of each other's needs and feelings. By stepping back and avoiding the things that interest him, I'm not showing him just how much I care about him. We're both at fault, and if we want to build a strong foundation, we need to change our habits.

I want to give this relationship one more chance.

He nuzzles my neck, leaving a trail of light kisses over my throat. "You made me jealous. Why did you go to Xander's house instead of coming home? I figured you'd just sleep in the guest room."

"I didn't have keys with me." I sigh. "And I didn't have any other choice at two in the morning, so he let me sleep in his guest room."

"He's a good friend, and you seem to have grown on him."

At his words, a heat that has nothing to do with Jake or the way he's holding me rushes through my veins. The memories of Xander set my skin aflame.

"Where were you today?"

"I hadn't seen Aunt Millie in forever, so I went over there." I close my eyes, trying to force myself to enjoy the way his thumb caresses my skin. "She says hi."

"Was Ben there?" He pulls back, startling me.

I give him an awkward smile. "Yeah."

He shakes his head. "He never liked me."

A pang of guilt hits me, making me grimace. "Unfortunately."

I'm tempted to ask him about what Ben told me today, about the frenemies situation and Jake's broken nose. But if I bring it up now, it'll only lead to an argument.

"It's kinda strange, you know? I've never wronged him." He pulls me onto his lap so I'm straddling his legs. "Why do you think he doesn't like me?"

With one hand on his chest, I pull back and arch a brow. "You really don't know why?"

For a moment, he frowns, then a look of understanding crosses his features. "It's because of our breakup in high school. Isn't it?"

"Not so much the breakup but what you did *after* that. For someone who claimed to be crazy in love with me, you moved on incredibly fast."

That part of our past doesn't bother me. I'm the one who ended things. He was leaving for school, and I didn't want to hold him back. So I made the decision for both of us, and, in all honesty, it was the right choice.

"You know I didn't date anyone in college." He drinks me in, his expression lascivious as he grips my hips hard. "It was just sex; my heart has always belonged to you."

My stomach drops. "Liar." Just the other day, when he mentioned his rivalry with Xander, he said it was because he dated a girl Xander liked.

Before I can call him out, he pulls me in, his lips covering mine. He slips his tongue into my mouth, deepening the kiss. But that unease niggles at me, making it impossible to lose myself in the desire that usually flares to life when he touches me.

"Jake..." I breathe as he kisses my jaw.

"Babe, I don't want to talk anymore. I want you," he murmurs, his hot breath on my skin.

"You said you dated a girl Xander liked," I blurt out.

Abruptly, he pulls back, his eyebrows pinched together. "Er, what?"

"You told me the two of you liked the same girl, that she chose you. That you were dating." I study him, watching his reaction, noting the way he rapidly blinks. "You said you dumped her. But in order for you to break up with someone, you need to date them. Right?"

"Theoretically, yes, but–er, it was just...sex?" His tone is full of uncertainty, his eyes pleading with me to drop the subject. "It was nothing serious. I slept with her, went on a few dates. I didn't consider her my girlfriend."

Jake has always been a terrible liar. He's too vague, and when I fish for details, it's nearly impossible for him to provide them; he can say one thing, then totally contradict himself later. I've caught him in lies more than once, but they've always been innocent, so they were easy to disregard. This one, though, is much harder to minimize.

"What's with all the questions? My college days are in the past. You're my future." He sits up on the couch, taking my face in his palms. "You're the only person I want. I love you."

It's not the first time Jake has told me he loves me, and yet I can't find it in me to say it back. It's as if my heart is full of ice, incapable of love, yet I crave it. It's been my drug of choice since I realized my own mother doesn't hold an ounce of love for me.

Maybe if I tell him I love him, it will get easier. Maybe I'd believe it.

"I...I love you too." The lie slips out easily, yet nothing inside me changes. It's like paying the utility bills every month. Mundane. A task to be crossed off a list.

"Isabella." His voice cracks as he inches closer to me. He stares at me, as if he's afraid to blink. With his mouth a hairsbreadth from mine, he runs his tongue over my bottom lip, and I suck in a breath.

Eyes twinkling with playfulness, he pulls back. Then he dives in for real, his mouth covering mine. His kiss isn't urgent or forced—on the contrary, it's very gentle. Our lips move together, slowly and in total sync. Moaning softly, I finally let go of the worries that are plaguing me and wind my hands around his neck.

I don't have any desire to continue interrogating his college life. His lies. I don't want to care about anything right now.

CHAPTER 16

Blonde

BELLA

August

ALMOST TWO WEEKS HAVE PASSED SINCE XANDER'S PARTY, and my relationship with Jake has improved. Our interactions remind me of how it was when we were young, without a care in the world. We go to the movies and to dinner, soaking in the time together. We keep a low profile, so I feel at ease. I can't stop smiling. The effort he's put into our connection makes me feel better about my decision to give our relationship another chance.

The Warriors won their first preseason game against Dallas last Thursday, so the team is hyped about the game against Tennessee next week, and the fans are hopeful Xander will help them start the season strong.

While I'm thrilled they're doing well, the conversations that revolve around the game and the team are never-ending and inescapable.

What's more frustrating is how hard it has become to meet with Xander to work on his bathroom. He refuses to discuss things over text, annoying me to no end. I found the perfect vanity in three color choices, but I need him to pick one so I can order it.

And when he does have a little free time, I'm working. I knew it would be challenging, but I never imagined it would be this hard to even speak with him.

JAKE HAS plans to spend the day with his dad, so Meg and I hit our favorite pastry shop. While we sip on coffee, we talk about our jobs, my work on Xander's bathroom, and the new feud she and her sister are engaged in. This time, Liz is blaming her for the loss of one of their regulars.

We also talk about Marco and her crush on him. I can't remember the last time she was so obsessed with a guy.

"He's wonderful. He texts me every day, calls me when he has a free minute. We've gone out twice, and both times, everything was so easy. It kinda scares me." Meg lets out a nervous laugh and averts her gaze to a couple sitting two tables away from us. "What if I'm imagining things?"

"I don't think you are. I saw you two together at the club, and the way he only had eyes for you made me so giddy. The guy is into you, so stop questioning it." I put my hand over hers on the table. "Just have fun and enjoy yourself. I have a really good feeling about you two."

Expression relaxing, she entwines our fingers and gently squeezes my hand. "Thank you so much, Izzy. I really needed to hear that."

Before I can respond, my phone buzzes in my purse. I dig it out, and when Xander's name flashes on the screen, I sigh and slide my finger over the screen to answer. "Hey."

"Hi, Bella. How are you?" His deep voice sends warmth through me, as if I'm hiding under a blanket.

Meg sits back, sipping her coffee and eyeing me over the rim.

"I'm fine. How about you?"

"Good. Tired, but good. I'm on my way home. Any chance you can stop by my place?"

I wince. "Sorry, I'm with Meg. We're at Thierry's Bakery."

"Hm, that's not far from my house. Mind if I join you? We could discuss the vanity, and I wouldn't mind a little break. I think I've forgotten how to talk about anything but football."

Fighting a smile, I say, "Wait a minute. I'll ask Meg."

I mute the call and ask. Meg gives me a mischievous smirk. "Of course he can join us."

Xander has to stop by his house to pick up Milo and measure the space for the vanity, but he promises he'll be quick.

When I end the call and put the phone down, Meg is scrutinizing me. "Do you still think Xander is an asshole?"

I blow out a breath as I consider my answer. Xander is...complicated. He's cocky, for sure, and definitely a flirt, but an asshole? No, I don't think so.

Eventually, I shake my head. "I was wrong about him."

"You like him?"

"I'm with Jake." The words fly out of my mouth so quickly, it even surprises me.

She only arches a brow in response.

Straightening and steadying myself, I try again. "Xander and I... we're getting along better now."

"I noticed." She takes a sip of her coffee. "It was great, the way he stood up for you at the club. I'm thankful he did, because I was a few seconds away from scratching Jake's eyes out."

Though nerves skitter through me at the idea that my best friend feels that way about my boyfriend, I force a chuckle. "Since Xander's party, Jake hasn't been going out. We've been spending more time together, and we're both making an effort."

She hums, her attention focused on the liquid in her mug. "If you say so."

My phone vibrates again, this time with a call from Jake. "Hey."

"Hi, babe. Are you on your way home?"

"No, I'm still at Thierry's with Meg. We're waiting for Xander."

"Walker? What for?"

"To pick out a vanity for his bathroom. I thought I mentioned it to you."

In fact, I know I did. Just last night, I was telling him how ready I was to get this part done and move forward with the project.

"Yeah? Guess I forgot." He laughs.

I exhale, unwilling to get riled up over such a small thing. "That's fine. I won't be long. What about you?"

"I need to take Dad home, so I'll probably be late. You know how Mom is...and she'll be asking about you."

"I'm free tomorrow if you want to visit them. Or Monday. Whenever you want."

"Thanks, babe. See you at home."

I put the phone down again and smile at Meg. "Any fun plans for tomorrow?"

"Actually..."

MEG IS STILL GUSHING about her upcoming plans with Marco when the ding of the bell over the door draws my attention. Xander strides in smiling with Milo on the leash. When our eyes meet, tingles spread all over my body, and lightness fills my limbs. A feeling of weightlessness settles in the pit of my stomach. I'm happy to see him, and even happier to see Milo. That dog is absolutely precious.

"Hey," he calls as he approaches.

"Hi, Alexander." Meg grins. She stands and picks up her things, like she's getting ready to bolt.

Confused, I scoot to the edge of my seat. "Meg?"

"Sorry, Izzy. I forgot to tell you that...um, Liz sent me a message. I need to get back to the shop."

This treasonous woman. Now I know why she was grinning—she's leaving me alone with him on purpose. I'm going to strangle her, I swear.

"Have a nice evening, you two." She presses a kiss to my cheek and whispers, "Call you tomorrow."

"Bye," Xander says, completely unbothered by her sudden retreat.

He lowers himself into the chair Meg just vacated right across from me.

Mouth suddenly dry, I watch my best friend leave. *Shit.* I consider going to the bathroom just so I can get up and put some space between me and the man across the table.

When a wetness on my leg registers, I look down and find Milo watching me, tail wagging.

My mood instantly lifts, like it always does when I see him. I lean over and scratch behind his ears. "Aw, I'm so happy to see you, buddy. I missed you."

"He missed you too." Xander's voice slices through my skin, a delicious poison injected directly into my veins.

My heart flutters. Hooking one leg over the other, I tighten my core muscles, willing the throbbing to stop. My body's reaction to this man's presence still throws me off, but I'm determined to put a stop to it.

"How are you?" I ask. Then a server comes to our table.

Xander orders an espresso, and as she walks away he zeroes in on me, an easy smile on his lips. "I'm good. Been busy with the start of preseason."

"You don't say." I unlock my phone, navigate to the side-by-side comparisons of the vanity choices, and set it in front of him. "Check these out and tell me what you think."

For a long moment, he studies the image, using his fingers to resize it a few times. Finally, he looks up. "I like the second option the most."

Eyes dancing with mirth, he turns my phone around. There, on the screen, is a selfie I took in the dressing room while Meg and I were shopping earlier. "But I like this one too. Red looks stunning on you."

With a groan, I snatch my phone from his hand. "I don't remember saying you could look through my pictures."

He throws his head back and laughs. "Isn't that why you gave me your phone?"

Gah, he's impossible!

With a shake of my head, I open my Notes app, determined to stay on topic. "Did you take measurements?"

The server delivers his espresso, and when he thanks her, she walks away smiling from ear to ear. The way she throws glances at him over her shoulder leaves no doubt she finds him attractive.

He takes a sip of his drink and finally nods. "I did."

As he rattles numbers off, I type them into the app. Then I find the vanity dimensions to make sure it'll fit.

"Looks like it'll work perfectly in that space. Now we can finally move forward."

He lets out a deep chuckle. "I thought we were moving forward when you ordered the rug."

"We were," I confirm, sitting back in my chair.

It took five minutes to complete a task he's been putting off for almost a week. It's like he was doing it on purpose...but why?

I open my mouth, ready to call him out, but I snap it closed again. Riling him up will only encourage him to flirt.

He's watching me over the rim of his espresso when a curvaceous girl with long blonde hair walks into the shop. She's wearing a tight black dress, nude stilettos, and a wide, familiar smile—and she's laser-focused on Xander.

I frown as she approaches.

Who is she?

CHAPTER 17

She's Jake Miller's Girl

XANDER

August

THE SOUND OF HEELS CLICKING ACROSS THE FLOOR PULLS my attention away from Bella. As I turn, a woman appears at my side, someone I met at the club after the Warriors party. She was hanging out with the team, and from the way everyone spoke to her, it was clear they all knew her.

She pulls her shoulders back and breaks into a seductive smile. "What a nice surprise! Hey, Xander!"

"Hi...Cindy, right?"

"It's so sweet of you to remember." She juts out one hip, making her dress rise a little. "How are you?"

"Not bad." I sneak a glance at Bella.

Across the table, the woman I can't get my mind off watches the newcomer. She's wearing that closed-off, distant expression again, and there isn't a hint of a smile on her lips.

Fuck. This is the last thing I need when I'm trying to get Bella to trust me. This girl needs to leave.

I clear my throat and turn back to Cindy, eager to get the interaction over with. "What are you doing here?"

"I'm going out with my girls later. Figured I could use some caffeine first." She bites her bottom lip and arches her eyebrow. "Any chance you wanna join?"

Wow. The blatant disregard for Bella is actually astounding. I hate when people are rude for no fucking reason.

"Sorry, no." I plaster a smile onto my face. But my heart isn't in it, so it probably looks like a grimace. "I'm actually busy." I nod at Bella and pick up my espresso again.

The corners of Cindy's mouth drop, but only for a heartbeat before she quickly smiles again. As if she's just now noticing I'm not alone, she whips her head to Bella.

"Oh, I'm sorry. I was so excited to see Xander, I forgot my manners."

I have to hold back a snort. Does she really think either of us believes that?

"I'm Cindy."

Bella's expression remains neutral. "Hi."

Cindy narrows her eyes, her lips thinning, as if she's annoyed that Bella doesn't introduce herself.

Why would she, after the way Cindy ignored her?

When Bella doesn't give in, Cindy turns back to me. "I gotta run. Sorry for the intrusion. I hope to see you soon." She turns, but before she makes it more than a step, she peers over her shoulder, wearing a calculated smile, and homes in on Bella. "Oh, by the way, tell your boyfriend Cindy said hi. I'm sure he remembers me."

"My boyfriend?" Bella asks.

"Yeah. You're Jake Miller's girlfriend, aren't you?" Cindy bats her eyelashes. "I recognized you right away."

"Sorry, I can't say the same."

"Aw, that's okay. I wouldn't expect you to know who I am. Jake mentioned you're a homebody, and we both know he's quite the party animal."

Bella smiles broadly, but it doesn't reach her eyes. "Definitely." She nods. "Goodbye, Cindy."

"Bye," Cindy mewls as she finally walks away, her heels clacking as she approaches the counter. A few minutes later, she's gone, thank fuck. The ding of the bell announces her departure.

The whole time, Bella sits ramrod straight, her focus fixed on something behind me. The vacant expression on her face has goose-bumps erupting all over my skin.

Suddenly, as if she's a machine that has just been rebooted, she blinks and peers at me. "Do you mind if I go?"

"Are you okay?"

Standing, she smooths the front of her skirt. "Everything's fine. I just want to call and get the vanity ordered."

She slips her phone into her purse, then crouches in front of my dog and pets him gently.

"You're such a good boy, Milo. I was really happy to see you. Bye, buddy."

When she stands, she gives me a small smile and takes a step.

Before she can go farther, I hold out Milo's leash to her. "Wait. We'll go with you."

Though her expression is wary, she takes the leash.

"I need to pay for my coffee; then we can go."

With a silent nod, she guides Milo out of the shop. The dog is smitten with her, and I can't really blame him.

I quickly pay for my coffee, stuff a twenty into the tip jar, then stroll out the door. The warm late-August air makes my skin hum. Or maybe it's being in Bella's proximity. She stands a few feet away, watching Milo roll on the grass as if it's the most fascinating sight in the world. I stop by her side and assess her. She's dressed in a white T-shirt, a skirt that's dotted with little red flowers, and beige platform sandals. Her hair is in a high ponytail, giving me a view of her delicate neck.

Her chest rises and falls rapidly—she's nervous. But why?

Because of me? Miller? What Cindy said?

When she notices me, she holds out Milo's leash. I take it, brushing her fingers on purpose. The contact makes my fingertips tingle, yet she looks absolutely unaffected.

With a deep breath, she takes a step away from me. "I gotta go."

My gut plummets. *Go?* No. I'm not letting her leave in this state.

I catch her elbow. "Stay."

"Xander, I'm—"

"Stay," I urge and turn her to face me. "Talk to me."

"There's nothing to talk about."

"You're a bad liar," I tell her in a quiet voice. "You're hiding behind your fake smile, but I see the real you."

With a scowl, she yanks her elbow out of my grip. "You're imagining things."

"Talk to me. Is this about what Cindy said?" I furrow my brow, studying her.

God, she has always been hard to read, but this is taking it to a new level. She's like a trap, showing me the tiniest glimpse of her true feelings before snapping closed the moment I reach out.

She doesn't feel like she can trust me.

I need to change that.

I grab her hand and pull her away from the shop, away from our cars. Just down the block, there's a little park tucked between two buildings.

She tries to free her hand, but I only tighten my grip on her.

Once we're standing in the grass, I finally release her. Milo sniffs around us, and I give the retractable leash a little more slack. He happily struts forward, and we follow.

I figure Bella will bolt. Instead, she sticks to my side but remains quiet and aloof, as if she climbed inside herself and shut the door.

"You know," I say, "a few years ago, I saw a therapist. I was surprised by how easy it was to open up."

She peeks up at me, her lips parting in surprise. Because I'm openly admitting to seeing a therapist, maybe?

"She told me it's normal to open up to new people. Our problems wouldn't affect strangers much. They don't care about the consequences of their help for us. Our past, our expectations for our future, it all means shit to them. They only focus on our present, on the immediate problem we're facing. The problem we need their help with."

Milo stops to sniff the grass, so Bella and I pause too. She watches me, but she doesn't say anything.

I give her a minute, and when she stays silent, I take the hint. She doesn't plan to respond. "I'm basically a stranger. I don't judge. You don't need to tell me about your past or your plans for your future. Talk to me about *now*. Tell me what's wrong."

Shoulders slumped, she shakes her head. "It's probably stupid."

"Or maybe it's not," I counter briskly. "C'mon. Tell me. Even if it is stupid, I promise I won't laugh."

She inhales and lets the air out of her lungs slowly. Then, finally, in the quietest of voices, she says, "Did you hear how Cindy talked about Jake? As if she knows him. Not in some friendly way, but as if she *knows* him...on an intimate level."

A lump forms in my throat, making it hard to breathe. I want to expose Miller, but only when the time is right—and now is not that time. So, I keep my thoughts to myself and stick with asking her questions. "Do you think Jake is cheating on you?"

"Maybe," she whispers. "I don't know."

"Cindy likes attention. That was obvious within minutes of meeting her," I say as Milo takes off again, leading us across the park. "She wasn't happy that I kinda dismissed her in the coffee shop. And she definitely didn't like when you acted indifferent toward her. I wouldn't let her response bother you. Don't drive yourself crazy trying to read between the lines. She's no one, just a girl who doesn't like to be told no."

"She's exactly your type, isn't she?" The words are so quiet, I barely make them out.

Frowning, I examine her closed-off expression. "Did Miller tell you that?"

She shrugs. "He said enough."

"Your boyfriend knows nothing about me that doesn't relate to football." I halt in my tracks and turn to her.

Bella does the same, her stormy eyes on me.

"But sadly, he doesn't know you either."

I press a palm to her cheek.

Rather than flinch away or back up like I expect, she stays rooted to the spot, watching me. A rush of electricity courses through me, and the world around us slows. Tingles assault my body, an exhilarating sensation I've never experienced before. The more I look at her, the more my skin burns.

Fucking hell...I'm in so much trouble.

I'm attracted to this woman. I have been since the moment I laid eyes on her at the welcome party.

Dammit. I'm screwed.

She's Jake Miller's girl.

I can't be attracted to her.

Slowly, I take a step back and drop my hand. "Cindy was at the club after the Warriors party, but I didn't see her with Jake. I can say with certainty she left the club with a guy, but it wasn't your boyfriend."

Bella nods, taking in the quiet park. "Thank you so much, Xander. I really appreciate it."

When her gaze lands on Milo, her lips finally tip up a fraction. The tiny giggle that escapes her slides right under my skin, making me feel featherlight.

"Your dog is something else."

"Milo is the best."

"He sure is." She cocks her head and threads her fingers through her ponytail. "I'll call you when I have a confirmed delivery date for the vanity."

"Awesome." I don't want her to go. "But will you stay for a little longer? Milo and I are going for a short walk before we head home."

"I'd love that." That flicker of a smile returns.

My chest tightens in a way it shouldn't. "Then let's go."

CHAPTER 18

Dead Inside

BELLA

August

THE HOUSE IS DARK AND SILENT WHEN I ARRIVE. JAKE MUST still be with his dad.

On my way up the stairs, a calm sensation engulfs me. It's strange, considering how disturbed I felt after Cindy walked out of Thierry's, how exposed I was when Xander read me like an open book. His ability to break through my defenses, to make me talk to him, is astonishing. No one has ever had that effect on me.

I learned how to hide my emotions long ago. Some days it's a blessing, but most days it's a curse. I've forgotten how to be open, how to trust. I've worn a fake smile for so long, it has become welded to my lips.

My life is nothing but a big pretense, and I'm the biggest hypocrite of all because I'm never honest. My desperate need to be loved turned me into someone I don't recognize.

A fraud.

That's who I am, and I don't know how to stop.

Truthfully, I've always preferred to be alone, where I could hide in my own thoughts. But the night my stepfather walked into my room, my aloofness became my armor, and when my mother refused to believe me, I turned in on myself completely.

"You've always been desperate for attention, but this is next level. If you ever say something like that again, or if I find out you're talking to others about this nonsense, you best believe I'll turn your life into your worst nightmare," Mother says just before she walks out of my room.

I sit on my bed, staring at the wall for hours, numb to everything. My life is already my worst nightmare. I'm not sure I have it in me to deal with anything worse.

So, I won't talk about it.

I'll remain quiet.

It's the only way to survive.

In the shower, I go through the motions, staring blankly at the wall all the while. Afterward, I slip into a nightie and comb my hair until it's smooth, like silk under the light of the moon. For a long time, I sit in front of the mirror, staring at my reflection while thoughts swirl in my head, bringing memories to the surface.

The ones I keep locked away.

Tonight, though, they've escaped, and they are invading my mind.

In the beginning, Kevin was great. My mother was the one who caused problems. She wanted him all to herself.

When I was thirteen, Kevin took my mother and me to New York. The trip had all the makings of a cherished memory—right up until my mother's outburst. Kevin had taken us to a Broadway show, and, in her opinion, he'd paid too much attention to me. She was awful to me all night, and before we left, I stepped into the bathroom. When I came out again, they were gone.

I ran out of the theater and scanned the sidewalks. I spent the next five hours searching, wandering. It was a miracle I found my way back to the hotel. Close to hysteria and shaking with fear, I knocked on the door of our hotel room.

Only when my mother calmly answered the door did I realize they hadn't been looking for me.

She told Kevin I had thrown a tantrum and insisted on walking back to our hotel alone. She lied to him, made me out to be a brat so she could have her husband's undivided attention. I can't imagine why he wasn't concerned when they returned to our room and I wasn't there.

That night, I sobbed silently in bed; if Kevin or my mother heard me, they'd yell, but I was unable to stop the tears. I felt like the loneliest person ever.

After that day, my whole life changed. Kevin clearly got the message my mom was sending and stopped treating me like his daughter. My mother was even more awful. She made it clear I was a burden to her.

That was when I lost hope of ever finding a person who would love me for who I was. Because if my mother couldn't do it, how could anyone else?

So, I became a different person. I became malleable, perfected the ability to meet the needs of those around me. Anything to be convenient. I adjusted myself for others to ensure I wouldn't cause trouble. I was deathly afraid of being left alone again, so I would put up with anything, do whatever was asked of me in hopes I wouldn't be tossed aside.

I lost my sense of self, decimated any self-esteem I still had. I let the real me disappear.

For most of my adolescence, I was invisible to Mom and Kevin. They didn't talk to me unless they absolutely needed to. They didn't care what I was doing, what I was wearing, about my grades or whether I had eaten. I was just there, always lonely but never alone.

The irony isn't lost on me. Life with Jake isn't all that different.

The ringing of my phone brings me back to reality. I pick it up, and Jake's picture stares back.

Xander's words about Cindy come back to me. I believe him, but that doesn't mean I don't want to ask Jake about her. After the incident at the club with Regina, I can't help but be suspicious.

I press my phone to my ear. "Yeah?"

"Isabella, baby, I'm still at my parents' house. Mom asked me to stay for dinner, and you know how that goes."

In the background, his mother laughs, and his dad responds, though I can't make out the words.

I stand and cross the room. "Are you staying there tonight?"

"Probably. That way I won't wake you up."

"Okay." I ease onto the bed and lie back.

"Did Walker give you the measurements you needed?" He's being polite. He doesn't give a damn about my work. When I tried to show him, he didn't want to see the designs his friend chose or what I liked the most.

"Yeah, everything's fine. Actually..." I take a deep breath and garner the strength I need to force the next words out. "When we were at Thierry's, a girl came in, and when she recognized Xander, she came to our table. She asked me to say hi to you. She said you know her. Her name is Cindy."

"Cindy?" he asks, his voice a little too high. "What does she look like?"

"She's blonde. Curvy, with big boobs and long legs." I don't mention that Xander told me everyone on the team knows her. This is Jake's shot to be honest with me.

"I don't think I know her. If I do, I can't place her," he says dismissively.

"Hm. Xander said she was at the club with you guys the night of his welcome party."

He's silent for a moment, and when he speaks again, his tone is harsh. "Well, if *Walker* told you that, then *of course* she was with us, and *of course* I know her. How could I not, right? Who fucking cares?! There were all kinds of people partying with the team. I'm Jake Miller. I should know everyone—every random bitch, every stupid fucker."

I lick my lips, my heart thudding loudly in my ears. "Why are you being so defensive? All I said was—"

"I heard what you said. I'll be home soon." With that, he hangs up.

I put my phone on the nightstand and crawl under the covers. Closing my eyes, I shut everything out, mentally removing myself from the situation I created by bringing up Cindy. I lie quietly, unmoving, begging for sleep to take over.

"ISABELLA..."

My eyes flutter open, and for a moment I don't know where I am. The room is dark and quiet. Behind me, the mattress dips, then Jake is hovering over me, his brow wrinkled. "Did I wake you up?"

"Uh-huh." I cover my mouth with one hand to stifle a yawn.

"I told you I'd be home soon. Why didn't you wait up?"

"Sorry. I accidentally dozed off." It's a lie, but it's easier this way. I prop myself up on my elbows.

He backs off a little, his grayish blues roaming over my face. A very calculated breath leaves his mouth, and he asks, "Why did you ask me about that girl?"

Hurt and irritation battle inside me. "Because I've never seen her before, yet she somehow recognized me. She asked me to say hi to you. She said you told her I was a homebody."

"Wow, so I not only know her, but I also talk about you with her?" He throws his head back and barks out a laugh. "Isabella, do you have any idea how nuts that sounds?"

"But Xander—"

"What?" he all but growls. "Xander what? Did he tell you I was cheating on you?"

"No." I force myself to stare Jake down, keeping my emotions in check. "He told me Cindy was partying with you guys at the club, that she left with someone from the team but it definitely wasn't you."

He chews on his bottom lip, as if my answer surprises him. Then he narrows his eyes. "Do *you* think I'm cheating on you?"

I shrug half-heartedly, my body sagging against the headboard.

"Baby, this is—" He shakes his head. "That's so messed up."

"Why?" Pain stabs my heart, like lightning piercing the sky during a storm. My feelings mean nothing to him. It's all about him.

"Because I already told you I didn't cheat on you. Yeah, I love to party, and there are lots of beautiful women around, but you're the only one I want. I've loved you since high school. I couldn't forget you, no matter how hard I tried."

"I'm the one who got away," I whisper hoarsely. "Is that what you called me in college?"

"Fucking Walker! He should've kept his big mouth shut." Jake rears back, grasping my forearms and forcing me to face him abruptly. "I'm not a cheater," he grinds out.

"Then why did you get so defensive when I mentioned Cindy?" I don't know why I'm asking. My gut tells me I already know the truth, but confirmation will help me decide what to do with him.

"For fuck's sake!" He shakes me, his fingers digging in hard enough to bruise. "Maybe this chick and I were at some of the same parties. Maybe I slept with her before you and I got back together. I have no fucking clue; that's why I didn't tell you anything. But also because, knowing you, you'd have hidden back in your head again if I told you I knew her."

I don't believe him. Lies slip through his every word, like water from a sieve.

My mother was my teacher. She lied so masterfully, blaming me for disappearing in New York even though *she* was the one who abandoned her own daughter. Since then, I've paid close attention, and I've learned how to tell when people are lying to me.

It may have taken me some time, but now I can spot Jake's lies too.

I take a deep breath and welcome the indifference that washes over me. I just want it all to end. I want to be left alone. My lips tremble, but I won't allow myself to cry. Instead, I force on the most convincing smile I can muster.

"Sorry," I say. "I don't know what came over me. I never should've doubted you."

"Bullshit." He scowls. "You're not fucking sorry at all." Closing his eyes, he takes a deep breath. When his eyes open and he focuses on me again, his voice goes soft. "You should've come with me to my parents'. If you had, you never would've met this Cindy person at all." His lips break into a smug smile as he pulls me to his chest. "See what happens when you don't come to stuff with me? I wouldn't put it past anyone to try to get between us, to lie to your face to make you doubt me. All I need is you."

"Uh-huh." His words do nothing to persuade me, but I don't tell him that.

Every one of them sends me back in time, to when Kevin would turn the tables and put the blame on me. Nausea claws at my insides. This moment is far too reminiscent of so many others I've tried to forget.

Jake tugs on my nightie and squeezes my breast, his eyes hooded with desire. "Fuck, I want you. Fighting with you makes me so fucking hard." He buries his face in my neck.

I want to vomit, to scream at the top of my lungs. Instead, I remain still, too scared to push back.

Fear permeates my veins, making my blood freeze. I'm back in my room with my drunk stepfather.

Some people are strong enough to fight back. I'm not one of them.

I am a coward.

"Avoiding me isn't going to work, Isabella." Kevin's hot breath on my cheek brings a wave of repulsion. "You don't want to be on my bad side, do you?" He wraps his hand around my throat, squeezing so hard my vision blurs. "You need to fix what you've done to me. Drop to your knees and be my obedient little whore."

I couldn't tell anyone what was happening, so instead I turned off my emotions, hid my secrets, and let him get away with that transgression and so many more.

Now, I'm letting Jake do the same thing.

"Whatever you want," I mutter.

He molds his mouth to mine, his kiss hard, demanding, but I don't feel anything. People who are dead inside can't feel.

They just want it to end.

CHAPTER 19

I Care About You

BELLA

September

HANDS ON THE STEERING WHEEL, I STARE AT XANDER'S house. The bathroom vanity should be delivered today, and I promised I'd be here for it.

But in all honesty, it's the last place I want to be.

For the past two weeks, I've been holed up at Jake's house. It's the easiest way to avoid seeing people. I haven't seen my aunt or Ben, though I've talked to him about work-related stuff. There's a big event coming up, but luckily I could send invites and order food and supplies from home. The client is paying twice our usual fee since it was a last-minute arrangement, and Ben trusts me to handle it on my own. I even refused to go to the movies with Meg. All I want is to be alone, to avoid questions and lectures about my decision to be with Jake.

My phone buzzes with an incoming message, startling me out of my stupor. As I jump out of the car, a warm wind gusts over me, and a little smile prods at my lips. Though it's September, it still feels like summer, and seeing as how summer slipped away from me this year, I relish the heat of the day.

As I approach the front door, I take Xander's house key out of my purse. He asked Jake to pass it along to me, since we haven't seen one another in weeks.

He probably thinks I've been ignoring him, and while that's part of it, my bigger motivation has been to give myself time to find a solution to the situation I got myself into by moving in with Jake.

After days and days of mentally running through scenarios, I'm still at a loss, and it feels like my brain is about to explode.

He won't let me go easily.

With a shake of my head, I banish those thoughts and force myself to focus on work.

AN HOUR LATER, the vanity has been installed. It looks incredible. Once the mirror and a light fixture have been installed, the room will be complete. Unfortunately, I've shown Xander a dozen options for both, and so far, he hasn't liked a single one.

When Milo darts out of the room barking, I follow and find Xander in the entryway. His dog is at his feet, jumping around and trying to get his attention. But he only has eyes for me.

My lips stretch into an uncontrollable smile. "Hey."

"Hey." He puts his duffel bag on the floor. "It's been a while."

"Two weeks." I shrug. My heart picks up its pace, thrashing against my rib cage. A combination of nervousness and excitement courses through me, making my knees go weak. "Your bathroom is almost finished."

"Really?" He crouches and continues to love on his dog. "So you found a mirror and a light fixture you think I'll like?"

"Not yet."

"Then it's still nowhere close to finished."

"You're being a pain in the ass." I laugh for probably the first time since I saw him two weeks ago.

"Maybe." With a wink, he stands and steps closer. "Your boyfriend went to his parents' house after practice."

"I know." I nod, my smile slipping away.

Xander narrows his eyes, his expression too damn knowing. "Have dinner with me."

My heart stutters, and a hint of longing works its way through me. I fight the sensation. "That's a bad idea. I better go."

"It's an *amazing* idea. I could really use the company. Pretty please?" He ducks his head and gives me puppy dog eyes.

"What's your motive here? I need to know what I'm signing up for." I squint, tilting my head.

"Hmm." He taps his index finger on his bottom lip, and then his face lights up with the most handsome smile I've ever seen. "That's for me to know and you to find out."

"Xander." I drop my head back and groan.

He skirts me and strolls toward his bedroom, Milo scampering after him. "I'll order pizza."

I stay rooted to the spot, watching him go.

Is it a bad idea for me to stay? Yes. Will I regret it? No. Xander makes me feel safe. Pizza might be a good distraction too.

"LOOKS like we have similar tastes in just about everything, huh?" He grins, sipping on his juice.

I guffaw. "Other than margherita pizza, I'm not sure we have all that much in common." I grin. "For instance, I don't like grape juice."

"What do you prefer?"

"Apple juice, or just water."

"And what's your favorite food of all time?"

Head tipped back, I survey the ceiling while I consider the question. "Probably mac and cheese. It's so simple, but my aunt's recipe is incredible." I arch a brow. "What about you?"

"Oven-fried chicken with mashed potatoes. My mom's is perfection. It's crispy and spicy..." He closes his eyes, a crooked smile growing on his face. "Damn, even thinking about it makes my mouth water." Straightening, he turns contemplative again. "What's your favorite dessert?"

"Are we playing Twenty Questions or what?"

"Why not? We're friends."

Are we?

"We're getting to know each other." He lifts his shoulder, his dashing smile disarming me. "So, I'll ask again: What's your favorite dessert?"

"Lava cake," I tell him, feigning annoyance when in reality I'm a thousand times happier than I've been in months.

"No way! Mine too." Xander wiggles his eyebrows.

I burst into laughter. It's impossible to remain serious around him.

"And what's your favorite season? Mine is fall."

"Spring," I say. "Now it's my turn to ask." I tilt my head to the side and consider my options. Eventually, I ask, "What's the most random thing you've ever bought online?"

He presses his lips together in thought. "A helmet," he says. Then, in slow motion, the corners of his lips tip up. "For Milo."

I rear back, my eyebrows pulling together. "What for?"

"For safety. I tried putting it on him once, but he just stared at me like I was the biggest disappointment of his life. I couldn't blame him; he looked ridiculous." Eyes shining, he leans forward. "If you were an ice cream flavor, what would it be?"

"Why is it always about food with you?" I shake my head.

With one finger pointed at me, he gives me a mock stern look. "I didn't criticize your question about my online shopping, so please, no judgment."

"Okay, okay." Giggles bubble out of me, making me hiccup. "I'm sorry. I love chocolate ice cream, but cherry is a close second. My favorite would probably be a mix of the two."

"I'll remember that for next time. Chocolate is my favorite too."

Next time. My heart tries to skip a beat, but I refuse to allow it. Instead, I roll my eyes.

"Why are you rolling your eyes at me? Did I say something stupid?"

I let out a long breath. "Just stop pretending, Xander. When your bathroom is finished, I'll be out of your life for good."

"You're wrong about that." He sets his pizza slice on the plate and wipes his mouth with a napkin.

"Other than your bathroom, the only thing we have in common is Jake, and I'm not—" I snap my mouth shut. *Shit.* I almost put my honest thoughts out there.

"You're not what?" He shifts an inch closer. "Did you ask him about Cindy?"

Unease washes over me. "I did, and I told him what you said about her."

"Oh." He lifts his chin. "That explains why he's been so hostile toward me."

My unease turns into dread. *Dammit.* Once again, I've caused problems for someone who has been kind to me. All I wanted was for Jake to tell me the truth. I didn't realize he'd retaliate—

"Don't look at me like that. Miller and I went through a lot of shit in college, so his little tantrum didn't bother me at all. Besides, we're good now. We're in sync on the field. That's what matters. Seriously, Bella, don't worry about it." The smile he gives me is meant to be reassuring, I'm sure, but it does nothing to calm the storm in my chest. "Anyway," he says. "What did he say about Cindy?"

I clear my throat. "He claimed he couldn't remember who she was, then swore that even if he did sleep with her, it was before me." Lungs tight, I take a moment to force a deep inhale. "He said he isn't cheating on me, that I was being ridiculous."

Xander frowns, his foot tapping the floor. "Wait, so he said he didn't remember her, told you he didn't cheat on you, and that's it? You believe him?"

With a nod, I pick up a napkin, needing an excuse to avoid his scrutiny.

"Do you realize how wrong this is?"

My stomach sinks. "Xander, don't."

"Miller is—"

"It's none of your business." Teeth gritted, I stand.

He jumps to his feet too, the corners of his mouth tugged down. "But—"

I scoff. "There are no buts." Cursing myself and him, I stalk to the front door.

This was a mistake, one I keep making over and over.

"You're not going anywhere when you're upset like this." He catches my elbow and whirls me around.

Anger boils in my veins. "Says who?" I pull my elbow out of his grip.

"Bella, please, *stay*." His voice softens. "I-I'm trying to show you that I'm here for you no matter what. You rarely talk about yourself. Do you realize that? Tonight was the first time you opened up about the things you enjoy. You clearly don't like being in the spotlight, and I don't think you mind being alone, but you're lonely. Opening up would be good for you. Like I said last time I saw you—sometimes it's easier to talk to people we aren't close with."

"You're not the first person to tell me that, but in the end, no one stays." The words spill out before I can stop them. *Dammit.* I swore I wouldn't be vulnerable like this again. I suck in air, trying to push the tears away. Why am I crying in front of him? *Oh my God.*

Xander cuts the distance between us and takes my face in his palms. "I will stay. I'll be here whenever you need me. I *am* your friend."

For a long moment, he holds my gaze, exuding calm and focus. The heat of his skin on mine is like a brand, but I don't pull back. Everything about him—his voice, his stance, the sincerity in his expression—makes me believe him. The realization shakes me to the core.

I wrap my arms around his torso and hide my face in his chest. Closing my eyes, I inhale and hold my breath. His sandalwood and cinnamon scent surrounds me, filling me with an unfamiliar feeling of comfort.

With his arms around me, he rests his chin on the top of my head. "You don't have to tell me your secrets if you aren't ready, but don't close yourself off out of fear you won't be understood. Sometimes, just talking about things helps."

"Another tip from your therapist?" I ask.

He huffs a laugh. "No, it's all me. I'm just that awesome."

Slowly, I untangle myself from him. He lets me, taking a step back and smiling at me gently.

I can't help but smile back.

"Finally." He ducks a little so our eyes are level. "Do you feel better?"

I nod.

"Good. I knew my cuddles would have that effect."

Laughter spills out of my mouth. "You're something else."

He's so good at reading me.

What happens if I let him turn the page? I'm afraid to imagine it, because somehow, I'm sure he'll be the one to carry all my secrets while also becoming one.

My phone buzzes in the living room, breaking the spell between us.

"You should answer that." He lowers his gaze to his feet.

I dart to where I stowed my purse on the chair and dig it out, finding Jake's picture on the screen. "Hey."

"Hey. I'll be home in about an hour." Just the sound of his voice makes my body go numb. "Are you still at Xander's?"

"Y-yeah, but I'm leaving now." I keep my tone neutral. "See you at home." I end the call and take a shaky breath. "I have to go."

Xander takes a single step closer. "Bella?"

"Yes?" I tip my head and smile.

"Be careful with Miller," he says, hiding his hands in his pockets. "He's good at making people do what he wants."

I lower my gaze to my hands, my chest caving. "Why are you so worried about it?"

"Because I care about you," he says matter-of-factly.

My breath catches. "Xander," I say, forcing myself to look up, "you don't know the real me."

"I beg to differ. You're kind, smart, and funny. I feel good around you. It's like you have this innate ability to lighten my mood. And you're one of the most gorgeous women I've ever met."

A grin tugs at my lips despite his warning.

"Just like I told you after the party...I don't know you *yet*."

I press my teeth into my bottom lip and shake my head. "For someone who isn't interested in being in a relationship, you sure do pay a lot of attention to me."

His jaw goes rigid. "I just care about my friends, that's all."

"Okay," I breathe, taking a step toward the front door. "Bye."

"Bye, Bella." He slips his hands in his pockets, watching me with a ghost of a smile on his lips.

As I step out onto the porch, I can't resist sneaking one last look at him. Instantly, I regret it. His hair is tousled, the stubble on his cheekbones visible even from here, and his tattoos only add an edge to his character. His presence brings me a kind of comfort and light I've never felt before, but it's time to get back to reality.

CHAPTER 20

You Knew

BELLA

October

WHEN MARNIE WAS THERE IS PLAYING WHEN I RETURN TO the living room with a glass of apple juice. I've already seen it more than once. It always brings me comfort.

Right now, comfort is exactly what I need.

The instant the front door opens, my insides churn. I lower myself onto the couch as an iron fist clenches around my gut, and I struggle to breathe.

Jake saunters in. His face is drawn, and there are dark circles under his eyes as he drops onto the cushion beside me. "Hey."

With a thick swallow, I plaster a relaxed expression onto my face. "How was your day?"

"A fucking disaster." He meets my gaze, his lips tugged down, and props his feet up on the coffee table. "Mom's throwing a birthday party for herself in two weeks, and she wants you to invite your parents."

The lead fist squeezes painfully. "I don't think that's a good idea."

"That's what I told her. I explained, again, that you don't talk to your mom." He trails off, frowning. "She thinks that since we live together, we're ready to take our relationship to the next level. And if we're going to be a family, you should try to mend your relationship with your parents. My mom knows your—"

"I can invite Aunt Millie and Ben," I blurt out, grasping for an acceptable alternative. "But inviting my parents is out of the question."

With a grunt, he sits up, his hands balled into fists. The move makes my hands go clammy and my heart rate take off.

Shit.

"Look at it from my perspective," he says, his blue eyes icy. "My parents have been happily married for twenty-seven years. For them, it's important to have a good relationship with *all* family members... and if you're going to be my wife one day, it means your parents will be part of that family."

My mouth goes dry. "Your wife?"

We've never talked about marriage. Where is this coming from?

"Yes, my wife. And once we're married, your parents will be my family too."

"If you keep pushing me to spend time with my parents, I highly doubt I'll agree to be your wife." With a huff, I stand and walk away. This conversation is pointless.

"You can't be fucking serious," he growls behind me, his voice getting louder. "And where the fuck are you going?"

I halt in my tracks and whirl around. My heart pounds painfully against my breastbone as he strides toward me.

"We're in the middle of a conversation. Why are you walking away?"

"I told you I'm not going to invite my parents—"

"No. You told me you don't want to be my *wife*!"

Breath held, all I can do is stare at him. "I told you I won't agree to be your wife if you push me to spend time with my family."

"For fuck's sake! Is it that hard to sit through one fucking dinner? One fucking dinner is all I'm asking!" His face contorts in anger, red painting his cheeks.

"My mother and my stepfather have no intention of being a part of my life. I can't even remember the last time I talked to them," I snap, blood rushing in my veins, my hands trembling. I've never been so pissed at him.

"I don't get it. They raised you; they did everything for you. Kevin even paid for college—"

"*Kevin?*" I all but screech. "Aunt Millie paid my tuition with the money she inherited after my father's death. Kevin had nothing to do with it. The only thing he's ever done for me is ruin my life."

Jake invades my personal space and grasps my wrists tightly. "Look, I know they left you on your own a lot, or with your aunt. Sure, they weren't the most attentive, but saying Kevin ruined your life? That's a bit of an exaggeration, don't you think? It's silly that you're still holding a grudge. It's time to let go."

I clench my jaw, my pulse racing. "My mother and Kevin never treated me like a part of their family. So trust me, they won't be upset about not being invited to your mom's birthday."

"Isabella." He softens his voice, and his hold on my wrists loosens. "My mom will eat me alive if your parents aren't there. Please. It's only one dinner."

I pull my hands out of his grip and take a step back. "No."

I won't do it. Not even with a gun to my head.

"Babe." He moves closer to me, craning low to look me in the eyes. "Sorry for being so pushy. But please, for me, won't you try to look past your issues with your parents?"

He doesn't understand that no means no, and maybe that's my fault. Maybe I give in too easily. But not this time.

"Jake, I said no. That's final."

"Okay, okay." He hauls me into his chest, holding me close.

I go numb. It takes what little strength I have left just to remain on my feet.

"I'm sure my mom will understand. She loves you, Isabella," he whispers in my ear.

If I still possessed even an ounce of energy, I'd probably shudder.

His mother doesn't think I'm good enough for him, and she doesn't hide that opinion. Back when Jake and I were just friends, she fawned over me, always talking about how she wished she had a daughter like me. That all changed when we started dating his senior year of high school, and all her concerns about me were connected to my mother. Now she suddenly wants to be friends with her? It doesn't make any sense.

"You smell like coconut," he says, planting a kiss on my cheek.

This sudden change of subject is so typical for him, it doesn't surprise me anymore.

"I just got out of the shower."

"How is the bathroom design going? Is everything ready?" He holds me at arm's length, his expression hardening again. "If I'd known it would take you this long, I wouldn't have suggested you help Xander."

My hackles raise at the slight. "All I need now is Xander's approval on a mirror and a light fixture." As I say the words, my chest pangs. This project has been the perfect excuse to spend time away from Jake, and I'm not ready to give it up.

As if he hasn't been listening to a word I said, he takes my hands in his, smiling. "Wanna watch a movie and order takeout?"

I let out a relieved breath. "Takeout sounds good. I've been watching—"

"Babe, no, please. You know I don't like those stupid cartoons." He grimaces.

I roll my eyes. *Whatever.* Watching anime with him is torturous anyway. He makes fun of the characters and the plot the whole way through, as if his favorite blockbusters are fucking masterpieces. Bullshit.

As I follow him back to the couch, one thought becomes louder in my head: I'm pretty certain I don't want to be in this relationship anymore. But I'll have to stay somewhere else while I search for affordable housing, so maybe a break will do for starters, and I'll need to be very careful figuring out my next steps.

Because Jake's behavior concerns me more every day.

I CHEW on my bottom lip as I take in my reflection. My floral lace midi dress is white with a surplice neckline. I feel like a princess in it, elegant and poised. The material is soft, and my nude stilettos are as comfortable as stilettos can be.

Despite all that, I worry I won't look proper enough for Jake's mother.

My hair cascades down my shoulders, and I've combined two little braids into one to make a halo. The style is effortless and a bit messy. It's perfect for me. For makeup, I stuck with black mascara and a nude lip gloss only. Jake's mom hates when women wear too much makeup, so I decided to play it safe.

Downstairs, Jake is on the phone, his loud voice echoing off the walls. "Yeah, I couldn't agree more. The bastard brought us luck." He barks out a laugh. "We've got Tampa Bay in the bag... You too, man. You've been on fucking fire this season, Garcia."

I stop at the threshold of the living room just as he finishes the call. "I'm ready."

He stalks toward me, his eyes sparkling with excitement. He's dressed in a white shirt and beige pants. The whole outfit is tailored to fit him perfectly, and he looks good. "You look absolutely amazing, baby."

For a week after he brought up my parents, he tried one approach after another to convince me to invite them. When guilting me didn't work, he tried begging. But my answer stayed the same, and he finally backed off. For the past week, we haven't had even the slightest argument. It's like we're tiptoeing around each other, like one spark will be enough to start a fire that would demolish everything in its wake.

This is all a pretense. A façade. On the outside, everything is perfect. On the inside, it's all crumbling—like my whole life at this point.

"I hope your mom thinks so too." I give him a small smile.

With his hands on my hips, he kisses me. It's slow and sweet, and it takes me by surprise. Recently, he hasn't been particularly gentle with me. When I found bruises on my ass cheeks after we had sex a few days ago, he said he got carried away, that he didn't actually want to hurt me. I like it when he's rough with me, but I don't tell him that. If I do, I worry he'll take it too far. The bruises on my ass are definitely not the first ones I've found on my body after sex.

"Nothing can spoil my mom's good mood. She went all out." He grins at me and takes a step back.

"Thank you for understanding. I'm sure my parents won't be missed."

With a shrug, he shifts his attention to the bookcase. "You said you didn't want to invite them, so...it's okay." He looks around the room, chin lifted, as if searching for something. Then he brings his gaze back to me. "Sounds like Walker is happy with his new mirror and the light fixture you ordered. It was delivered and installed yesterday, and he couldn't stop blabbering about it in the locker room."

A small smile tugs at my lips. At the same time, my heart aches. I haven't seen Xander since the day his bathroom vanity was installed. It's my choice, but it still hurts.

"He said you should stop by and check it out." With his hand in mine, he leads me to the front door. "I was surprised you didn't want to be there for the install, so you could take pictures of the results or whatever."

Head lowered, I swallow past the lump in my throat. "It's okay. We're both so busy. Our schedules never seem to align."

I saw Xander from afar at the Warriors game a couple of weeks ago, and it honestly made me sad.

I miss the time I spent at his house.

I miss Milo.

And, though I shouldn't, I miss Xander himself.

Jake lets me out first and joins me on the porch a moment later. "Have you noticed that since you stopped hanging out with Walker, things are better between us?"

Annoyance courses through me. Of course he'd blame someone else for his faults. "I think it has more to do with the both of us realizing just how much is at stake, don't you?"

"Maybe you're right. If a future with you is at stake, I'll do whatever it takes."

In response, I fake another smile and head toward his car.

FOR THE LAST TEN MINUTES, Jake and his dad have been talking nonstop about the upcoming game against Tampa Bay. Mr. Miller is very proud of his son. It makes my heart feel full. No matter what I think about them, I can appreciate that Jake's parents love him to bits. He's where he is now because they believed in him, and they did everything in their power to make his dreams of playing in the NFL come true.

"There you are!" Mrs. Miller calls from behind me.

When I turn, my heart drops straight to the floor. Lungs seizing, I yank on Jake's hand.

This can't be happening.

"Look who came to wish me a happy birthday!"

My mother follows Mrs. Miller out of the house. Her gaze is fixed on me. She surveys me, taking in my dress and my hair, her nose wrinkling. Then she shifts to look at Jake, a silly smile on her lips. In her opinion, the only thing I've ever done right was date Jake.

"Honey, you look fabulous," Mother says as she leans in and kisses my cheek.

The strong aroma of her perfume engulfs me. I hold my breath to avoid the dizziness it's sure to bring.

"With a boyfriend like Jake, you always need to look good. Otherwise, another woman might steal him away from you!"

"I don't need anyone but Isabella." Beside me, Jake frowns at her.

She takes a step back from me and kisses his cheek.

When she releases him, he gives her a polite smile. "It's nice to see you, Samantha."

"It's nice to see you too. Both of you, actually. I can't remember the last time I saw my daughter. Apparently Kevin and I aren't good enough for our beautiful Isabella." Eyes the same blue as mine flash to me.

"Or is it the other way around? Am I not good enough to be your daughter?" I ask, not a care in my voice.

Mother's expression turns pinched, and her smile slips.

She wasn't expecting that. I've always just taken her insults silently, preferring to avoid any form of confrontation. But not today. Today, I'm too fucking angry to let the slights and the backhanded remarks go.

"Isabella!" Mrs. Miller gasps. "It's my birthday, and this is my house. Please behave. You don't want to embarrass Jake, do you?"

"Of course not," I mutter, hands gripped tightly in front of me.

God, I hope she's here alone. If Kevin is here too, I'll snap.

"You have such a beautiful house, Caroline."

That fucking voice...

My knees go weak, and my vision goes spotty as my stepfather steps out of the house. His white shirt and black pants are fitted, flaunting his muscles, as always. He's more concerned about his looks than just about anything, and I guess he has to be. My mom would've left his miserable ass if he didn't take care of himself. Everything in her world must be perfect.

"We've done a lot of renovating since Jake started playing for the Warriors—all of which he insisted he pay for," Mr. Miller says, his chest puffing out.

Kevin's smile is wide, but it doesn't reach his dark brown eyes as he looks from person to person. He envies Jake's parents...and he envies Jake, a guy in his twenties who has achieved way more than he has at fifty.

"It's very nice of you to invite us." Kevin shakes Mr. Miller's hand and then turns to Jake. "I love watching you on the field. Your game is incredible."

"Thank you." Jake holds out a hand.

With every step closer he gets, my muscles tense further. My heart pounds painfully, and blood rushes in my ears. If I thought I could move, I'd probably run. Instead, I'm frozen in terror.

"Isabella, my sweet girl. It's been so long." Kevin pulls me into his arms.

Once again, I hold my breath. This time, I worry that if I catch the scent of his cologne, I'll vomit right here in front of everyone.

"You look breathtaking." The words are whispered in my ear, his breath hot on my neck.

Through gritted teeth, I hiss, "Get your hands off me."

"Isabella, Isabella. You know I just miss you," he murmurs sweetly, finally releasing me.

With that, he turns and launches into a conversation about the people in attendance, clearly assessing their statuses and whether they're worthy of his time.

While the five of them yammer on, I stand there, quietly seething, praying our parents walk away so I can speak to Jake.

But where my mother is concerned, my prayers are never answered.

She leans in, her eyes narrowed to slits. "Next time you decide to open your fucking mouth and be nasty to me, I'd advise you to think twice. I have no problem telling everyone what a vindictive little bitch you are." Her words are pure venom. "I doubt it would take long for Caroline and Dave to kick you out of their house and out of their son's life. You don't want that, do you?"

"Honestly?" I can feel Kevin's gaze on me, but I keep my focus trained on Mother instead. "By all means. Do whatever you want."

Her lips flatten, and her nostrils flare. "So incredibly selfish and ungrateful. As always. I shouldn't be surprised."

She turns back to Kevin and slips her hand around his elbow. He watches me again, eyeing me up and down as he runs his finger along the edge of his shirt collar. Finally, he turns back to Jake, who's still droning on about the Warriors this season.

I hate it here.

When dinner is served, I tug on Jake's sleeve, stopping him from going inside.

"Why are they here?" I ask once we're alone.

"Baby, I'm so sorry." He moves closer.

On instinct, I step back.

He frowns but stays where he is. "I told Mom you wouldn't be comfortable with them here. She swore she wouldn't invite them, but two days ago, I found out she did it anyway."

The numbness has returned, causing my extremities to tingle. "So...you knew?"

"Well, yeah. I didn't know how to tell you, and with the game, it kinda slipped my mind." He licks his lips.

Liar. He knew I wouldn't be here if he had told me the truth, and he didn't want to upset his mother.

"I'm so sorry, really. But it's just dinner, right? Please, babe, just ignore them. It'll be fine."

Taking a deep breath, I fold my arms over my chest. "No. I made it clear I don't want to see them. You only made things worse when you didn't bother to tell me they'd been invited. So no, I won't bear the presence of the two people I hate most in the world." My skin is buzzing, and pure fury flows through my veins. "I'm going home."

"Isabella," he mutters, reaching out. "I'll make it up to you."

I take a step back. "Don't bother." The words come out before I can process what I'm saying. "I need a break from this relationship, some time to think about what I want for my future."

I turn on my heel and head for the house, but I only make it a step before he catches my elbow. His fingers dig into my skin as he pulls me back, making me stagger.

"What do you mean you need a break?" he all but shouts. "Are you breaking up with me? *Again*?"

I shake my head. "I just need some time to myself. Away from you."

"What am I supposed to do without you?" he rasps. He already has on that hangdog expression he always uses to make me feel bad.

This time, I refuse to fall prey to his tricks.

"And for how long? A day or two? A week?"

With a sigh, I lift one shoulder. "I don't know. Maybe a month." *Until I can find an apartment I can afford*. But I don't say that aloud, for obvious reasons.

"*A month*? What are you talking about?" He steps up close,

towering over me. "You're breaking up with me over some stupid dinner?"

Behind me, the door opens, and Mr. Miller calls out, "What's taking you so long? Everyone's waiting on you two."

"I'm sorry, Dave. It's my fault." I force an apologetic smile. With my chin lifted, I head inside, not bothering to look at Jake or his father. In a few minutes, I won't have to deal with any of them. I don't care how pissed Jake will be. I don't care what he tells his parents when I leave.

None of it will mean shit.

I'm done here.

CHAPTER 21

Two Sides of the Story

XANDER

October

"Seriously, I don't understand why you're so worried about me." With my phone pressed to my ear, I watch Milo roll on the grass. *At least one of us is having fun.*

"Alex," my sister says, "every time I call, you're at home. You don't go out; you don't spend time with your friends. All you do is practice and sit around that big, empty house."

"And?"

"And who are you and what did you do with my brother? Because the Alexander Walker I know is the life of the party."

My chest tightens a fraction. "Maybe I'm growing up?"

"No, I don't think you are. I don't know what's going on with you, but I'll find out."

"Whatever, Audrey." I laugh and tug on Milo's leash, getting his attention. "Let's go home, buddy."

"I'm gonna visit you soon, so be ready to answer a ton of questions."

I huff another laugh as I head around the house to the front door. "Whatever—"

All my breath escapes me at what I find on the porch, and my heart pounds in my ears.

"Alex?" Audrey asks, breaking my trance.

I clear my throat. "Y-yeah, I'm here. I gotta go. I'll call you tomorrow."

"But—"

I hit End then quickly pocket my phone, my palms starting to sweat.

I can't believe she's here. Is my imagination playing tricks on me?

Why is she here?

She hasn't seen me yet, so I stay where I am and take her in. She's sitting on the steps, the porch light illuminating her white dress, a small suitcase at her side.

Unwilling to wait any longer for an answer, I tug gently on Milo's leash. "Do you see who's here?" I point at the house, and his head instantly snaps in her direction. The fast wagging of his small tail makes me chuckle.

I crouch and unclip his leash. Once he's free, he takes off, running straight to Bella. He barks and yips, and a moment later the air fills with her laughter. The sound causes warmth to spread in my chest.

"Goodness, Milo, stop," she giggles. Despite her command, she holds him close.

"He's happy to see you," I say as I approach.

She looks up, and a smile brightens her expression. "Hey."

"I'm surprised you're here. Wasn't Miller's mom's thing tonight?"

"Yeah." She stands slowly, keeping Milo in her arms.

I drink her in, and when I notice stains from Milo's paws on her white dress, I reach out. "Put him down. He's ruining your dress."

"It's fine. I don't care."

"Why are you here?"

With her lip caught between her teeth, she shrugs. "I don't know."

Thrown off by her answer, I ask the first thing that comes to mind. "Did something happen at the party?"

She focuses on Milo, avoiding looking at me. "I just... I have nowhere else to go, so I thought... Never mind. It's stupid. I'll call another Uber."

My whole body feels weighed down, and a sickening sensation washes over me. "Bella, you can stay as long as you need, but please, tell me what happened."

Shoulders slumping, she sighs and peers down at Milo. "Jake's mom invited my parents...after I made it clear I didn't want them there. And J-Jake knew about it."

Stepping closer, I take Milo from her and set him on the ground. She doesn't put up a fight. When I straighten again, her arms hang awkwardly at her sides.

I hover close, studying her gorgeous sapphire eyes. "C'mon. Let's get you inside. I bet you want a cup of coffee."

Her lips tilt up in the tiniest of smiles. *God, she's cute.*

"Thank you, Xander," she whispers.

I grab her suitcase on my way to the front door, surprised by how heavy it is. This is definitely more than a couple days' worth of necessities.

Did she break up with Miller?

"Let me wash Milo's paws, and then I'll make a pot."

Ahead of me, she wrings her hands and scans the entryway like she's never been here before.

"Why don't you wait in the living room?" I put her suitcase in the hallway and head to the bathroom. Fuck, I wish I could turn off my mind—the number of crazy theories in my brain is insane.

I need to talk to her.

TEN MINUTES LATER, I find Bella in the living room, her eyes closed and her head resting on the back of the couch. The sheer exhaustion radiating from her makes my heart squeeze painfully. The more time I spend with her, the easier she is to read, but right now, she's a closed book.

"Coffee's ready. Let's go to the kitchen," I suggest, lowering myself onto the couch beside her.

She opens her eyes and rolls her head to the side until her gaze is fixed on me. "I don't have the strength to move, honestly."

"Okay." I turn to face her and take her in again. "You look amazing."

"Thank you." She gives me a tired smile and sits up straighter. "So," she says, "do you really like your bathroom, or did you just say that to make me feel good?"

"I never say things I don't mean. I love the pieces you picked, and I was bummed when you didn't want to see the final result."

"I'm sorry." She sighs. "My life has been a mess lately, and I didn't want to drag you down too."

I swallow thickly. "Talk to me. You can trust me with any of it. All of it. It'll stay between us."

Knee bouncing, she looks away from me.

Desperate to help her but at a loss, I put a gentle hand on her thigh to stop the movement.

With an audible exhale, she turns back to me.

"Remember how I brought you home after Miller was an ass? You can trust me," I reassure her, meaning every word I say. "I'm here for you, Bella."

A barely-there smile tugs at her lips, her eyes softening. Taking a deep breath, she covers my hand with hers and laces our fingers together. A jolt of electricity runs through me, spreading all over my skin and down to my toes. One simple touch, and this girl brings me to my knees.

She's my friend.

But fuck, am I attracted to her.

I was a fool to think I could use her to make Jake pay for what he did.

"My mother..." She lets out a shaky breath. "In her eyes, I'm not good enough. She hates *everything* about me. She can't help but make comments about my body, my hair, my choice of clothes, my makeup. Today, she made a snide comment about how some other woman might steal Jake from me if I don't keep my appearance up...as if who I am on the inside isn't enough for him."

She bows her head and takes several breaths before she looks at me again, her expression flat.

"She treated me horribly when I was a kid. She intentionally left me at a theater in New York when I was thirteen, then told my stepfather I was the one to blame. Kevin stopped trying to be a father to me after that. When I was fifteen, they took an extended vacation to Europe, and I stayed with my aunt for two months."

She falls silent, chewing on the inside of her cheek. This time, though, her eyes are glossy.

"Was your stepfather at the party?"

Muscles tensing, she nods. "My mom never goes anywhere without him. He's her accessory." Her lip curls on the last word. "Imagc is everything to them. He takes good care of himself; he wears his fake smile and his designer clothes. He practically lives at the gym after my mother said she would divorce him if he gained weight. His colleagues admire him, our neighbors adore him. Everyone thinks he's a great man. They don't know who he really is."

Her chest rises and falls rapidly as she wets her lips.

In response, my lungs constrict, making it hard to breathe.

"What did he do to you?" I move closer, trying to catch her attention.

Rather than look at me, she focuses on the black screen of the TV. "There are two sides of the story."

"What's yours?"

"Mine?" Finally, she peers at me, the anguish in her eyes making her irises a stormy blue.

I hold my breath, gaze trained on her, cataloging every detail of her expression, the pain roiling in her eyes. I pinch the skin between my thumb and forefinger, an itch forming in my limbs. I need to get up, move, do something, because I have a feeling what I'm about to hear will send me spiraling.

"When I was seventeen, I came home from a party. Kevin came

into my room while I was getting ready for bed. He..." She takes a deep, shaky breath.

My vision blurs, and a flashback hits me: a bloody scene. I shut my eyes tight. When all I see are black dots, I let myself open them again. My muscles and veins strain against my skin. It's like I'm reliving my old nightmare...even though Bella's circumstances are totally different.

"He was drunk and pissed off because my mother had berated him for something she didn't like. He said he wanted to punish her. I guess he thought the best way to do that was by using me."

She blinks at me, her face drawn. All I can do is squeeze her hand to let her know I'm here.

When she clears her throat and straightens her spine, I know she's about to break my heart. "He decided...the best way to get back at her was by forcing himself on her daughter. My stepfather raped me. I only told one person, and when I told her, sh-she didn't believe me." Every word is quieter than the last, as though they're hard to get out. "My own mother called me a pathetic liar. She said a man like Kevin would never look at me...let alone touch me. My stepfather is a rapist, and no one knows." Her voice cracks at the end, a lone tear rolling down her cheek.

I'm speechless at first, the pounding in my ears too intense to talk over. Pure rage courses through me. Her fucking mother and stepfather don't deserve to even breathe the same air as her. They should rot in hell, without any chance at redemption.

"Bella..." When I finally find my voice, it's hoarse. "I'm so sorry that happened to you. No one should ever experience something like that. I understand why you want to stay away from them." I clear my throat. "You didn't tell anyone else? Your aunt? Your cousin?"

"I told you, this story has two sides. *His* is completely different." She bows her head again and picks at an invisible piece of lint on her skirt. "I stayed at my aunt's as often as I could. I only went home when I was certain my mother would be there too. None of it mattered. It didn't stop him. It was killing me, Xander. I was living a nightmare. He once said he was teaching me how to please a man, that

I should be thankful for him...for all his lessons. He told me if I ever told a soul, he'd say I was the one who seduced him. It didn't stop until I left for college."

"What a sick fuck. I want to beat the hell out of him for everything he put you through." Teeth gritted, I release her hand. My rage is so strong, it takes everything I have not to get in the car, drive over to Miller's parents' place, and kick her stepfather's teeth in.

Instead, I get up and pace, hands trembling and anger flowing through me. When I stop, I realize I also have tears in my eyes. I rush back to the couch and drop to my knees in front of her, taking her hands in mine.

"You've endured so much. You deserve nothing but happiness and love, maybe more than anyone I've ever met."

She gives me a sad smile. "Some things just aren't meant to be."

My heart clenches. "You're wrong." I inch closer and press my palm to her cheek.

She leans into my touch, sighing deeply.

"Your mother thinks you aren't good enough for Miller? Truth be told, he isn't good enough for you."

"Xander." A lone tear rolls down her cheek.

"Since the day I met you, I've been asking myself: What is a girl like her doing with Jake Miller? You're stunning and kind, and despite all the shit you've been through, your soul is pure." I brush my fingers down her jaw and gently cuff the nape of her neck. "You're amazing, and it fucking pains me that you don't see it. You deserve so much more than Miller could ever give you."

Eyes glistening with tears, she smiles faintly. "I told him I needed a break."

My heart stutters. "You broke up with him?"

"Not yet. I told him I needed to think. Really, though, I need time to find an apartment." She swipes her tongue along her bottom lip. "That's why I came here. He won't think to look for me at your place. If I went to Meg's, or my aunt's, he'd be on the porch tomorrow, demanding I talk to him. I don't want that. I'm never going back to him."

I pinch my eyebrows together. "Why do you—"

I scrutinize her quietly, my fingers rapping on my thigh. There's a question burning on the tip of my tongue, and the longer I keep it to myself, the hotter it turns my blood. So, I force it out.

"Are you afraid of him? Is that why you don't want him to know where you are?"

Her gaze flickers to me then darts away. "It's complicated."

"There's nothing complicated about this. Yes or no, Bella? Are you afraid of him?"

"He'll be angry when I break up with him. He recently started hinting about marriage..." She presses her trembling lips together. "But I'm afraid of who I am when he's around. I'm—"

I haul her to my chest and hold her close. "Don't ever talk bad about yourself. You're nothing but amazing, do you hear me?"

When I release her, she nods. I'll take the win, regardless of how small it is, because changing how she talks about herself is one of the first steps to changing how she views herself.

Hugging her tight, I hide my face in her hair and inhale her sweet scent. Coconut and strawberry, and something stronger that makes me a little dizzy. An overwhelming wave of warmth crashes into me and seeps into my bones.

She's here because she trusts me to keep her safe.

CHAPTER 22
Have Fun with Your Bitch
BELLA

October

My racing thoughts kept me up all night. I've been staring at the ceiling for hours, and now that it's light in Xander's guest room, I prop myself on my elbow and grab my phone. It's still in airplane mode.

Before I turned it off, I gave Meg a heads-up and texted Ben and told him to email me if he needed anything. Because they're incredible friends, they were supportive. They offered to help in any way they could, though neither one liked that I wouldn't tell them where I was. Thankfully, they eventually let it go.

I lie back and take a deep breath. Everything's going to be fine. I did the right thing. After all I've been through with Jake, I need to take this step back and reevaluate.

All night, anxiety plagued me. He won't react well when I break the news to him, but I can do it. I've been through much worse.

I should've brought more of my things, but I was afraid he'd come home any minute, and I wasn't sure Xander would let me stay. Hiding may be childish, but I can't risk confronting Jake until I've figured out how to break up with him for good.

Despite the concerns I can't shake, I feel secure here. Xander has a way of doing that, but I fear it may be causing a whole new host of issues. Because I like him. A lot. Way more than I should like a friend.

Telling him about my parents was easier than I thought it would be. I should've guessed, knowing how safe I feel with him. It's as if nothing can hurt me when he's around, like I can be myself without judgment.

After the run-in with my mom, my emotions threatened to boil over. Turns out anger and disappointment only fueled my determination. I left the house without a word, leaving it to Jake to explain my disappearance. I have no doubt he came up with some bullshit story in which he doesn't look like the bad guy.

The fifteen minutes I spent in my mother's presence brought up all kinds of memories I'd suppressed. I can't remember ever feeling like my mother actually loved me. According to Aunt Millie, my parents were happy together and thrilled when I was born, but when my dad died, my mom became a different person.

After that, she scolded me for every slight misstep. All I wanted was for her to love me, to be there for me when I needed her, but she never was. After she met Kevin, she paid even less attention to me.

Years later, I still feel like a burden, an inconvenience to those around me, useless and weak. I'd give anything to go back and change things—

A sniffing sound on the other side of the door cuts through my thoughts. Instantly, my heart lifts. Smiling, I throw the blanket aside, but before I can stand, hurried steps stop me.

"I told you I'm taking you for a walk," Xander says. "Let Bella sleep, buddy."

I grin at the way he speaks to his dog. His affection is clear in every word.

A moment later, the front door closes, and I haul myself out of bed, pulling on a pair of blue shorts and a white tee.

Last night, Xander insisted he didn't need anything from me, but I want to repay his kindness. Surely he won't mind if I make breakfast, right?

In the kitchen, I find he already started the coffee, so while I wait for it to brew, I search the pantry for what I need.

"WHAT DO you want to watch next?" I ask a shirtless Xander, who's sitting beside me on the couch.

Since breakfast—blueberry pancakes, which he loved—he hasn't left my side, save for taking a call from his mom. We've spent hours talking, laughing, and watching Netflix, and what blows my mind is that he acts like he's enjoying my company. He *wants* to be here with me.

"Whatever you want." He pops a cherry tomato into his mouth and winks. "I'll watch whatever you want."

"Be careful, or you may sentence yourself to an anime marathon."

He lifts a shoulder, unbothered. "Cool. I like anime."

Laughing, I swat his chest. The craziest kind of heat flows through my veins the second my fingers brush his bare skin. "Liar. You have no idea what I'm talking about, do you?"

Xander grabs the remote from the coffee table and scrolls through the list of movies. "Hm," he says noncommittally. "Do you want something specific?"

"*Spirited Away*." I beam, pulling my legs under my butt. "I've seen it at least a dozen times, and I still love it."

"Okay, if you say so." With a serious look on his face, Xander skims through the movies.

I use this moment to study him. Impossibly long eyelashes frame his deep blue-green eyes, and there's the tiniest smattering of freckles over his nose and cheeks. For the first time, I realize there's a little scar crossing his eyebrow. So many new things, the smallest details... I'm devouring every bit of information I find about him.

"Why are you staring at me like that?"

Busted.

I smile through the embarrassment. "Just observing you."

He shakes his head. "I don't get you."

"Really? I'm an open book when I'm fed, hydrated and my needs are taken care of. There's nothing to get."

He watches me in silence, his finger hovering over the Play button.

My needs are taken care of? Why the hell did I say that?

I worry my bottom lip, wondering how to play it off, and his gaze instantly drops to my mouth. A powerful rush of energy travels between us, and heat pools in my lower abdomen.

"So this is...the happy version of you?" Xander breaks the silence, arching an eyebrow.

"Uh-huh." A full-blown smile blooms on my lips. "And I'll be even happier if you agree to watch anime with me."

With a chuckle, he presses play, though within minutes his phone buzzes, and he pauses it again. He snatches the device from the coffee table and stares at the screen, his lips collapsing into a frown.

He turns the screen to face me, and when Jake's name registers, my stomach twists painfully.

"Hey, man." Xander puts the call on speaker, his focus intent on me but his tone easy.

"Hey, Walker." Jake's booming voice vibrates through me, and I shudder. "How about hitting the gym in a few hours? Might be good before tomorrow's practice."

"That's a great idea, but I'll pass."

"For fuck's sake, don't tell me it's because of some chick. I already heard that bullshit from Garcia."

"Well, actually, yeah. I have a guest, and hanging out with her is far better than hitting the gym."

He bursts out laughing. "Is it Cindy? She was asking about you the last time I saw her. She definitely has her eye on you."

Breath caught in my lungs, I gape at Xander. Jake claimed he didn't remember who Cindy was. It just confirms what I've known all along: He's nothing but a liar.

"No," Xander says, his tone a little sharper. "It's not Cindy."

He snorts. "Your loss. She's great in bed."

Xander's gaze focuses on me. He's studying my reaction to Jake's words, his expression intense, tearing down all my walls and staring right at my battered soul.

"No offense, but I prefer the company I've got," Xander says.

"What does she look like? Maybe I know her."

He searches my face, as if he's memorizing every detail. "She's the most beautiful girl I've ever seen."

My cheeks heat.

"Too cheesy, dude."

"How was your mom's party?"

Relief washes over me when Xander changes the subject, and I can't help but wonder whether Jake thinks I'm at home.

"It was good. Stayed up too late drinking with my dad," he mutters. "I'm on my way home now."

"I thought Isabella was with you." Xander puts his hand on my knee and squeezes it lightly, tipping his head to the side.

"She was, but then she pulled her usual shit. Played the victim and bolted, leaving me to deal with my parents," he grumbles. "I tried calling her, but her phone is off. She's probably at her aunt's. If it wasn't for the game on Sunday, I would've headed to the club after the party, to have a little fun before having to deal with her again. The girl has looks, and she's great in bed, but, man, she drives me nuts."

Xander holds my gaze and says, "Then why don't you break up with her?"

"Are you fucking insane? Why would I do that?" Jake laughs. "She lives with me. I'm gonna pop the question soon, and then I'll just knock her up again and again and again."

"Ah, so she's gonna be your trophy wife then?" Though his tone is cheerful, the look on his face is murderous.

"Glad you get it." The laugh Jake lets out crawls inside my skull and makes my vision blurry. "Anyway, have fun with your bitch. I'm heading to the gym."

When the call ends and we're plunged into silence, I realize I'm trembling. I hug myself tighter, but the shaking only grows stronger. Such a short call, but so many things to unpack.

Xander wipes his hands on his sweatpants and exhales deeply. "Are you okay?"

"So he *did* sleep with Cindy."

He shifts, threading his fingers through his hair. "Sounds like it, but I'm not really in the loop when it comes to that shit. Especially after he found out what I told you about her."

"And maybe because of your history. What happened there? Ben said—"

"I promise I'll tell you everything. Just not right now."

Disappointment forms like a lead ball in my gut. "You want me to open up to you, but you're not doing the same."

"Bella, I will. I just need some time to work up the nerve. I worry it'll change things." He curls his hands into fists but quickly loosens them again.

"Whatever." I sigh and take the remote from him. "Let's watch the movie."

The last thing I want is to tank my mood further.

CHAPTER 23

You're Not a Mistake

XANDER

October

When I step through the front door, Milo is sitting in the foyer, focus fixed in the other direction, his leash beside him. Only when I say his name does he wander my way, finally acknowledging my presence.

I drop my duffel bag and kneel so I can pet him. "Hey, bud. What's going on here?"

"Sorry I made you wait, sweet boy," Bella says as she comes down the hall. When she sees me, she halts in her tracks. "Oh, you're home."

"The game ended two hours ago."

As she approaches, I take her in. She's in a black hoodie and leggings, holding a ball cap.

"Why do you need that?" I nod at the cap.

She slips it onto her head and pulls her hood up. "I just don't want anyone to recognize me. If the paparazzi followed you home and are waiting outside... I don't want to create more problems for you."

I stand up and level her with a glare. "You're not creating problems for me. I'm glad you're here."

The corners of her mouth tremble, but a small smile graces her features.

"And I'm glad you're getting out. You haven't been outside in, what? Three days?"

"I figured I'd take Milo for a walk. I wasn't sure when you'd be home, but now that you're here—"

"No, no, no. You're not bailing on Milo. He's been patiently waiting for you. No need to upset him." I pick up my bag and sidestep her. "Actually, I'll go with you. Wait for me, please."

"Okay, but hurry up." She pushes up the sleeves of her hoodie. "I'm getting hot."

Chuckling, I jog to my bedroom. *Fuck yeah.* Having her here makes me happier than I could have imagined. The rest of the team went out to celebrate our win, but all I wanted was to get home to Bella.

Fuck, I'm digging myself a grave.

She's a friend. A friend who has been through a lot and doesn't need to add any of my shit to her plate.

I've been tossing around ways to expose Miller without Bella's involvement, but I haven't settled on one. Now, it's time to get serious about it.

As we come to the intersection, Milo stops and sits without being told.

With a huge smile, Bella crouches and presses a kiss to his head. "Aww, he's a smart boy."

The way she praises my dog makes my chest feel lighter, and I can't help but smile. Something is seriously wrong with me...but I don't care.

For a while, we're quiet, walking close, my shoulder almost touching hers. Milo slows us down, stopping here and there to sniff things or roll in the grass. His happy yips mix with Bella's laughter, melodic and soft. What happened in college completely fucked me up, but watching them now heals the wounds of my soul just a little.

"Oh God!" Bella yelps. She scoops Milo up, then spins to me, wide-eyed. "What do we do?"

Dread fills me, but when I realize what the issue is, I smile. A German shepherd without a leash is ambling his way toward us.

"Everything's fine. Put Milo down."

The crease between her eyebrows deepens. "No way. What if he gets attacked?"

"He won't." I wrap my arm around her shoulder and hold her close. "Trust me."

Tension rolls off her, and rather than put my dog down, she pulls him closer. I rub a hand up and down her arm, soothing her while we wait. If I know my neighbor, he'll be out here any second. Typically, he only lets Pup off his leash to let him play, and he never lets him go too far.

"Pup!" A booming voice startles us as an older man runs toward us. "You're a bad boy, Pup. You shouldn't have run away from me."

When Mr. Jensen catches up to his dog, he quickly clips the leash on and straightens.

"Hi, Mr. Jensen."

"Xander, hey." He breaks into a wide smile. "I was so worried Pup would scare someone, I didn't realize it was you and Milo." His eyes settle on Bella, and he grimaces, probably because she's still locked up tight, Milo pressed to her chest. "Er, Miss, I'm very sorry if Pup scared you. My grandson put on his leash, but clearly he didn't fasten it properly. He would never hurt you, I promise. He's friendly and old, just like me. And he loves Milo." He takes a step closer and holds out a hand. "I'm Mr. Jensen."

She takes it but keeps Milo in her other arm. "It's nice to meet you, Mr. Jensen. I'm Isabella. I was just worried this little guy would get hurt." She untangles herself from me and puts Milo on his feet. He instantly walks up to Pup, and they sniff each other, tails wagging.

"Pup would never hurt Milo. They're old friends." Mr. Jensen smiles warmly, his gaze shifting to me. "Congratulations on your win, by the way."

"Thank you, sir."

We chat for a minute, and then Mr. Jensen heads home for dinner.

The mention of food makes my stomach growl, so Bella turns around with a laugh. "C'mon. Looks like it's time for us to have dinner too."

"XANDER?" Bella calls from the guest bathroom.

When I step through the open doorway, Milo is standing in the shower, his head tilted to the side.

Bella is standing near him, wringing her hands, her cheeks the most adorable shade of pink. "I said I'd wash his paws, but...can you please show me how?"

I can't stop the loud snort that escapes me in response.

Eyes narrowed, she takes a step forward, bumping into my shoulder. "Go away. I'll figure it out."

I don't budge. Instead, I move forward, forcing her to step aside.

"I'll show you." I grab the showerhead, but before I can turn on the water, she snatches it from my hand.

"I said I'd do it."

Damn, is this woman gorgeous. Her hair is loose now, cascading over her shoulders. She doesn't have any makeup on, just a simple white tee and black leggings. She looks absolutely breathtaking.

Caught in her gravitational pull, I reach for the showerhead. Instead, my fingers slip, and I turn on the faucet.

Bella yelps and, with a jerky movement, directs the stream of water down. It hits Milo, startling him, and he bolts out of the shower and down the hallway, leaving a wet trail behind him.

With a huff, she turns off the water and gapes at me. "You..." she mutters, shaking her head. "You..."

Like I'm drawn to them, I can't help but drop my gaze to her tits. *Fuck me.*

She's not wearing a bra.

"Why did you do that?"

“I didn’t—” I lick my lips, distracted by her hard nipples poking through the fabric of her tee, the outline of her areolas in the damp white cotton. *Dammit.*

I force my attention up to her face, only then realizing she’s ogling my chest in the same way I was ogling hers.

Slowly, she creeps closer. Her eyes flicker up to mine, then to my lips. It’s pure torture, how long it takes her to press her lips to mine, but when she does? Holy shit. A spark ignites inside me, and all rational thought leaves my mind.

I return her kiss without hesitation. I’ve been waiting for her to give in, to take that step and cross all her fucking boundaries. I slide my fingers through her hair and grip the back of her head.

In response, she lets out a quiet moan.

My heart thumps loud and fast, a ticking time bomb in my chest.

Her lips are my new addiction.

She sighs into my mouth, and I slip my tongue over hers. They dance, curling around each other, setting our bodies on fire. The sensation is exhilarating. Never in my life have I experienced a kiss like this.

I move my lips along her jaw, then nip at her earlobe. With the tiniest moan, she tilts her head, giving me better access.

“God, you’re perfect,” I whisper in her ear.

A loud bark from the doorway makes us jump apart. In unison, we turn to find Milo watching us.

“I better change.” She hands me the showerhead, ready to flee the scene, but I block her path. “Xander...please.”

“Bella.” I keep my tone soft. “Don’t run away from me.”

“I shouldn’t have done that.”

A bitter laugh escapes me as I give her a once-over. “Do you regret it? Was this a mistake?”

With a single step closer, she brushes the hair from my eyes. “I could never regret kissing you,” she confesses. “And you’re not a mistake.”

I wind my arms around her waist, pulling her to me. My body is desperate for her, my skin buzzing for more. Instead of doing what I really want to do, I hold her close and relish the way she buries her face in my chest. Holding her like this is peaceful and pleasant, like a sunny day after weeks of rain.

"Milo is still here," she whispers against my pec. "He probably thinks we've lost our minds."

A low chuckle rumbles from my throat as I look down at her. Her deep blue pools shine brightly as she stares back at me.

"Or he's wondering whether we're ever going to wash his paws."

Her lips stretch into a genuine smile, and she takes a tentative step back.

"Go," I say. "I'll take care of Milo."

"You sure?" She nibbles on her bottom lip.

"Yes." I nod at her translucent T-shirt. "Like you said, you better change."

Bella glances at her chest, and when she looks up, to my surprise, she's grinning. "Don't tell me you weren't enjoying the view."

"Of course I was." I lick my lips, taking advantage of the moment and getting one more peek in.

"Good to know." With a wink, she's gone.

When I'm alone, I brace myself against the wall and bow my head.

I don't do relationships. I fuck.

But that kiss? Hands down the best kiss of my life.

CHAPTER 24

Keep Your Eyes on Me

BELLA

October

WITH A SPOON IN MY MOUTH, I HEAD TO MY BEDROOM, carrying the pint of ice cream. I stop abruptly when my eyes lock on Xander in the foyer. He's looking absolutely delicious in a white shirt, black pants, a black buttoned jacket, and a duffel bag in his hand.

It's not fucking fair to be that gorgeous.

I pop the spoon out of my mouth. "Leaving already?"

Goodness, Bella, as if it's not obvious.

"Yeah, my flight is in two hours." His gaze drops to the chocolate ice cream in my hand. "Looks like we'll need to restock when I'm back tomorrow."

"I'll buy groceries while you're away. Don't worry about stuff like that. You have a game to win. Focus on that."

"Will you turn on your phone?"

I frown, a droplet of water sliding down my fingers as the ice cream starts to melt. "No...why?"

"So I can call and make sure you and Milo are okay."

Heat pools in my lower abdomen, and I squeeze my thighs together in hopes of stopping my core from throbbing. "We'll be okay."

Xander takes a step closer, leveling his gaze with mine. "Please. Turn on your phone for me."

My heart is ready to jump out of my chest. His proximity is too much. Warmth creeps onto my cheeks, and I lick my lips and nod. "Okay. I'll do it later."

"Good girl," he tells me with a flirtatious lilt to his voice.

If my panties weren't damp before, they surely are now. *Fuck.*

"Well, off you go." I force a smile and skirt him.

He chuckles. "Not even a 'Good luck, Xander'?"

I glance over my shoulder. He's already by the door, ready to walk out, but his gaze is on me. "Good luck."

"That's better." He steps outside. "Don't forget to turn on your phone." He winks at me, and in the next moment, he's gone.

This away game against LA came right on time. Even one day away from him will do me a lot of good. I need to collect myself—it's been four days since our kiss, and that's all I think about. The kiss that left me wanting more. Every day, it gets more challenging to remember why I shouldn't have done it. Kissing someone never felt so fucking right.

"Stop it, Bella," I scold myself for the thought as I slip into my room. Netflix and ice cream should help...at least, I hope they do.

I LEAN BACK on the couch, legs tucked under me, my phone in hand. A little break from work won't hurt, especially since I've spent the past two hours searching for one tiny error. It's only a matter of five dollars, but God, does it irk me.

Teeth sunk into my bottom lip, I can't resist checking the highlights from the game. The final play, the last and winning throw. I watch transfixed as the camera zooms in on Xander. He takes his time, snaps his arm forward, and the football soars through the air. The next moment, the announcer shouts, "Touchdown! Another win for the Warriors!"

A smile tugs at my lips. My phone vibrates in my hand. As I close the replay video and open the text, I scowl. Another text from Jake. He's called a dozen times since I turned on my phone yesterday, and he's sent me fifty messages, if not more. Some have been demanding. In others, he begs me to talk to him and give him a chance to explain himself. Other times, he acts as if nothing happened.

JAKE:

Miss you babe. The win doesn't taste as sweet when you're not with me

I snort. Yeah, right.

I lock the screen, set the device down, and focus on my laptop again. Work is my savior these days. It keeps me from stressing too much about how few apartments are available in my price range.

And it kept me from talking myself into stopping by Jake's to pick up some of my stuff. I could use a few more outfits, and I definitely need my car. Yes, the team has been in LA since last night, so I wouldn't see him, but if I pack up more of my things, then what? It doesn't feel right to bring it all here. This is a temporary arrangement, and I'll move out the moment I find a permanent place.

If I find one...

I hide my face in my palms and groan. This is why I need to stay focused on work. Otherwise, I become a hostage to my own mind. Hopelessness fills me, making it hard to breathe. I know I'm going to break up with Jake, but God, do I wish I could just disappear from his life without confrontation.

After another thirty minutes of searching for the five-dollar mistake, I give up and snap my laptop closed. It's the weekend. I can figure this out on Monday.

I've been at Xander's place for nine days already. Everything about him puts me on high alert now. His voice, his laughter, his smell, his eyes on me, his presence in the room. I swear, the man never wears a shirt at home, so I can't do anything but ogle him. And when he catches me? The smile that blooms on his face makes my knees weak.

He's gone quite a bit, either at practice, the gym, or his parents' house, but when he's home and I'm not working? We spend all our time together. Our evening walks with Milo are becoming my favorite time of the day, simply because it feels normal. I've even watched football with him. He's patient with his explanations, and his commentary and jokes make the experience surprisingly enjoyable. It has never been like that before.

I miss him.

HOLDING a wineglass in one hand and petting Milo with the other, I force myself to focus on the final few minutes of *Kiki's Delivery Service*.

It's been a challenge, since Jake sent me two more texts an hour ago. I turned my phone off, but I'm still stewing over his shitty messages.

The front door opens and closes, and a minute later, Xander appears. "Did you turn your phone off? I tried to call." He's dressed in a white shirt and black pants, his black jacket casually draped over his arm.

My mouth waters...because damn, the man is hot.

"Oh, uh, yeah. I shut it off a while ago. Sorry."

With a chuckle, he heads my way. He assesses me, smiles at Milo, then arches a brow at the bottle of wine on the coffee table. "Decided to let loose a little?"

"A little." I hold up my wine. "This is my first glass."

He tosses his jacket over the back of the couch. Then he plops down beside me and places his hand on Milo's fur, trailing it up until it covers mine. A rush of hot energy spreads from my fingertips to my toes, making me clench my legs tighter.

He's my friend.

Kind, caring, and extremely hot...but a friend nonetheless.

Do I want him to be a friend, though?

"How are you?" His hands are calloused, but his touch is surprisingly featherlight and gentle.

"Good," I say hoarsely. "You were incredible on the field."

"Did you watch the game?"

I shake my head. "Just highlights. I don't think I'm ready to see... him."

The corners of Xander's mouth drop, and his fingers stop moving. I hold my breath, hoping he won't retract his hand. He doesn't, and when he threads his fingers through mine, I exhale.

"No one knows you left Miller—not even him. He said some shit to me and Garcia about you waiting for him at home."

"That's my fault. I told him it was a break, not an actual breakup." I eye my phone. "He's been calling and texting. That's why I turned it off again."

He arches a brow. "What does he want?"

"Depends on the day. He wants me to come home. He wants to talk, to sort out our issues. He wants me to stop acting stupid, and he wants to remind me that I'm risking losing the best thing that ever happened to me. No one will ever want a girl like me if I'm not with him."

Xander's eyes bulge. "He said that?"

"It's fine." I shrug. "I've heard worse."

"That's not right. This kind of belittling and humiliation is disgusting."

Annoyance flashes through me. "I'm trying to figure it all out. There's no need to lecture me."

He slumps back and drags a hand down his face. "That's not my intention. I just want to help you see that *Jake* is in the wrong, not you."

I pull my hand away and haul myself up, intending to escape to the guest room, but I'm not fast enough. Xander catches up to me and grabs my elbow, and in one swift motion my back is flush against his chest. My skin hums, and a fire forms in my lower abdomen, like it did the other day in the bathroom.

I want him.

"I've only been gone for two fucking days," he says, his lips brushing the shell of my ear, "but it feels like an eternity. Not seeing you, not talking to you, not hearing your voice? It's torture. I'm fucking obsessed with you, Bella, and when you're around, I lose my goddamn mind."

"Why?" Without my mind's permission, my body takes over, and I grind my ass over his groin, feeling his hardness through his pants. Just that hint of friction is enough to make my eyes roll back.

"Because all I want is you, and it's driving me absolutely crazy." He cups my breasts, making my skin buzz.

Head tipped back, I sigh. "I—"

"But you've been drinking." He pinches my pebbled nipples through the fabric of my tee. "What if you forget this tomorrow morning? Or, worse, regret it?"

"I didn't even finish my first glass of wine. I'm not drunk." I look over my shoulder, my gaze colliding with his. "I could never regret you."

Covering his hand with mine, I guide it from my breast to the waistband of my shorts. I keep my focus fixed on his face as I ease his hand into my panties until his long fingers brush my slit.

"You're so fucking wet for me." He moves his fingers in a slow, unrelenting motion.

"Xander, please," I whisper, breaths coming quicker as pleasure builds in my core.

He takes his hand out of my panties and turns me around. The hallway is dark, but the lights coming from the living room allow me to see the longing in his eyes.

"Tell me you want me." He grips my hips and squeezes.

"I want you."

"Tell me I can kiss you."

"You can kiss me."

His lips crash onto mine. It's feverish, sending a delicious thrill through me and setting my skin on fire. His kiss is like oxygen. It's vital. I've never experienced anything like it.

He lifts me with ease, and I instinctively wrap my legs around his hips. Then my back is pressed to the wall with enough force to drive a gasp from my lungs. For a moment, all I can do is watch him. My chest rises and falls quickly, my heart ready to jump out of my chest.

And all he did was kiss me.

A satisfied grin plays on his lips. *Dear God, he's gorgeous.* Slowly, he lowers me to my feet, his hands dropping from my sides.

I swallow my disappointment and take a step back. What's he playing at?

He grasps my arms to stop me, leaning in close to lick a trail from my collarbone up to my ear. "Remember when you walked away after our first kiss? How you left me alone in the bathroom?"

Breath shuddering, I nod frantically.

"I'm finally going to do what I wanted to do then." He slips his hand into my panties again. "Stick my tongue in you until you come all over my lips." Groaning, he moves his middle finger through my slick folds, teasing my opening. "So wet, and just for me."

I bite my bottom lip, and when he presses his thumb to my clit, I can't stop a moan from rumbling out of me. He works me over with precision, sending me hurtling toward my orgasm at breakneck speed.

Then, without warning, he stops.

I make a noise that's half anger, half grief.

Handsome smirk in place and eyes sparkling, he slowly kneels in front of me. As he goes, he curls his fingers over the waistband of my shorts and pulls them down along with my panties. When I'm bared to him, all he does is stare.

Under such intense scrutiny, it's hard not to squirm. I giggle, hiding my face in my palms.

"Bella, look at me," he demands in a hoarse voice.

I obey, drinking him in. A gorgeous guy in an expensive shirt and pants is on his knees for me. The Boston City Warriors quarterback. Jake's teammate. My friend. I should probably feel ashamed or embarrassed. Instead, I feel pretty, and that means more than I can put into words.

"That's better. Keep your eyes on me, baby. Don't look away."

As soon as those words leave his mouth, his tongue brushes my aching clit.

"Oh, fuck!" I cry out. With a hand on my breast, I squeeze hard. The pain mingles with the pleasure Xander gives me as he works miracles on my clit. He sucks and licks, increasing his tempo until I'm writhing and babbling incoherently. Then he backs off, depriving me of my orgasm and driving me out of my mind.

"God, you taste so sweet," he murmurs, never breaking eye contact with me. It's the most intense experience I've ever had.

When he dives in again, he adds a finger, curling it inside me as he works me over with his tongue. I play with my nipples, twisting and pulling through my tee.

Xander adds a second finger, and the heat in my core goes molten. "Fuck, you're dripping all over me."

With one hand around the back of my knee, he drapes my leg over his shoulder. I'm wide open for him, and the sounds he makes while he devours me are about to push me over the edge. He keeps a steady pace, his fingers hitting the perfect spot inside me, making my knees quake. When my body starts to shudder, I lift my hips in time to his movements and grasp his hair roughly, holding him where I need him most.

"I'm so close."

"Then come for me," he encourages. To emphasize the point, he sucks my clit into his mouth and releases it with a pop. He does it again, over and over, while his fingers relentlessly move inside me.

My pussy tightens around his fingers, and an intense orgasm slams into me like a tsunami. Letting go, I pull on Xander's hair, making him hiss. My body trembles, and I can't keep my eyes open no matter how hard I try.

"That's right, baby, give it to me," he coos. He doesn't stop licking and sucking, drawing my orgasm out.

When my spasms have subsided, he lays a kiss on my thigh and sets my foot on the floor. Then he helps me into my panties and shorts before he stands. He slips his palm to the back of my neck and hauls me to him for an open-mouthed kiss. When I taste myself on his tongue, a raw sensation scatters all over my body, leaving me wanting more.

Groaning, he breaks the kiss and presses his forehead to mine.

"You taste even better than I imagined...and I have a pretty fucking good imagination."

I snort, wrapping my arms around his torso. "Looks like I owe you an orgasm."

He rears back, his brows pulled together. "Don't say it like that. It's not some kind of debt. I wanted to give you pleasure, and I did. If we don't do anything more tonight, I'd be perfectly content." Delicately, he tucks a stray strand of hair behind my ear and angles in closer. "Although," he rasps, "I'll never say no to waking up with you in my bed." He takes a step back and extends a hand. "Sleep with me, Bella. Please."

Without hesitating, I let him lead me to his bedroom.

By his side is the only place I want to be.

CHAPTER 25

Only for You

XANDER

October

When I open my eyes, the first thing I see is Bella. She's still asleep, lying on her right side, both hands hidden under her pillow. In the morning light, I take my time admiring every little detail of her face.

Her lips are full; their subtle red reminds me of delicate rose petals. Soft and inviting, and so fucking kissable. Fuck, it was nearly impossible to stop last night. I swear, I haven't made out like that since I was in high school.

I'm fucking obsessed with her, and that was never part of the plan.

She stirs, and I instantly tense. The irrational fear that she'll hear my thoughts hits me. Fuck. If she knew the truth, she'd probably hate me. My priorities have changed, just like my intentions, but I'm not sure she'd care about that if she knew my initial reasons for getting close to her. And now, I can't lose her. If I do, it'll be my fucking downfall.

"Watching people sleep is creepy." Her hoarse voice rips me out of my thoughts. "What time is it?"

Hand splayed on her hip, I pull her closer. "It's not time for you to wake up. Go back to sleep."

She buries her face in my chest and sighs. "I haven't slept that well in days. This bed is amazing."

A deep chuckle rumbles out of me. "That's why I've been telling you to sleep with me."

She tenses just a fraction but quickly relaxes again. "I didn't want to cross the line."

"Until last night." My tone is a little firmer than I intend. "Do you regret it?"

She leans away, her eyes meeting mine. "Ask me again if you can kiss me."

My grip on her hip tightens. "Can I kiss you, Bella?"

"Yes," she whispers.

This kiss isn't anything like our others. There's no rush or desire to possess each other. It's slow and gentle, building anticipation. She parts her lips, giving me access to slide my tongue into her mouth.

She trails her hand down my side to the waistband of my briefs. The gentle sensation stirs a deep need inside me. When she slips her hand beneath the fabric, finding me already hard for her, she groans.

Her nipples are puckered beneath her T-shirt, rubbing against my chest as she strokes me and presses a kiss to my jaw. She works her way down, leaving a trail of hot breath and wet, open-mouthed kisses down my neck and chest. When she reaches my nipple, swirling her tongue around it before she grazes it with her teeth, I thread my fingers through her hair.

"Bella." In one quick move, I turn onto my back and pull her with me until she's straddling my hips. She looks down at me with a seductive grin playing on her lips. I swear, my fucking skin hums as goosebumps spread all over my body.

I'm a lost cause when it comes to her.

She grasps the hem of her loose tee and yanks it off, sending it flying to the floor. Her dark brown hair spills over her shoulders and down her naked breasts, making my mouth water. I drink in the sight of her full tits, her hard, perky nipples like pink buds against her skin.

"Do you like what you see?" she purrs.

"Hell yeah." I sit up, one hand on her waist and the other buried in her hair again, and pull her mouth to mine. She greets me with the same vigor, slipping her tongue inside my mouth. Last night, we kissed for what felt like hours before we drifted off, but I still want more. Way more.

Bella sucks my bottom lip inside her mouth and sinks her teeth into it. Then, with her hands on my chest, she pushes me down onto the mattress.

I obey, ready to do anything she wants.

"You're going to lie here"—she scoots back and tugs my briefs down—"and watch me suck you dry."

Once she's settled between my legs, her eyes never leaving my face, she gives my shaft a few light pumps.

My body is vibrating, shuddering in anticipation. Fuck. Her taking initiative is the most powerful thing I've ever seen.

She takes just the head at first, sucking on it slightly before releasing it with a pop. Next time she lowers her head, she takes me deeper into her mouth, her tongue swirling around my length. She sucks and licks, one hand cupping my balls, kneading them slowly.

"Yeah, baby..."

She peers up at me, hand sliding up and down. Then, with a wicked smile, she bends and takes my entire cock inside her mouth, deep enough to make herself gag. Her eyes fill with tears, but she doesn't slow down.

One hand balled into a fist to fight the desire to thrust up into her mouth, I use the other to push her hair aside.

She releases my dick but continues stroking me, her hand gliding faster. Her cheek is pressed to my shaft, her eyes glistening, her lips plump, a string of saliva on her chin.

When she goes back for more, a tingling sensation starts at the base of my spine. I'm close.

"Fuck..."

She pops off my dick again and squeezes so hard I fucking see stars. She swirls her tongue around the head, then takes me deep again.

"Baby, do that again..." I beg, breathless.

And she does. She squeezes then laps at my crown. When she takes me deep, I explode, spilling my cum inside her mouth. My hips jerk forward, and a loud groan springs from my lips.

When she sits up, I'm levitating, still riding high. I breathe hard, my brow covered in sweat. "Open your mouth," I tell her.

She does, sticking her tongue out, and fuck, if my dick doesn't thicken again. Her tongue is coated with my release, my cum slowly dripping down her chin.

She closes her mouth and swallows, a triumphant smile on her face, before she wipes her bottom lip and chin and pops her finger into her mouth.

"Delicious."

There's no stopping my urge to pounce on her. I flip her onto her back and hover over her, taking in her swollen lips. Balanced on one forearm, I blindly open the top drawer of my nightstand and search for a condom.

My recovery period is the best it's ever been as I force myself onto my knees and yank her panties down. I quickly sheath my cock and nudge her legs apart until I'm nestled comfortably between her thighs.

With a seductive grin, she slides her hands down my ass and digs her fingernails into my flesh. I press my lips to hers, kissing her hard and fast, tasting myself on her tongue. I feel euphoric—not only because the orgasm was mind-blowing, but because she took control and did what she wanted.

I zero in on her wet little cunt, and I'm a fucking goner. One time with her will never be enough.

Slowly, I push the tip of my cock into her warm pussy. A raw sensation ripples through my veins and lights up my insides. I keep my movements controlled and gentle at first, giving her the chance to get used to me. Little by little, I thrust until I'm balls deep inside her.

"Fucking perfect."

Bella moans, her hands wandering over my biceps, my shoulders, my back, exploring every inch of my body. I fuck her nice and slow, thrusting my cock into her tight pussy over and over. She's so fucking wet, her arousal drips down my dick, the wet sounds loud in the early morning quiet.

Hands looped around her legs, I spread her wider and watch the way her cunt swallows my dick.

"You're taking me so well, Bella." I tighten my hold on her thighs, my fingers sinking into her skin. "Your pussy was made for me, so greedy for my cock."

Hovering closer, I seize her lips in a feverish kiss, silencing her moans. My mind goes totally blank, and my vision goes dark. Sex has never felt this good. Bella is divine, fucking exceptional.

"Xander...more. Please."

Straightening, I take a handful of her ass and roll my hips, stabbing into her harder, burying my cock inside her pussy at full force.

Her moans mixed with my groans and the sloppy sounds of her pussy are like music to my goddamn ears.

"Fuck, you like it hard?" I murmur, half surprised but also feeling smug.

"Yes...harder, Xander..."

"You're a needy little slut, aren't you?"

Her eyes flare, her mouth falling open. I smile, waiting for her to prove me wrong but knowing I'm right. Pressing my fingers to her clit, I keep my pace steady. Her body glistens with sweat, her hair clinging to her forehead. She's close to her orgasm, I can fucking feel it in my bones.

But instead of pushing her over the edge, I stop.

"Xander." With her brows knit, she searches my face. "Why did you stop?"

"I asked you a question." Fuck, I'm liable to go over my own edge right now with the way her pussy throbs around me. "I'm not getting you off until you say it."

I pull out and slide her legs off my shoulders, my eyes locked on hers the whole time.

Chest rising and falling quickly, she licks her bottom lip. "Ask me again."

Inching forward, I tower over her, the crown of my cock teasing her entrance. "You like it when I fuck you hard?"

She nods and swallows thickly.

"Are you a needy little slut?"

Chin lifted, she holds my gaze. "Yes...but only for you."

Grabbing her hips, I haul her to me, sinking my cock deep inside her pussy. I pound her greedy cunt, and she lifts her hips, meeting me thrust for thrust. Her moans become louder, and the slapping sound of our bodies drives me into oblivion.

"Please, Xander," she breathes, her back bowing off the mattress. Her pussy contracts, strangling me as she cries out and her body shudders underneath me.

"That's it, Bella. Come for me." I choke on my words, on the precipice of my own release.

With a hand wrapped around her throat, I capture her lips with mine, stifling her moans. It's fucking everything. Waves of pleasure wash through me, making all my muscles flex. All the tension, all the anticipation, finally reaches its peak and erupts. I soar, sliding into an ocean of pure bliss.

"Fuck, you're perfect." I cover her mouth with mine in a long, slow kiss.

Only when my lips feel numb do I move away. Beneath me, Bella glistens with sweat, her chest still heaving, her hair a tangled mess on my pillow. Her eyes shimmer, and she's all I want to look at.

"I'm tingly all over," I confess. "This is the best way to wake up in the morning."

She giggles and presses a hand to my face. "What time is it?"

"I have no clue. I just know I've never come so hard before."

For a moment, she watches me in silence, biting her bottom lip. Then, abruptly, she rolls out of my bed and dashes out the door, throwing "I need to use the bathroom" over her shoulder.

I dispose of the condom and then sit with my back pressed to the headboard, wearing what I'm sure is a ridiculous grin.

When she returns, her naked body has me forgetting my fucking name. She has an hourglass figure, a narrow waist with a flat stomach and round hips that make my dick twitch even though I've come twice already. And don't get me started on her fucking tits. But the most gorgeous thing about her is that genuine smile.

She climbs onto the bed and straddles my legs, wrapping her arms around my shoulders. "Ready for round two? Or three, in your case?" She cocks an eyebrow at me, wiggling her fit ass over my dick.

Hell yes, I want her again.

For a moment, we just stare at each other, totally lost in our own bubble of lust. After taking her once, I'll do anything to have her at my mercy again. Touch her, fuck her, caress her skin. Pleasure her slowly, taking care of her and making her come over and over again.

Unraveling her is fucking liberating. Bella is irresistible, and I'm weak for her, ready to worship the ground she walks on.

Because that's exactly what she deserves.

CHAPTER 26

Good Boy

XANDER

October

"WANT ANOTHER GLASS OF WINE?"

Bella insisted we watch a movie I like, so we settled on *RocknRolla*. Her love for anime is pretty much like my love for Guy Ritchie movies—unmatched.

She's tipsy, her eyes sparkling devilishly. I love when she's uninhibited like this. She talks more, smiles wider, and laughs easily at my jokes.

"Nope." Bella shakes her head and points a finger at me. "A sober person isn't good company for a drunk one."

"Are you drunk?"

"A little bit." Giggling, she pulls off her scrunchie, and her hair spills over her shoulders. The sigh that escapes her is almost pornographic as she sinks back into the couch. "God, that feels heavenly."

I catch a lock of her hair between my fingers and gently twirl it—it's silky to the touch and smells like strawberry. Just those simple sensations make my pulse pick up and send heat rushing through my veins. Why would I need alcohol when I can get drunk on her?

"What do you want to do then? Watch another movie? Go to bed?"

"You should go to bed; you have an early morning. I'll stay out here and read for a bit." She nods at the purple paperback on the coffee table.

"Read? What's your book about?" I lunge for it, but she's faster. In the blink of an eye, the paperback is pressed against her chest.

"You won't like it."

Brow quirked, I hover a little closer. "Why?"

"It's romance." She shrugs, her attention drifting to something behind me. "Jake used to call it porn. He'd make fun of me every time he saw me reading."

Anger seeps into my veins, the way it does every time she brings that fucker up. "Why would he say that?"

She shrugs. "It's nothing like porn. In these stories, people fall in love, have sex, and then get their happily ever after. The guys treat their women with love and respect. They'd basically burn the world for them."

Intrigued, I scoot a little closer. "And how detailed are the sex scenes?"

Bella blinks at me and then bursts out laughing. "That's the part you picked up on?"

"I'm just curious, baby." I wrap my fingers around the spine of the book. "I'm not making fun of you, and I'd never judge you for what you love. I just want to know more about the things you enjoy."

I ease the book from her hands and look down at the title. "What is it about?"

"It's a billionaire romance with a love triangle. The female main character has two love interests. One is the perfect guy, respectful and kind—who happens to be her new boss. The other is her ex from high school. Her first love, who's also a real asshole from time to time."

I flip through the pages. It's just a book, and I'm far from the perfect guy, but I see parallels between this story and her life. Jake and me. Old and new. Bad and...bad, because I'm no better than Miller.

I let it happen. I let him get away with it.

I blink away the thoughts and clear my throat. "Do you know how it ends?"

"Yeah." She nods, bottom lip caught between her teeth. "I have a bad habit of checking the ending before I finish the book."

"And?" I arch my brows. "The good guy wins?"

She shakes her head. "No. She goes back to her ex...and he becomes the perfect guy—for her."

Could Miller be her perfect guy? Maybe now that he realizes he really could lose her, he'll treat her right. If he did, could he win her back?

"Xander." The book is plucked out of my hands, and a moment later Bella's face appears in front of me. "What's wrong?"

"It makes me think about you and Jake." My words come out easily, as if they were already on the tip of my tongue. "What if he tries to win you back?"

Lips trembling, she climbs into my lap and frames my face with her hands so I'm forced to meet her eye. "You know what this book and my situation have in common?"

She's quiet for a moment, and when I don't answer she tilts her head to the side, her hair cascading over her right shoulder.

"A choice." She presses her forehead to mine. "And as long as I have a say in what I want to do with my life, I'm not going back to Jake. I promise."

Closing my eyes, I inhale deeply. Her sweet, fruity scent engulfs me, and I can breathe freely again.

I don't know what it is about her that has me so out of my mind.

I've always fucked around. In high school, in college, after graduation. Girls have always gravitated toward me. I never minded. Until Bella...

What the fuck am I thinking?

A storm brews in my chest, growing from a light gust to a torrential downpour.

With my arms wrapped around her, I shift so she's on the couch and I'm on my knees in front of her. I want to give her all the power, let her do whatever she wants with me. She's confident and bold; she just needs to see herself the way I see her.

"Use me," I tell her. "Do whatever you want with me. Do what the girls in your books do to their men if you want."

Bella studies me with a calm expression before she pushes me away and stands. I stay on my knees, watching her walk out of the room. She saunters to the dining table and turns a chair around before she sits and spreads her legs wide.

"Crawl to me, Xander."

My heart skips a beat, and heat creeps up my neck. I stare at her, caught in her trap. The power she exudes rewires my brain.

Every day, she tightens her hold on the reins of her life. It's sexy as hell. I'd do anything for her. So, I get on all fours and crawl to her.

"Take off my shorts," she commands the moment I reach her.

When her shorts land on the floor, she shifts to the edge of the chair, her pussy in my face.

I wet my lips, dying to taste her.

"Make me come, Xander...with only your tongue."

With a smirk, I dive in. Her sweet scent overtakes me, the taste of her enough to make me rock-hard. I suck her clit then release it. With my lips and teeth, I work her over, adding more friction, winding her up. Anytime I suck her clit into my mouth, she trembles.

"Good boy, Xander..." Bella whimpers, her eyes falling closed.

I double my efforts, and she comes in minutes, hard and intense, her legs shaking. I don't move. My cock is rock solid; even my balls are tight while I wait for her next command.

When she stands, her legs wobble. It takes effort not to steady her, but she hasn't given me permission. Once she regains her bearings, she peers down at me. "Sit."

I stand and slump into the chair she just came on, and when she straddles my lap, I bury my hand in her hair.

"Use me," I beg, my words raspy.

Bella doesn't say a word; she just watches me.

Hand at her nape now, I force her face down until our eyes are level. "Use me," I whisper more urgently. "Take what you need from me and use me."

I wait. I've never been a patient man, and already my patience is wearing thin. Just as I'm about to give up and make a move myself, she angles in and captures my lips with hers.

She presses her hands to my face, her lips desperate for mine. I tug on her hair, opening for her so she can explore my mouth with her tongue. She's in control, deepening our kiss one moment and almost pulling away the next.

I groan in disapproval when she moves back again. Desperate for more, I lunge forward, but she pushes me back with a hand to my chest.

Her breathing is fast as she sits perched on my lap, eyebrows knitted together. "You told me to use you." She clutches my hands and removes them from her hips, dropping them so they dangle at my sides. "No touching."

"That's not fucking fair."

"No touching, Xander, or I'll stop."

Swallowing the instinct to take over, I nod. With a smirk, she pulls her tee over her head, and her round tits and puckered nipples are on display, making me salivate all over again.

Bella shimmies off my lap and picks up her shorts. When she drops them again, she's holding a condom. She pulls my hard dick out of my sweatpants and sheaths my length; the whole time, I keep my teeth clenched tight, my hands balled into fists. Fully naked and with a naughty smile, she climbs onto my lap again. Her light peck on my lips is not nearly enough.

Hoisting herself up, she wraps her hand around me and slowly lowers herself. She shudders, and my eyes fall closed when she's seated completely. *Fuck.* My skin feels like it's on fire. My desire to touch her just might be the death of me. That, or the loss of my sanity.

As she works herself up and down, my mind goes hazy. She moves slow and steady, her breasts bouncing, making my urge to disobey grow. Her pebbled nipples are inches from my face, but I'm not allowed to touch them. *Goddamn.*

She's gonna pay for this, and I know exactly how. It'll still be all about her, but I will be the one in control.

"Such a good boy," she praises. Her cheeks are flushed, her hair is messy, but her smile? Immaculate. "You want to touch me?"

I nod.

"Say it." Her words are followed by a loud moan.

"I want to touch you."

"Then beg for it."

Never in my life could I have imagined myself begging someone, or crawling to them, but that was then...before her.

"Please, Bella. Please let me touch you. I want it so bad, baby."

"Thank you for begging so nicely." She slams her lips to mine.

I kiss her with the same passion, the fire inside me flaring hotter. Finally, I touch her, caressing her smooth skin, playing with her nipples. Her tongue battles mine, twirling and curling until she's out of breath.

She lifts and drops herself down harder, arching back and resting her hands on my knees. Her moans and whimpers, the sloppy sounds of her pussy dripping down my cock, fill the space.

With a hand at her throat, I squeeze, and when the corners of her mouth tip up, I add a little more pressure. She's altering my brain's chemistry. This is all new, this wildness, her insatiable nature that pushes my limits.

And I'm fucking happy about it.

Her movements become more frantic, her pelvis grinding against mine as she chases her orgasm. "Oh my God!" she cries out, throwing her head back. "I'm so full..."

"My dick is soaked with you, baby... You feel like heaven." I squeeze her throat until her face flushes a shade darker, her smile broader. "You like that?" I breathe out.

"I love it," she moans. "The best necklace I've ever worn..."

Holy. Fuck.

Every day she weaves a little more of herself into my being, into my life, stealing my senses and my reservations as well as my sanity.

I let go of her throat and push her hair off her face. Sweaty, skin on fire, she watches me, her eyes hooded with her almost-there orgasm, and fuck, if this isn't the most beautiful sight in the world.

"I'm coming." She throws her head back as her insides spasm, pulsating until I explode too.

When my breathing calms, I kiss her again. It's slow and gentle—the total opposite of how we started.

"You like to be on top," I say.

"Yes."

"Is this your favorite position?"

"No, but you're about to find out what is," she answers playfully. "And, uh"—she tucks her chin and focuses on my lap—"I think I ruined your sweatpants."

"If it means I get to see you like this again, wild and unpredictable, you can ruin all my clothes. Don't be afraid to be a mess for me, baby."

Cradling her face, I kiss her again, just to feel her mouth on mine.

"I didn't expect you to listen or beg...or to crawl," Bella confesses once our lips part. "But you were a good boy. You did exactly as you were told."

This woman. She's trying to get a rise out of me. She's goading me into doing what she wants. I could easily teach her a lesson, but why should I?

Standing, I grip her ass and haul her up with me.

She wraps her legs around my hips and clings to my neck. "Where are we going?"

With a swat to her ass, I say, "To my bedroom."

"And what are we going to do there?"

"You're going to sit on my face, and you'll scream my name as loud as you can while I make you come."

CHAPTER 27
Where's Bella?

XANDER

October

Fuck, I can't wait to get home and take a hot shower. Practice went well, and the whole team is pumped for Sunday's game against Miami. Their record is similar to ours, so it'll be tough, but we are determined to win.

This season, the Super Bowl will be ours. I can feel it.

I slip my hoodie over my head while Drew Carter talks about his plans to go to the movies with his wife. He's our middle linebacker, and so far, he's the closest thing I have to a friend on this team. Garcia's a good guy too, but his bond with Miller is a big red flag for me.

As much as I hate that the entire team thinks Jake and I are old friends, I'll keep the lie going, for Bella's sake.

"Garcia. We going out tonight?"

My teeth grind at the sound of Miller's voice. He has dark circles under his eyes, and he looks like he's lost weight since Bella left two weeks ago. Since then, he's only gotten more aggressive and vile, even to his teammates.

"Yeah, why not?" Garcia calls out as he slips into his leather jacket.

"I figured you'd blow me off like you have every other time I've asked these past two weeks."

Garcia shrugs, his expression easy. "Meg's shopping with Isabella, and then she has plans to meet with her sister, so I've got time."

"Really? Isabella didn't mention it." Jake hides his hands in his pockets, his cold eyes calculating. "Do you know where they went?"

Garcia, oblivious to his friend's scheming, says, "Not a clue, man, but Meg is meeting up with Liz soon, so they may be finished."

"Never mind. I'll ask Isabella when I see her." Miller picks up his duffel bag. "I'll wait for you in the parking lot." With that, he strides out of the locker room, not bothering to say goodbye to anyone else.

I can't say I hate to see him so miserable, but his calls and texts to Bella are becoming more desperate, and that has my hackles raised.

She's doing her best to guard her peace and mentally prepare herself for the inevitable breakup. I just wish she'd do it already.

She's been apartment hunting this week, but all her options are either too expensive or in terrible condition. I refuse to let her live in a place where she isn't safe—which is also why I want her to stay as far away from Jake Miller as possible.

He's fucked up and manipulative, and I worry if he gets anywhere near her, he'll know exactly what to do or say to make her come back to him. She claims she'll never go back, but that doesn't stop me from worrying. The fucker has a knack for putting the blame on her, making her feel bad about herself, and treating her like she's his property. It kills me how easily he gaslights her, has her believing she's overreacting. He might not know the details of what her family put her through, but he learned how to tap into her wounds and exploit them, and that disgusts me.

A guy doesn't treat the girl he claims to love like that.

For now, I push the spiraling thoughts out of my head and pick up my bag. Once Carter and I have made plans to meet at the gym in the morning, I give my teammates some quick backslaps and fist bumps and head out.

The time alone in the car to cool off will do me good.

JUST AS I park my car in my driveway, my phone rings. When my sister's name flashes on the display, I tap Accept.

"Hey."

"Hey," Audrey says, her voice coming in loud and clear through the car's speakers.

"How are you?"

"Spent the day doing nothing, waiting for Ryan to fly back home." She sighs. "I can't wait until we can finally move back to Boston. I miss everybody."

Audrey is four years older than me, and though I'm almost twice her size, she's still overprotective. That's just her personality. She's nosy and overbearing, but she means well.

"You've got, what, six months? Mom said her agent found a house that's perfect for you—"

"Yeah, she sent me the details, but I don't think I like it. It's too far away from your neighborhood."

I roll my eyes. "But it's close to Mom and Dad. What if I get traded? Then being in my neighborhood wouldn't mean shit."

"I'll think about it." She huffs. "Any fun plans for tonight?"

"Nah. I just got home. I'll probably watch a movie." *With Bella*, though I don't tell Audrey that, not yet. Not until Bella leaves Miller for good. Just the sound of Jake's name would send my sister into a full-blown tirade.

"When was the last time you went out?"

"Eh, it's been a while, but what's wrong with staying home?"

"Nothing. It just isn't like you; it weirds me out. Are you really okay?"

"I'm tired, that's all," I bite out, anxious to get inside and see my girl. "Hey, listen. I need to run."

"Already?"

"Sorry, yeah. I'll call you later. Bye."

"More like nev—" I tap End before Audrey finishes talking. It's rude, and she'll be royally pissed, but that's the least of my concerns.

Inside the house, Milo click-clacks across the floor, his little tail wagging. I crouch and pet him, listening for Bella, but the house is silent.

Shit. I thought she'd be home by now.

Miller knows she went shopping with Meghan. What if they're still out and Jake finds her?

Fuck.

I spin around, ready to flee, but a loud bark stops me in my tracks.

Milo. Shit. He hasn't been out in hours.

"Sorry, buddy. My brain is all over the place." I snag his leash from the table by the door, and then we head out. As we hit the sidewalk, I pull my phone out of my pocket and type a text to Bella.

BELLA:

I'm still with Meg. She had a change of plans, Liz is busy.

ME:

Think you'll be much longer?

BELLA:

I'm headed to my aunt's next. Should be there in about forty minutes

ME:

Send me the details. I'll come pick you up

BELLA:

Why? I'll call an Uber or ask Meg to give me a ride

ME:

Because I miss you

BELLA:

Miss you too, but I'm not buying it. Why?

ME:

Miller knows you're with Meg. I don't want him to corner you. Let me pick you up

A moment later, a text with an address appears. *Good girl.*

ME:

I'll be there in thirty. Wait for me

BELLA:

Yes sir

Puffing air out of my lungs, I slip my phone back into my pocket and follow Milo's lead. I just hope Miller thinks Bella and Meg split up earlier and he isn't out looking for her.

MEG HUGS BELLA TIGHTLY, and when she pulls back, they're both laughing. As Bella heads my way, her friend gives me a small wave then makes her way to her car.

"Did you have fun?" I ask as she slips in beside me.

She holds my gaze as she buckles her seat belt, a genuine smile on her face. "I did. Meg and I haven't spent enough time together lately."

I dip my chin. "Glad you had the chance, then."

Bella folds her arms over her chest and sticks out her bottom lip, feigning a pout. "I really could've called an Uber. What can Jake possibly do to me in public?"

With a press of the ignition button, I sigh. "I'm worried he could follow you somewhere private."

Rather than respond, she lowers her head and taps out a text on her phone. Then, like I figured she would, she changes the subject. "My aunt asked me to stay the night. I said yes."

As happy as I am that she has her aunt in her corner, someone who loves her unconditionally, I'm still worried about Miller. He could easily show up there.

And, selfishly, I'll miss her…even though it's just one night.

"What if Jake shows up?"

"He looked for me there twice already. I doubt he thinks I'm staying there."

When the light ahead of us turns red, I bring the car to a stop and narrow my eyes on her.

"You need to break up with him for real. Why prolong it if you know you don't want to be with him?"

Her shoulders slump. "That's one of the reasons I want to see my aunt, to talk to her about it. Meg let me bounce ideas off her too. I don't know exactly how I'll do it yet, but it was helpful."

Ten minutes later, I pull up in front of her aunt's house and survey the façade, realizing there isn't a single light on. I unbuckle my seat belt and turn to look at her.

"You sure she's waiting for you?"

"Yeah, she responded to my text when you picked me up. She probably went to lie down," she mutters. "I'll let myself in. I don't want to trouble you more than I already have."

"It's not a problem, but I selfishly want you to come home with me. Any chance I can convince you to change your mind?"

Though a spark of interest ignites in her eyes, she quickly blinks it away. "Sorry. I haven't seen Millie in weeks. I miss her."

I put my hand on the back of her head and draw her face to mine. Our kiss is slow, and it awakens something primal in me. I suck on her bottom lip and sink my teeth into it before releasing it again.

"God, what am I going to do without you?" I press a kiss to her jaw, then her neck.

"I'll make it up to you," she mewls, sounding as turned on as I am.

I cover her mouth with mine again, and when I pull away, we're both short of breath. My heartbeat is like the revving engine of a Formula 1 car, fast and intense.

"What are your plans for tonight?" Bella asks, fixing her hair.

"I hadn't thought about it, but your words about your family made me realize I could actually visit mine. Mom will be happy."

"I'm sure your parents miss you." She checks her reflection in the car visor and turns to me. "I feel bad; you've barely seen them since I started staying at your place."

"Stop. I talk to them every day. They know how busy I get during football season." I catch her hand and hold it between my palms. "Plus, I'm happy you're staying with me."

"Me too." She plants a light peck on my lips then grips the door handle. "I gotta go."

I hop out too and round the car so I can walk her to the door. Just as I take her hand, I look up and find Bella's cousin watching us. His eyebrows reach his hairline, and the guy beside him stops short and gawks, his mouth agape.

I lift my free hand and thread my fingers through my hair. "Hey, Ben."

CHAPTER 28

Got It?

BELLA

October

My stomach drops. *Shit.* I wasn't prepared for these two men to come face-to-face. I mentioned Ben to Xander, and he remembered him from college, but just vaguely.

"Hey, Ben." I wave awkwardly and then greet his boyfriend. "Hey, Tom."

"Hey," Tom mutters, looking surprised. "What are you guys doing here?"

"I promised Aunt Millie I'd visit. Xander just offered me a lift."

My cousin narrows his eyes, like he can see right through me.

I lower my gaze, hoping I can avoid giving anything away, and press my teeth into my bottom lip. A pain shoots through me, and I gasp, bringing my fingers to the place where Xander bit me.

"Let me see." With a hand on my wrist, Xander gently turns me. His gaze coasts over my face, a small smile curving his lips. "I'm sorry, baby."

"I'm not." I smile back.

This moment is like so many we've shared. When we're together, the world around us disappears, and it's just us, safe and sound in some kind of bubble. His touch on my wrist spreads warmth through my veins, and the way he looks at me makes my heart skip a beat. He's going to be my undoing, I have no doubt, and somehow, it doesn't scare me.

"If you want to visit my mom, we'd better head in. She's probably about ready for bed," Ben rasps harshly.

"But—" Tom tries to protest, but when my cousin hits him with a cold stare, he snaps his mouth shut.

I give Xander a sheepish smile. "Bye."

"See you tomorrow." With a nod at Ben and Tom, he takes a step back.

"Goodnight." Tom grins, and it makes me smile. He has so much energy and compassion, and he's always happy to share it with everyone around him. He's such a cheerful, nice guy, and I love him for that.

"Bye." Ben's response is much more subdued as he stalks to the front door.

Tom drapes his arm over my shoulder and kisses my temple as we climb the stairs. "I missed you."

"I missed you too," I murmur, snuggling closer. "Where have you guys been?"

"Penny and Christina are getting married, so they threw a little celebration." He glances over my shoulder as Ben finally unlocks the door. "Alexander has the hots for you, my dear, and it turns me on."

"Tom!" I push him away, giggling. "You're being ridiculous."

"Ridiculous?" Tom gasps dramatically, a hand pressed to his breastbone. "Have I ever lied to you?"

"You're overdoing it a bit," Ben huffs.

His boyfriend immediately bursts out laughing and pulls me into his side again. "Bella knows I'm joking, right?"

"Of course."

As I step into the house behind Tom, I finally dare to look at Xander. Black sweatpants, a black hoodie with a white T-shirt underneath, and white Nike Air Max sneakers—he's effortlessly hot, even with his tattoos hidden.

He lifts his chin when he catches me staring and mouths *goodnight* before rounding his car.

"Do you want some coffee?" Tom asks.

Ben adds, "Mom's probably upstairs."

"Yeah, coffee would be great."

"I know you're staying at Alexander's house to avoid seeing Miller," Ben says as I follow him to the kitchen, where Tom is already working on the coffee, "but I thought you were smarter than that. What if Miller showed up?"

I drop into a chair, elbows on the table, and hang my head. "Jake found out I was out with Meg earlier, so Xander was worried he'd track me down. All he did was pick me up and bring me here."

Tom sets two mugs of steaming coffee on the table, then goes back for his. "That man is even hotter in person," he says as he joins us with his own cup.

"He may look like a sex god, but that doesn't make him a good person," Ben snaps.

My heart pinches at the disgust in his tone. "You don't know him."

"One year of college was enough. I know how guys like him operate. You've known him for what? Three months?"

"People change." Tom brings his mug to his lips and takes a slow sip.

"Not him. Rumor on campus was that he dumped a girl and she tried to commit suicide. Guess he's the one who found her. He ended up saving her life."

Silence settles in the kitchen. My shoulders tremble, and I swallow the bile climbing up my esophagus.

"Do you think he had something to do with it?" Tom asks. "With her trying to..."

"I'm not sure. After it happened, he was broody and distant with everyone, even his teammates. As I mentioned, he and Miller got into a fight. But then...things kinda went back to how they were before, like he just switched his emotions off. He acted completely unbothered." Ben covers my hand with his. "I'll never force you to do anything you don't want to do. I'm not judging you if you have something going on with him. Just be careful, and remember I'm always here for you."

Heart lodged in my throat, I nod once. "I know."

"No, you don't. When shit happens, you shut us all out, as if it'll be easier to deal with it alone. That's an illusion, Bella. I'm not only family, I'm your friend too, and I'd do anything for you."

My heart swells with tenderness. "Thank you, Ben."

"I love you two so much," Tom murmurs, putting his palm over ours.

"We love you too." Ben tilts closer to his boyfriend and pecks his lips.

Warmth blooms in my chest. I've always admired their relationship. It's built on friendship, mutual respect, and trust. Their love is precious and strong. It's what I long for myself.

"When are you two going to get married, huh?" I ask, needing to change the subject. "Penny and Christina aren't the first of your friends to tie the knot."

"We don't want to rush anything," Ben says.

"Rush anything?" I frown. "You've been together for close to three years."

"We want to live together first," Tom says. "We found a lovely apartment and can move in next month."

"Does Aunt Millie know?"

Ben's expression darkens. "Yes, and she's not happy about it. She says Tom should just move in here, that the house is big enough for all of us." He sighs. "She means the world to me, but I'm ready to start my own life with Tom."

"I could talk to her." She and I planned to talk about living arrangements anyway. She suggested I move in with her while I save for an apartment. If I'm here, it will be easier for her to accept Ben moving out.

"You'd do that?" Tom leans forward, beaming. "Yes. Please, we'd be forever grateful. If you can get her on board, I'll buy you anything you want."

"Hold your horses, cowboy." Ben lets out a deep laugh. "Mom adores Bella, but it might not be enough."

"We'll never know unless we try," I murmur.

"You are our savior, Bella." Tom stands and stretches. "I need to go to bed."

I stand and collect our mugs. "And I need to see Aunt Millie before she falls asleep."

"Go ahead. I'll take those and make sure the guest room is made up." Ben carefully takes the dishes from my hands, then nudges me toward the living room. "See you tomorrow."

"Goodnight, boys."

"Babe," Tom says, catching my arm. Leaning in so Ben won't hear us, he whispers, "Alexander likes you. Trust me—I can sense these things." When he steps back, he gives me a gentle smile.

My heart pangs. Talking about their relationship distracted me. It was a reprieve from my concerns about Xander and the plan I still need to make for my breakup with Jake. Now? All those gloomy thoughts fill my mind again.

"Night, Tom." All the way up the stairs, I think about what Ben said about Xander, about that girl who tried to commit suicide and him being the one to rescue her. Something is missing, and I can't figure out what. How does Jake's broken nose fit into the picture? Is she the girl Jake told me about when we first talked about his friendship with Xander?

God, I need the whole story. I'll ask Xander for *all* the details about his past with Jake. These little bits of information aren't enough.

As I close the door to Aunt Millie's house behind me, I turn and close my eyes, soaking in the sun's rays. The weather is unusually warm for the end of October, but the wind that scatters over my skin still makes me shiver. I zip up my leather jacket then pat my pockets, looking for my phone so I can order an Uber.

Movement in the driveway startles me, and when my gaze clashes with Jake's, my pulse skyrockets.

He's leaning against his SUV with his arms crossed over his chest, looking far too casual.

I thread my fingers through my hair, only to pull my hand back and fist it when I realize it's trembling.

This is not how I wanted to see him for the first time in two weeks.

With a deep inhale, I steel my spine and force myself to move his way.

"What are you doing here?" I ask, making sure to keep a couple of feet between us.

He raises his brow, his scowl deepening. "That's what you want to know?"

"Yeah." I swallow thickly. "Because I remember telling you I needed a break."

"The break is over. It's time to stop this bullshit." He drops his hands and pushes off the car, towering over me. "I've given you more than enough time to get your shit together, and I've let all the unanswered calls and texts slide." He flings his arms wide, and I flinch on instinct, taking a step back. "I'm done being patient. It fucking stops now."

I wince at his loud voice but force myself to stand tall. "That's not how—"

He wraps his palm around my wrist and hauls me toward him, knocking the air from my lungs. In a voice so cold it freezes the blood in my veins, he whispers, "You're not listening, Isabella. *You are my girlfriend*." He squeezes my wrist, his digits sinking deep into my skin. "My girlfriend who left me all alone at my mom's party for everyone to see, including my parents. I don't particularly like being a laughingstock."

I grimace. My resolve slowly evaporates. "Jake, let me go."

"Tell you what," he continues, as if he doesn't hear me. "You can play this game for three more days. I'll leave you alone until Sunday, but then you'll bring your ass to the stadium and watch me play. You'll sit with the other girlfriends and wives and cheer us on. Got it?"

A memory resurfaces in my mind, and my skin crawls.

The bathroom door opens, and Kevin steps inside. He turns the lock then zeroes in on me, eyes burning with an energy I'd recognize anywhere.

"Your mom went to see her friend."

He steps into me, and I shuffle away until my back hits the wall.

"Stop these games, Isabella. We both know your cunt is desperate for my dick."

He grabs my shirt and hauls me to him. I push him away, pounding at his chest. It only makes him laugh.

"Let me go!" I protest.

He whirls me around and pushes me facedown into the countertop. Then he lifts my skirt and slaps my ass with his open palm. I bite my bottom lip, stifling the sounds, knowing they only rile him up more.

"Next time you pull something like that, you'll regret it. Got it?"

Got it? Those two words are like icy daggers to my heart.

Jake is just like Kevin, always has been. My coping mechanism, my ability to retreat when I'm hurt or triggered, has caused me to miss vital red flags. My fear of being left alone and my need to be loved have led me here, to this dark full-circle moment.

"Jake." My voice is weak, just like my legs. I'm outside, yet it feels like the walls are closing in on me, making it hard to breathe.

"I asked you if you understand," he says, raising his voice.

My body trembles, and my breakfast threatens to reappear, but I will my mind to stop its spiraling. Breaking up with Jake at the stadium after his game is what Meg suggested I do yesterday. That way, there will be other people around. He wouldn't dare make a scene in public, but right now I just want him to leave. I want to escape him and his threats by any means possible.

And so I let him think he's got the upper hand.

I nod, avoiding looking him in the eyes. "I understand."

He grabs my chin and lifts my face to his. His lopsided grin makes me sick to my stomach. "I'm glad we're finally on the same page, baby. See you on Sunday." He kisses my lips briefly and takes a step back.

I stay where I am until long after he's gone.

When I come back to myself, I press a palm to my forehead and take a deep breath.

Everything's going to be alright. Meg will be with me on Sunday. I can do this.

An ache in my wrist draws my attention, and when I tug up the sleeve of my hoodie I see red, blotchy skin. I lower my sleeve, feeling nauseous all over again. That will surely turn into a bruise. When the queasiness becomes unbearable, I whirl to my left and rush to the nearest bush, emptying my guts into it.

CHAPTER 29

Take Me Home

XANDER

October

"Hey. When did you get back?"

Bella gives me a gentle smile and closes her laptop. "Ten minutes ago." Standing, she stretches then shuffles my way. But instead of greeting me, she crouches to pet Milo. "I figured you took him for a walk. I missed you, little boy."

I smirk. "Didn't you miss me?"

Honeyed laughter spills from her lips as she straightens and wraps her arms around my torso. "You too."

I lower my head and capture her lips with mine, kissing her slowly. Instantly, my body grows warm. It's been a good day, but *this*? This is the fucking highlight.

I lean away and look down at her. "How was your day?"

"It was fine." She untangles herself from me, and as she steps back she tugs on the sleeves of her white hoodie so only her fingers are visible. "Wanted to go to the movies with Meg, but she's busy."

"Movies? What did you want to see?"

"There's a new Charlie Hunnam movie…" She grins, her eyes twinkling with mischief.

"Oh yeah? How about you and I go?"

Her smile drops, and she bites her bottom lip. "I don't think that's a good idea." She shifts her weight from one leg to the other. "What if someone sees us together? What if they take a picture?"

My stomach sinks with disappointment. "We can go in separately and then sit together once the theater goes dark."

Eyes averted, she says, "That sounds like a date."

For whatever stupid reason, my heart skips a beat. I swore off relationships years ago. My own ignorance and inaction caused another person so much damage, and I can't forgive myself for that. But I want to go on a date with her, even though it scares me.

"Because it is." I smile, though nerves skitter through me. "A friendly date. What do you say?"

She contemplates me for a moment, then smiles. "Okay. I can be ready in twenty."

"Glad I could change your mind." I wink at her.

With a peck to my lips, she scurries to the guest room to change.

"I TOLD you it'd be fine." I lean over the empty seat between us and grab a handful of popcorn from the bag on her lap.

She swats my hand away and furrows her brow.

"What?"

"What's the point of coming in separately if you're going to sit so close and steal my snacks?"

"There's a whole seat between us, Bella." I grin and toss the popcorn into my mouth. "It's almost empty in here anyway, and I'm pretty sure that couple"—I point at two girls sitting two rows below us, their lips locked—"came here to make out."

With a huff, Bella turns back to the screen, like she actually cares about the commercials playing on repeat before the previews start. Her plaid skirt rides up her thighs, and the view of her toned legs sends a wave of heat right to my dick.

"The guy who sold you your ticket recognized you. He's a Warriors fan. What if he decides to come looking for you?"

"Then it's a good thing I'm not sitting back there in my reserved seat." I thumb over my shoulder then hold out my hand. "Can I?"

"Sure."

Just as I've stuffed another handful of popcorn into my mouth, the lights dim and the previews begin.

AN HOUR and thirty minutes later, my blood is boiling. I hate how Bella looks at Charlie fucking Hunnam. The parted lips, the excited glint in her eyes, *the giggling*. You know the type—when a girl is fascinated by something, or, in this case, someone.

I am jealous...of an actor on a screen. What a bunch of crap.

Huffing, I shift in my seat and fold my arms over my chest, wishing that instead of watching this sex scene, I could whisk Bella away from this place and distract her from the screen.

When she releases a long, shaky breath, an idea comes to mind, and I can't stop myself from grinning.

I know how to make her forget about this guy.

Ducking low, I scoot over to the seat we've kept between us. She turns to look at me with her eyebrows pinched together, a question in her eyes. In answer, I take her chin between my thumb and index finger and drink her in. It's dark in here, but even in the glow from the screen, she's a stunner. When I look at her, everything else dissolves into thin air. It's just her and me, and it's enough.

"Xander..." she says softly.

I press my mouth to hers, and her lips part for me. Our tongues move as one in a slow, tantalizing motion. Already, my dick is painfully pressing into my zipper. *Damn*. If we were at home, she'd be on my lap, and I'd have my hands on her hips, rocking them back and forth to grind her wet pussy over my cock. But burying my dick in her little cunt can wait. Now, it's all about her.

As I drag my lips to her cheek, then to her ear, she grips the armrest that separates us, and when I suck her earlobe into my mouth, she lets out a moan that's a little too loud.

"Spread your legs for me," I whisper.

Bella leans away, eyes searching mine before she scans the dark, mostly empty theater. "What if someone sees?"

"As long as you keep quiet, no one will notice a thing," I say. "Spread your legs, Bella."

Hesitantly, she leans back and shifts her hips forward, spreading her legs.

Fuck yes. My body goes warm as I ghost my fingers up her thigh and under her skirt. "I want you to keep your eyes on the screen and watch your favorite actor while I'm getting you off."

Her breaths come faster, her gaze feverish—burning, even.

I don't move my hand; I just keep my focus fixed on her face until she turns back to the screen.

Only then do I trail my fingers up to her panties. They're soaked.

Damn, girl.

"Be a good girl, baby, and keep quiet," I murmur in her ear. "If you do that, then I'll play with this pussy until you're coming all over my fingers."

With her panties pushed to the side, I trace her slick folds. My breath is ragged now too. For a moment, I stop and focus on inhaling through my nose and exhaling through my mouth. With her, my self-control is shit. When I've regained a fraction of it, I nuzzle her throat and press my thumb to her swollen clit.

She sighs, and her hips buck forward, desperate for more. *So needy.*

God, I love that about her.

Moving my thumb over her clit, I ravish her throat before I move down and sink my teeth into the sensitive skin at the crook of her neck.

With a gasp, she turns to me.

I stop. "Eyes on the screen if you want me to continue."

She shakes her head but turns away again.

"Good girl," I praise her, rolling her clit between my fingers.

Her chest heaves with harsh breaths, and her fingers dig into the armrests of her seat. The slapping sounds coming from the screen hide her whimpering, but they also mean the scene will end soon—and that means I need to redouble my efforts.

I work her clit faster and inhale her intoxicating scent. *Fuck.* She makes me lose my shit more than anything in the world.

"Xander..." She wiggles her ass, following my movements.

"My little slut wants more?" I ask, my lips ghosting over her ear.

"Yes."

"Good, because you're about to come undone in the middle of this movie."

I massage her clit harder, and she trembles in response before she jerks in her seat, chin lifted, neck elongated, lips clamped shut. I caress her as she rides out her orgasm. I only retract my hand when she stops shuddering, sucking my fingers into my mouth. Then I cuff her neck and force her to look at me.

Mouth open, eyes hooded, she stares at me, disoriented. A few locks of hair have fallen out of her ponytail, framing her face.

My chest expands. Now, anytime she sees this Charlie guy, she'll be reminded of me.

I kiss her hard and fast, not letting her push me away. Fucking heaven. I don't care that my dick is about to explode. This moment is perfect.

"I bet you don't mind that I switched seats now," I say against her lips.

"Aren't you arrogant."

"For good reason." I grin and slip back into the other seat. "I just got my girl off."

We left the theater separately, and we didn't make the ten-minute walk to where I parked the car together. I've been waiting here for a solid five, and Bella is nowhere to be seen.

I'm considering going back to find her when she rounds the corner. Her plaid skirt swishes with each step, her loose strands of hair floating around her. Her leather jacket is zipped up, and when a gust of cold wind envelops her, she crosses her arms over her chest.

Bella stops in front of me, a gentle smile lifting the corners of her mouth. "Sorry."

"I was about to head out on a rescue mission."

"You have zero patience."

"Not true." I grip her hips and pull her to me. "I have zero patience when it comes to *you*."

Head tilted back, she sighs. "That makes me feel special."

"Because you are." I press a kiss to her forehead. "Did you like the movie?"

Bella nods.

"Did you like coming all over my fingers while watching it?"

This time, her cheeks go pink, but she nods right away.

I take her mouth in another hard kiss. Fuck, she's like a dose of something vital. She's a need, and I've never been more desperate than I am with her.

"Get in the car," I whisper against her lips.

Eyes burning into mine, she opens the door and climbs into the backseat. I squeeze in behind her and lock the doors. Though I'm eager to touch her, I sit still, keeping my hands to myself, waiting for her to tell me what she wants.

Slowly, Bella palms my groin, tracing the outline of my dick through my jeans. We work in tandem to lower my pants and my briefs to my knees.

When she grips my shaft and strokes it, excitement builds inside me; just the thought of fucking her in my car has me worried I'll blow my load early.

She shimmies along the seat and takes my cock into her mouth, her tongue curling around the crown. From root to tip, she licks me, teasing the hell out of me, taking her time, as if she's savoring each moment.

"That's it, baby. You're doing so good," I whisper.

With my balls cupped in one hand, she tugs, and as she grazes her teeth up my shaft she clenches the base of my cock and jerks me. Hissing, I fist her hair and throw my head back.

A moan escapes her lips as I tug on her ponytail, and then she doubles down. She deepthroats me, gagging as she does. Then she does it again. She increases her pace, taking me like a champ.

"Bella, you're fucking...a-amazing..." My release looms, but before it can wash over me, she slows her movements. "Please," I beg her.

Straightening, she strokes me lightly and leans in, tangling her tongue with mine. When she squeezes my cock, I groan against her lips, sucking her bottom lip inside my mouth and biting hard.

She's going to be the death of me.

With one last flick of her tongue in my mouth, she drops and takes my dick as deep as it'll go. She gags, but that doesn't slow her down. No, she fucking loves it. Her moans and hitched breaths are louder than any sound I make.

"Babe...I'm gonna come," I groan. "Let me come, please."

She squeezes my balls and grazes her teeth over the sensitive tip of my cock, twisting her wrist and pumping my shaft. That's all it takes for stars to dance in my vision, for me to unleash inside her mouth.

She swallows it down, prolonging my release and milking me until I'm fucking empty.

"Wow," I exhale as she pulls back. "That was the best blow job I've ever had. You are fucking perfection."

"I'm glad you enjoyed yourself," she murmurs, her lips curved up in a devilish smirk.

"Enjoyed myself?" I pull her onto my lap, making her straddle my legs. "You sent me over the fucking edge; I can't think straight. Fuck, baby, you are magic."

The kiss we share is slow but arousing. Already, my cock is thickening again, my head spinning.

"God, I want you," I whisper against her soft skin.

"Take me home, Xander," she says, rotating her hips over my hard length. "I want you to blindfold me and fuck me so hard I won't be able to walk." Her lips hover over mine. "Can you do that for me?"

"Who am I to say no to you?" I murmur, pulling her face down and kissing her slowly. "Let's go home."

CHAPTER 30

Audrey

BELLA

October

A KNOCK ON THE DOOR WAKES ME. I INSTANTLY SIT UP IN bed, startling Xander.

"What happened?" He yawns.

"Someone's knocking."

The knock sounds again, and Milo scrabbles to his feet and starts barking.

Shit. My stomach roils with nerves. Is it Jake?

God, please don't let it be him.

We both fall silent, looking at each other, and when we hear the knock again, Xander sighs and rolls out of bed.

He puts on his sweatpants, and as he heads out of the room, he says, "It's okay. No need to panic. I'm sure it's not Miller."

My gaze drops to my wrist, where the signs of Jake's grip are evident now that the concealer I used to hide it from Xander has washed off. I'll need to cover it up again.

Just the thought of going to the game makes me nauseous. I'll do everything in my power to stick with my plan and break up with Jake after it, but it won't be easy.

When Xander and I got home last night, we fell into bed, and after a round of sex we fell asleep almost immediately, he with his arm around me and me with my back pressed firmly to his chest. I didn't have time to tell him about Jake's visit, so I'll have to work up the nerve today. He won't be happy.

I pull on a pair of leggings and a loose blue T-shirt, then rush to the guest room so I can comb my hair. It's a tangle of knots after last night's activities, so I collect it into a loose bun.

Not wanting to greet Xander's company looking like I just rolled out of bed, I pop my head out the door and peer down the hall. It's empty, and Milo's happy squeals are definitely coming from the living room. With an exhale, I dart to the bathroom and silently close the door behind me. *Phew.*

I wash my face, then study my reflection in the new mirror. My cheeks are tinged pink, my blue eyes clear and lively. Being around Xander is good for me.

I can't say the same for him. All I've done is drag him through my shit. I apply concealer to my wrist to hide the bruising, blowing on it so it dries quickly. Then I give myself a silent pep talk. *I can step out there. It's time to face reality.*

"Bella?" The bathroom door opens, and Xander pads inside, his gaze roaming over my face and down my body. "Planning another escape?"

"No," I mutter, entranced by his captivating eyes. Just being near him heightens all my feelings. I've never had such powerful emotions for a person. *I can't possibly be falling for him, right?* "You have a guest, so I thought... I thought I'd stay out of the way. Besides, I have work to do."

He cocks a brow. "At seven a.m.? You don't usually start until ten."

"Oh. I didn't realize it was that early," I chuckle.

In one stride, he steps in close and pulls me against his chest, covering my mouth with his. The kiss is gentle, slow, and sweet enough to make me melt on the spot. I have no desire to leave this room, and I don't care who's here. All that matters is him.

Unfortunately, he's got more of a level head. With a sigh, he backs away and palms my cheek.

"I couldn't resist."

"I'm glad you didn't," I whisper.

The bathroom door bursts open, making us jump away from each other. A beautiful brunette stands in the doorway, her jaw slack.

"Alex?" she asks, her voice melodic and deep.

My stomach plummets. Who is this woman? Why is she here so early?

"Old habits die hard, I see."

"Stop being dramatic." He saunters over to her and drapes an arm over her shoulders.

Heart twisting painfully, I study them. It only takes a moment for relief to wash over me. They've got the same deep blue-green eyes, the same pouty bottom lip, the same straight nose with a smattering of freckles.

"Will you introduce me to your girl, or will you pretend she's not here?" his sister asks, her tone a little too snide for my liking.

"This is my friend Bella. She helped me finish this bathroom." Xander holds an arm out, gesturing to the space. "She's staying with me while she looks for an apartment."

Brow arched, she assesses me before she breaks into a gentle smile. She untangles herself from Xander and holds out her hand. "I'm Audrey, this idiot's sister."

"I'm Isabella—Bella." I return the smile even as nerves ricochet through me. I'm not in any position to meet his family. "Erm, I don't want to bother you two."

"You're not a bother. Have breakfast with us," Audrey suggests.

"I'm not—"

"That's a great idea. You've got plenty of time before work anyway." Xander breaks into a lopsided grin.

Beside him, Audrey's eyebrows are raised expectantly, so I nod. "I'd love to."

Xander grins and spins his sister around by her shoulders. "Why don't you go wait in the kitchen? I'll be right there."

Rather than leave, Audrey grasps my hand and tugs me along with her. Clearly, the impatience is hereditary. So is the demanding persona.

"Do you want help?" I ask as she goes straight to the fridge.

"No." She waves a hand. "Sit."

I plop myself down on a chair and stroke Milo's back. "Xander said Milo was a gift from you."

Crouched in front of the open fridge, Audrey looks at me over her shoulder. "Yup. I thought they'd be good for each other. My little brother can play the cool dude, the heartless jerk, but in reality, he's a softie."

"A softie? Really?" I chuckle.

Audrey meets my eye and bursts out laughing. "Right? With all his tats and muscles, you'd never guess it."

"He definitely gives off a bad boy vibe," I murmur, remembering seeing Xander for the first time.

"He's not perfect, but he has a kind soul and a very big heart. It's impossible not to love him." She starts preparing toast with peanut butter, and Milo barks. Grinning, she peers over the island at the dog. "Do you really think I don't see you?" She pulls some lunch meat from the fridge and tosses a slice of ham at him. Milo practically inhales it.

"Now I see why Xander calls him a glutton."

"He's been like that since he was a puppy." Audrey's expression is tender as she surveys the dog, but it turns shrewd when she fixes her gaze on me. "How long have you known my brother?"

"Three months or so, I guess. I helped him with his bathroom, and...well, he's my friend now."

"Just a friend?"

Unease sweeps through me, but I tamp it down. "Just a friend."

Eyes narrowed, she scrutinizes me. It's like she's trying to see through me, but she doesn't know how good I am at hiding behind easy smiles.

"What are you two up to?" Xander appears, dressed in gray sweatpants and a light-blue tee.

"Just talking." Audrey shrugs.

I relax, thankful she's not going to press the issue further.

"Bella's trying to convince me she's just your friend and nothing more."

My jaw unhinges, and all my breath escapes me. She's worse than her brother when she wants to know something.

Xander guffaws, sitting down beside me. "Bella *is* my friend and nothing more."

"Uh-huh," she deadpans. "And I'm the Pope."

"God, sometimes I forget how stubborn you can be." Xander shakes his head, still laughing. "Bella, tell my sister about your—*ahem*—boyfriend. Maybe then she'll believe us."

"Boyfriend?" Audrey frowns, her eyes dancing between her brother and me. "You have a boyfriend, yet you're staying at Alex's house."

"I'm taking a break from the relationship while I decide what to do," I mumble. "Jake Miller is my boyfriend. Do you know him? Xander's teammate?"

Audrey's confused expression morphs into a menacing scowl. "Jake Miller," she hisses through clenched teeth.

Xander holds his sister's gaze, but neither one of them speaks. It's like they're having an entire conversation without saying a word. Discomfort seeps into my veins, and I shift uncomfortably.

"Let's just say...I don't like your boyfriend," she eventually grits out.

"That's fine." I shrug. "My cousin isn't very fond of him either. I'm used to the hate."

The kitchen falls into silence for so long, I itch to jump up and run away.

Milo's bark startles us all.

Audrey jumps. "Shit, Milo. Here." She holds out another piece of ham to him.

"Is all this for him too?" Xander teases, pointing to the three plates of toast Audrey has lined up.

"Of course not. These are for us." She sets our food in front of us then goes back for hers. Once she's slumped into the chair across from me, she gives her brother an innocent smile. "Maybe you could make some coffee?"

"I should've guessed you'd want that."

While he gets to work at the counter, I smile awkwardly at Audrey, not knowing what to say to her.

"Why didn't you tell me you were coming to town?" Xander asks.

"Wanted to surprise you." Audrey shrugs. "Plus, my flight was disgustingly early. I didn't want to call from the airport and wake you up."

"You couldn't have told me when we talked yesterday?"

She deflates. "Alex, I miss you. It was a last-minute decision to fly in. This way, I can go to your game on Sunday."

Xander turns, his expression softening. "I miss you too. I'm glad you're here. Just surprised, is all."

"Aww, isn't he the sweetest?" Audrey murmurs.

"He is." I nod, my eyes locked with Xander's.

He opens his mouth but shuts it again. Then, with a wink at me, he turns back to the coffee maker.

I shift in my seat. The butterflies in my stomach are keeping me from thinking clearly. Audrey, however, wears a sharp expression.

"So," I say, scrambling for a suitable topic, "you live in Florida?"

"Yep, my husband and I moved to Miami three years ago." Head tilted, she studies my face. "How long have you and Miller been together?"

Though Jake is the last thing I want to talk about, I explain how we dated in high school then got back together last winter.

"He called her 'the one that got away,'" Xander says without turning to look at us.

Audrey nods. "Did he break up with you the first time?"

"No. I thought a split would be best since he was leaving for college and I was still in high school."

A triumphant smile blooms across Audrey's lips. "I'm sure he only called you that because you hurt his ego. He's the great Jake Miller, and you dared to dump him. I like you more now, Bella."

I force a smile onto my face, but I'm not sure how I feel about her words.

Xander sets two mugs of steaming coffee onto the table then goes back for his own. When he settles, he picks the chair next to mine. This close, his body heat soaks into me, calming me.

"IT WAS NICE TO MEET YOU," I murmur as we stop in the foyer.

"You too." She steps closer and plants a kiss on my cheek. "I know you're taking a break from Miller, but is there any chance I can convince you to go to Sunday's game with me?"

"Audrey." Xander's voice is low and quiet, but it's definitely a warning.

I keep my focus fixed on his sister. "I already promised my best friend I'd go with her, but it'd be fun if you came along too."

Without a word, Xander shifts closer. His shoulder brushes mine, sending goosebumps skittering all over my skin.

"Awesome." Audrey beams. "Let me get your number?"

She and Xander make plans to have dinner with their parents tonight. Then she gives her brother a hug and walks out of the house, humming under her breath.

The second Xander closes the door, he turns to me. I lock my hands in front of me and shuffle my feet, suddenly nervous.

He comes closer, hovering over me. "What's this about you going to the game? I thought you weren't ready to see him."

"I've decided how I want to tell him we're over." I swallow around the lump in my throat and tilt my chin to look him in the eye. "I'll break up with him after the game. Meg will be with me."

With an arm around my waist, he pulls me against him. "Are you sure?"

I am, but I'm also scared.

"Yeah."

He presses his lips to the corner of my mouth and then moves them to my earlobe. "I know Milo needs to go for a walk...and you need to work..."

I shiver even though the anticipation of what's to come makes my skin sizzling hot.

"But maybe I can convince you to take a shower with me first? Two birds, one stone."

The feeling of his already-hard cock pressed to my leg sends all my rational thoughts to the dumpster.

Winding my hands around his neck, I whisper, "Why not?"

And, like it always does, the world around us disappears. Nothing matters except this man and his hands on my body.

CHAPTER 31

Just Sex

XANDER

October

After dinner with my family, I find Bella in the living room, watching yet another anime, *Princess Mononoke* this time. I quickly change into a pair of gray sweatpants and cuddle up close to her on the couch. When the movie's over and she's queued up her next one, she tries to get up, but I hold tight.

"Where do you think you're going?"

She clutches my arm and tugs, but I don't let go.

"I'm thirsty," she says. "You won't let me go long enough to get a drink?"

"Nope." With a grin, I hop up and lift her, guiding her legs around my waist. Instantly, goosebumps spread over my whole body. She's dressed in nothing but my T-shirt and her panties, and her bare skin on mine makes me shiver.

I stroll into the kitchen and hold her with one arm under her ass as I open the fridge.

She tightens her hold on me, as if she's worried I'll drop her. "What if I fall?"

"I'll catch you." I set her on her feet and press my forehead to hers. "No. I take that back—I'll never let you fall."

Then I kiss her. The feeling of her soft mouth against mine sets my body on fire, but rather than give in to the temptation to devour her, I take a step back and grab the apple juice.

She pouts. "Turning me on and then leaving me is so unfair."

"You said you were thirsty, so I brought you in here for a drink."

She shrugs, taking a step back. "Sorry…it won't happen again."

The words leave her mouth automatically, as if I've sneezed and she's saying *bless you*. She says it because it's expected of her. Out of habit. And that pisses me off.

Sighing, I set the apple juice on the breakfast bar and cup her face. "You sound like a robot. I want the real woman, the one who was laughing with me a few minutes ago. The one who loves reading romance novels and watching anime. Who was making incredibly sexy faces when I was inside her this morning. Who opened up about her past and let her guard down around me. Be that girl, Bella. Please."

Her eyes well with tears, but she blinks them back, and her lips tip up. "I will. I promise." She tucks her hair behind her ear.

Before we head back to the living room, I grasp her wrist so I can pick her up again. When I make contact, she flinches and pulls back.

What the fuck?

I grasp her arm, more gently this time, and a little higher.

My blood turns to ice. There's a big fucking *bruise* wrapped all the way around her wrist.

"Where did you get this?" I ask quietly.

Bella pulls her hand out of my grip and stares blankly at me. "I hit it when I took Milo for a walk."

I snort as fury builds in my chest. "Try again."

"It doesn't matter." She tries to skirt around me, but I block her path, caging her between me and the breakfast bar. "Xander, let me go."

"Tell me what happened, and I will."

"Nothing happened." She pushes against my chest. "You're making a big deal out of nothing."

Unbelievable. Twisting my lips into a scowl, I study her in silence.

Her behavior doesn't make any sense. "This kind of bruise"—I take her hand again—"happens when someone snatches your wrist, hard."

Bella tugs, but I don't release her.

She steps closer to me, her tits pressed against my chest as she says, "Let me go."

"Tell me what happened."

She throws her free hand in the air. "Jake happened, okay? He was waiting for me when I left my aunt's place. We talked, and he left," she grinds out. "Happy now?"

With a harsh breath, I let her go. "Why wasn't it there earlier?"

"Because I covered it up. I showered while you were gone and forgot to put concealer on again. You weren't supposed to see it." Bella folds her arms over her chest. "Can I go now?"

I nod and take a step to the side.

She stomps past me while I stay still, stewing in the thoughts that war inside my head. But before she has a chance to leave the kitchen, I turn. "What did he want?"

With a sigh, she stops. "He came to convince me to go to the game."

My anger and frustration mix into a dangerous cocktail, making it impossible to think clearly. In two strides, my chest is pressed to her back. Wrapping my hand around her throat from behind, I lower my head to her ear.

"I fucking hate that you didn't feel safe enough to tell me," I whisper hoarsely. "Why did you hide it? You don't trust me?"

"Xander, that's not why."

I whirl her around and cuff the back of her neck, keeping her close. Our gazes lock, and, like it always does, everything else disappears. Her eyes usually remind me of sapphires, but right now they're the color of the deepest ocean. My lungs hurt; taking a deep breath is impossible. The beating of my heart echoes in my ears, loud and demanding.

"Then why?" I ask.

"I didn't want you to know because I was afraid you'd hurt him.

And if that happens, everyone will know the truth...about us," she says.

I trace the delicate skin of her throat, my thumb hovering over the vein on her neck.

"If people found out you were fucking your teammate's girlfriend, it would damage your reputation."

"You're not his girlfriend," I argue. "He doesn't deserve to breathe the same air as you."

"Break or not, to the world, I am still his girlfriend, Xander." Bella splays her hand over my heart. "If this got out, I'd be a whore who cheated on her boyfriend, and you'd be a traitor who fucked his teammate's girl. No one would care to hear our side of the story. I don't know the details of your contract, but it sounds an awful lot like misconduct," she says quietly. "I know what I'm doing when it comes to Jake."

I thread my fingers through her hair. "If he hurts you like this again, please tell me. You don't have to deal with him on your own."

"He won't," Bella says, lifting her chin. "I already asked Ben to meet me at Jake's house immediately after the game so I can get my stuff."

I shake my head. "If Miller feels like he's being backed into a corner, he'll be unpredictable. Trust me."

Bella chews on the inside of her cheek, and I swear I see the wheels in her head turning. Then she shrugs. "Okay. Once I break up with Jake and move in with my aunt, you won't have any reason to put up with me. You won't need to worry about me anymore."

I stagger back, feeling like I've been stabbed in the gut. "Wait... you're moving in with your aunt?"

"She suggested it. Said I can stay with her for as long as I need."

My heart sinks. So we're just not going to see each other anymore?

Bella tries to untangle herself from me, but I'm not letting her. "I'm curious," I say. "Why do you think we won't see each other after you dump Miller?"

Her lips part, and she shifts, causing her pebbled nipples to brush my chest.

Dammit. I'm seconds away from fucking her in my kitchen.

"You told me yourself," she says, her tone derisive. "You have no interest in a relationship. So that makes us friends who fuck, and I'm sure once I'm out of this house, you'll have a ton of girls eager for a chance with you. You won't even notice I'm gone."

Wow.

The knife lodged deep in my gut twists painfully.

It shouldn't hurt. She's not wrong—that's exactly what I told her. Yet I hate it. Confusion is my strongest emotion right now. I've never been captivated by someone like this.

Bella is absolutely not what I thought she'd be. She's beautiful and powerful, yet tender and unassuming. She doesn't see how incredible she is. She is kind, loyal to the people she loves, and so fucking smart.

But she's wounded. The emotional injuries she suffered as a kid are still there. Since the moment I found out about what she endured, I couldn't help but compare Bella to *her*. They're so alike—gentle, caring, uninterested in football, and they've both been through so much.

And goddamn it, what if I hurt Bella the same way I hurt her?

Fuck, I still have nightmares about that night. I'm still processing it despite all the therapy.

It would ruin me if my actions ever put Bella in danger.

She's right. We should just be friends who occasionally fuck.

It should just be sex.

I tilt her chin up to me and cover her lips with mine. She opens for me, and my tongue slips inside, curling around hers. A growl escapes my throat as I deepen our kiss. It's fast, powerful, and hot. She turns me on so damn much, I can barely remember my own fucking name.

Dick already rock-hard, I lift her and set her on the barstool.

Her eyes snap open, and her forehead creases as I kneel in front of her, yanking her panties down with me.

"We should go to your bedroom," she croaks.

"Fuck no. I'm starving, and the kitchen is the best place to eat."

I put her leg on my shoulder, opening her wide for me as I plant a swift little kiss to her thigh. Then, head lowered to her cunt, I curl my tongue around her swollen clit, toying with it slowly, and when I suck it into my mouth, her hips jerk.

"Such a delicious little pussy," I murmur.

I back off and trace a finger down her slit to her opening. She's so wet, my finger slips inside without any resistance. Then I dive in again, lavishing her clit with my tongue. Another finger slides inside her, and she instantly fists my hair.

"Oh God, you feel so good," she whispers breathlessly.

I suck and lick, teasing with my tongue and my teeth while I relentlessly move my fingers inside her.

Within minutes, she's close, writhing and moaning, her pussy quivering.

"Do you want my cock inside you?" I taunt her, fucking her with my fingers and relishing the way her walls spasm around me.

"Yes," she pants, head thrown back. "Yes, I want your cock."

A smile curves my lips. "Then come for me, baby. All over my face and tongue. Give it to me." I suck her clit into my mouth again, drawing a long, loud moan out of her.

Pussy pulsing, she scrabbles for purchase, grasping the breakfast bar with one hand and tightening her hold on my hair with the other. She keeps me in place like that, grinding her pussy into my face. I lap at her little nub, prolonging her orgasm as I move my fingers inside her until I feel like she's had enough.

For now.

Standing, I drag the back of my wrist over my lips. "Open your mouth."

Chest heaving, her pebbled nipples poking against her tee, she obeys.

I slide my fingers into her mouth, and she sucks her arousal from them, cleaning up the mess her greedy pussy made. I pop my fingers out of her mouth and capture her lips with mine.

Without breaking the kiss, she slips a hand beneath the waistband of my sweatpants and strokes me gently through my briefs. When she finally slips her fingers under the thin fabric and touches the head of my cock, I groan into her mouth.

I step back, fish a condom out of the drawer I stashed them in the last time we fucked in here, and shuck off my pants. Once I'm sheathed, I settle between her legs. Our eyes meet again, and I can't look away. Slowly, I ease inside her, inch by inch, until she's full.

"You feel amazing," I murmur.

I start slow. It's taunting, but it feels like heaven. A bead of sweat drips down my back, and my every nerve ending lights up. I straighten her legs and wrap my hands around her ankles, holding her wide open as I thrust harder, finding a new rhythm.

"God, I love the way you feel. I could live in your greedy little cunt forever. You're doing so well, Bella," I praise her. "Touch yourself, baby. Let me see."

Without hesitation, she rubs circles around her clit. I watch, spellbound yet again. There's no better view than this—her pussy swallowing my cock.

"Such a good girl you are."

Tingles at the base of my spine signal my impending release. I grit my teeth and hold it back, putting her legs on my shoulders and inching forward until our lips collide.

I'm desperate for her.

"Xander, I'm gonna come," she pants, damp hair clinging to her brow.

"Come for me, baby."

I dig my fingers into her ass, my balls slapping her skin as I bury myself inside her again and again. Her walls squeeze rhythmically, her hot pussy choking the life out of me. I thrust into her hard and rough until I spill into the condom with a guttural groan.

My head spins like I've just consumed my favorite drug as I step back and steady myself.

Just sex.

That's what this is supposed to be.

But it's not enough.

Even if I'm not ready to tell her that yet.

CHAPTER 32
Isabella Is Yours
BELLA

November

"IZZY, STOP." A WARM PALM COVERS MY BOUNCING KNEE. "Everything's going to be alright, I promise."

I take a deep breath and will my mind to stop racing. Keeping my head on straight was pretty easy...until it wasn't. The second Jake zeroed in on me in the stands, my heart started racing. Ten minutes later, it's still hammering in my chest. I'm a mess, and if things don't go the way I planned, I'm gonna lose it.

Jake Miller is my ex-boyfriend...he just doesn't know it yet.

"Bella!" At the sound of my name, I turn and find Audrey approaching with the brightest smile on her lips. She's wearing a cute denim dress, her long hair loose around her shoulders.

"Damn, you're like a needle in a haystack. For a second, I was worried you changed your mind and stayed home."

I introduce her to Meg, and she settles beside me.

She scans the crowd, then peers up at the suite designated for players' families. "I figured you'd be up there rather than in the stands."

"We prefer to sit here." Meg gives me a sly wink. I'm glad I'm not the only one who thought Audrey sounded a bit snobbish.

Oblivious, Audrey leans into me. "Do you think the Warriors will win?"

"Of course. They're amazing, especially your brother."

She smirks. "I heard at least five girls talking about him while I was searching for you. God, they were a mess, like they'd pee their pants if he spoke to them."

"We did too," Meg chuckles. "One said she wants to wait for him in the parking lot."

"Ugh, it's like my college days all over again. He was still in high school, but more than one of my friends was dying to hook up with him."

I don't blame them. Xander is the hottest guy I've ever seen, and I thought that before I got to know him.

Smiling to myself, I focus my attention on the field.

I hope the Warriors win.

WITH THREE MINUTES left on the clock, they're ahead by a single point.

I can't stop shifting in my seat. I'm a wreck. The game could go either way, and I can't stand the anticipation. The offense is lined up. Helmet tilted as if he's scanning the defense, Xander is crouched behind their center, TJ Harris.

"Bella?" Audrey says, bumping my shoulder. "Do you have plans Wednesday evening?"

"Not really. Why?"

"It's my birthday, and I'm having a small gathering. I'd love for you to come."

"Oh." I straighten. "I'd love to come..."

"But?" She smiles at me with faux innocence, batting her eyelashes.

My defenses are up, because what the hell is she up to? I swallow thickly. "You don't know me. Why would you want me to come to a party with your close friends and family?"

She bursts into laughter. "Based on how comfortable you and my brother are around each other, I have no choice but to like you too."

"That doesn't explain anything."

"Alex was broody as hell at dinner the other night. I don't want him to be like that at my party, so inviting you is my best bet."

Could that really be it? She looks sincere, and I could see myself doing something like that for Ben. Maybe I've become too guarded. I can't imagine what ulterior motive she could have.

"Okay. I'll come."

"Yay! I'm so happy to hear that." She wraps her arm around me, hugging me tightly. "I promise you won't regret it."

Nodding, I turn back to the game, hopefully signaling I'm done speaking. The party is three days away, and for now I have more important matters to attend to...like breaking up with Jake.

Just as I'm focusing on the field, Meg clutches my hand and shouts, "Oh my God! It's a quarterback sneak!"

There, running down the field, is Xander. He's got the ball tucked under one arm. Holy shit. If he scores, they'll win. The offensive line crashes forward, and he's right behind them.

Focus fixed on him, I sit at the edge of my seat, my knees bouncing. He's unstoppable as he races to the end zone. I have never watched Jake play with as much interest as I watch the Warriors' quarterback.

The thought settles, and I forget how to breathe. I'm enjoying watching football because I enjoy watching Xander.

Just as he runs into the end zone, the clock runs out. The ref throws his hands in the air.

On either side of me, Audrey and Meg jump up, screaming and clapping.

My heart roars like thunder. I can't move a muscle because it's just hit me: I'm in love with Xander.

This simple thought crashes against my insides and makes my body shudder. How did I let this happen? I'm an idiot.

Mustering all my strength, I put my emotions in a box and lock it up tight before I stand and do my best to show enthusiasm. The

Warriors, with forty-one points, are celebrating their win. They deserve all the praise for a well-played game. That's all that matters now.

MEG WALKS in front of me, her fingers curled around mine. I'm dragging my feet, dreading the inevitable talk with Jake. Audrey's chatter helps, distracting me and easing my anxiety a fraction.

When we enter the family waiting area outside the team's locker room, some of the players are already here. Audrey rushes to Xander and throws her arms around him, diverting his attention solely to her.

Biting my bottom lip, I scan the crowd until I spot Jake. He's standing a few feet from Xander, talking and laughing with Marco and Drew Carter. Meg leads me over to them and gives my hand a firm, reassuring squeeze. I flash her a cautious smile and let go of her hand so she can congratulate Marco on their win.

Inhale.

Exhale.

You've got this, Bella.

I touch Jake's arm, and he turns.

"Congratulations! You were incredible." I turn to look at Marco and Drew. "You guys too."

"We came determined to win." Marco winks at me and hauls Meg into his arms.

The way she beams makes my heart ache. Seeing her so happy puts a smile on my face, loosening the tight knots in my rigid muscles.

"Yeah, we stepped onto the field knowing we would be winners." Jake loops an arm around my waist and kisses the top of my head. "You're my lucky charm, babe."

This man owns so many of my firsts: my first kiss, my first sexual experience. My first love. In high school, I dreamed about one day becoming his wife. Now that the dream has the potential to become a reality, it's the last thing I want.

With Jake, my dreams will turn into nightmares.

He's manipulative and authoritarian, abusive and cruel. His gaslighting and unfaithfulness are just a few of so many red flags I've ignored. I have more than enough reasons to walk away and never look back.

And the cherry on top? I've managed to fall for his teammate.

"We're having a celebratory dinner. Are you guys coming?" Drew asks, eyeing Jake and me.

"Of course!" Jake confirms, his fingers digging into my side. "It's perfect, because we're about to have another reason to celebrate." He squints at me, his lips curling into a grin.

How did I ever think that expression was a kind one? Where I used to see affection, now all I see is malice.

"What do you mean?" Marco asks.

Suddenly, I feel like I'm floating above my body. What happens next plays out in slow motion. Jake kneels in front of me and holds out a little velvet box.

My vision darkens, and my lungs constrict. *This can't be happening.*

"Isabella, if there's anything I love in this life, it's football...and you. You're everything to me, and with each day that passes, I fall more and more in love with you."

The room is silent, suffocating. Every eye is fixed on us, making my skin crawl and my legs quiver.

"Will you be my wife?"

"Oh shit," Meg says quietly.

Unshed angry tears blur my vision. He trapped me so easily. I was a fool to think I'd be safe in public.

"Isabella, baby, will you be my wife?" he repeats, his eyes flaring in warning.

If I humiliate him in front of his teammates, he'll make things so much worse for me, especially considering how upset he was when I left him at his mom's birthday dinner. He'd raise hell if I said no to him now.

Be convenient.

The words that have run through my head on repeat for years

surface, but for the first time in my whole life, I mentally bat them away.

Fuck no.

Flexing my jaw, I force a smile. I'll play by his rules for now, because the consequences of saying no scare me more, but I'm not changing my mind. Ben should be at Jake's place already, waiting for me so I can get my stuff. This proposal changes nothing. I'm done with him and this relationship.

I nod, wearing the fakest smile. Like a mantra, I tell myself over and over that this means nothing.

He jumps to his feet and slides a huge diamond ring onto my finger. It's heavy and sparkly, but I can't bring myself to care. He steps closer and scoops me into his arms, covering my mouth with his. It's a show. He wants everyone in the room to know I belong to him, that I'm his property. His future trophy wife. A lesser human he can order around and force to do whatever the hell he wants, including giving him babies...just like he told Xander.

The kiss lasts an eternity. A very strange eternity, because as my lips are fused to his, the gaze of another person burns into me like a brand. Finally, Jake breaks the kiss and peers at me. His breathing is erratic, and his hard cock strains against my hip.

I fight back a shudder.

It means nothing.

"Miller, don't you think that was a bit much?" Xander's voice drifts to me. "That level of PDA was way more than my poor heart can handle."

"Sorry, I got carried away," Jake quips, pressing me harder against his chest.

"Don't worry. We all know Isabella is yours." Xander's eyes find mine, and my heart plummets. Those blue depths swim with so much hurt. "Congratulations, you two." He nods, a tight smile plastered onto his mouth. Then he turns around and heads into the locker room.

The next few minutes are a blur. Congratulations, kisses on my cheek, hugs and shaking hands. My brain barely registers what's going on around me. I'm just playing along for now so I can fix it later.

"Wait for me here," Jake tells me as he steps back, ready to follow his teammates into the locker room.

"Sure." I soften my voice. "Meg will keep me company. Maybe Audrey too."

"Audrey?"

I nod. "Xander's sister."

He scoffs. "I don't want you spending time with that bitch. She's scheming and manipulative."

Look who's talking.

"She's been nothing but nice to me. I think you're wrong."

"I'm never wrong, Isabella." He glances at someone behind me and purses his lips. "Wait for me. I'll take you home so you can get ready for dinner. You'll need to dress up. We're celebrating our engagement."

With one more brief kiss, he trudges into the locker room.

I exhale a shaky breath and turn, coming face-to-face with my best friend. Meg hugs me tight, whispering over and over that everything's going to be fine. I hold on to her for a moment before I step away, needing one to myself.

A fucking avalanche of regret crashes down on me, poisoning my mind. Thinking I had everything under control was a huge mistake. Getting involved with Xander was my undoing.

More than anything, I need to make things right.

I don't know what it will cost me or how Jake will react when he sees Ben at his house, but this fake engagement ends tonight.

I'm done.

CHAPTER 33
Doesn't a Winner Deserve a Kiss?

BELLA

November

MINDLESSLY, I WALK DOWN THE HALLWAY IN THE STADIUM, breathing in and out to calm myself. The anger inside me grows stronger, mixing with disappointment. I should've known Jake would pull some trick on me, but I was too busy getting lost in my own head, too upset he was ordering me around about attending the game while I wanted to end things on my terms.

And he did it again.

I chose the safest option and went along with his proposal, but I'm still going to break up with him today. His little trap bothers me less and less with each passing second, though my frustration with myself only grows. I can't believe I let everyone think I'm gonna marry him.

I let Xander believe it.

My heart constricts painfully. I hurriedly blink away the tears veiling my eyes.

What does Xander think of me now?

Halting in my tracks, I turn and press my back to the wall. I hang my head low and breathe. My reaction today came from the deeply rooted beliefs of my childhood, just like my reasons for staying with

Jake. I want so desperately to be loved, I fooled myself into thinking abuse was my love language. I confused someone's presence with love. Confused sex with love.

Anything to make me feel wanted.

I was starved of love for years, and Jake filled me to the brim with his manipulations and gaslighting. He excels in his art of putting the blame on me, of turning tables and making me believe I was wrong.

It hurts so much, but I only have myself to blame.

I need therapy. I can't handle it on my own.

"Running away again?"

Breath hitching, I look up and come face-to-face with Xander. A small smile pulls at my lips. He's still in his jersey, number seventeen; his hair is a mess, and his eyes gleam with something I don't recognize.

"I needed to think."

His shoulders droop. "Miller is boasting in the locker room about how he got himself a fiancée."

"I can imagine." With Xander this close, the rigidness of my muscles loosens a little. "Why are you here?"

"I wanted to make sure you're alright."

"I'm alright."

He frowns like he doesn't believe me, his blue-green eyes slowly wandering over my face.

"I'm being honest."

"Have you already forgotten that I can see right through you?"

"You're—"

"Unbelievable? Yeah, the most stunning girl in the world has told me that a few times already."

He says it so simply, and my whole body comes to life. My skin buzzes with the need to tell him.

I love him, but I can't let him risk his career over this. Over me.

"Are you riding with Meg?" He peers over his shoulder, as if looking for her.

"No. I'm waiting for Jake."

His only response is the narrowing of his eyes.

Unease ripples through me, but I clear my throat and straighten.

"Thank you for checking on me, but I think you should go. You don't want anyone to see you with me."

"Since when do I care what people think?" He arches an eyebrow, stepping closer.

Butterflies take flight in my belly. I'm not sure whether they're from nerves or excitement. Maybe it's both, but it's not a good combination. It has caused me a lot of trouble in the past.

"Why did you say yes? Do you really want to be with him?" His questions come in a pained voice, and my knees give out. Thankfully, there's a wall behind me.

"Xander," I whisper, my throat clogging.

"Why didn't you say no?"

"He did it on purpose...right in front of everyone, so I'd agree."

His jaw ticks, but he keeps his tone even. "You could've said no."

"You don't understand." I shake my head. "He was angry when I left him at his mom's party. Can you imagine how furious he'd be if I said no in front of his teammates? I was afraid of what he'd do if I publicly humiliated him, because that's exactly how he would've seen it. And so I said yes...even though I meant no."

Xander swallows, his Adam's apple bobbing. When he speaks, his voice is quiet. "I understand. You did what was right...but I don't like it."

"I'm sorry." I clasp my hands together to stop myself from reaching out. Then I step away from the wall and move around him so I can return to the family waiting area. "You should go. I heard you're all going out. You were amazing out there today, and you deserve to celebrate your big win."

"That win meant shit after Ben showed up to collect your things this morning. And now? After what happened with you and Miller?" He ducks his head and shakes it, hands clasped behind the nape of his neck.

I'm frozen in place. "Xander..."

"Doesn't a winner deserve a kiss?" He looks up, blue eyes blazing.

Without giving myself a chance to overthink it, I cradle his face with my palms. The world around me is nothing but a blur, all sounds muffled like I'm underwater. There is only this man and me.

Leaning forward, I press my mouth to his. The second he parts his lips, I sweep my tongue between them, brushing his. He tastes like mint and smells like sandalwood mixed with cinnamon and comfort.

He wraps his strong arms around me, holding me firmly to his chest.

This kiss is passion in its purest form. Sizzling hot lava spreads through my veins and sets my skin aflame. He came to make sure I was okay even though my actions hurt him. God, it's everything I've ever dreamed of—

"Alex!" a familiar voice echoes through the space.

I step back abruptly, my vision still clouded. Xander looks dazed, lips parted, breath harsh. I whirl around and lock eyes with Audrey.

"What the fuck?" Face flushed with anger, she storms toward us. "What if someone sees?" she hisses. "She just got engaged to your fucking teammate! Do you understand what would happen if word got out you were banging Miller's girlfriend behind his back?"

Heat creeps up my neck.

"She's not his girlfriend," Xander bites out.

"Ha." Audrey snorts. "Yeah, my bad—she's his *fiancée*."

He stomps forward until he's nose-to-nose with his sister. "Stay out of it, Audrey. I know what I'm doing."

"Alex." Her voice softens. "Don't do this to yourself."

Xander runs a hand through his tousled hair and glances at me. "I'm fine," he says as he skirts around her. Then he's gone, striding down the hallway without looking back.

My chest is heavy. Shame. Guilt. Remorse. A cocktail of emotions brews inside me. It's the last thing I need before I face Jake.

"The second you told me you were Miller's girlfriend, I knew nothing good would come of you getting close to Alex," Audrey hisses, balling her fists. "I wanted to be wrong because I saw how he looks at you, but I should've known better. Everything Miller touches is rotten, corrupted to the core with his filth. You are no exception."

My heart lurches at the venom in her tone. "Audrey—"

"Do you know what Miller did to Alex?"

Though it's warm in here, goosebumps scatter all over my skin. I've gotten bits and pieces, but no, I don't.

"He fucking broke him when they were in college." She looks me up and down, scowling. "And it looks like you're dead set on ruining the only thing he still loves. Football is everything to him. Do you not understand what would happen to his career if someone saw you with him the way I just did? Though," she huffs a sardonic laugh, "if you're as selfish as your fiancé, you probably don't give a shit."

I shake my head, taking a step back from her on instinct. "I had no idea Jake was going to propose. I came here to break up with him; my cousin is waiting for me at his house so I can collect my things." The words rush out in one breath. My heart is drumming against my rib cage, and my hands are trembling. "I never wanted to hurt Xander—"

"But you *did*," she spits. "You didn't see his face when Miller dropped to his knee."

My stomach twists into a painful knot. "I'm leaving Jake today. I'm done with him."

"Then what? Are you going to keep living at Alex's place?"

"No. I'm moving in with my aunt. I understand the risks, and I don't want to hurt Xander's career. I swear."

Audrey watches me from under furrowed eyebrows. Eventually, she rubs her hands together and sighs. "Alex is as stubborn as a mule, and for some reason he's willing to put his whole future at risk *for you*. So, come to my party. I invited you knowing it would make him happy. This is your chance to prove *to me* you're nothing like Miller."

I shuffle back another step. "You still want me to come?"

"Are you dumping Miller today?"

I nod, my breath catching.

"Then yes, I want you to come. I want to see what my little brother sees in you...and I better be convinced." With that, she turns and leaves as abruptly as she came.

I remain rooted to the spot, my feet too heavy to move.

With a shake of my head, I breathe in and out through my nose, centering myself. I need to focus on the reason I came here in the first place. Breaking up with Jake is step one. I'll deal with the rest once that's done.

"WHERE WERE YOU STAYING?" Jake taps his fingers on the steering wheel as he waits for a red light to change.

I hit Send on my text to Ben, then slip my phone back into my purse. "Why does it matter?"

His expression darkens, and his eyes go hard. "I'm just compiling a list of people who lied to me about your whereabouts." The light turns green, and he speeds through the intersection. "So far, I suspect it includes your aunt and your cousin."

"Wrong." I tell him my carefully prepared lie. "I knew if I went to Aunt Millie's or Meg's, you'd find me. I was staying at a hotel. Thankfully, there's no shortage of them in Boston."

"So you *were* hiding from me."

"I was taking a break." I fold my arms over my chest and watch the scenery go by. The sidewalks are busy, and the leaves on the ground mix in a kaleidoscope of reds, oranges, and yellows. Boston is full of life, full of vibrant colors. It brings a smile to my face and fills me with hope.

"Good thing your break is over," he mutters, his lip curled.

I stay silent. Nothing I say will defuse the situation. We're almost at his house, and soon this farce will finally be over.

CHAPTER 34

Breakups and Setups

BELLA

November

"WHY IS YOUR COUSIN HERE?" JAKE PULLS INTO HIS driveway and comes to an abrupt stop.

I bite my bottom lip to hide my growing smile. With Ben by my side, everything will be fine. "I asked him to come," I say, making eye contact.

He scowls. "Why? We're leaving for dinner in two hours. You won't have time—"

"I'm not going to dinner." I throw open the door and climb out of Jake's SUV.

"Hey." I wave at my cousin, focusing solely on him.

Ben uncrosses his legs and straightens from where he's been leaning against his car. As he heads my way, hands hidden in his pockets, his calm demeanor transfers to me, helping me gather the courage to stand up for myself.

When a car door slams shut behind my back, though, an intense shiver runs down my spine, making it hard to hold on to that resolve. I don't need to look at Jake to know he's pissed.

He stomps after me and grips the nape of my neck, making me stagger back.

"What's gotten into you?" he hisses in my ear.

My back collides with his chest, and a gust of air escapes my lips.

Ben darts forward, his face murderous. "Miller, let her go."

Jake only squeezes harder, his breathing going ragged. I wince, certain he'll leave a bruise.

"You're hurting her."

Before Ben can physically intervene, Jake lets go of me and steps back.

I release a shaky breath as relief slowly swims through my veins, letting my body relax. *Everything is fine.*

I turn around and am immediately caught in his glare. Anger shimmers behind his irises, far too familiar to mean anything good.

"What's going on?" He tightens his hands into fists at his sides.

I look at him, mustering the courage to say the things I need to say. With a deep breath, I take off the ring he gave me and hold it out to him. "This ring...isn't for me."

His eyes go wide, then narrow to slits. "What the fuck are you talking about?"

"We're done. We aren't right for each other, and we never were. Getting back together was a mistake—"

"Since fucking when?" he barks. "You're the only girl in the world who would dump someone like me. Twice!"

"You'll find someone better than me, someone who shares your interests, who wants to go out at night, who will be happy with your expensive gifts. You don't need me."

"I don't need you? What the fuck?" He lunges forward, but Ben steps in front of me.

I fist the ring, its diamond digging into my skin. It's painful, but at least it helps me stay focused.

"Fuck off, Ben. Let me talk to her."

"No."

"Who do you think you are?" He puffs up and gets in Ben's face, trying to intimidate him. Jake is undoubtedly bigger and taller, but Ben stands his ground, squaring his shoulders and lifting his chin. "*Step back.*"

"*You* step back, and calm the fuck down."

Jake snorts. "Are you for real?"

"She's my family, Miller. I won't let you hurt her."

"I don't want to hurt her!" Jake rakes his fingers through his hair, the vein in his neck pulsing. "I want to talk."

"Then act like it," Ben grinds out.

A heavy silence settles among us. Every muscle in my body is tense. His reaction is worse than I thought it would be. He's barely controlling himself, his knuckles turning white as he pulls on his hair. If not for Ben...I don't even want to think about it.

Slowly, Jake lowers his arms, breathing heavily. The feverish glint in his gaze makes my skin crawl. It's like a fixation, and I'm the center of his attention. Nothing else exists for him in this moment.

"Isabella, can we talk?" he asks in a strained voice. "Please?"

I watch him intently, then nod. "Yes, but let me get my things first."

His eyes flash with anger, but the expression is gone as quickly as it came. Then he slips on one of his many masks, this one full of sorrow. "Okay."

When Jake steps aside, Ben shifts, still shielding me. He doesn't trust him, and I don't blame him.

His shoulders are hunched as he stomps to the front door. After he disappears inside, Ben gives me a small, reassuring smile and guides me into the house.

Physically, the place hasn't changed. All the pieces I picked are in place, but all the happiness and excitement have disappeared. It feels shallow and unwelcome inside. Was it always like this? Could I have been delusional enough to not notice?

"Where's your stuff?" Ben asks.

Jake replies before I can. "Upstairs." He keeps his focus on me. "I didn't touch anything."

"Thanks," I say, heading toward the stairs. "We'll get all my stuff, and then we can talk."

"I'll wait for you in the living room."

Twenty minutes later, my meager possessions are boxed up and loaded into Ben's car.

Ben stands in the front yard with his phone to his ear, and I stand a few feet away, staring at Jake's house. The sky is already deep blue, the last remnants of daylight peeking through wisps of clouds. An oak tree from his neighbors' lawn looms over the house, casting long shadows. Inside, the lights are off, which means he's sitting in the dark. That doesn't bode well. I have no idea what's on his mind, but I know what's on mine.

I need to be out of his life as soon as possible, or he will ruin me completely. I can heal from what's happened, but I'm afraid if I drag this out any longer, there won't be anything left to recover.

Running my hands over the skirt of my dress, I straighten and stride toward the house.

"Bella..." Ben says behind me.

Over my shoulder, I respond, "Wait for me in the car."

"No way. If I wasn't here, he would have hurt you already. I'm not leaving you alone with him."

I pause. "Maybe you can wait for me in the hallway? Just in case."

Lips pressed together, he searches my face, then nods. "Okay."

With a deep breath, I step inside. From the sounds coming from the living room, it's obvious Jake's watching game footage on his phone. At least that's normal.

"Mind if I turn on the lights?" I ask.

"Sure." He shrugs and tosses his phone onto the cushion beside him.

I turn on the lights, sit on the opposite end of the couch, and set the ring on the table.

Jake swallows loudly, his fists tightening again. "Why?"

Nerves skitter down my back, but I work to keep my voice even. "We aren't right for each other."

"No, Isabella. I've heard that one before, and it's fucking bullshit.

You just told me you'd marry me, and now you're breaking up with me? You gotta give me a better reason than that."

"You've been cheating on me," I say simply. The words don't affect me in the slightest. It's just a fact, and it doesn't matter what he might say. I know I'm right.

His eyes go wide. "What?"

"I said you've been cheating on me."

Breath ragged, he drops to his knees in front of me. "Baby, please, don't do this to me. I'm far from perfect, but I love you. I've always loved you, and I'll go crazy if you aren't with me. It happened to me once, and *fuck*—I can't go back to that. I need you, only you."

Tears stream down his face, but all I feel is indifference.

"I can't be with you. I can't stay with you without breaking myself. I revert to the old Isabella when I'm with you, the one who kept quiet so she didn't cause any trouble, the girl my mother loathed and treated like shit. That version of me needs to stay in the past."

"You should've told me how you felt. I would've..." He trails off.

I have to bite back a laugh. It's textbook victim blaming—I wouldn't expect anything less from him. "You would've what? Treated me differently?" I smirk, avoiding his eyes. "Since the moment we reconnected, you've been manipulating me. Gaslighting me. Cheating on me. Do you think anything I could say would've changed that?"

He hangs his head. "I'm sorry. You're right. I-I cheated on you a few times. I always justified it because it wasn't sex—just a blow job, just a kiss. But you didn't deserve that. I'm sorry."

His admission does nothing to me. Little by little, he has killed all the affection I had for him. There's nothing left.

"Baby, what am I going to do without you? No matter what you think, I love you." He takes my hand in his, holding it between his palms.

"You'll be fine. It'll be lonely, and you'll hurt for a bit, but...you'll be fine. You're Jake Miller!" I say, probably sounding like a robot. "You always get what you want."

"But not you."

"Not me. We aren't right for each other. It's for the best." I nod at the ring on the table. "You can probably still return it."

He zeroes in on it, lips pursed, then picks it up and holds it between us. "It's my gift to you. Take it."

"No. It's too expensive." I try to stand, but he grasps my wrists, holding me in place.

He turns my palm up and puts the ring in it, then closes my fingers over it. "Take it. Do whatever you want with it—sell it, give it to someone else. Hell, throw it away. Whatever. It's yours."

Hands in my lap, I study him for a moment. He does look miserable and apologetic, but after everything I've been through—with my mom, with Kevin, with him—it's hard to accept. His apology has come too late.

Still, I nod.

With a groan, he stands, pulling me up with him. With his hand on my nape, he angles my face up until our mouths are only inches apart.

I press my open palms to his chest and push. "Let me go."

His fingers skim over my neck as he holds my gaze, his dilated pupils making his blue-gray eyes almost black. "Let me kiss you."

"No."

"Let me kiss you, Isabella. Please." He angles closer and inhales; an eerie smile blooms on his face. "You're making me crazy... Let me kiss you one last time."

"Jake." With more force this time, I push at his chest.

He only squeezes harder.

"Miller." Ben's voice rings in the air. "Let her go."

With a glare at my cousin, Jake finally takes a step back and slips his hands into his pockets. "I got carried away." The way his lip curls up sends a wave of unease through me. This is all a game to him. "It won't happen again."

"I hope so." I take a step back, then another before I turn and walk away.

"Isabella?"

My heart pinches, but I stop. "Yeah?"

"I have no right to ask this, but...can we please not make our breakup public yet? I'll look like a fucking loser if it gets out that you dumped me right after I proposed."

More than anything, I want to say no. He deserves whatever he gets. But if it means he won't bother me anymore? I'm willing to take that risk.

"Okay. You have one month." I turn on my heel and head out of the living room.

FOR TWO DAYS, I hide out at my aunt's house, thankful for her and Ben and Tom and all the ways they've worked to distract me from my thoughts.

It's incredible, this true freedom from Jake. But without Xander in my life, there's an ache in my chest that won't go away.

Audrey texts a couple of times, reminding me about her party and sending me the address. I consider bailing, pretending I'm sick. But I want to see him, and this is the best way to make that happen.

NERVES RUSH through me as I knock on the front door. I can't imagine I'll know anyone here but Xander and his sister, and honestly, I don't even really know Audrey—and from what I do know, she's not all that fond of me.

With any luck, Xander will keep me company, but what if he doesn't want to speak with me? With zero communication between us since Sunday, it's a possibility I can't ignore. And what if he brought a date?

"Isabella!" Audrey opens the door and looks me up and down. "I'm glad you decided to come."

"Happy birthday," I say, my muscles tensing.

"Thank you." She steps back to let me in. "Is that for me?" She tips her head toward the bouquet in my hand.

"Yes." I give her the flowers, and she instantly buries her nose in them. "Peonies are my favorite. Hope you like them too."

"I *love* them." She smiles, though I can't help but remain on edge in her presence. After Sunday, I can't trust that she's being genuine. "Come on, I'll introduce you to everyone."

On the terrace, we make our rounds. I meet close to a dozen people. Her parents aren't here due to an unexpected trip to Washington, but at least her husband flew in.

"Bella?"

I look over my shoulder and lock eyes with Xander. He's standing in the doorway, gaping at me in surprise.

My heart sinks.

He didn't know I'd be here, did he? Audrey set me up.

CHAPTER 35

Harder

BELLA

November

"Hey." I wave awkwardly and sneak a glance at Xander's sister, who's standing several feet away with her husband and a couple of friends.

Audrey catches my gaze with a smug smirk. I might be misreading the situation, but it feels like she insisted I come not because she wanted to get to know me, but because she figured Xander would be angry with me for showing up unexpectedly.

What the hell is wrong with her?

"Hey." Xander's tone is subdued, and his posture deflates as he heads in the opposite direction.

My heart pangs, and my chest constricts painfully. His reaction speaks volumes. Now I know how he feels about me. Shrugging, I focus on Jess, a cute girl with red hair who has been friendly.

"How long have you known Audrey?" she asks.

"I just met her. I guess we've hung out, like, three times," I answer with a smile.

"Three times?" Jess blinks in confusion. "What do you mean?"

I huff a little laugh. "I met her at Xander's house last week. We sat together at the game on Sunday. This party makes three."

"Oh." Jess briefly looks over my shoulder before focusing on me again. "Looks like I asked the wrong question. How long have you known Alex?"

"Three months."

Eyes twinkling, she says, "Three is your lucky number, isn't it?"

I chuckle. "You could say that, yes."

"Are you and Alex a thing?" She arches a curious brow.

"No," I reply truthfully. "We're friends."

"Audrey is so overprotective of him. Has she threatened you about hitting on him yet? She once told me she'd never speak to me again if I tried."

A thread of jealousy weaves its way through me. "Are you interested in him?"

"I thought I was once." She smirks. "Audrey and I grew up together, so I've known him forever. He's a few years younger than me, but when he turned eighteen it was hard not to let myself think about it. He never showed any interest in me, and he's picky, especially when it comes to women. So if he calls you a friend, it means he likes you."

"I'll take your word for it."

We chat for a few more minutes before someone calls her name and she excuses herself.

As she walks away, I heave a sigh, not knowing what to do next. From the sound of things, dinner will start soon, but for now I occupy myself by looking around.

I take in all the small details of the house. The place looks wonderful, full of light and thoughtful choices. It's a rustic design based on wood accents, lots of modern furniture mixed with natural materials, and a neutral color scheme. It's beautiful and cozy, oozing comfort, and it immediately eases my anxiety a little.

When I come across the bathroom, I lock myself inside and splash some water on my cheeks, avoiding my eyes so my mascara doesn't run. After I'm finished, I take a cleansing breath and open the door.

A figure looming in the hallway startles me, and I yelp.

"Xander?" *What's he doing here?*

Arms crossed, he gives me a once-over, and that familiar lopsided grin forms on his lips.

"How do you like it?" He lifts his chin, gesturing to the bathroom behind me, his eyes sparkling playfully.

"It's beautiful. The same neutral colors as the rest of the house."

"What do you think about Jess? I saw you talking to her."

"She's nice."

He only nods in response, not taking his eyes off me.

Shoulders pulled back, I step closer. "Can you please move? I want to go back to the terrace."

"No."

I huff, annoyance spilling in my veins. Twenty minutes ago, he acted like he barely knew me; now he won't let me walk away? I press my hands to his chest, making him keep his distance. "Back off. I'm not in the mood."

He cocks an eyebrow as an amused smirk lifts his lips. "Why should I?"

"Your reaction to my presence spoke volumes."

"Forgive me, Bella, but your reaction to my reaction also speaks volumes." He looms closer and leans against the doorframe. "My sister set us both up—she loves to meddle. I didn't know she invited you, and I'm thinking you thought I did. Am I right?"

"Maybe," I scoff.

"Where's Miller?"

"Probably at home."

"Probably?"

"I don't know *where* he is because we broke up."

"What?" His eyebrows pinch together, and his lips part. "At practice yesterday, he told Garcia you were waiting for him at home."

Lips twisted into a scowl, I cross my arms. "He asked if we could keep the breakup a secret for now, and I agreed."

Xander inches even closer and says, "I have way too many questions. Looks like you're coming home with me tonight."

"Says who?" I snort, surprised by the confidence in his voice.

"Your friend," he murmurs, leaning in so close I can feel his breath on my skin. "Your lover."

Without my permission, my core throbs. Xander's proximity is my worst enemy.

He has done nothing wrong; still, I can't get caught in his snare again. "Go to hell, Xander."

"I'll go wherever you want, but only if you keep me company." His lips find mine the moment he stops talking. It's just a peck, but my knees go weak immediately. Why do I always react to him this way?

Taking a step back, he holds his hand out. Rather than take it, I walk past him. Behind me, he chuckles, and the next thing I know, he has his arm casually draped over my shoulder.

"You won't get rid of me that easily," he whispers in my ear, freeing the butterflies in my stomach.

Though I do my best to keep my feelings in check, my heart wants to explode with happiness. His affection means way more than his words about not wanting a relationship.

We stop at the door that leads to the terrace.

"When did you break up with Miller?"

"At his house after the game. It went about as well as I could have hoped." It's not exactly the truth, but he doesn't need to know that, especially not now. It's Audrey's party, and I don't think she would appreciate me ruining his good mood.

Xander watches me, poking his tongue into his cheek. "He didn't try anything with you—"

"Ben's presence helped." That part, at least, is the truth. The bruise on my neck isn't that big, covered by a thick layer of concealer. I'll show it to him later, when it's just us.

Untangling myself from him, I say, "Let's go, or there won't be any food left."

"We're going to my place," Xander says as we leave his parents' house around midnight.

"Why?"

"We need to talk." He stops and extends his hand, his handsome smile taunting me, so easily knocking down all my walls. "Please, Bella."

With a sigh, I take it, and he entwines our fingers like it's the most natural thing in the world. He pulls me into his side and guides me to his car, where he insists on opening my door for me. Once he's sure I'm safely strapped in, he traces the skin on my wrists. A dashing smile lights up his features. I'm not sure I'm making the right decision, but the two glasses of wine have dulled my nerves a bit.

Keeping his eyes on the road, Xander says, "Did you have a good time?"

"I did. What about you?"

"My day significantly improved when I saw you...alone."

I focus on the scenery outside. "I told you I was going to break up with Jake. Don't know why you're so surprised."

"I'm not surprised. I'm just proud of you."

I turn in my seat to peer at him. "Will you finally tell me what happened in college?"

His jaw clenches, and his smile drops. "I will." His tone is sharp, his posture instantly rigid.

But he doesn't speak, so I take my phone out of my purse and text Ben to let him know I'm not coming home tonight.

BEN:

I'll never understand your love for terrible decisions. Tell Alexander I said hi

I roll my eyes and slip my phone back into my purse. Ben is always going to be Ben. He only wants what's best for me, but sometimes he forgets that what he thinks is best isn't always right.

My eyelids are heavy by the time we step into Xander's house, but I'm determined to power through. He wants to talk, and I'm tired of being in the dark. I want to know the truth so I can understand his rivalry with Jake, because it has become clear to me that it's no longer a friendship.

I'm not sure it ever was.

When Milo rushes me, I feel lighter. I kneel, petting him and soaking in his warmth. "Did you miss me? Because I missed you, buddy."

In response, he whines and rolls over, showing me his belly.

"He did," Xander says, crouching next to me. "He likes you."

"I like him too," I whisper.

Xander leaves us to check Milo's food and water, and I take my shoes off and settle in the living room. The couch in here feels like a safe place for me. It's where I finally opened up and talked freely about my past. All the hurt is still with me, and I think it will be there for a lifetime, but Xander's willingness to believe me made a huge difference. It set me free.

The curtains are drawn and the room is dark, but when Xander returns, he turns on the light and sits beside me. He's still in his white shirt and dark blue jeans, his sandalwood and cinnamon scent drawing me in, enveloping me in comfort.

"Did you make up the guest room for me?"

"You're staying with me," he replies, unbothered. "In my bed."

My stomach dips, but I keep my expression neutral. "Bold of you to assume."

He slides off the cushion and kneels between my legs, his eyes burning into my soul.

I fidget, anxious for his next move.

"I said we need to talk...and we will." He rests his hands on my legs, his fingertips disappearing beneath the hem of my skirt. "For now, I want to devour your delicious cunt. I missed the taste of you. These few days without you have made me fucking feral."

He inches his hands higher and tugs at my panties. I arch my back so he can slip them off and spread my legs. It's not what we should be doing, but resisting him has never been easy.

Holding my gaze, he brushes his index finger over my clit. That alone is enough to make me break into a full-body shiver. He slips it down to my slick core, watching me the entire time.

"I love how you react to my touch, to my voice. It's so raw and real." Head lowered, he kisses the inside of my right thigh.

When he moves to the apex of my thighs, I hold my breath in anticipation. To start, he tongues my clit, lapping and curling around it in slow circles. My eyes roll back in my head, and I grip the edge of the couch, already wild with need.

"Such a sweet little cunt," he coos, blowing hot breath on my sensitive skin.

When he plunges two fingers into me, I grip his hair with both hands, keeping him in place. His tongue, his lips, and his fingers work relentlessly, driving me to my orgasm.

God, I want to come. I want to kiss him and taste myself on his tongue. I want him inside me...and I just want him for good.

My insides spasm around his fingers, and my eyes snap open.

I love him, and it's stronger than anything I've ever experienced before.

"You taste so good. I could eat you for breakfast, lunch, and dinner and never get tired of it. Never." He pulls himself up, one hand on the couch to brace himself, and hovers close, his lips an inch away from mine.

I put my hand on the back of his neck and kiss him without holding back, as if this is my last moment with him. For all I know, it could be. Jake and I aren't together anymore, but that doesn't mean Xander and I are free to date. A relationship between the two of us could put his career at risk.

Not to mention his aversion to commitment. Regardless of how attracted he is to me, I don't know if he'd break all his rules for me. I don't know if he'd deem me important enough.

We aren't meant to be. The realization hits hard, making me lose all my restraint, urging me to enjoy my time with him while I can.

Soon enough, our clothes are scattered all over the floor. We touch every inch of one another, barely coming up for air.

When I stroke him, he trembles. His breathing becomes erratic, and he drops his head to my shoulder. His release is approaching, but I don't want him to come yet.

So, I push him back and make him sit on the couch. He looks disoriented, as if he's drunk on us.

Roles reversed—now I'm the one on my knees before him—I curl my tongue around the head of his cock and run my hand up and down his length.

Xander brushes my hair off my face, his gentle fingers caressing my skin. "God, you're gorgeous," he breathes. "And my fucking dick in your mouth is a sight I'll never forget."

He lifts his hips, driving his cock into my mouth. His moans and grunts mix into each other, and beads of sweat run down his chest. Thank God he turned on the lights; watching him while I give him pleasure brings me close to my own orgasm again. He's the most handsome man I've ever met, and he's totally at my mercy.

"You on your knees for me, my cock down your throat... I want to memorize every detail so I can revisit this memory whenever I want," he tells me. "Your mouth feels so good, baby. I'm gonna come so hard—"

Xander puts his hand on the top of my head, and a guttural groan slips from the back of his throat. His cock throbs as his cum fills my mouth, and I barely have time to swallow it before he yanks me up and kisses my lips.

With my legs straddling his hips, we fuse our mouths together. When I'm out of breath, I lean away. Desire clouds Xander's gaze; the way he's looking at me sets my mind ablaze. He's devouring me mentally, examining every inch of me.

He grabs the back of my neck to bring my face to his, and a sharp pain radiates out from the base of my skull. Before I can stop it, a gasp escapes me. Xander rears back and releases my neck, frowning down at his hand.

"What is this?" he asks, holding up his concealer-covered fingers. "Did you cover something on your neck?"

I blink, trying to collect myself. *Fuck.* I'm sweating with exertion; the concealer must be melting off. Dread engulfs me as I steel myself to open up. This is not how I wanted him to find out about the farewell gift from Jake on my neck.

"It's a bruise," I admit.

"What?" Xander puts a finger under my chin and forces me to look at him. "Show me."

I know better than to argue with him, so I push my hair aside. He leans forward, examining it so closely his breaths feather the hairs at my nape.

"Did Miller do that to you?" His voice drops an octave lower.

"Yeah."

He goes rigid beneath me. "But you said he didn't try anything—"

"I didn't want to upset you at Audrey's party. I planned to bring it up when we were alone. But like I said, Ben's presence helped."

I can only hope Xander keeps his cool. I don't want him to wreak havoc on Jake. The past needs to stay in the past, and I can't let him endanger his future, his career.

"He wasn't happy when I walked away from him. He grabbed the back of my neck to stop me. Ben stood up for me. I have no idea what would've happened if he hadn't been there."

Xander frames my face with his hands, anguish written in every line of his face. "What else did he do?"

"Nothing, I swear. Ben helped me pack my things, I talked to Jake, and we left."

He eases me off his lap and paces across the room, totally naked.

I stand too. I turn off the light and wrap my arms around him from behind, halting him in his tracks.

"I know it's not okay, and I swear I wasn't going to hide it from you. I was waiting for the right moment."

Xander carefully turns around and presses me to his chest, holding me tenderly. We stand like that, his fingers threading through my hair as his heartbeat slows. "I hate Miller for everything he did to you. I want to hit him until he fucking bleeds."

"It's over now. I don't want you to risk your spot on the team for this. He's not worth it," I tell him. "Just be there for me, okay? It's enough."

"Always." His gaze falls to my mouth, and he pounces.

Feral, he devours me, all lips and tongue and teeth. When he breaks the connection, he turns me and pushes me gently toward the couch. He guides my elbows to the back cushions and presses down on my spine, encouraging me to arch my back to give him the best view of my wet pussy. There's a rustle of clothing, the tearing of a foil packet. Then, he's behind me, his sheathed cock pressed to my entrance.

"How do you want me to fuck you?"

"Hard," I whisper.

"Want to be my fuck toy tonight?"

"Yes." I rotate my hips, desperate to feel him deep inside me.

He trails his palm over my ass and then digs his fingers into my flesh. "So impatient... Don't you worry, baby. I'll do anything for my little slut." With that, he drives his full length inside my pussy in one stroke.

"Oh, God, yes!" I moan, shutting my eyes.

Xander fists my hair, pulling my head back. A light prickle at my roots travels all the way down to my lower abdomen, making my clit pulse with anticipation. His other hand is planted on my ass, his fingers kneading my skin. He fucks me slow and steady at first, and I don't mind it one bit. I'm still a little high from my previous orgasm, and I don't want to come too fast.

"You're soaked," he growls. "Fuck, your cunt feels incredible."

"Harder," I tell him.

He puts his leg on the couch and tugs my head back, and I see stars. His dick is so deep, hitting that little spot inside me with a precise roughness. My moans, the slap of skin on skin, the sloppy sounds of my pussy, and his groans are all I hear.

"Harder," I chant, and Xander happily obeys.

"Touch yourself, Bella," he orders, out of breath.

I sneak my hand between my legs and rub the sensitive bundle of nerves there. My eyes roll to the back of my head, and my lips part. Then, I come so hard my whole consciousness becomes fuzzy. It's like I'm not in this room anymore.

"Yes, yes, yes..." I cry out, my insides spasming. "Xander, I'm coming..."

He thrusts into me over and over, prolonging my orgasm until I'm ready to pass out. Then, with a guttural groan, Xander comes too.

He slips free of me before he helps me to stand. When he turns me around, we're both panting and covered in sweat. A devilish smirk prods his lips, and I smile back as he cups my face with his palms and presses his forehead to mine.

"I don't want this night to end yet," I confess.

"Me neither," Xander whispers. "Though my dick needs a little break."

I chuckle. "A little break won't hurt. I want to take a shower."

"Shower sounds great." He slides his hands down my waist and lifts me, making me wrap my legs around his hips. "How about I join you?"

"I'll never say no to that."

CHAPTER 36

Stacey

XANDER

November

Waking up with Bella may be the highlight of my life. Her body is pressed to mine, my hand possessively splayed over her hip bone, her skin warm and velvety to the touch. She's wearing my tee and her lacy red panties, and fuck, is it the sexiest thing I've ever seen. Her dark brown hair is spilled over my pillow, tickling me.

I don't want to leave her side...but I can't be late for morning practice.

I ease out of bed, making sure she's undisturbed. When I press my lips to her forehead, the corners of her mouth tremble, and a full-blown smile stretches across my face. How am I supposed to focus on the game against Washington when all I want to do is climb back in bed and spend the next few hours fucking her, tasting her, kissing her?

As much as I'd love to fuck with Miller, I'll have to wait. I can't stop myself from comparing this to a turnover. No one knows Miller lost Bella, but I've already intercepted, caught her in my arms, and I don't plan to ever let her go.

I can only hope that when I finally tell her about what happened in college, she won't push me away. Thinking about our upcoming talk makes me feel like there's a rock in my stomach.

Shaking my head, I force myself to focus on getting dressed. I've got the leash clipped to Milo's collar when an idea strikes me. I leave him waiting near the front door as I rush into the kitchen and write a little note to Bella, explaining where I'm going and asking her to wait for me. The inevitable truth looms over my head like the sword of Damocles, but I can't let my past rob me of my future.

I just hope she'll understand.

"PRACTICE WAS A LITTLE ROUGH TODAY, don't you think?" Carter asks me, tearing me out of my thoughts.

I force myself to smirk at him. "I didn't notice."

"You're too cocky. If you're not careful, it could be your Achilles' heel." He chuckles. "Though maybe you're just speaking your truth. You've been the star of our team since the moment you got here."

"I'm trying my best, man. Hoping we can push through the rest of the season and make it to the Super Bowl."

"I admire your determination." He wraps a towel around his waist and heads for the showers. "See you tomorrow."

Despite the grueling practice, as I walk to my car, my mood is good, my mind clear. Miraculously, Miller's presence didn't bug me one bit today.

Revenge is a dish best served cold, and I think I served mine frozen solid.

When I press the ignition button, the engine comes to life, and a Post Malone song blasts from the speakers. All the way home, I tell myself Bella is there waiting for me. She has to be.

Seeing Miller propose to her gutted me. So did walking away from her after Audrey caught us kissing. As much shit as I've been through, nothing compares to the pain I felt when I thought I'd lost Bella.

I'm in love with her. It hit me hard when Miller dropped to one knee in front of her, and I've been dazed ever since. I was worried I might have lost my chance with her. For years, I've told myself I don't do relationships, certain I didn't have the ability to fall in love.

But I did, and it's the most overwhelming feeling I've ever experienced.

I sit in my car for a moment, willing the anticipation stewing inside my chest to settle. I'm ready to cross my fingers, ready to pray to God that I'll have the chance to explain myself to her. She needs to know the truth about my college years, about Miller. I want to explain my behavior too...but that might change the way she feels about me. It might ruin my life and our potential future, but I have to be completely honest with her. I'm ready to risk it all for a chance.

I walk into the house, and when the sound of the TV registers, my heart fucking flips over itself.

She's still here.

Scared shitless but wanting to take the leap, I head straight for the living room. I'm tired of hiding the truth from her. She doesn't deserve it.

She's on the couch with Milo, her hair in a messy bun on top of her head, a few wild locks framing her face. When she sees me, she takes the remote from the coffee table and presses pause. My dog lifts his head and finally notices me, his tail wagging lazily.

Yeah, buddy, I'd prefer her company over mine too.

"Hey, you're back," Bella says as I trot to the couch.

"And you're here." I sit beside her, taken by her beauty. She's still in my tee, her bare legs pulled up beneath her. Milo's head rests on her lap, her fingers deep in his fur. She feels like home, full of comfort and hope.

I'm not my usual self when I'm with her, but I like this version of me better. It's who I was before all the shit that went down in college. Bella brings out the best in me.

"How was practice?"

"It was great. I have a good feeling about the game this weekend." I squint at the TV. "What are you watching?"

"It's *Howl's Moving Castle*, my all-time favorite anime. I've probably seen it fifty times. The books are great, but the movie? Unmatched."

"I'm intrigued." I settle beside her and lean back against the cushions. "Mind starting it again?"

"Sure, but...maybe we can talk first?" She shifts so she's fully facing me.

My pulse picks up, and a lump lodges itself in my throat. This is what I wanted, but I'm still nervous.

"Sure." I stand a little too quickly. "I'll go change my clothes and be back, okay?"

I don't wait for her to respond before I dart from the room.

It's time to tell her everything.

"So..." I sit on the opposite end of the couch and turn to get a better look at Bella.

She turned off the TV, and now she's cradling a steaming mug of coffee between her palms. Her blue eyes are like the sky on a clear summer day.

I rough a shaky hand down my face. "Did Jake try to convince you to stay?" That was not what I planned to say, but I go with it. "I saw him today, and it made me think..."

She snorts. "He knew we were done, but yeah, he did. He also admitted he cheated on me."

"God, he's stupider than I thought." I shake my head. "I would never cheat on you."

Bella sets her mug on the coffee table, averting her eyes. "'Never' is a very strong word."

Fuck, I didn't think I could hate Miller more than I already did.

"I never say words I don't mean."

"I know. Just..." She looks up, her expression full of apprehension. "Can you please tell me what happened, like you promised?"

With a nod, I trace my front teeth with my tongue. I take a minute to collect my thoughts; then, with a deep sigh, I lean back on the couch. "I'm sorry I didn't do this a long time ago, but I wanted you to make up your mind about Miller first. To decide for yourself that he wasn't right for you, not because I told you what he did."

She dips her chin in confirmation but doesn't speak.

"In high school, Jake and I played for rival teams. Then we ended up being college roommates. At first, it was great. We had similar interests. Football, obviously, and we both majored in finance. But after a while, our personalities clashed.

"My freshman year, I focused on football and my classes. That was it. I was set on being at the top of my game, and I was. I was the best quarterback the team had seen in years." I chuckle. "It sounds cocky, but it's the truth. Not gonna lie—it boosted my ego. Miller was impressive as fuck too, and Coach was always saying he hit the jackpot when he recruited the two of us. It was like that until Jake and I started causing problems—because of girls.

"During my freshman year, I hooked up with girls pretty regularly. I was a typical college jock, I guess. But things changed sophomore year. I started off focused on football again, even to the point where I sort of ignored my family. I was the big man on campus; I was unstoppable on the field and could get any girl I wanted. I had it all. Life was perfect—until Miller and I set our sights on the same girl."

I take a deep breath. I don't dare to look at Bella, choosing my clasped hands instead. It doesn't help. Her gaze is burning holes into my skin. My heart has climbed all the way up my throat, and I can feel my pulse in my fingertips.

"What happened next?" she asks in a quiet voice, giving me the push I need to continue.

"Neither one of us had slept with her, and it quickly became a competition. He and I razzed each other, fucked with each other. Once, we got into a fight. It was stupid, but that's when we really became rivals. Frenemies. We'd smile at each other while holding knives behind our backs, ready to strike any minute.

"Coach noticed. The team atmosphere became toxic, and being in my room was stressful. We were competitive, and neither of us wanted to be the one to back away, which added to an already enormous pile of problems. Miller was the one who suggested a solution: the first one to fuck her wins, and afterward we'd forget about the whole ordeal no matter what the results were.

"I won. It should've been the solution to our problem, a one-time thing. Instead, it started something way bigger and way darker. It became our routine: find a new girl and see who would score first. Sometimes it was me; other times it was Jake. On our more successful days, it was both of us. At the same time."

I've broken out in a cold sweat, but I make myself look up at her. She has her arms wrapped around her middle, her face drained of color. My head pounds, making my vision blurry.

But I have to get it all out, regardless of how badly I want to shut up.

I take a shallow breath, my chest caving as I divert my attention back to my hands. "It lasted for two years. We visited Europe, where we continued our sick games. I didn't think we were doing anything *too* bad, you know? It didn't occur to me that we were using these girls, that we were treating them as if they didn't deserve respect. I thought it was okay."

In my periphery, Bella visibly shrinks, catching my attention. Her expression is distraught, and a dark energy lurks behind her irises. I was a disgusting pig back then, and now she knows it.

Fuck.

I'd do anything to make her see me the way she did before, but it's not possible. If I want her in my future, I have to tell the truth, and so I open my mouth and continue.

"Things really took a turn during our senior year. On my way to class one day, I bumped into a girl...a very beautiful girl. Her name was Stacey. We'd had the occasional class together, but I'd never paid much attention to her. This time, though, I couldn't take my eyes off her. From that moment on, I couldn't stop thinking about her. So, I invited her out for coffee."

A ghost of a smile quirks my lips, but it disappears almost instantly as the vivid memories reappear in my mind.

"Stacey was smart and gentle. She had a kind heart and always wanted to see the good in people. What I felt for her was different than anything I'd ever experienced before. As I got to know her, the parties, the alcohol, the hookups—they didn't mean anything. When we officially started dating, I abandoned that altogether. I focused more on my grades, and Coach was thrilled with my performance on the field, as well as my attitude.

"Audrey met Stacey when she came home with me for winter break; my sister absolutely adored her. They became friends pretty quickly, and for the first time in my life, it didn't bother me that Audrey was meddling. I was happy.

"Jake, on the other hand, was not. He became my worst enemy. Sabotaging me. Bad-mouthing me. Giving me shit constantly. Calling me a pussy for changing my ways. I didn't care. I was done with him and our friendship, but he wasn't done with me."

Bella kneads her chest with the heel of her hand, watching me with a pained expression. Everything in me crumbles, the truth wrecking me all over again.

"Miller started flirting with Stacey, making suggestive comments and touching her inappropriately. I told him to stop, more than once. He never listened. He swore Stacey was no different from all the other girls we'd been with, and he promised to prove it to me. One day, I walked into our dorm room and caught them fucking on my damned bed—"

"Oh my God," Bella gasps, her hand flying to her mouth. Unshed tears glimmer in her eyes.

I lick my dry lips, locking my hands back in front of me. "I was pissed. Well, no—I was heartbroken. I went home. I needed to be with my family. Stacey called me, sent me text after text. I deleted them without reading. I didn't want to hear anything from her. I felt betrayed, and I promised I'd never let any girl make me feel like that again. I was bigger than that. I was Alexander Walker, a winner, not a loser. I got over it.

"What's crazy is that things between Miller and me chilled out after that. He said he did it to prove I couldn't trust her. I didn't believe him, not for a second, but for the sake of my future, I made my peace with it.

"Two months later, Stacey sent me one simple message. All it said was, 'Goodbye.' I couldn't tell you what made me go to her room. I hadn't spoken to her, and yet...I rushed over."

My throat closes before I can get the next words out. The image of blood on the tile, of her in the bathroom, haunts me to this day. The nightmares still make me sick to my stomach. They're just as vivid as they were back then. No amount of therapy, no amount of support from my family, has helped me forget what I saw. Because *I* ruined her life.

"She... Stacey tried to commit suicide. She slit her wrists. I did everything I could to keep her alive. Fuck, I was so scared. I rushed her to the hospital, and the doctors were able to save her. She recovered physically, but I don't think she ever did mentally.

"Her mother thanked me for saving her, and she begged me to talk to her daughter, to listen to what she had to say. I did, for her and for me...I needed closure. That's how I found out that Miller had drugged her. He made her believe she was with me. Miller broke her because he couldn't handle the idea that there was someone in my life more important than him. It was a betrayal in his mind, and he wanted to make me pay. So, he used Stacey. He ruined our relationship like it was nothing.

"I broke his nose the day I talked to Stacey for the last time. He apologized, over and over, but it wasn't enough. It's never been enough. I wanted to make him pay for what he did."

CHAPTER 37
Hook, Line, and Sinker

XANDER

November

"WHAT DO YOU MEAN?" BELLA ASKS.

Milo jumps off the couch and trots to the kitchen, as if sensing the change in the atmosphere.

"When the truth was revealed, I cut him out of my life. I didn't want anything to do with him. If he'd seduced her and she'd given in, that would have been one thing, but drugging her? I couldn't forgive that."

"Jake tells the story differently. He said he was the one who dated her, and you were the villain who wanted to snatch her away." She hugs herself again, running her hands up and down her arms, trying to warm herself up.

I want to move closer and comfort her, but I keep my distance. I'm not sure she wants me to touch her.

"I didn't believe him. Something about his story was off." She tilts her head to the side. "Why are you still talking to him?"

"I couldn't avoid him, even if I wanted to. It was the last semester of our senior year, and we were still roommates. He and I slowly started talking again. It wasn't the same, and I knew it, but I tried to be civil. Miller thought I'd already moved on, that I'd forgotten everything...and I let him believe that." I peer at Bella. She looks miserable.

"Did you agree to play for the Warriors so you could get back at him?" She furrows her brow.

"No. I love football. I'm good at it. Coming here was a step forward in my career. This is what I need to be at the top of my game. Plus, my parents live here. I made that decision with a clear mind." I wet my lips. "If anything, Jake was the reason I hesitated when I got the offer. I wasn't sure I could handle being his teammate again."

"Did you stay in touch with him after graduation?"

"We talked from time to time, had drinks when one of us was in the other's town. No more than that."

"And...what was your plan then?"

"Honestly?" I scrub a hand over my face. "I didn't have one at the welcome party. I convinced myself I could do it—I could be a professional and put my personal feelings aside, focus only on the team's success. But all night, he went on and on about our college days, and it hit me like a semitruck. All these years, he's lived guilt-free, as if nothing happened, as if he did nothing wrong. The comment I made about you eye-fucking me? It was shitty, I know, but I did it to test the waters. And, sure enough, it proved to me he hadn't changed at all. I looked at him, and all I saw was blood on the floor, and Stacey, skin ashen, body limp. After that, I was determined to show the world who he really is...and I wanted you to help me."

"Ben was right," she whispers, her features etched with devastation. "He told me I should be careful around you."

"Bella, no. It's not like that," I say, hands clenched though I'm desperate to touch her. "I wanted to expose him so the world would know what he did. I wanted your help, but that dinner at his place changed things. When I saw how he acted while you weren't around, and more so when you *were* around, I wanted nothing more than to convince you to leave him."

"Well, I left him. Congratulations." The tears in her eyes wreck me. With each one that falls, my heart cracks a little more. "How do you feel now?"

"When I got to know you and saw how he was treating you, my plan evolved. Miller was destroying you, and I couldn't let that happen. I couldn't let him do to you what he did to Stacey." I turn to face her, massaging my throat in hopes it'll make talking easier. "My motivation was no longer about revenge. I wanted you to leave him for *you*, for your own sanity, your own well-being. Miller doesn't deserve you."

"That's why you were flirting with me..." Her voice quavers with each word.

"No. Bella, no! I'm not Jake. I was flirting with you because I liked you. I wanted to get closer to you, to make sure you were okay. I wanted to earn your trust so I could eventually reveal his secrets and show you who he really is," I rasp, the words clogging my throat. My heart pounds against my sternum, and blood rushes to my head, making me dizzy. "The day you walked out of my house after I promised to be there for you whenever you needed me, I acknowledged a few things. It wasn't just an attraction anymore. It was deeper. It was so wrong of me, and yet...I wanted you so badly. I'd never wanted to kiss anyone more than I wanted to kiss you." I set my elbows on my knees and lean forward, holding her gaze. "I want you for you, for the person you are. It has nothing to do with Miller or what happened in college."

Bottom lip caught between her teeth, she scrutinizes me. I can't blame her for being apprehensive. After what I just revealed, she's probably second-guessing everything that happened between us, wondering how many lies I've told her.

In the end, the truth is simple.

My attempts to convince her I don't do relationships were ridiculous. From the moment we first kissed, I couldn't imagine being with anyone else.

"I haven't been with anyone since that morning at Miller's house." I clear my throat, my mouth dry and my voice hoarse. "Only you."

"Why?" She looks at me with such intensity, I swear she can see down deep, all the way to my soul.

I straighten, hoping like hell she can feel my sincerity. It's the only way I can make things right. "Because I fell for you, hook, line, and sinker."

Eyes widening, she lets out the tiniest gasp.

"The only lie I ever told you was the one I told myself as well. I said I don't do relationships, but I was a fool. I want to do relationships...but only with you. I'm in love with you, Bella."

As tears stream down her face, she gapes, bewildered. I sit still, watching her. I understand her reaction. All her life, she has been treated as if she's nothing. She has been told over and over again that she isn't enough. Her soul is so damaged, yet it's also beautiful. I see light in there. I see hope. I've never loved anyone the way I love her.

She is my perfect match.

"I love you. Only you," I confess again.

"I...I l-lov-ve y-you-u too," she sobs.

In one smooth motion, I move closer and haul her onto my lap. She wraps her arms around my shoulders, hiding her face in the crook of my neck.

I close my eyes and massage her back with my palm. "Shh, baby, shh. Don't cry," I whisper. "I'm here. I'll never let you go. Never. You're mine, Bella, and I don't need anyone else. Only you."

I have no idea how long we sit like this, tangled in each other. Bella's crying subsides, but even after she quiets, I don't let her move.

"Will you stay?" I ask. "Or do you want me to take you to your aunt's?"

Pulling back, she worries her lip. "I want to stay."

My heart sinks at the hesitation in her voice. "But?"

"What does all this mean? Who are we to each other?"

"I'm your friend," I say confidently.

She leans away. Her eyes are puffy and her face is tearstained, her brows pulled low.

"I'm your lover," I continue. "And your soon-to-be boyfriend."

She blinks and then bursts into giggles.

Relief washes over me like a wave. Finally, this is my girl. *My Bella*. I'm the happiest when I'm with her.

There will no doubt be days when she falls back into her old habits, but I'll be there for her. Our love will help us overcome anything, and I'll be a better version of myself. For her.

"Aren't you afraid of risking your place on the team? You're okay breaking the rules? Just for me?"

I press a thumb between her brows, smoothing out the crease there. "I'll break all the rules for you, Bella. There's nothing I won't do for you. You're single; I'm single. There's no misconduct there," I tell her with conviction. "I don't fucking care if anyone has a problem with it, including Miller. He, on the other hand, is in a precarious position. You hold all the cards there. You could go public with what he's done to you."

She shakes her head. "No. If he keeps his distance, I'll keep it to myself. All I want is to move on and forget it." She looks away for a moment, her teeth sinking into her bottom lip again. "It's just...if he knows—"

"He's a douche," I grit out. "Are you trying to tell me that we're in love with each other, but we can't be together because of Miller?"

"No. That's not what I'm saying." She frames my face with her hands.

Instantly, my body sags with relief. She knows all my buttons, where to press so I'm totally at her mercy.

"Just...I don't want to go public for now. I told Jake I'd wait a month before announcing the breakup—"

My heart lurches, and I rear back. "You gave him a month?"

"Yeah, he said he'd look like a loser getting dumped immediately after proposing, so I gave him one month. If you and I go public too soon, he'll be painted as the victim, and you'll be the villain who snatched your teammate's girl away from him. No one will care to listen to what really happened."

"But I want you to move in with me," I blurt out.

Bella's lips ease into a big, radiant smile. "Really?"

"Really."

"We can make it work, but we'll need to be extra careful. You have a Super Bowl to win. People look up to you. The last thing I want is bad press."

"Miller will find out eventually." Fuck, I hate the idea of hiding, and I'm not sure it'll be as easy as she thinks.

"And he will be furious about it," she says, tipping her head. "It's better if he finds out later; hopefully, he'll have already moved on."

I scoff. "I don't fucking care how any of this affects him. I'm not going to sacrifice my happiness or yours because his ass can't keep his shit together."

Bella snickers, ruffling my hair.

"All I care about is you." I hug her tight. "And my only concern is making you happy."

Bella smiles brightly before she lowers her gaze to my lips. That one little look is all it takes for my heartbeat to quicken and my dick to wake up.

"I know a few things you can help me with," she murmurs.

I lower my hands to her ass and squeeze. "Anything."

"I can't tell you here. We have an eavesdropper."

In unison, we look down at Milo, who's sitting at my feet, watching us with great interest, and fall into a fit of laughter.

"Can we go to your bedroom?" Bella chokes out between giggles.

I haul myself up without letting her go and bury my face in her hair. Her fruity scent is like an aphrodisiac, making me hard in an instant. I'm drunk on love. This girl is my everything.

I glance over my shoulder at Milo and smile apologetically. "Sorry, buddy. I think we're gonna be busy for a while."

With a sigh, he lies down and rests his snout on his paws.

The world outside this house doesn't exist. Our little bubble is full of love, heat, and pure passion.

With any luck, Bella's here to stay.

CHAPTER 38

Seductive Destruction

XANDER

November

"What do you need my help with?" I shove my hands into the pockets of my sweatpants, my dick already rock-hard.

Bella walks past me to my walk-in closet, a hint of a smile dancing across her lips. She's up to something, and I'm impatiently waiting to find out what it is.

When she returns, her hands are behind her back, her expression pure mischief.

"What do you need my help with?" I ask again.

"What do you think about ties?" She holds up a familiar strip of black silk.

Damn. Is it just me, or is it suddenly too hot in here?

I take the tie, making sure my fingers brush hers. "To tie you up so you're at my mercy?"

"Yes." She steps closer, and when her mouth meets mine, a fire ignites within me. She moves to my jaw, using her tongue to trace a line down to the hollow of my neck. I shudder, goosebumps spreading over my skin.

Her touch disappears abruptly, and when I open my eyes she's watching me, her irises a deep, dark blue, all-consuming and full of sexual energy.

I pull her against my chest, and when her breath hitches I can't help but grin. We're in this together, enjoying the moment. There's no need to rush things. We have our whole lives ahead of us. Today, I want to explore her body, to test her limits and discover new things about her.

I pull the T-shirt—my shirt—over her head and drop it to the floor, leaving her standing before me in nothing but a bra and a pair of panties, her chest rising and falling erratically.

As I touch her, I soak in her warmth, relishing the way she trembles with desire. I grip her hips tighter and walk her back to my bed. To *our* bed.

God, that simple phrase turns me on even more.

She shimmies her panties down and unclasps her bra, tossing it to the floor. As she eases herself back onto the mattress, her hard nipples catch my attention. I desperately want them in my mouth. I take her wrists and carefully tie them together with my tie, stretching her hands above her head.

"Does that hurt?" I murmur in her ear.

She shakes her head and smiles, reassuring me she feels safe.

As I strip off my tee, I keep my focus fixed on her. I watch the way she drinks me in, lingering on the tattoos on my chest, then on my abs and the V that disappears beneath my waistband. I shuck off my sweatpants and kneel beside the bed, between her thighs.

Her pussy is already soaking wet, and I haven't even done anything yet.

Time to change that.

I trace her slick folds, teasing her opening. Bella gasps, and when I slide two fingers inside her, the sound morphs into a moan. I pump my digits into her slowly, deliberately avoiding her clit.

I want her to beg.

I quicken my pace, each movement rougher than the last, faster.

Bella moves her hips up and down, as if she wants me deeper. "Xander, please," she pleads.

"Please what?" I whisper against her sex, close enough that my lips barely brush her folds.

"Please touch me."

I give in more easily than I intended, but fuck, I can't deny her. I flick my tongue over her soft spot, and she arches her back. I suck and lap, fingers thrusting into her.

"You taste so good." I blow on her clit, and when she writhes beneath me, I know she's close. She pulls against the tie, as if trying to free her hands, rocking her hips against my mouth and making little groans of pleasure. I suck harder, curling my fingers, finding her sweet hidden spot with ease. Bella's whole body stiffens, and she arches her back, screaming my name as she comes. I don't stop, prolonging her orgasm and enjoying the taste of her.

She tastes like mine.

My cock is painfully hard. I want to be inside her so badly—Bella's warm pussy is where I belong. I hover over her, bracing myself with an arm on either side as I take in her beautiful face.

Six months ago, if someone had told me I'd end up falling in love with Miller's girl, I would've laughed in their face. But the second I laid eyes on her, I knew I was screwed.

Then, when I saw how she looked at me, I knew she could be my forever.

Beneath me, her pupils are blown, her breathing erratic. With my lips against hers, I devour her, nibbling on her bottom lip and sucking it into my mouth. Again, and again. When my tongue tangles with hers, electricity sparks through me.

I shift so I can touch her. I need to touch her. With her nipple caught between my thumb and forefinger, I pinch.

She moans against my lips. A little bit of pain mixed with pleasure is exactly what gets her off.

Slowly, I lean away and wet my lips. "Can I fuck you bare tonight? I've never done it with anyone, but it's all I want with you," I confess hoarsely. "I get tested regularly."

Breath hitching, she nods. "I'm on the pill."

I smash my lips to hers and push my entire length into her in one thrust, a groan ripping from my throat. I sink my hands under her butt, lifting her hips so I can pump deeper.

"God, you're perfect." I dip my head down, leaning closer to her. I ravage her neck, licking the delicate column of her throat and sinking my teeth into her flesh, leaving marks on her skin.

Bella pulls on the tie again, wrapping her legs around my hips. "Harder," she moans. "Please, make me come. Make me come so hard."

Dangerously close to losing it, I bite her bottom lip and then let it go, coming deep inside her in hot bursts. I growl as absolute ecstasy overwhelms me. Her orgasm hits her a second later, and her pussy tightens around me. We're somewhere in the middle of our own universe, oblivious to any sounds but our breathing and the beating of our hearts.

When her spasms ebb, I pull out and drink her in. She lies on the covers, breathing hard. I nestle between her legs again, focusing on her cunt. My cum leaks from her opening. It's the hottest thing I've ever seen.

I dive in and lap at her until there isn't a drop of either of us left, my cum mixing with her juices.

Bella gasps and rolls her hips. "I want to taste us... Let me taste us."

Hovering over her, I lower my head, and when she parts her lips, I spit the mess we made into her mouth.

"Now swallow, baby," I tell her, tugging on her nipple. "Show me what a good little slut you are."

With a smile, she does as I tell her.

Watching her like this, my heart grows two sizes. I press my forehead to hers and inhale deeply. This thing between us is beyond my understanding, making me doubt everything I thought I knew about myself.

"I love you."

"I love you too," she says softly.

Cock already hard again, I release her hands, and Bella instantly pulls me to her for another mind-blowing kiss. She's insatiable. I break our connection and flip her onto her belly, slapping her butt before I lower my head to her ear, my tongue tracing her earlobe.

"Do you want me to be rough or gentle this time?" I sneak my hand under her belly and help lift her ass up.

"Rough, please." Her shaky voice makes me smile. Slowly, I slide into her from behind. Her hot, wet pussy clenches around my shaft so hard my body trembles. "I want you to use me... Make me your filthy slut..."

Gripping her ass tight, I slam my hips against hers over and over. I close my eyes, spurred on by the sweet sounds she makes.

"Don't stop," she begs, her voice low as she hides her face in my pillow.

"Anything for my beautiful slut."

"Yes, please," Bella breathes.

I spank her and watch her skin redden. It's a very thin line—to be rough with her like she wants but not hurt her. I increase my tempo, ramming into her pussy and slapping her over and over, using her little whimpers as cues.

Suddenly, she trembles and cries out, "Oh, God!" and I'm hit with a gush of warm liquid.

Fuck. It takes all my self-control not to come on the spot. I pull out and roughly flip her so she's on her back.

Her eyes are wide, her chest rising and falling violently.

I grin at her. "Is that the first time you've ever squirted?"

"Yeah. I had no idea I could do that." She bites her bottom lip, and pink creeps into her cheeks. "I'm sorry for ruining the sheets."

I put my finger under her chin and make her look at me. "I don't care about the sheets. You are the only thing that matters to me." With that, I flip her again. "Ass in the air, baby."

She grips the headboard this time, and I put my hand on the small of her back, urging her to arch deeper.

I find my rhythm again quickly, hunched over her so I can rub her clit between my fingers. When her insides start spasming around my dick again, she buries her face in my pillow, muffling her sounds.

Immediately, I slow and lightly slap her cunt. "I want to hear you come on my cock."

She glances over her shoulder and nods.

"Good girl." Keeping a steady pace, I massage her clit, my fingers moving frantically.

When she comes, screaming my name, I grip her hips with both hands. My fingers dig into her skin as I let the wave of heat rush over me, my cum spilling inside her. It's so intense, it clouds my mind.

When I've been emptied out, I roll onto my back beside her, pushing away the hair that sticks to her sweaty forehead.

"You were incredible," I whisper, caressing her face.

I can degrade her all she wants in the bedroom, but deep down I know she has power over me like no one's ever had before. She is the queen of my heart, my body, my mind. Her reign began the second she kissed me, and I've worshiped the ground she walks on ever since.

When I'm with her, I have everything I need.

WE CLIMB INTO BED—WITH a clean set of sheets—a few hours later, and I cuddle her to my chest, hiding my nose in her hair. Her scent is all over me, mingling with mine, full of spice and sex and promises.

"Bella?"

"Yeah?" She presses her body closer to mine.

"How long have you been on the pill?" I ask quietly.

"Since my first time with...erm...since my first time."

She was going to say Miller's name. *Fuck*. I shut my eyes. I need to remember that they have a history together, that they shared some pivotal moments of their lives.

"Did you love him?"

"Xander." She shifts and peers up at me, resting a hand on my cheek. "Jake was my first love, but you're the one I want. I'm in love with you...and my feelings for you are so much stronger and deeper than anything I ever felt for him."

"I've never loved anyone more than I love you, so I know the feeling."

Eyes softening, she presses her lips to mine for a slow kiss. When she pulls back, I drag her over my body until she's straddling my legs. "I've been thinking...I'd like to introduce you to my parents."

Her whole body goes tense. "Wh-what?"

"When you're ready, I want to take you to meet my parents. They're great, I promise." I put my hands on her sides and slowly lower them to her hips. "What do you say? Wanna meet my folks?"

"I'd love to. Just give me some time." She inhales deeply, worrying her lip. "Maybe a few weeks."

"Whenever you're comfortable. There's no pressure."

We stay tangled in each other for a long time, our soft caresses turning needier with each passing minute. With her hands roaming over my chest, tracing the ink on my skin, she murmurs, "Mind if I tie you up?"

Pulse stumbling, I snag the tie from the nightstand and hold it up. In seconds, she's straddling me again, leaning over me, tying my hands together. I catch her nipple in my mouth, my teeth grazing it.

She grips the headboard as she ties my hands to it. "Now it's time for you to play by *my* rules, Mr. Quarterback."

Goddamn. This girl is fire, a tornado, a seductive destruction. She's everything.

CHAPTER 39

It's His

BELLA

November

THE WHOLE WAY TO HIS PARENTS' HOUSE, I PLAY IT COOL. I happily listen to him tell me about how he almost face-planted in the driveway when Milo pulled on the leash while he was texting with Drew. I make sure to smile when he mentions the *Lord of the Rings* marathon he's planning. It's one of his favorite franchises, and apparently he watches all six movies at least once a year. He has yet to do it this year, and since it's almost December, it only feels fair that we binge them next week.

He never says no when I ask for anything, and I'm trying to emulate that. This relationship deserves all the time and effort I can give it. I am his first serious relationship, and even though he isn't mine, he's the first man to treat me with respect and care. Obviously, not all days are perfect; we learn by trial and error, but what I feel for him makes it all worth it.

"How do you feel?" he asks as he rounds the car and meets me at the passenger door.

I shrug. "I'm good."

"So you're not nervous?" He drapes an arm over my shoulder.

I chuckle, cuddling closer. His hoodie smells like him—woodsy, with notes of tobacco. I love it.

"A little bit."

"You have nothing to worry about. My parents already love you," he says. "Besides, Audrey and Ryan are here too. Familiar faces should ease your fears, right?"

Everything in me stills.

Audrey's presence does the opposite of ease my fears—it puts me on edge, but I don't mention that to Xander. His sister means so much to him, but the woman doesn't like me one bit, despite how often he tells me otherwise.

I hum noncommittally. "Are they still looking for a house?"

"Yeah. Audrey is next-level picky. She wants something big and spacious but also cozy and comfortable. She vetoed the last one because it didn't have a pool."

"I thought she was dead set on a hot tub, not a pool."

"Exactly." He kisses my nose. "I'm not sure she knows what she wants. Other than the location, since she's looking for a house in our neighborhood."

His words send a shiver down my spine. The idea of having her so close makes my stomach roil.

As if he can sense my unease, he holds me closer. "Everything's going to be fine, I promise. You're safe with me."

I want to believe it, but a little voice in the back of my head questions his words. I force myself to smile. "I know."

The house is gorgeous. It's white with a black roof. Its modern details work surprisingly well with the classic New England vibe. The lawn is manicured, and the cobblestone driveway looks recently redone. The solid wood door is decorated with an adorable Warrior-themed wreath, the pine needles adorned with a red and white bow and dotted with little footballs.

"Is this their tribute to you?"

"Yeah, Mom made it herself," he answers as he knocks on the door. "She said she made one for us too."

"Oh, that's so cu—"

The door opens, and I find myself face-to-face with Audrey, who's smiling from ear to ear in light blue jeans and a beige cashmere pullover.

"Look who's finally here," she announces, her eyes on her brother.

"We're right on time." Xander pulls me into the house, then releases me to kiss his sister on the cheek. "It's good to see you home again."

"Better get used to it. March will be here sooner than you think." She turns to me then, and the corners of her mouth drop a little, but she forces another smile almost immediately. "It's nice to see you, Isabella."

"You too."

Instinctively, I move to Xander, and he laces his fingers with mine.

"Where is everyone?" he asks.

"Dad and Ryan are in the living room, Mom's in the kitchen."

The living room is light and inviting just like I remember it, with a big gray couch and large windows that flood the space with natural light in the morning. The fireplace is surrounded by built-in shelves with rows and rows of books and framed pictures. The TV is on, the volume turned up loud as Ryan and Xander's dad watch hockey.

As we step farther into the room, Xander's dad jumps to his feet, a radiant smile on his lips.

"Alex, Isabella!" He hugs his son, then holds out his hand to me. "I'm Greg."

I slip my palm into his and I'm instantly struck by how much he looks like Xander. Dark hair. Blue eyes. Sharp jaw and straight nose.

"We're so happy you're here."

"Thank you so much for inviting me." I smile.

His gaze is warm, and the smile lines bracketing his mouth deepen as he grins. "Alex has talked our ears off about you. Glad we're finally meeting."

"Oh, I've heard so much about you too."

"I hope only good things?" A petite blonde shuffles into the room, her blue eyes sparkling and her smile bright. Her bottom lip is a bit fuller than her upper lip, and it's pouty, just like her son's.

"Definitely," Xander comments. "I don't have a mean bone in my body."

His mom snorts and fixes her warm gaze on me. "We are so happy you agreed to come. We've been waiting for Alex to introduce us since the second we saw his bathroom. You did such a wonderful job, dear! I love it!"

My heart warms at the simple compliment. It's so genuine, so kind.

Xander hauls me to him. "Looks like Mom forgot her manners," he teases. "Bella, this is my mom, Pauline."

"Oh my God!" She smacks her forehead and laughs. "I was so excited to finally meet you, I forgot to introduce myself." She closes the distance between us and wraps me in a hug. "Thank you so much for coming, Bella."

"I'm so happy to be here," I say as she steps back.

"Well," she says, hands clasped over her chest, "let's go. Dinner is ready."

After Pauline's delicious dinner, I put the dishes into the sink as she instructed, finding it hard not to smile. I'm content here, in this house. Almost as content as I am at my aunt's.

This house is a home, full of warmth and comfort, love and happiness. It seems silly now, how worried I was about meeting them. They welcomed me, and they treat me with respect and kindness simply because Xander loves me.

"Did you have a good time?"

Startled, I turn and find Audrey in the doorway. "Yeah. Your parents are amazing."

"They are," she says with a nod.

Silence follows her words. At a loss for how to fill it, I straighten the invisible wrinkles from my skirt and cross my legs at my ankles.

"I was wrong about you." She lifts her chin, assessing me. "You are nothing like your ex, and you...you love Alex. I believe you."

She believes me?

Relief washes over me. "Thank you."

"I still don't like the way you two got together. Sneaking around, hiding from everyone. It looks more like an affair than anything, and it makes Alex look bad." She folds her arms over her chest. "People love him. I just hope it stays that way once you two go public."

A lump forms in my throat. "I hope so too."

Audrey narrows her eyes then sighs. "As long as he's happy, I'm happy. It's nothing personal, Isabella. I just want to make sure my brother doesn't get hurt."

"I love Xander; hurting him is the last thing I want." I uncross my legs and head to the doorway. When I pass her, I pause and hold her gaze. "I'm not your enemy."

She nods and steps aside to let me through.

In the living room, Xander pulls me down next to him on the couch. The moment we're touching, the stiffness in my shoulders dissipates. Exhaling, I put my head on his shoulder and listen to him and his dad talk about the team's chance at the Super Bowl.

"Love you." His whisper caresses my skin as he kisses my temple.

"I love you too," I whisper back.

He is my constant, always on my mind. He has burrowed so deeply into my soul that as long as I have him, I'll be content. Xander is the sweetest poison, filling the world around me with vibrant, eye-catching colors and warmth.

He stole my heart...and I'll gladly let him keep it.

CHAPTER 40
The Cards Are on the Table

BELLA

December

"Time for a walk," I say, rushing inside. I only have a couple of hours before Ben's party. I've spent most of the day with Aunt Millie, helping her prepare for his surprise. Xander left for practice before I woke up. Practice, gym, strategizing—football is the only thing he thinks about these days.

I just hope he'll be home on time.

Milo walks over to me, yawning and lazily wagging his tail.

I smile at the sight. He has become my almost constant companion. When I work, he's always near me, putting his head on my lap or trying to catch my attention so I'll play with him. Thanks to him, I never feel lonely, even when Xander is out of town. He's my little savior.

Outside, I let Milo lead me down our usual route, anxious for tonight. Tom is planning something big—if I had to guess, he's going to propose to Ben.

When my phone buzzes, I assume it's Xander, calling to confirm he's picking up the cake I ordered. Instead, I find Meg's name flashing across the screen.

"I don't want to freak you out," she says when I answer, "but I think Jake knows about you and Xander."

A ball of lead sinks in my stomach, and a cold sweat breaks out across my skin.

"Izzy? Are you still there?" Meg asks.

"Y-yeah, s-sorry," I say, even as the world around me goes blurry. "Why do you think that?"

We've been careful. Xander jokes that he's a special agent on some super secretive mission with all the precautions we've taken. I never go to his games; we've never been photographed together. My car is always parked in his garage. I thought we had it all covered.

"I'm at Marco's place, and I overheard him talking to Jake. Miller said he should've guessed you were helping Xander with more than just his bathroom. I hope I'm worrying you for nothing, but Marco says Jake is acting weird."

"Fuck," I mutter, glancing at Milo. He's carefree, but I'm suddenly engulfed in panic. Taking a deep breath, I close my eyes and count to ten.

"Izzy," Meg pleads. "Are you alright?"

"Just considering how to handle things if he actually does know." I hesitate, my hand curling harder around the leash. "I need to call Xander."

"Sure. I'll call you later. Just know I'm here for you, okay?"

My chest pinches with affection and a little fear. "I know."

I'm navigating to Xander's contact info when a voice behind me makes me freeze.

"Didn't think I'd be so lucky."

Heart pounding, I turn around, finding myself face-to-face with Jake.

"Hey," I say, fear churning my insides.

He looks like a madman. There's a strange glint in his eyes and a menacing scowl on his lips. "What are you doing here?"

"What am *I* doing here? Really, Isabella?" he hisses, taking a step closer.

I stand my ground, refusing to show him how scared I am. My fear is his fuel, and I don't want to give him any power.

"A little bird told me Walker got himself a girlfriend...*my* girlfriend."

"We broke up," I remind him, casting my gaze down to Milo. He's sitting by my feet, staring intently at Jake, unusually quiet and unfriendly.

"Yeah, you left me to spread your legs for my teammate."

"I left because we—"

"Aren't right for each other. I heard that." Another step in my direction. "After everything we've been through, after all the things I did for you...you betrayed me with that fucking asshole!"

"That's not true." My own anger settles in the pit of my stomach, mixing with my fear.

"Stop lying." He clutches my wrist and pulls me to him. "How do you think I felt when I found out you were playing house with Walker? I refused to believe *my Isabella* would ever do that. I was sure it was just a misunderstanding. So, I came here." He narrows his eyes, his nostrils flaring, and squeezes my wrist tighter. "And what did I find? You walking his damn dog like a fucking whore."

I wince and try to pull my wrist from his grip, but it's no use. "Let me go. You're hurting me."

"Am I?" Brow arched and focus fixed on me, he adds more pressure, a sadistic smile blooming over his lips. "I just want to show you how I felt. The love of my life broke my heart—not once, but twice. You broke off our engagement and immediately jumped into bed with the guy who has been pretending to be my friend for years, who probably only did it to get back at me for fucking his nerdy girlfriend in college. That slut was happy to wet my dick, but he still put the blame on me."

Milo stands and barks. The piercing sound is enough to startle Jake into releasing me. I dart to the house, dragging Milo and his too-short legs with me. It only takes a second for Jake to catch up and yank my hair from behind. The leash falls from my hand, and I yelp as he drags me into his chest and wraps his other hand around my neck.

"Where do you think you're going?"

"Isabella, is everything alright?" Mr. Jensen's voice makes my heart beat faster. From time to time, I see him out with Pup, and we chat. He's a good man, and I've never been happier to see him.

Jake turns us around, faking a smile. "Hello," he says.

"Jake Miller?" Mr. Jensen furrows his brow in confusion.

"Yep, that's me." He bends down, finds Milo's leash, and straightens again. "Everything's alright. We were just on our way inside."

"I asked Isabella, not you," Mr. Jensen says, his voice cold. "Isabella?"

Jake squeezes the back of my neck hard enough to make my vision darken around the edges.

"I'm...f-fine." Despite my words, I widen my eyes, hoping he reads my silent plea and calls Xander.

"We gotta go. Goodbye." Jake forces the leash into my hand before dragging me to the house. On the porch, he leans in so his mouth is at my ear. "Open the damn door, Isabella."

With trembling hands, I work the knob, and he stomps inside with me in tow. He slams the door with enough force to make the house shake, then stuffs Milo into the coat closet.

Holy shit.

Keeping my emotions in check, I pull my shoulders back. "What do you want?"

"You." He shrugs, suddenly nonchalant.

What the hell? His change of attitude gives me a whiplash.

"That's not going to happen."

"Isabella, baby, did you already forget that I know you like the back of my hand?" He smirks. "One touch to your clit, and you'll be dripping wet for me, ready to fuck."

My stomach roils. "Is that what you said to Stacey?" I ask. "Xander told me everything. Absolutely everything."

His anger contorts his face, his eyebrows pulling together. "Did he mention we spent our college years competing to see who could fuck girls first? That we banged more than a few together?"

Chin lifted, I nod. His eyes flare for a second, but then he's smirking, his fists clenched at his sides. He leans into me, and I take a step back, only to bump into the wall.

He clutches my chin and forces me to look at him. "In that case, you know what—"

"What the fuck are you doing?" a familiar voice booms.

I practically jump out of my skin, and my heart takes off, but when I realize who the voice belongs to, relief washes over me, making my knees weak.

Xander.

"I'm claiming what's mine." Jake doesn't bother to look at him. He remains fixated on me, his pupils so wide, his usually grayish-blue eyes look black.

Xander grasps Jake's shoulders and turns him around right before his fist connects with Jake's jaw.

I jump away as Jake's back hits the wall.

Xander delivers another punch, and the sound of bones cracking is deafening. Blood drips down my ex's face as he slides to the floor. Just like that, all trace of the strong, powerful man who tried to exert control over me vanishes. He crumples like a paper bag, moaning as he brings a hand to his nose and tries to stop the bleeding.

"How dare you force yourself on her?" Xander bellows. "What's wrong with you?"

"Xander," I call out to him quietly.

As if he can't hear me, he yanks Jake off the floor and cocks his fist back, ready to punch him again. All the rage he's kept locked up erupts. If he doesn't stop, the consequences could be devastating.

"Xander, please!"

He looks at me over his shoulder.

"Please," I plead.

Reluctantly, he takes a step back, chest heaving.

"Isabella is the love of my life," Jake roars. "And you fucking took her from me. I was sure she'd give me another chance until Cindy told me she saw you two together at the store. I thought the slut was lying, but it's the fucking truth!"

"You thought you'd show your love for me by hurting me? By raping me?" My voice trembles, my body shuddering.

"I wasn't going to rape you." He takes a step toward me, but Xander blocks his path. "Let me talk to her!"

"No." Xander squares his shoulders.

"It's not for you to decide, Walker!"

I lock eyes with Jake over Xander's shoulder. He looks pathetic. Perhaps we should've sat him down and told him ourselves. Not because he deserves it. Not because I owe it to him. No, because Xander and I don't deserve to have to deal with him. We deserve to be free of him once and for all.

Slowly, I step forward and put a hand on Xander's forearm. He squints at me, his lips pursed into a thin line.

I give him a small smile.

"Bella..." he warns, shaking his head.

"It'll be okay." I slide my hand down his arm and lace our fingers.

Xander sighs, his gaze softening. "Fine, but he's talking to both of us."

"Of course," I say. "Let's go to the living room."

Jake's gaze darts to our entwined fingers. Anger flares in his eyes again, but he tempers it and nods. "Fine."

I let Milo out of the closet while Xander herds Jake to the living room. Then, Xander and I shuffle into the kitchen. I leave him there and go in search of the first aid kit in the primary bathroom. Xander plucks a few supplies from it and takes them to Jake. When he returns to me, I tend to his knuckles. They're bloody, but the sight of them causes warmth to spread through my veins. He defended me without a second thought, putting his career and reputation at risk simply because he loves me.

"We need to call the police." Xander's voice is just above a whisper.

I shake my head. "No. You've already risked enough for me. If he presses assault charges, it could ruin your career."

"Bella, if I hadn't gotten here when I did—"

"I know." I look up at him. His eyebrows are pulled together, a deep wrinkle crossing his forehead. "But think of all the ways the press can twist this. They could label Jake the victim, while you got involved with your teammate's girlfriend. They'll say you hurt your team's wide receiver and weakened the Warriors' chance at the Super Bowl. Fans wouldn't appreciate it, and neither would management. I don't want you to put your whole future at risk."

"Then what do you suggest we do? Let him get away with it? *Again*?!" Xander snaps, his hand trembling in mine as I blot at his knuckles with a cotton ball.

"We're going to tell him that if he tells anyone you hit him, I'll go to the press and make a statement about how he treated me when we were together."

"And I'll go to management and the rest of the team."

"That too." I smile, caressing his wrist.

Xander chews his bottom lip. "For the record, I don't like it, but okay. Let's do it your way."

"Thank you." I thread my fingers through his and pull him toward the living room.

Xander and I sit on the couch across from Jake, our hands locked together.

Through hard, slitted eyes, the man I once thought was my forever scrutinizes me. He claims he loves me, but he only wants to possess me, control me. I know the difference now.

"How long have you been together?" Jake asks.

"For about a month," I lie, holding his gaze. There's no way I'm telling him the truth—that Xander and I have basically been together since I told him I needed a break.

"You were single for a month after our breakup?" he deadpans.

"Yes."

"Was it... Did you..." Jake takes a deep breath and clears his throat. "Was there something between you two while we were together?"

I shrug. "No. We became friends while I worked on his bathroom, so when we reconnected after you and I broke up, I realized I was attracted to him, and I decided not to resist it."

Jake and I stare at each other for a long moment. His stormy eyes only accentuate how miserable he looks. Then he shifts his gaze to Xander.

"Is this because of your ex? Did you want to get back at me...for what happened in college?"

"No. I thought Bella was stunning the moment I saw her at the welcome party. My relationship with her has nothing to do with college, or you. It's about me and her. That's it." Xander leans forward, putting his elbows on his knees. "I desperately wanted to make you pay for what you did to Stacey. I wanted everyone to know the truth about you, but Bella changed my mind. She changed my whole life. Now, I couldn't care less about you. Though, I must admit, seeing you like this is...satisfying."

"I gave you everything you needed for payback. I shouldn't have come here." Jake hangs his head low. Deep down in my gut, I don't believe the act. He's manipulating us because he knows he's at a disadvantage. We cornered him, and he's playing his part. "When are you going to go public?"

Xander shrugs. "When Bella is ready."

Jake peers at me, his eyes coasting slowly over my face, as if he's memorizing my every feature. "I'm sorry, Isabella...for hurting you. I've always been territorial, and when I found out you chose Walker, my jealousy blinded me."

"I didn't choose Xander. I chose myself." I take a deep breath, the plan Xander and I discussed ready to spill from my lips. "I won't press charges this time, but only if you promise not to reveal that Xander broke your nose—"

"And swear to stay the fuck away from Bella. If you even look her way, I'll go to Coach, to management, to our teammates, to the press —to anyone ready to listen. I'll expose you. I'll make it my life's mission to ruin your career."

A dark ugliness flares behind Jake's eyes, but he quickly suppresses it and nods. "Okay." His gaze ping-pongs between Xander and me. "What happened today won't happen again. I swear."

"You better keep your promise, Miller." Xander straightens. "I would've done so much worse if not for Bella."

"I'll keep my mouth shut," Jake promises, rising to his feet.

Xander stands too. "I'll walk you out."

On his way to the foyer, Jake sneaks one last glance at me. It's full of sorrow and what might be remorse. "Bye, Isabella."

"Bye, Jake." I look him in the eye when I say it.

Once he's out of sight, the adrenaline drains from my body. Then, Milo is there, trembling and pawing at my leg. I pull him onto the couch, and he rests his head in my lap. "It's okay, Milo. Everything's fine. You were so brave, trying to defend me."

The couch beside me dips, and two muscular arms envelop me. I close my eyes and relax into him.

"I wanted to kill him when I opened the door and saw him all over you." Xander nuzzles my neck, inhaling deeply. "He looked like a damn psychopath."

"I know," I whisper. The image of Jake's bewildered look appears in my head. "What does it mean for the Warriors? His broken nose, I mean."

"It will be fine, even if he's out for a few games. We have Isaiah Gibson—he's got a ton of talent. We won't suffer." He hugs me tighter. "Did he hurt you?"

"He could hardly control himself," I say, knowing Xander won't like hearing it.

He crouches in front of me, assessing my face before working his way down my body. When he notices bruises on my forearms, he clenches his jaw.

"Mr. Jensen said he pulled your hair," Xander hisses through gritted teeth.

I bow my head and nod.

With a curse, he snakes his arms around my waist. The move dislodges Milo. Then, Xander is lifting me. "We still have a few hours before the party. What do you want to do? Will you let me take care of you?"

"Will you just hold me?"

Mouth tilting up at the corners, he cups my cheek and caresses my skin. "Whatever you want."

Angling closer, I brush my lips over his, erasing the memories of my encounter with Jake. I replace them with memories of my time with Xander, allowing his love to flow through me. With him, I can overcome anything.

With him, I feel loved.

CHAPTER 41

My Man

BELLA

December

I've just hung up with Meg as Xander parks his car near my aunt's house.

My best friend was enraged when I told her what happened with Jake, but she was ecstatic about the part where Xander came to my rescue. She shrieked when I finally gave her permission to tell Marco about my relationship. With how chatty Meg is, I'm impressed she lasted this long.

"Are you okay?" Xander asks for what has to be the tenth time. It's adorable how worried he is about me.

"I'm fine." I give him a gentle kiss. "I want to enjoy this party and forget what happened with Jake while I can."

"While you can?" He pushes his door open and signals for me to wait for him. When he opens my door, he says, "What do you mean?"

I hold up a finger. "Cindy saw us." A second finger. "Meg will tell Marco." A third. "You told your agent you broke Jake's nose. Do you really think our relationship will stay hidden much longer?"

"When you put it that way…" He scratches the back of his neck. "Is that a bad thing?"

"I don't think so." I shake my head. "Your family knows we're together. Aunt Millie, Ben, and Tom know too. The same goes for Meg." I smile brightly at him. "I think I'm ready to go public with you."

He gently lifts the cake out of the backseat. "Are you ready to officially be introduced as the girlfriend of Alexander Walker, the star quarterback of the Boston City Warriors?" He arches an eyebrow, breaking out a cocky grin.

I step closer and press a hand to his wildly beating heart as I wet my lips. "I'd love to know more about all the perks I'm signing up for beforehand."

"The perks? How about this: I'll fuck you nice and hard all night long, exactly the way you like it. I'll always take care of you and keep you safe." Xander ducks so we're eye level, forcing the butterflies in my stomach to take flight. "And I'll never stop loving you."

"Bella!" The sound of my name makes me jump back.

Tom stands on the porch, his face etched with panic. "Get in here! Ben is on his way."

"Sorry, Tom, it's my fault." Xander winks at me as we stroll toward the house. "I got distracted by this beauty."

WITH A GLASS of wine in one hand and Xander's arms wrapped around me from behind, I feel at ease. The warmth of his embrace makes me forget about everything else, transporting me to our bedroom, to the world we create when we're together. Our own universe full of love, passion, and care.

"Don't get me wrong, guys. I'm not judging what you do behind closed doors, but..." Tom sits beside me on the couch, a sly smile playing on his lips. "You could've hidden the bruises on your neck better."

"Bruises on your neck?" Ben looms over Xander and me with a deep frown.

Ben is typically easygoing, but when it comes to the people he loves, he will never hesitate to speak his mind. Telling him Xander and

I were dating was the most intense and rewarding experience. Though he voiced plenty of reservations, he also pledged his support. Then he threatened Xander's life if he didn't treat me well.

"Jake did that, not Xander," I remark.

"Excuse me?" Ben drops to the coffee table in front of us. "You dumped him two months ago."

"He found out about us and came over. Caught me walking Milo."

"File a restraining order," Ben seethes, his fists clenching. He shifts his gaze to Xander, glaring at him. "Do a better job next time."

"I will. This time, I broke his nose." Xander shrugs.

Ben's jaw unhinges. "For real? Again?"

"I would've done so much more, but Bella stopped me," Xander says. "She didn't want to call the police."

"*What?*" Ben and Tom yell simultaneously, drawing attention.

I sigh. "I don't want to put Xander's career at risk," I explain. "We told him if he tells anyone Xander broke his nose, or if he comes near me again, I'll file charges, and Xander will tell management the truth."

"I don't like it." Ben narrows his eyes at me.

"I don't either, but I won't make decisions for her." Xander pulls me into him, holding me close to his chest.

"Bella, baby, you're unbelievable." Tom shakes his head, glancing discreetly at Ben, suddenly looking hesitant.

I stand and hold out a hand to him. "Will you accompany me to the kitchen? I need to check on dessert."

"Sure."

Behind us, Ben and Xander talk in hushed voices. As I pass Aunt Millie, who's talking to Tom's parents, I smile warmly at her.

"You seem really happy," Tom says when we're alone.

"I never could have imagined being this happy in a relationship."

The second I laid eyes on Xander, my whole existence shook. He was dangerously gorgeous in his black jacket, tight white shirt, and black pants. I couldn't avert my gaze, even if Jake was standing right beside him.

Xander is everything I've ever wanted, and now, he's mine.

"My intuition was right, as always. Do you remember when I told you he had the hots for you?"

I bark out a laugh. "Of course I do. But he didn't admit it until I broke up with Jake. Before that, we were just friends with benefits."

"And now here you are, with the freedom to touch that gorgeous man any time you want." Tom licks his lips.

"Should I tell Ben you're having fantasies about my man?" I tease.

Instead of laughing along like I expected, he instantly pales, his eyes darting around the kitchen.

I grasp his arm as my stomach sinks. "What's wrong? I was just joking. I didn't mean to offend you."

"No, no. You did nothing wrong. It's me. I screwed up." He lowers his gaze as he sighs.

I cup his face, forcing him to look at me. "What happened?"

"I wanted to organize something special for Ben's birthday. I-I asked my parents to come because I want to propose."

My heart leaps. I was right.

But why the hell is he so reluctant?

"I wondered when you'd finally do it." I speak in a soft voice. "Are you having second thoughts?"

"God, no. No. It's just...you know Ben. I should've realized this before. I don't think he'll like a grand gesture." Tom looks up at the ceiling, sighing deeply. "What if he says no?"

"He won't. He might be a little shocked, but he won't say no."

His shoulders droop. "I don't know."

"Tom Hayes, don't be a chicken," I rasp. "You love Ben. He loves you. Just do it. You won't regret it."

Tom gapes at me. Then he breaks into a big, lopsided grin and pulls me in for a hug. "I love you, Bella," he whispers.

"I love you too." I hug him back.

"Ben," Tom calls, pulling me with him as he strides toward the living room. At the threshold, he lets go of my hand and eats up the space between himself and Ben.

"Yes?" My cousin cocks a curious brow at his boyfriend.

"To hell with it," Tom mumbles. "I'm in love with you," he says, looming over the couch. "And it's driving me nuts. Literally. I can't imagine my life without you. You're my every day. You're my past, and, most importantly, you're my future. Every freaking day is better than the last because of you, because of your love and support. I'm the luckiest guy to have you all to myself. You're my friend and my lover… and I hope you'll agree to be my husband."

Tom lowers to one knee and holds out a small box. "Will you marry me, Ben Lawson?"

The room falls silent, but in my mind, it's a riot. God, this is the most beautiful moment.

Ben's throat bobs as he swallows. He's nervous. I cross my fingers, hoping with all my might I know what his answer is.

After several long seconds, he sighs. "I should've known you wouldn't be able to resist making a scene." He chuckles. "Yes, Tom. I'd be happy to call you my husband."

The moment those words leave his mouth, the room erupts. Ben stands and helps Tom to his feet. Then, hand in hand, they stare at each other, lost in their own bubble. Tom slides the ring onto Ben's finger, and then he captures his lips in a heated kiss. My heart is ready to jump out of my chest. I'm overwhelmed by happiness.

As if he and I are opposing magnets, I can't stop myself from searching for Xander. When I find him, those gorgeous blue-green eyes are locked on me, his face bright. God, he's so handsome, so kind, so incredibly caring. He's my light, guiding me through the darkness. Never in my life have I been happier than I am with him.

CHAPTER 42

Last Love

BELLA

January

"Okay, I give up." I pout. "Please tell me why we're going to Miami."

"Wish I knew. My sister hasn't given me specifics." Xander buries his nose in my hair and inhales. "A couple days away from Boston will do us both a lot of good, though."

"Are you sure?" I glance at the runway out the airport window, watching a plane land.

"Yes. After divisional playoffs on Monday and all those articles and paparazzi, I'm exhausted, and I can imagine you need a break too."

He's not wrong.

I had my worries about Jake and his promises, but the day after he attacked me, Xander and the whole team got an email from management. I was bowled over. Jake went to rehab, claiming he'd had a nervous breakdown after our breakup. In his statement, he was very apologetic about letting down the fans and not being able to help the Warriors make it to the Super Bowl. He promised to get better and come back refreshed.

The support he got from management and the fans was astounding; in reality, it was just a PR stunt. Rumor is, Jake's agent hired a crisis PR company to help navigate it all and make sure his reputation remains intact. And it worked.

The news about me and Xander broke two weeks later, right before the last game of the regular season. Since then, we can't go anywhere without being hounded by paparazzi. Gossip magazines are sensationalizing our relationship, spinning lie after lie, each one worse than the last.

I turned off my DMs and comments on all social media; the messages I was getting were more than enough to disturb what little peace I'd found. To the world, I'm at fault for it all. I'm a cheating whore who ruined Xander and Jake's friendship and put the Warriors' chances for the Super Bowl at risk. Receiving death threats was the last straw for me.

Therapy is a priority, but with this public backlash, with Xander's games and practices, with my own job, there just isn't time to find a reputable therapist I mesh with.

Xander has helped me stay focused on the important things. He helps me remember that, even on the cloudiest of days, the sun is still there. I just can't see it. He is my rock, despite how hard it all is on him as well.

Meg sent me an article in which the journalist dug into Xander and Jake's college days and how much time they spent partying. Miraculously, he didn't discover anything about Stacey. She definitely doesn't deserve to be dragged into the spotlight.

Jake made a public statement through his rep the day after the first article about my relationship with Xander was published, insisting he respects my decision and wishes me nothing but happiness. He reassured the public that Xander wasn't the reason we broke up.

Isabella was my first love. I naively thought we could build something new when we reconnected as adults, but we became different people during the years we were apart. I'm not the right guy for her. I never was.

Things have improved since then, but not much. We're still

villains in the public eye. Speculation that Jake was covering for us, that we are the reason he had a breakdown and went to rehab, is still rampant. Every day, I regret keeping my mouth shut about Jake's attack.

"Yeah, a little break will be nice," I say.

"Coach is a good guy. He didn't have to give me the time off so close to the Super Bowl." Xander sighs, placing his chin on top of my head. "Situations like ours aren't easy for the team, but, thanks to him, the atmosphere in the locker room and on the field has improved a ton. Thanks to Isaiah too. He's been invaluable since he took Miller's place."

"Do the guys talk to you?"

"Yeah." Xander massages my back. "Meg told Garcia about Jake's cheating, and she hinted at how he was treating you. It didn't take much for them to see through Jake's bullshit. Most of the guys on the team are family men. They didn't appreciate what he did to you."

"I should've pressed charges," I mutter.

Xander leans away and gently takes my chin between his fingers. "Everything is going to be alright. We'll win the Super Bowl, and I'll make the haters eat their words. For you."

"If you win, can I make a wish?" I ask, an idea forming in my head.

He chuckles. "Why not?"

THE POOL HOUSE where we're staying is small and tidy, with floor-to-ceiling windows and beige walls. The living area is filled with a spacious couch, a big TV on the wall, a PlayStation, and a kitchenette in one corner. Beyond a half-opened door is a luxuriously made bed flanked by nightstands.

"Did my sister overwhelm you with all her blabbering?" Xander whispers after the door is closed behind us.

"A little," I laugh.

"That's what she's like when she's up to something." With a smirk, he sets our bags on the floor.

Then he pulls me in close, his lips finding mine, and I sigh into his mouth. I've never been with a guy like Xander before. He occupies all my thoughts, and he has stolen my heart with no intention of giving it back. He's under my skin, flowing through my veins.

He's everywhere.

"She was the same way on the day of her birthday party. I should've guessed she invited you."

"What would you have done if you'd known I was going to be there?"

Xander shrugs. "Made you jealous."

I narrow my eyes. "What?"

"I would've made you jealous to gauge your feelings, especially after you agreed to be Miller's wife right in front of me." His lips hover over mine, his warm breath caressing my skin. "I hoped you'd fallen for me, so I needed confirmation. I needed to know I wasn't in this alone." He presses his forehead to mine, sliding his hands down my hips. "I want to sneak out with you tonight. The beach is a short walk from here. We can be alone there, no prying eyes."

"The pool isn't enough for you, Mr. Quarterback?" I tease, standing on my tiptoes.

"Never enough." He seizes my lips in a feverish kiss, and the rest of the world stops existing.

MOST OF THE people here know each other, but Jess has taken pity on me and is keeping me company. She tells me about the project she has been assigned to, about the nutrition course she's taking. I tell her about my job and my love for interior design.

"Have you thought about taking classes?" Jess asks, head tilted, red curls veiling her shoulders. "On interior design, I mean."

I take a sip of my drink. "No."

"Why not?" She arches an eyebrow. "You clearly love it. Why not learn more so you can do it full time? Maybe work for yourself?"

I ponder her words as I sneak a glance at Xander, who's engrossed in conversation with Ryan. If I wanted to study interior design, would he be on board? With a sigh, I turn back to Jess.

"I don't know. I never thought about it." I lift my shoulder. "I'm mostly self-taught, though I've learned a lot from my cousin and magazines."

"Think about it." She smiles, clinking her glass against mine. "When you're ready, I'll be your first client, and you can do a badass design for my little studio. Deal?"

I laugh. "Deal."

Around us, conversations die, and when I look up, Audrey and Ryan are standing in the middle of the room.

"We have news," Audrey chirps.

Ryan winds his hand around her waist, holding her close.

"As you all know, Ryan finally got a promotion, and we're moving back to Boston in March. Going back to our roots."

Xander drapes his hand over my shoulder, smiling like the Cheshire cat. I chuckle, remembering how excited his parents were about finally having both their kids in the same city again.

Ryan smiles. "We wanted to have you all here tonight since, once we move, we won't see most of you often. But there's a second reason we invited you...Audrey is pregnant. We're going to be parents."

All around the room, people laugh and whoop and clap. Xander stands up and rushes over to his big sister, pulling her in for a hug and whispering in her ear. She breaks into a giddy smile and bounces on her toes.

He'll be the best uncle, I have no doubt. The broodiness is nothing but a façade; he's the sweetest guy I know.

After the party, we stroll along the sand. The beach is lit up by the moonlight, and the only sound is the lapping of waves on the shore. It's peaceful and secluded.

"So your parents knew? How did they manage to keep it a secret?"

"I don't have a clue. When we dropped Milo off yesterday, they didn't say a word," he mutters, chewing on his bottom lip. "Makes me want to get back at them for keeping the news from me."

"Got anything particular in mind?" I snort, amused by his childish behavior. Drunk Xander is hilarious.

He stops abruptly and takes off his T-shirt, then his sweatpants. "When I have something big to announce, I'll keep it a secret too." He pouts. He's adorable, like a little boy who didn't get what he wanted for Christmas.

Then he scoops me up, throws me over his shoulder, and runs into the sea. I laugh, my mood light and cheerful. Once he's waist deep, he drops me into the water fully clothed. When I surface, I rub my eyes and cough salty water.

"Dammit," I sputter, still laughing. "You should've told me to wear a swimsuit."

He traps me in his big arms as his lips leave a trail of hot kisses down my neck. "Sorry, baby. Where is the surprise if you knew we were going for a swim?" A low chuckle makes my throat vibrate as he guides my legs around his hips.

With one arm looped around his neck, I push my hair off my face and drink him in under the light of the moon. I can't get enough of him. Every day, every hour, every minute...it's never enough.

I want more of him.

I need more.

I don't know who moves first, but soon our lips are locked in a passionate kiss.

Our bodies rock against each other, my center sliding along his hard length. He sneaks his fingers under my panties and caresses my clit. I float in an ocean of pure bliss, oblivious to our surroundings. The only raw emotion still here is desire.

I let him do things to me that I never thought would excite me. This man is everything I never dared to dream about. Now, he's painting my world in thousands of different colors with nothing more than his fingers on my skin.

Clinging to his broad shoulders, I deepen our kiss and move my hips in time with his fingers. Breath hitching, I bite his bottom lip, sucking it into my mouth.

"Baby." Groaning, he breaks our kiss.

Then, in one fluid move, he impales me. He moves slowly, his lips sliding along my jaw. His tongue brushes my earlobe, making me shudder. He's touching my very soul and pulling at my heartstrings.

When he sucks on my neck, leaving a hickey, I moan louder, encouraging him to do more, to mark my whole body. I am his, body and soul, now and always. The heat, the desire we both feel, is overwhelming, freeing. His thrusts become rougher, deeper, and when he tugs on my hair and nips at my collarbone, my eyes roll back in my head.

"Bella." My name on his tongue mixes with his guttural groans.

Then he's throbbing inside me, triggering an orgasm so powerful it makes my toes curl.

"You're driving me insane," he says as we come back to the present.

"Why?" I ask, readjusting my hands around his neck.

"I just wanted to swim a little, to kiss you under the moonlight and go back to our warm bed. But the moment I had your legs wrapped around my waist, my mind turned into jelly." Xander laughs, spinning us around. "God, I love you. I have no idea how I survived all these years without you. I wasted so much time on the wrong people."

"All those wrong people led us here, to this moment." I cradle his face, forcing him to look at me. "And now you're stuck with me."

"And you're stuck with me." He steals a quick kiss before leaning back. "You're my perfect match, Bella."

I close the distance between us and kiss him, over and over again. I don't want to let him go.

Love is a simple, four-letter word...but the feeling it signifies bestows the power to change everything. Xander's love for me has turned me into a believer. I believe in our love for each other. I believe in us, in our future.

He's my second-chance love. Our bond is way stronger than anything I've ever felt before. It's deep and overwhelming. Our love makes me feel like I'm losing my mind.

To be loved by a man like him is exhilarating—a man who can touch my soul with his words, heal my wounds with the touch of his fingertips, ease my pain with just a peck on my forehead. He's an attentive lover, caring boyfriend, and wise best friend. He's my everything.

Xander is the place my mind wanders to when it needs a break from my racing thoughts. He makes me happy in a way no one else ever has.

There's no one else for me.

He's my last love.

CHAPTER 43

You Owe Me a Wish, Mr. Quarterback

XANDER

February

"HOW DO YOU FEEL?" GARCIA STOPS BESIDE ME. WE'RE shoulder to shoulder, watching people fill the Sharks' stadium in Miami.

"Good. Ready to get that trophy."

"I thought you got your trophy when Isabella agreed to be with you."

"Bella isn't my trophy." I turn to face him, arms crossed. "I'm not with her because of how she looks. She's my person."

"Wow." Carter whistles, joining us. "Sounds to me like you're ready for the big step." He gives me a hard slap on the back before he puts me in a headlock and runs his knuckles over my hair. "Are you going to steal the show and propose to your girlfriend?"

"Steal the show? Nah." I laugh and push him away. "Happiness loves silence. Do you remember Logan Jones from the Beavers?"

Carter huffs a laugh. "How could anyone forget? The guy helped his team win three Super Bowls. He's a fucking legend. Why?"

"He proposed to his girlfriend after that first win, but no one knew until months later. He did it in the middle of the empty stadium so the moment could be just between the two of them."

"So...are you planning to propose to Isabella or not? You lost me." Garcia frowns. "Meg loves grand gestures. She wouldn't mind if I proposed for everyone to see."

"Bella is the total opposite. And no, I don't have plans to propose." The thought flashed in my head when I saw her reaction to Tom getting on one knee for Ben. It'd be the most logical continuation of our love, but it's too soon.

"Like, never?" Garcia scratches his jaw.

I groan. "Just not now. This whole thing with Miller..."

The fucker didn't pay for any of his wrongdoings. He didn't pay for drugging Stacey. He didn't pay for all the abuse he inflicted on Bella. Even now, in "rehab," he's posting Stories about his everyday life on Instagram. He kept his place on the team because management didn't want backlash, and with Isaiah Gibson helping us get here today, they're happy. I was so fucking tempted to tell them the truth about Miller. My words could easily be his undoing, but he outplayed me with the help of his agent and PR company, and I was forced to stay quiet.

Garcia's face pales. "Sorry, man. I shouldn't have brought it up."

"Thanks."

"You okay?" Carter asks in a quiet voice.

"I'm fine." I give him a half smile. Somehow, this guy has become my best friend.

After everything with Miller went down, Carter has been by my side. He and Garcia are the only people on the team who know the real reason behind Jake's rehab stint, and they hate him just as much as I do.

"That's good to know." He nods.

I nod back, my insides warming. I cherish all the relationships I have on this team, but with Carter? It's the kind of friendship I've longed to have for years.

"Should we go?" Garcia asks. "We have a Super Bowl to win."

"Hell yeah, we do!"

The three of us head to the locker room. It's time for the big game.

Our center, TJ Harris, stands in front of me. I flex my hands. A powerful energy courses through my body. The roar of the stadium is deafening, but in this moment I can hear everything. Every breath. Every shift of weight from the defense.

TJ snaps the ball and I catch it, drop back three steps. The line collapses around me; everyone is moving. One of Atlanta's linebackers breaks through, coming way too fucking fast.

I spin left, barely missing the outstretched arms reaching for my jersey. The clock is running out. I scan the field, the tingling in my fingers intensifying. And finally I see him—our wide receiver. Isaiah Gibson is cutting toward the end zone. Ten yards, five...

Fuck, it's now or never.

I stop, set my feet firmly, inhale harshly, and throw. The ball slices the air like a knife. Everything around me slows down; the stadium goes silent. I watch as Isaiah leaps up and fucking catches the ball.

Expelling the breath I've been holding, I see the ref throw his hands in the air.

Touchdown.

That means...we win. We fucking win! We earned it. The whole team was in sync. Final score: 31 to 20.

I'm buzzing with adrenaline and excitement. *Fuck*. My very first Super Bowl.

Tonight, all those journalists who said I'm nothing but a pretty face are eating crow.

"We fucking won!" Carter barrels into me, knocking me over and yelling in my ear like a banshee. "Walker, we won!"

I laugh and push at him, but he doesn't budge. A moment later, I'm in the middle of a mob of red and white, the whole team chanting.

When I'm finally on my feet, Coach is soaking wet from head to toe, shaking his head but grinning. More and more people have joined us on the field, but I'm only looking for her. I desperately want to take her in my arms and kiss her lips for all these people to see. I want to show the world she means everything to me.

"Alex!" My sister runs toward me, our parents and Ryan on her heels, smiling from ear to ear. She leaps into my arms, hugging me tightly and blabbering about how proud of me she is.

"Oh my God, Alex! I was biting my nails the entire game!"

"Why?" I laugh, my head lolling back. "Did you doubt me?"

"No. These stupid pregnancy hormones make me extra anxious, especially about you." I put her on her feet, and she instantly palms my face, tears streaming down her cheeks. "You've been through so much shit the last few weeks, so I'm just...I'm so, so happy you won. You won the Super Bowl!"

"Audrey," I murmur. "You're a mess."

"I know," she sobs as she steps away, still smiling.

Ryan claps me on the back. "You were incredible." He moves away and wraps his arm around Audrey's waist.

My dad is next, pulling me in for a tight hug. "You were great. Probably need to work on your spiral a bit, but—"

"Greg!" Mom yelps, swatting Dad on his shoulder. "Leave him alone."

I rake a hand through my sweat-soaked hair. "Mom, if Dad didn't give me shit, I'd think his body had been taken over by aliens."

"I'm so happy for you," she says, pushing her way between us. "And so proud." She kisses my cheek before stepping back.

I try to keep up with what they're saying, but my mind is elsewhere. The only person I want to see is Bella, and she isn't here.

"You're coming to our house tonight for a little party..." Audrey says as I survey the field.

Bella is somewhere here too. Did she get lost in the crowd? I glance over my shoulder, seeing Marco with our teammates, and it eases some of the tension. Meg isn't here either.

"...and it will be incredible!"

"I don't think Alex is listening," Ryan laughs, pulling my sister to his side.

That catches my attention.

Her face falls, and her eyes go hard. "Do you have more important priorities than celebrating with your family?"

"Sorry, Audrey. Just...have you seen Bella?" I look from one family member to another.

"Sorry, man. Bella didn't sit with us." Ryan gives me an apologetic smile.

"Did she even come to the game?" Audrey asks, arms crossed over her chest.

I frown. What the hell is wrong with her?

"Bella is here with her best friend, her cousin, and his fiancé. They chose to sit in the stands," I grit out. Then I focus on my parents. "See you later, guys. I need to get back to the team. We're gonna take pictures in a few."

"Of course." Mom smiles and takes Dad's hand. "See you later."

"See you." Ryan turns and drags my sister away, trailing after my parents.

They're still within earshot when Audrey says, "She's the reason Alex has been through the wringer, and she couldn't be bothered to show up and support him? I'm telling you, she's no better than her ex."

Clenching my jaw, I focus on my breathing. Audrey's words boil my blood. I'll talk to her later, make sure she understands that I won't put up with her speaking about Bella like that. It's cruel, and incredibly far from the truth. My sister should know better.

I've almost made it to where the team is gathered when the sound of Bella's voice makes me stop in my tracks. I whirl around and barely have time to throw my arms out before she's launched herself at me. She hugs my neck, peppering my sweaty face with light kisses. I slide my hands down to her butt, keeping her close.

This right here is just as significant as the moment we won.

My heart beats out of my chest, and my throat is tight with emotion. I've never gotten high in my life, but I can imagine it feels something like this, like I can do absolutely anything. I'm unstoppable, invincible, immune to anything bad when she's with me.

She's my light, my personal sunshine. She's my partner in crime, my seductive mistress, my sensitive girl. Bella makes me feel complete.

"I was worried you bailed on me," I whisper in her ear.

She pulls back abruptly, her sapphire eyes raking over my face, a worry line between her brows. "Never," she murmurs. "Meg and I got a little lost trying to find our way onto the field. She's with Marco now."

"Where are Tom and Ben?"

She rolls her eyes then leans in close. "Tom, apparently, has never had sex in a public place, and he wants to change that today."

I throw my head back and guffaw. "No way."

"Yes way." She nods. "You owe me a wish, Mr. Quarterback, remember?"

"What will it be?" I set her on her feet and clasp her hands. Like every time we're together, the rest of the world disappears.

"I'll tell you when it's just us." She brings her mouth to mine and slips her tongue between my lips.

Fuck. Controlling myself around my girl has proven to be impossible.

"Hey, lovebirds." Carter's booming voice brings us back to reality. "It's time for pictures, and we need our star quarterback."

I bring Bella's hands to my lips and kiss her knuckles. "Will you be okay?"

"Of course." She grins. "See you later."

"We're headed to Audrey's, I guess. She planned a small get-together."

"Oh." Bella worries her lip, brows pinched. "Okay, I'll find Ben and Tom and say bye."

"Why don't they come with us?"

"Ben made a reservation at some fancy restaurant he's been dying to try." She takes a step back. "Go. I'll figure everything out. Don't worry."

"Love you," I murmur.

Her lips stretch into a gorgeous smile. "Love you too."

THE NEXT HOUR passes in a blur. Picture after picture. Interview after interview. At the end of it all, I'm stumbling around in a daze, so much so that I genuinely wonder why the field isn't green. Good thing I keep my question to myself, because once I blink away my dizziness, I realize it's confetti.

"You know what I'm the most excited about?" Garcia asks as I pass him on my way out of the stadium. He has his arm wrapped around Meg. "Super Bowl rings!"

I snort, though I'm excited for that too.

"I can get behind that," I say as we fist-bump. "See you guys."

The moment Bella comes into view—sitting in the car we rented—all my tiredness disappears. She's here, waiting for me. My girl... The concentrated look on her face is my addiction.

"Hey, you." I climb into the car, catching sight of the book in her hands. It's filled with colorful tabs, as if she's found something interesting on every page. "Sorry you had to wait so long. Hope you weren't too bored."

"Nah, I had my book boyfriend to keep me entertained." She twists at the waist and sets the book in the backseat. "Ready?"

"Book boyfriend?" I eye her, fighting the urge to pick up the book and flip through it.

"Jealous?" She waggles her brows. "Actually, I was reading about the history of American interior design." She pulls her seat belt across her torso and clicks it into place. "Thank you for picking this car instead of the fancy one your agent insisted on."

"Your love for simple things amazes me. You could have it all, yet you're always so content with the understated. It's one of my favorite things about you."

"I hope so. For a second, I thought you were judging me," she remarks.

"Never." I put my palm on her thigh. "You're remarkable."

DURING THE HOURLONG drive to Audrey's place, Bella asked a million questions about what it was like on the field.

"Were Tom and Ben okay without us?" I ask as we walk hand in hand to Audrey's front door.

"I'm pretty sure they were grateful to have a break from us."

"Ouch. I thought they loved me." I bring a hand to my heart and wince.

Bella smacks my forearm. "They do, but they don't love all the attention you attract."

I turn the knob and guide Bella into the house with my hand on the small of her back. Instantly, I'm blinded, disoriented by the dozens of people chanting my name and clapping.

What the hell? So much for a small gathering.

Bella curls in on herself, her hold on my fingers tightening as a quiet "Oh" escapes her.

"I didn't know she invited so many people," I mutter, squeezing her hand.

"It's okay." Bella gives me a small smile and closes the door.

It's not okay. Audrey should've warned me the party would be so big. She always does this, and I get wanting to celebrate, but I specifically told her I wanted something small.

WHEN I FINALLY CLOSE THE door of the guest room at three a.m., I'm exhausted yet still a bit hyped. I tried to confront Audrey, but Mom intervened, insisting that my emotions were heightened after the game and reminding me that my sister did it because she's excited for me.

So, I let it go. But if it happens again, I won't let anyone shut me up. I don't need my big sister's protection, and I'm over her meddling. I haven't been a little boy for years, but she has a hard time accepting it.

"I'm beat." Bella drags herself to the bed and slumps onto it. "Today was too much."

"You're right." I plop down beside her.

"What were you and Audrey talking about? She looked hurt."

Thankfully, Bella didn't hear our conversation. She had run to the restroom, and by the time she returned, our talk was over, though my sister continued huffing, complaining I ruined her mood.

"I just told her a small gathering means a small gathering. Blindsiding us like that wasn't okay. I didn't need a party, and I didn't want to see all those people. Hell, I barely know most of them." I yawn loudly. "I had so many plans for tonight...for you and me."

"We have all the time in the world, Xander," she murmurs, turning onto her belly. Her eyes are sleepy, and a soft smile plays on her lips. She inches closer, kissing me slowly before she leans away. "Sometimes, these little moments mean more than big gestures."

"I know," I chuckle, my eyes growing heavy. "I don't think I have the energy to get up and wash my face, let alone take my clothes off."

"I feel the same way."

I haul Bella to my chest and bury my face in her hair. Yes, my plans to make love to her are ruined, but falling asleep with her in my arms feels just as good.

Bella stirs in her sleep, her pretty ass rubbing over my groin and instantly making me hard. Within seconds, she rolls over, tangling her legs with mine.

"I want you." Her hot breath fans over my face.

My lips tremble as a smile forms. "I want you too."

With one warm hand, she pops the button on my jeans and lowers the zipper. When she palms my cock, tingles dart up my spine. For a moment, she moves her hand, jerking me off with her hand down my jeans. Then, once I'm completely at her mercy, she pulls my jeans and my briefs down, freeing me.

The second she takes my dick inside her warm mouth, I'm a mess.

I rake my fingers through her hair, relishing the softness as she swirls her tongue around my crown. An erotic moan escapes her lips, making my balls tighten. She works me over, taking me deep before swirling her tongue over my head again and again as stars flicker across my vision. She's not just giving me a blow job, she's making love to my dick, and I'm in fucking heaven.

"Bella," I moan. "Please, don't stop, baby."

She deepthroats me in earnest, squeezing my balls. I want to last, but my restraint is so thin already. I'm in her possession, whimpering and rolling my hips, fucking her throat while fisting her hair as if it's the anchor keeping me on this Earth, keeping me sane.

I come hard and intense, my whole body stiffening as I let out a guttural groan. Bella doesn't stop. She strokes my shaft, sucking my head and licking my cock clean. This girl... There's no escape from my feelings for her. Every day, I fall more in love.

She's in my blood, in the air I breathe.

She's everywhere.

The curtains are closed, but from the natural light coming in around them, I'd guess it's early morning.

Bella sits up, staring down at me with a smile on her lips. Her hair is disheveled, but she looks happy, so damn happy, it makes my heart flutter.

"Bella, I thought we had this talk." I sit up in bed as well.

"What talk?" She gives me an innocent smile.

"I don't like to be the only one getting attention." I reach over, ready to yank her to my chest, but before I can she hops off the bed and looks at me with a naughty glint shimmering in her eyes. She takes off her dress using slow, calculated movements, and when it falls to the floor, she's in nothing but red lingerie.

"I don't know about you, but I could use a shower," she says, her tongue tracing her bottom lip.

She turns around and strolls to the bathroom door, sensually swaying her hips. Shower? I'd follow her into a bathhouse and beg a wicked witch to turn me into a fucking dragon if it meant I could keep Bella safe. I'd give Calcifer my heart in exchange for powers to help me protect my girl.

I huff a laugh. Damn, every one of my thoughts is anime-related, and I'm not mad about it. Anything that's important to her is important to me.

With a grunt, I climb off the bed. I strip quickly before I rush to the bathroom. She's already in the shower, facing the glass. Beneath the steaming spray, she keeps her eyes on me and rubs her clit. Water streams down her neck and over her hard nipples, all the way to her pussy. With her other hand, she cups one breast and squeezes it hard.

She's going to be the death of me.

While she pleasures herself, I stay rooted to the spot, stroking my dick. When she drops her head back and lets out a moan, my cock jumps.

In two strides, I'm at the shower door, pulling her out until she's standing on the bath mat. I take her chin between my thumb and index finger, making her look at me. When she's this close to her release, I can't just watch from afar. I want to be inside her, right this second.

I press my mouth to hers, my fingers sliding down her throat to her breasts, over her soft belly and down to her pussy. Fuck, her core is hot and wet, and not just from the shower. Groaning, I lift her and guide her legs around my hips. The sensation of her wet skin on mine sends tingles through my whole body.

I yank a towel off the rack. With one hand, I spread it over the marble countertop before setting Bella on top. She leans away, her lips stretching into a seductive smile.

"You owe me a wish, Mr. Quarterback." She brings a finger to the hollow of my throat and drags it down until she traces the word "Freedom" inked below my right nipple.

"What is it?" Feverish, desperate to sink deep inside her, I inch closer, my hands sliding down her hips and pulling her to me. "Tell me."

"I better show you." She pushes me away, hops to her feet, and turns her back to me. The mirror is misty with condensation, so I can't see her face, but the moment my eyes fix on her ass, I'm salivating.

The diamond peeking back at me can only mean one thing: a butt plug.

"When did you..." I can't finish the sentence. My thoughts are too scattered.

"I might've been up a little longer than you think." Bella looks over her shoulder, grinning. "And I might've been wearing it here and there for the past few days, to get used to it."

My heart stumbles. And I didn't notice?

"You were busy preparing for the Super Bowl," she says, as if reading my mind. "Plus, I've been sneaky. I didn't want you to know until after you won."

"Sneaky for sure." I rest a hand on her ass, gently tracing her skin. So soft and warm. I give it a good smack, and she hisses through her teeth. "Damn, baby. My handprint looks perfect on your skin. I'll never get tired of the view."

"What about my wish?" She twerks, and I break into a sweat. Just the thought sends me skyrocketing into outer space.

"Baby, we need lube. I don't think—"

She laughs heartily. "You think I wouldn't come prepared?"

I lift my chin in question, eyebrows pulling together.

"Check my toiletry bag."

Hand trembling, I pull the bag close. There, right on top, is a small bottle of lube. I set it on the counter then take a step back, admiring this gorgeous girl. I won't lie, I've dreamed about fucking her ass, but I didn't expect her to want it too.

But here we are.

I slide closer and cup her pussy from behind. Bella arches her back in response. "So greedy..." I murmur. I rub her clit until she's moaning and pressing hard against me. Her panting becomes louder, and I lightly slap her pussy before I pull my hand away.

Bella sags over the counter. "It's not fair."

"I don't want you to come yet." I pick up the lube and spread it all over my shaft. "Touch yourself, baby," I order.

With one hand pressed to the marble surface, she sneaks the other between her legs. Once she's panting again, I ease the plug out almost completely, but then I push it back in. A shuddering moan slips out of her mouth. God, there's nothing more satisfying than making her feel good. I repeat the motion several times, and when her legs are shaking and she's practically crying out for relief, I finally pluck it out fully and toss it into the sink.

I squirt a generous amount of lube on my fingers then push one inside her. When I find little resistance, I slip in a second one and thrust slowly, ensuring she's ready for me.

"Xander, it feels so good..."

My chest puffs with smugness in response to her breathy sounds.

"But I want your cock..."

With one hand on the small of her back, I rub my dick over her little ass. With calculated slowness, I withdraw my fingers and push the tip of my cock past that ring of muscle before pulling back out. When she whimpers at the loss, I do it again, over and over, until she's trembling once more.

This time, I go a little deeper, and a soft cry leaves her mouth.

"You're doing so good," I tell her.

It takes all my willpower to hold back my orgasm. Her ass is so fucking tight, welcoming me in perfectly. Eventually, I'm fully seated, and I can't resist letting out a loud groan of approval.

"Oh my God, I'm so full," Bella moans, her breathing erratic.

Fingers digging into her hips, I slowly rock against her, taking my time stretching her wide and enjoying our closeness. "You love my cock inside your tight little ass."

"Yes..." Her words are whispered, but her loud moans echo off the tile. "I love your cock in my pussy...in my mouth...in my ass... Please don't stop. I'm so close..."

All her sounds combine with the steady stream of water hitting the tile, clouding my mind as I rail into her, taking her deeper and more roughly with each thrust. I wrap her hair around my hand and fist it, pulling her head back.

She releases a long, guttural groan.

Desperate to see her face, I hunch over her and wipe off a section of the mirror. Our eyes lock instantly, hers flooded with just as much desire as I feel.

"Harder, Xander, please," she begs.

I grip her flesh hard enough to bruise and obey, fucking her harder. The satisfied smile on her lips tells me everything I need to know. She fucking loves this. When I slap her ass, she pulsates around my shaft, squeezing my dick like never before. Her legs tremble, and she grips the edge of the countertop, trying to steady herself.

"God, baby, you're fucking perfect," I praise her.

As I pound into her, I keep one hand in her hair and use the other to spank her. Every time I do, her back arches, and I admire how flexible my girl is. There are so many things I've yet to discover about her, all the ways she loves to be fucked.

I let go of her hair and wrap my hand around her throat from behind. Her ass contracts, strangling my cock with enough intensity to make my vision blur. I look down at where we're connected, at my handprints on her fine ass, and it's enough to send me into fucking oblivion.

"X-Xander, I'm gonna come. Oh, G-God, please make me come!" Bella cries out as her body spasms, her ass tight around my dick.

Her orgasm triggers my release, and I squeeze her throat, controlling her breathing.

"That's my girl," I growl. I come then, spilling myself inside her.

When I've finally emptied every drop, I gently ease out of her, pulling her with me until her back is flush with my chest. She breathes erratically, her mouth open. As we watch each other in the mirror, all I can think is that I love this woman. I'm so fucking in love with her, it hurts. I can't imagine my life without her in it. She's always on my mind.

Planning a trip? What will Bella think about it?

Hanging out with my friends? What if she joins me?

Talking to my parents about my future? Bella is a part of every sentence.

I want her with me twenty-four hours a day, seven days a week. She's the oxygen I'm in desperate need of.

I spin her and snake my arms around her waist, drinking in every detail I love so much—the long eyelashes framing her beautiful sapphire blue eyes, her perfectly shaped brows, her straight nose that's a little upturned at the end. Her puffy lips and the little birthmark on her right cheek.

I close my eyes and kiss her.

These days, the negative voices in her head bother her far less often than they used to. She's learning so many things about herself, rebuilding her identity, rediscovering all the things she loves and craves. It's fascinating to watch her rise like a phoenix from the ashes. It's the greatest honor to know that she finally believes she deserves to be loved, to be happy.

Bella deserves the world, and I'm determined to give it to her.

CHAPTER 44

New York, New York

BELLA

A year and five months later
July

"How do you feel about going back home?" Dr. Khan gives me a broad smile.

Her shiny black hair frames her face, ending at her collarbone. Warm golden-brown eyes assess me as she tilts her head. Natural light filters through the gauzy curtains, illuminating her light brown skin. She's a beautiful woman in her forties, elegant and always so attentive and kind. I love my sessions with her.

"Isabella?"

"Sorry," I say, chuckling. "I'm feeling good. Can't wait to finally go home, spend time with my family and my friends. I miss it. I miss Boston—more than I thought I would."

She examines my face. "You've made amazing progress."

I lift a shoulder. "I've finally learned how to love myself. I understand now that I'm enough. I don't need a person by my side to feel powerful, beautiful, or desired." I press my palm over my heart. "Everything I needed was in here, and you helped me realize it."

The corners of her eyes crinkle, and her lips ease into a big, genuine smile. "I'm proud of you. I can't wait to hear about where you go from here. You're still set on virtual visits for the time being?"

"Absolutely." I hook one leg over the other, sitting more comfortably. "I'll be busy—I have a huge event to organize in four weeks, plus schoolwork for my internship in May—but our sessions are already on my calendar."

Dr. Khan steeples her fingers, watching me intently. "We've talked about the importance of maintaining a healthy work-life balance, right?"

"We have," I confirm. "I'll do my best to have fun too."

"I'm glad to hear it." With a nod, she leans back, her leather chair squeaking. "How was your last day at school? Did it go the way you thought it would?"

I look around the room, lost in memories of my time at the New York School of Interior and Landscape Design. I've had my ups and downs, but overall, it's been a positive experience.

Pursuing my dreams has not only helped me grow and feel happy, it has also brought me some amazing new friends. I landed myself an incredible mentor in Professor Hopkins, and devoting my time and energy to school and my new friends has helped me move on from my past. It's a feat that, at first, I didn't think I'd accomplish.

I've finally become the person I aspired to be.

After living in the darkness of self-destruction for so long, I needed it.

Taking a deep breath, I focus on Dr. Khan and answer the question. This day ought to be good.

"LAWSON!"

I turn my head at the sound of my last name and break into a smile. Kaden stands next to his Nissan Altima, an iced latte in each hand.

Even in my four-inch heels, my steps are light—just like my mood

—as I hurry toward him. "Hey. How long have you been waiting for me?"

"Twenty minutes."

Arching an eyebrow, I tilt my head to the side. "I don't like it when you lie to me."

He barks out a laugh and extends one of the cups to me. "Five minutes, tops. I honestly wasn't sure I'd make it on time. The lease has been signed, thank fuck."

I bring the latte to my lips, taking a generous sip. "Exactly how I like it. Thank you."

Kaden smiles. "Ready for our walk?"

"Always."

He straightens and checks that his car doors are locked, and then we're off, heading toward Central Park.

The silence that settles between us doesn't bother me. The busy streets of New York keep me company, the cacophony a familiar comfort. It's hard to believe that when I first moved here almost a year ago, I hated all the noise.

So much has changed since.

"How are you?" Kaden finally breaks the silence as we cross into the park.

I sidestep an older couple. "I'm fine. Still coming to terms with going back to Boston, but at the same time, I'm happy about it. Ben needs me. He's been stressed out of his mind trying to plan his own wedding while still helping his clients. And since my internship doesn't start for another ten months, it's a win-win." I nudge him with my shoulder. "Can you believe we're done with school?"

"It feels strange." He grins. "But we killed it, didn't we?" With an arm draped over my shoulders, he pulls me to his side. "So, you're ready to go back to your hometown...even considering all the history?"

I rest my head on his shoulder, inhaling the scent of his cologne—citrus and spice mixed with a woodsy scent. He's handsome and fit, with a six-pack, muscular arms, and toned legs. His dark brown skin is warm to the touch, enveloping me in protection. We met during our first week of school, and he's been an incredible friend ever since. He's one of the few people I've met who couldn't care less about my past.

His indifference to gossip and his kind heart make it relatively easy to be comfortable in his presence. He's a good guy, and I've been lacking good people in my life lately.

"It's not like that history is going to give two shits about my return," I joke, unwilling to let my unease make its way out of the box I've shoved it in. "And, to answer your other question, yes, I'm ready."

Kaden squints at me, his deep brown eyes searching my face. Then he smiles and presses me a little closer to his side. "I'm really gonna miss you, Lawson. How am I supposed to spend time with my best friend when she's in another state?"

"There's always Zoom. And DMs, phone calls. A four-hour drive if you start missing me *that much*."

Throwing his head back, Kaden laughs. The loud sound is contagious, making me giggle. "You're impossible, but you're lucky. I love you, so I'll stick around."

"Love you too," I murmur. "And I'm glad you're here."

"Me too." With a kiss to my temple, he guides me along the path.

Two hours later, before we part ways, I snap another picture of the two of us for Instagram. It's become a tradition to take a picture every time we meet for coffee. I have dozens, and every time I look at them, they bring the biggest smile to my face.

Simply because I have the best friends in the world.

As I stroll to my apartment building, the warm July wind plays with my hair, encouraging me to slow my steps and enjoy the weather.

Memories of my first days in New York surface as I lift my face to the sky and relish the warmth. It's been less than a year, but it feels like an eternity has passed since I arrived. So many things have changed, some for the better, some for the worse. Still, it's an experience I'm grateful for.

If not for the hell I've been through in my life, I wouldn't be here, wouldn't have met such incredible people. Each one of them stepped into my life for a reason. Some of them left because it was time for me to let them go...including the ones I hoped to never say goodbye to.

When my phone buzzes and I find Meg's name on the screen, I smile. "Hey."

"I kept my distance like you asked because of your exams," she says, "but...you're done now, and I miss you."

"I miss you too," I answer softly. "I just needed time to focus. But I have my certificate now, so I'm good."

"You know what I think—you have a gift. You didn't need a certificate to work as an interior designer."

My chest tightens. "Thank you, boo, but you and I both know that's not true. You're—"

A deep voice cuts in. Marco. He wants to know if he should get me a ticket for the first preseason game in a few weeks.

Stomach tightening, I come to a stop outside my building. In all honesty, going to a Warriors game isn't on my to-do list.

"Izzy?" Meg says, her tone hesitant.

"Yeah?" I enter the apartment building and hit the button to call the elevator.

"Would you go to the game with me?"

"I'm not sure that's a good idea."

"I know the emotions are still raw," she says, "but you've come a long way. I'm incredibly proud of you, and I think it's time to own your life again."

"And going to the game will help with that?" I smirk, stepping into the elevator.

"Duh. It'll be an opportunity to face your past, to show them all what a gem you are. To prove to *her* she didn't break you."

I can't help but laugh. "There's no bad blood between Audrey and me."

"You're too forgiving. I hate that bitch."

Warmth spreads through my veins. Her words may be harsh, but her devotion means so much.

"Please say yes. It'll be for the best. I promise."

The ding of the elevator indicates my ride is over. Yet I don't move a muscle. Instead, I'm caught in a whirlwind of racing thoughts.

Am I ready to see Xander in person?

"I'll be there for you. I won't leave your side."

With a deep breath, I step out of the elevator and head to my apartment. "Fine. I'll go with you."

"Yes! You won't regret it," Meg cheers as I unlock my door. "I have so many plans for us, so many places I want to visit with you. Ugh, I want you to be home sooner."

"Hey, I just got home, and I want to work a little before I go for another walk."

"Sure, boo. Love you."

After I hang up, I throw my phone and my purse on the couch, moving to the window so I can look out over the lively streets of New York.

A year and a half ago, right after the Super Bowl win, I was blissfully happy with Xander. I got to know his parents, made plans for our future. I couldn't imagine I would lose him, couldn't dream there would ever be a time in which he wasn't around.

Yet, it happened.

I was the one who cut all ties. Last August, I broke up with Xander.

It was the hardest thing I've ever done, but I let him go.

The End of Book One

Afterword

THANK YOU SO MUCH FOR READING!

If you enjoyed **BREAKING RULES**, I'd be immensely grateful if you can leave a review.

Stay tuned for **CHANGING RULES**, the second book in the *Rules* duet. Bella&Xander's story will be concluded on July 9th, 2025.

For exclusive bonus content and new releases make sure to sign up for my newsletter via my website. Follow me on my socials for news, announcements and giveaways.

Acknowledgments

To *my husband and my son*, thank you for being so patient with me, especially when I'm chasing my deadlines. Love you both to the Moon and back.

To *Alwyn*, thank you so much for your help, your feedback and your support. You're the best, and I'm so excited for all your future projects!

To my rockstar editors: *Mel*, *Beth*, *Alexa* and *Caroline*, thank you so so much for your hard work, your professionalism and patience. Xander&Bella's story has my heart, and you helped me to turn it into its best version possible, the one I'm immensely proud of.

To *Leila*, the talent you have is mind-blowing! Thank you so much for this stunning cover—it looks like it came straight out of my dreams!

To *Jess* and *Ambar*, thank you so much for your feedback and your help with this story! So happy to be on this journey with you!

To my incredible beta-readers: *Emily*, *Emma*, *Jamie*, *Megan*, *Sam and Stephanie,* I'm forever grateful for your feedback and suggestions! I was living for your comments and reactions—Thank you!

To my darling *PA Kristina*, I have no idea what I would've done without you. Thank you so much for everything you're doing for me and your support!

To my superstar content creators: *Cassie* and *Mackenzie*, your talent, dedication and all the hard work you put into everything you do is astonishing. Thank you!

To *my content and ARC teams*, thank you so much for loving my characters, reading my books and for helping me spread the word about my stories! You're real MVPs!

To my beautiful *readers*, thank you from the bottom of my heart for being on this journey with me! For reading my books, for recommending them, and for loving my characters.
And to *every person* who once had a "Jake" in their lives—I see you, and I believe you! Your strength, your kindness, and your beautiful souls are shining even through the cracks. Never let anyone dim you light. You are perfect as you are, and you deserve love that gives, and never takes.

If you or someone you know is in crisis, these resources can help:
https://rainn.org, https://www.wannatalkaboutit.com

Also by Anastasija White

SIN-BIN: An Enemies to Lovers College Hockey Romance

BARN BURNER: A Fake Dating Hockey Romance

HALE: A Single Dad Sports Romance

BREAKAWAY: An Accidental Marriage Hockey Romance

POWER PLAY: A Second Chance Hockey Romance

Breaking Rules (Rules Duet, book 1, 2025)

Changing Rules (Rules Duet, book 2, 2025)

Title TBR (A Stepbrother Romance, 2025)

HADE: A Rockstar Romance (2026)

About the Author

Anastasija is an indie author who spends her days creating swoon-worthy and steamy stories that will make your heart race. Her writing is filled with flawed and relatable characters that you'll find yourself rooting for. Whether you're in the mood for angsty drama or steamy romance, her stories take you on a rollercoaster ride of emotions with guaranteed happy endings.

When she's not writing, she loves to lose herself in reading books, rewatching her favorite tv-shows and spending time with her son. She loves traveling and exploring the world, and then including places she visited in her novels.

If you're a fan of romance that leaves you breathless and begging for more, Anastasija is the author for you. Connect with her on Instagram and TikTok, where she loves to hear from her readers and share sneak peeks of her books and upcoming projects.

Made in the USA
Columbia, SC
30 May 2025

58677511R00202